Isla Gordon lives on the Jurassic Coast of England with her T. rex-sized Bernese Mountain Dog. *A Season in the Snow* is her first novel, inspired by life with an ever-growing puppy, and when researching the book in snowy Switzerland she fell in love with the country. And even more in love with cheese.

Isla has worked as a dance teacher, a manager, and an editorial assistant but has been writing professionally since 2013 (and unprofessionally since she can remember). She also has five romantic comedies published under the name Lisa Dickenson.

Isla can't go a day without finding dog hair in her mouth.

Also by Isla Gordon,
as Lisa Dickenson

ISLA GORDON

A Season in the Snow

sphere

SPHERE

First published in Great Britain in 2019 as an ebook by Sphere
This edition published by Sphere in 2020

1 3 5 7 9 10 8 6 4 2

Gloria Steinem quote as featured in the VICELAND At the Women's March series,
reproduced with the kind permission of the office of Gloria Steinem, and Vice.

Emma Watson quote transcribed from 2011 press conference for
Harry Potter and the Deathly Hallows, Part 2

A CIP catalogue record for this book is available from the British Library.

ISBN 978-0-7515-7449-4

Typeset in Caslon by M Rules
Printed and bound in Great Britain by Clays Ltd, Elcograf S.p.A.

Papers used by Sphere are from well-managed forests
and other responsible sources.

MIX
Paper from
responsible sources
FSC® C104740

Sphere
An imprint of
Little, Brown Book Group
Carmelite House
50 Victoria Embankment
London EC4Y 0DZ

An Hachette UK Company
www.hachette.co.uk

www.littlebrown.co.uk

Dedicated to my big puppy, Kodi-Bear,
and all the furry friends who make
the world feel brighter

Hope is a very substantial and
powerful thing.

Because if you don't have it, you're
defeated before you start.

The one thing that is worse than trying and
failing is not trying.

GLORIA STEINEM

Chapter 1

Alice put the world on mute, just for a moment, so she could soak it all in. A thousand colours stitched together with pink threads – from woollen hats to bright T-shirts stretched over the top of zipped-up jackets, to the splashes of paint on placards being held high into the sky, to the flushed cheeks of the women and girls and men and boys giving it their all on this frost-covered January morning.

Smiling faces, warm greetings, cold breath, little children through to elderly ladies, and even a few dogs, full of fight. There was anger here, and fury and fire, but there was also hope. There was camaraderie; a sea of strength and sisterhood. London, and the world over, was alive with the power of women. She felt ripples of optimism within her own blood.

And with that, she let in the roar. The noisy, excited, diverse, vibrant sounds of London's Women's March flooded her ears and she whipped around to face her circle of friends who she'd pulled along with her.

'Are you ready?' Alice shouted to be heard.

Jill, her closest friend in the whole world, the Amy Poehler to her Tina Fey, nodded, blowing into her gloved hands and jiggling to the loud music that blasted from erected speakers. 'Yes, let's get marching; anything but standing around.'

Alice handed each of them – Jill, Bahira, Kemi and Theresa – a placard that she'd been up late into the evening making, and they admired her handiwork for a moment. Alice's skills with illustration and amusing, catchy slogans did her proud, and the women pointed out details to each other – a resistance fist here, a rainbow flag there, a few cleverly placed pussycats.

A large group of women twirled past them dressed like the female wrestlers from *Glow*, chanting about pussy power, catching Alice's eye. She watched them as they laughed and jostled and placed their hands on each other's shoulders and lower backs with such casual ease.

'Next time we should do that,' she called to the others, who nodded, humouring their friend.

'Let's go,' said Jill.

Alice's grin spread, and she threw her arms wide, ready to jump into the throng. 'This is really cool, right? I know it's freezing, but look at this history we're part of.'

Jill laughed. Alice's optimism had always been infectious, and the five allowed themselves to be swept into the river of wonder women.

'Thanks for coming with me,' Alice shouted back at Jill as she was jostled forward and nearly poked in the eye by someone's banner, though Jill was just watching her mouth move, the noise was so overwhelming. 'This year is going to be a good one, I can feel it.'

Foot-sore and feeling on top of the world, the five women pooled into a Starbucks near Westminster a couple of hours later.

'We'll have five caramel hot chocolates please, my good lady,' Jill said a little too loudly, the volume of the music outside still ringing in her ears.

The woman behind the counter raised an eyebrow. 'What name please?'

'The Five . . . ' Jill faltered and looked at Alice.

'Pusscateers?' she suggested.

'You know what,' the barista said, putting the cups to the side. 'I think we'll find you. Take a seat.'

'Thank you, sister!' Alice said, her voice hoarse, and punched her fist in the air.

They found a table in the corner and spent a while propping up their placards and peeling off their layers of coats, scarves, backpacks and pink hats with cat ears that some of them had acquired.

'Today was so cool,' Alice enthused, shaking out her light brown hair. 'Women are so cool.'

'Women are the coolest,' Jill agreed.

'There were so many more people there today than I ever imagined,' Kemi said, flopping into her chair.

Theresa stretched out her arms and legs like a cat. 'I know, it was heaving. Fab idea, Alice.'

The drinks came and Bahira went back up to the counter to grab a bunch of cakes and cookies to go with them.

Alice bit into a slab of carrot cake and said through the crumbs, 'Didn't we meet some amazing people today?'

'The old ladies dressed as suffragettes,' said Bahira.

'Those kids with their sassy T-shirts,' Theresa added.

'I just wish I could spend all day every day with every single person I met, and you guys,' sighed Alice. 'I think I might have eaten too many of those sweets they were handing out.' And she chomped into another big bite of cake.

'Do you feel like you got lots of good material for *Funny Pack*?' Jill asked her.

Alice nodded, chewing on the cake, her mind whizzing with memories. She worked as a freelance cartoonist focusing mainly on political, satirical or positivity and aspirational art. But mostly she was in-house for an online magazine called *Funny Pack*, run by a collective of individuals motivated by finding the humour, or if not the humour then the optimism, in current affairs. Alice was a big believer in making people feel good in dark times, she was proud of her work, and she wanted to create some great depictions of the Women's March for the magazine.

'I'm going to head back to the flat after this and try and sketch everything out tonight while it's fresh in my mind.'

'That's dedication,' said Jill. 'I'm going to go and lie in one of my marble baths.'

They laughed. It was an ongoing joke that Jill lived in a mansion compared to the rest of them. It wasn't true, but due to the passing of Jill's grandmother the year before, Jill had been gifted her three-bed semi in Forest Hill, complete with driveway and enclosed, spacious garden. Alice's flat in Islington was the size of a box in comparison; Kemi and Theresa were both in house shares, and Bahira's home was a gorgeous, cosy townhouse in St Albans that she and her husband (and their dog) had fallen in love with when she was pregnant with her daughter Zara a couple of years back.

They rested in the companionable silence that came with knowing each other for over ten years, or in the case of Alice and Jill, their whole lives. Inseparable since childhood, they had gone to university together and met the other three there.

'What do you want out of this year?' Alice asked the group from behind closed eyelids.

Bahira piped up first, a woman who always knew what she wanted. 'A big family trip outside school holidays so I don't have to hang out with anyone else's kids.'

'I want to spend more time outdoors,' Kemi answered. 'I'm always at work or the gym so I might try running this year, maybe along the Thames.'

'I want to see you lot more,' Theresa said. 'Because you don't laugh at me when I get messy drunk like my other friends do.'

'We laugh at you a little bit,' Jill said.

'What about you, Jill?' asked Alice.

'A pet,' said Jill. 'A cat or dog, I'm not sure which yet.'

'You want a pet?' Alice asked, cracking open her eyes and looking at her friend. 'What's wrong with the orchid I got you?'

Jill laughed. 'It'll be nice to have some company in my mansion, and you won't move in with me, so . . . '

'I like my servants' quarters, thanks.' Alice smiled, closing her eyes again.

'And I want to travel more,' Jill continued. 'I want to be one of the Instagram goddesses that goes camping in the wilderness with their big dog and speaks in motivational quotes.'

'That's quite a lifestyle change, unless you were going to camp out in Hyde Park,' said Kemi.

Jill nodded. 'So what about you, Alice? What do you want this year to bring?'

She thought about it for a moment. 'A long, warm summer. And to travel more, too. And Michelle Obama to be president. And a Turner Prize for one of my cartoons. And the whole *Funny Pack* office to be given Women of the Year awards.'

Kemi drained her hot chocolate. 'Keeping the dreams small this year then, Ali?'

'I think every one of those things is going to happen for you.'

'Thank you, Jill, and I think you will get a cat-or-dog and be very happy out in the wild.'

That evening, Alice closed the blue door of her Islington flat and all was quiet again. Her home was how she'd left it, with the mug beside the kettle, the glue and scissors and paint and brushes spread over the small round table in her kitchen/living room area. Her washing was still damp on the clothes horse. If she switched on the TV, Netflix would still be waiting for her, ready with the next episode of *Grace and Frankie*. It was almost as if her spending the day marching through the streets of London with 100,000 like-minded souls had never happened.

So Alice sat down to work, humming the latest powerful track from Little Mix, mug of tea beside her, and looked up at the frame above her desk, like she did before every new drawing session. Inside it was her career highlight – so far: a cartoon that had been published the previous year in the *New Yorker*.

She yawned and rubbed her eyes while she swept her pen over numerous pages, rough-sketching ideas for cartoons before they ran out of her head, or she ran right out of energy.

Alice's mind kept bringing her back to the conversation with her friends, and what they wanted these next twelve months to bring. Maybe it was the Women's March, maybe it was the hope that comes with a brand new year beginning, or maybe it was just inside her, but Alice felt like she could take on the world.

Chapter 2

Springtime in London was the first sign of the heatwave that would bathe the capital until nearly September. It was only mid-March, but coats had been hung up, shorts had been pulled out of the back of drawers and bare arms were getting the first of their yearly doses of vitamin D.

Alice walked down Kensington High Street on her way to meet Jill, having left the *Funny Pack* office early that Friday afternoon. The incoming lighter evenings, with the low sunshine warming her face, made the winter months worth it.

She wanted to talk to Jill, seriously, about an idea they'd both skirted around for a couple of weeks, mentioning in passing, making quips about, but never really pinning anything down. So she'd suggested they meet at a bar in the sunshine for a glass of wine.

'Can you believe this weather?' Jill asked as a greeting, the same greeting all Londoners were using at the moment.

'If this can just last all summer I will have ticked at least one thing off my "what do I want to happen this year" list.' Alice sat down and they ordered a bottle of rosé to share, because when it feels like summer you may as well go all out.

'How was work today, honeypie?' Jill asked, as if she were Alice's husband.

'Just marvellous, thank you, darling. And you?'

'Same old, same old.' Jill worked as a web developer, usually on long-term retainers from tech companies, which gave her the sociability of an office environment with the freedom to dictate her own hours. 'So what did you want to talk about?'

'Okay,' Alice leant forward. 'You know we both said we wanted to travel more this year?'

'Yes, definitely.'

'And we keep bringing it up and saying how great it would be.'

'It would be great. You and I have a lot of fun travelling.'

Alice grinned. 'We have had some good adventures. I was thinking, shall we just do it again? Shall we just go for it?'

'Go backpacking again?'

'Maybe not *backpacking*, but have another adventure. For a month or two, like a road trip around Europe or something.'

'When were you thinking?' Jill asked, sipping her wine.

'Maybe after summer, so we have some time to save up a bit and book the time off work. What do you think?'

Jill hesitated, and Alice felt a drip of doubt sink into her. Maybe Jill didn't want to do something like this after all. She shouldn't have got so ahead of herself with hope.

'How do you feel about dogs, Alice?' Jill asked all of a sudden.

'Oh. Okay, we can talk about that. I like them . . . I don't know a lot of dogs.'

'Well, you know I said I wanted to get a pet this year?'

'Yeah.'

'I think I'm going to get a dog. This summer. In like, July.'

'That's exciting news,' Alice cried. 'Congratulations! Why July, specifically?'

'Because my puppy is already, um, baking, in its mum's tummy.'

'What?' laughed Alice. 'What kind of puppy is it? How did this happen?'

Jill looked a little relieved that Alice was taking this so well. 'A friend of a friend has a lady Bernese Mountain Dog and they wanted her to have one litter of puppies. Long story short, we got in touch and the friend said I was welcome to have one of them if I wanted.'

'What's a Bernese Mountain Dog?' asked Alice. 'They sound big.'

'They are big.' Jill grinned. 'Black and orange and white, sort of like a smaller St Bernard. With big paws and a big nose and a really lovely personality. It'll be born in May, and it's best to take home a new puppy eight weeks after. So, July.'

'That's so exciting you're going to have a puppy!'

'Thanks for not being mad at me!'

'Why would I be mad? Oh – because of the travelling thing? Don't worry about that, it was only a really vague idea, I hadn't even thought about it much.' Alice didn't mention that she'd wanted to meet here so they could hop straight over the road to a travel agent afterwards and start planning their route.

'I mean ...' Jill swirled the wine in her glass and stared into the distance for a moment. 'I did think it would be pretty cool to be one of those Insta-chicks who travels with her dog.'

Alice sat up a little straighter. 'You'd want to take him with us?'

'It's not the stupidest idea I've ever had. Where in Europe where you thinking?'

'I don't know. If we took a puppy I guess it would make sense to do more a countryside, beach, mountains-kinda tour than a bunch of cities strung together.' She paused and drank some wine. 'But that's definitely not a bad thing.'

'Could we do it by car? I don't know the logistics of taking puppies on planes.'

'A car might be a bit tight, but we could think about a campervan?'

Jill looked at her friend, a smile on her lips. 'Are you serious? Would you really be happy doing this plan with a dog in tow?'

Alice shrugged. 'What could go wrong?'

'Absolutely nothing.'

'It could be pretty funny.' A campervan filled with two women and a puppy, making their way around the Continent. It wasn't quite what she'd had in mind when she'd walked into the bar, but she was open to it. 'I think we should do it.'

'I think we should too!' Jill cheersed her glass. 'We have a lot to think about and plan. Where do we even start?'

Alice looked around, super-casual. 'Ohhhh, I don't know. I guess we could go over to that travel agent's and get some brochures?'

Chapter 3

Alice and Jill's travel plans were coming along nicely. They'd leave in September, when the sun was still warm but the French and Italian coasts had taken a breath after the August heat. Their route would then take them for a jaunt through the Croatian mountains, then up through Slovenia, Austria, Germany and the new puppy's home country of Switzerland.

Alice was working hard from her desk in the *Funny Pack* office, where the air conditioning was broken so all the windows were wide open letting in what little breeze there was on this stifling June day. She was on overdrive trying to get as many illustrations in the bank as she could so that the impact of taking two months off at the end of the season wouldn't be too noticeable. With the political unrest at home and overseas, plus the changes in the air from ever-growing social movements, she had plenty of material.

'This is your fault, you know,' Kemi said, calling her out of the blue.

'What did I do?'

'You wished for a long, hot summer,' she panted down the line. 'I just tried to go for a lunchtime run and have had to stop for a Frappuccino.'

'I take full responsibility for global warming,' Alice replied, taking a drink from her water glass and leaving yet another red lipstick print on it. Today was an endless cycle of hydrating, weeing and putting lipstick back on. 'Hey Kemi, have you heard about that outdoor concert they just announced for the summer?'

'I don't think so.' Kemi took a long slurp. 'What is it?'

'It's being put on by a women's rights charity in Brookwick Park in the first week of August. I thought I might go. Shall I ask everyone?'

'You can ask, but I think Bahira and her family are away that week.'

'Ah, they couldn't get a week outside school holidays in the end?'

'No, she said that was wishful thinking. But send over the date and info and we'll see.'

Alice hung up and sent the details straight over to her circle of friends. She was feeling fuelled by the same optimism she'd felt way back in January, but she just couldn't put her finger on what she wanted to do about it.

As it turned out, Bahira was away, Theresa didn't want to splash out on the ticket and Kemi had a family barbecue pencilled in with all her relations that day. Jill, though, good old Jill, was more than happy to chip a bit off their travel fund to go along with her. Before either of them could change their mind, Alice bought the tickets. Now she had something fun planned for August, before the big something fun that was planned for September.

Okay, back to the grind . . .

Alice had a car that she kept parked on a quiet street near her home that was used once in a blue moon. So the following week she was designated driver to head over to Tunbridge Wells with Jill for the first puppy visit, along with Theresa, who'd begged to come too.

'On a scale of one to ten puppies, how excited are you?' asked Alice on the journey.

'A million puppies. Apparently the mum had three, two girls and a boy, and the girls are going to family members. So ours will be the little gentleman.'

'Ours?'

Jill laughed. 'Yes, ours.'

'How old are they now?' asked Theresa from the back seat.

'About five weeks. I'm so sorry if I cry my eyes out or just make a run for it with all three.'

'Well, don't leave us there,' answered Alice. 'I don't know these people. Are you sure it's going to be okay you being away for the evening of the concert?'

'In August? Yes, definitely. Sam will be home from uni then so I'm going to ask him to come and stay for a few nights.' Sam was Jill's younger brother, and little did he know he was being lined up to be a dog sitter.

They pulled into the driveway of a large home, where they rang the bell and were ushered in by a grinning, but sleepy, gentleman who introduced himself as Max and showed them out into the shaded garden. He opened a door and out of the house came the most ginormous dog Alice had ever seen: glossy dark fur bouncing sunlight, paws as big as side plates and a tail like a plume of smoke rising from a chimney. Her chest was coated with the thickest white fur and she had orange splodges on each ankle and above her eyes.

She woofed at the three women, a low, warning woof that echoed around Tunbridge Wells.

'Sorry about that,' said Max. 'This is the mum, Betty. She's just being a bit wary and protective because of the pups.'

Betty woofed again and then went up to each of them in turn to have a sniff and peer up at them with big eyes that said, *can I trust you?* Alice sat on one of the garden chairs and Betty seemed to like this, turning her back to Alice and sitting a million kilos of dog on her feet.

'You've passed the test,' Max grinned. 'Shall I let the puppies out now?'

He opened the door again and three stumbling, chunky bear cubs tumbled out, their legs shorter than the threshold, their noses squished in and guinea-pig like. Jill almost fainted with happiness, and Theresa's phone camera began working on overdrive.

The puppies picked their way over the grass, bumping into chair legs and each other, clamouring over feet, chewing on each other's ears and trying to climb on Betty, who'd flopped down to lie on Alice's trainers by now.

Max scooped up the roundest of the puppies who was barging his way through the bowl of water that sat outside. 'This one's your little lad.' He handed the puppy to Jill.

Tears popped straight into and out of Jill's eyes. 'Oh my God. Hello, you.'

The puppy licked her face. Freckles were just visible in the folds of his snout, and he had a two-inch white splash of fur decorating the back of his neck, like somebody had spilt cream on him when they'd walked past.

After he'd cleaned away Jill's impromptu tears, the puppy wriggled free and scurried over to his sisters to push one of them over with his nose.

'So they're all healthy, they're all okay?' Jill asked Max.

'They sure are. And by the time you pick him up in three weeks all their vaccinations will be up to date and I'll give you a pack I've been putting together about his food and all that.'

'That sounds perfect.'

'Let me get you all a cup of tea,' Max said. 'And then you can get to know them all a bit better.'

'You've changed your mind, haven't you?' Alice joked to Jill when Max had gone inside.

'They're just so ugly,' she laughed back while one of the sisters chewed on the loose ends of Jill's hair.

Theresa stroked a passing fluffball. 'I want one too.'

'You can come over and play with this one whenever you want.' Jill was rolling a tennis ball gently towards her soon-to-be-puppy and watching him approach it curiously. Alice watched her friend, happy for her.

She looked down at the giant dog on her feet. It was a good job Jill had a big house.

Chapter 4

On the seventh of July, Alice picked up Jill at eight in the morning, hoping to avoid being in the car while it was too hot while they brought home Jill's new puppy. At eight weeks old, he'd grown into a squat little bear cub, with thick legs, round paws and a spindly tail. His nose, though still squashed, had distinct dots scattered on it and his fur was crumpled and plentiful.

In the car on the way home Jill cooed and chuckled over him as he settled himself into the foot well by her legs without a care in the world.

'He is possibly the sweetest puppy in the whole world,' Alice commented, glancing away from the road for a second. 'You're not going to be able to go anywhere without people wanting to stop you and pet him.'

'I know, but I get to have him all to myself for a month before I can take him out for walks,' Jill replied, obsessively playing with his silky ears. 'Oh my God, you are such a little bear.'

'What are you going to call him?'

'Bear probably, because that's how I've been referring to him over the past two months.'

'Like when pregnant people call their unborn babies "bean" or "pip"?'

'Yep.'

'Well, Bear certainly suits him,' said Alice, and Bear stared at her and started hiccupping. 'Hey, Bear, if you like this car journey, you just wait two months and you're going to go in a campervan.'

'That's right!' said Jill. 'Bear, we have big plans for you. You're going to see lots of the world, because Alice and I are having an adventure, and you're coming too. Are you excited?'

Bear looked up at her and yawned, before falling asleep against her ankles.

'He's excited,' confirmed Jill.

As July rolled forward, Alice took advantage of the long summer evenings to take her work outside. She loved summer in the city. Yes, the heatwave was prickling and the Tube was uncomfortable, but London was alive with tourists having a great time. Colourful outfits swirled in the streets, office workers made the most of short hours on a Friday, and ice-cream vendors popped up around the capital's beautiful parks.

And there was so much going on that she wanted to be a

part of – film festivals, photography exhibitions, panel discussions, fundraising evenings – it felt like getting involved was always within reach here, and in such vibrant ways, and she loved it.

Even more so, she loved the ever-closer extended holiday she and Jill were going to be taking. By the start of August all details were nearly finalised, and they were hanging out at Jill's big home one late afternoon to choose the accommodation for their last stop in Switzerland.

'I definitely think somewhere in the Bernese Oberland,' Jill was saying as they got to her back door after taking Bear for his first 'outdoors' walk. 'It would be a nice ending, you know? Especially if they had snow there already.'

'Doesn't Vanessa live somewhere around there?' Alice asked.

Vanessa was a girl she and Jill had met on their gap year, on a South American tour. They'd become close friends on the trip, and had stayed in touch since, but the ten-year gap between seeing each other meant they'd naturally drifted apart somewhat.

'It would be so good to see Vanessa again,' Jill enthused. 'Let's get in touch and find out exactly where she is.' She entered the house and then laughed, her hands on her hips, while Bear sat down on his tufty, muddy bottom and grinned up at her. 'Look at the state of you. It's the middle of a beautiful summer and you found the one puddle of mud in all of London.'

'You can't even see the white blob on his neck any more,'

Alice said, gingerly moving some of his fur aside. He turned around and dug pin-like teeth into her hand. 'Ow!'

'Sorry, he's chewing everything at the moment. He doesn't mean anything by it. Just don't roll your sleeves down, he'll never let go.'

'You're a menace to society,' Alice said, booping Bear on the nose.

'There's only one thing for it, mister, you need a bath. Will you help me bath him?' Jill pleaded.

'Sure . . . where?'

'In the bath.'

'Oh, in the actual bath?'

'What did you think I meant?'

'I assumed you'd use the hose or something.'

Jill mock-gasped. 'He wouldn't stand for it! Come on.' She picked up Bear, and he wriggled in her arms to make extra-sure she was covered in mud. 'Ali, the dog shampoo and conditioner are in the cupboard under the kitchen sink. Don't look at me like that because I have dog conditioner. Can you grab it plus a couple of those old towels?'

Upstairs Bear watched with suspicion as they filled the bath a few inches with cool water. He was sure something fishy was going on, but he didn't want to leave the action, so he paced about the bathroom, sniffing the air.

'All right, you muddy little Bear,' said Jill, picking him up at cooing at him as she lowered him into the bath.

When his feet touched the water he stood stock still for a minute, and Jill took the opportunity to dump a splodge of shampoo onto his back. And that's when all hell broke loose.

Four slipping and sliding paws resulted in splashes flying and an instantly soaked dog. Mud splattered on the tiles. The shampoo bottle was knocked off the side and into the bath. Claw marks scraped trails into the porcelain of the tub as he tried to scramble out.

'Oh shit shit shit,' cried Jill. 'Alice, turn the shower attachment on, we can't let him out with all the foam on his back.'

Alice obeyed but this just freaked out Bear more, and Alice made a snap decision.

Standing up she whipped off her jeans and climbed in the bathtub in her knickers and T-shirt. Bear scrambled up her like a totem pole, holding on to her for dear life against the evil pool of water below. The claws on his hind legs dug into her bare thighs and she wondered why the hell she hadn't suggested Jill do this instead of her. Or why she hadn't just kept her jeans on and put up with the horrid feeling of damp denim against her skin.

'Shhhh,' she soothed him as she scooped small trickles of water into her hands to remove the suds.

Jill helped from the other side, gently cleaning his legs and the back of his neck, while he was distracted by licking the water off Alice's face.

When he was sud-free Jill lifted him from the bath and he went for a shaking rampage around the house, furiously rubbing his nose against anything and everything to dry it. Jill helped Alice out of the bath.

'Thanks for that,' she said. 'Nice pants, by the way.'

'Slightly regretting my life decisions right now,' replied

Alice, inspecting her arms and legs, now covered in tiny scratches.

Jill laughed and held the towel out in the air for Bear to rocket face-first into as he sped back into the bathroom. 'You're going to make a brilliant dog mum one day.'

Chapter 5

A couple of days later it was Jill's turn to come up to Alice's flat in Islington, leaving Bear at home under the care of her brother, Sam.

'Thanks for coming with me today,' Alice said as the two of them got ready to head out to the concert in Brookwick Park that would start in the early afternoon. 'I'm really looking forward to this. Shame the other three couldn't make it, though.'

'Let's do something as a group next week. But maybe something indoors, I'm not sure how much more I can stand of this heat!'

It was 37 degrees Celsius and the capital city was airless. Hot tarmac could be felt through sandals and even when people tried to stand apart there was an uncomfortable closeness in the air. Skin was permanently sticky, brows consistently furrowed against the sun, heads aching and noses pinked. Even the jokes about how British it was to complain about the weather being *too* nice had long since gone, burnt away like the blades of yellowed grass in the city's parks.

Alice finished layering on the factor fifty sun lotion and handed it to Jill. 'You want to borrow a hat to wear?'

'Yeah, I think I'd better, if that's okay. It won't really go with my outfit, but that's probably not the most important thing.'

'They'll let us take in water bottles, right?'

'I'm sure they will, in this heat. Or at minimum they'll be giving them away.'

'I know I am such a summer girl, but right now I would happily stick my head in a pile of snow,' said Alice, slicking on her signature lipstick and then putting it in her crossbody bag. 'Are we nearly good to go?'

Jill faced her and nodded, smiling at her friend. 'I can't wait to push your face into the snow on our trip.'

Alice laughed a happy laugh. 'But first, we dance!'

'But first we dance,' agreed Jill.

The concert was a much bigger operation than Alice had expected. Thousands of people swarmed over the parched grass of Brookwick Park, closing around the stage with its looming, black sound system and video screens. Food vans sizzled and spat hot smoke towards the queues of people, and enormous crates of bottled water stood unmanned, a last-minute free-for-all thanks to the organisers. Alice and Jill's own water bottles had not been allowed in, so they'd gulped them down before entering, their throats already dry.

But the atmosphere was electric, the pre-concert music

thumping joyously out of the speakers and through the soil so you could feel it in your heart. Attendees fanned themselves and picked their hair off the back of their necks, but with smiles and excitement on their faces.

'Shall we head towards the stage now so we're as close as possible to the front?' Alice said, shouting to be heard.

Jill nodded and gave her a thumbs up. 'Let's just get a bottle of water first.'

Alice was so, so pleased she'd come to the concert. This was the most stirring event she'd probably ever been to, and she knew she'd remember it for a long time. It didn't matter that her make-up had run, or that her shoulders were probably tinting a little pinker than they should be in the unshaded sun. Right now, all that mattered was that she felt so lucky to be in one of the world's greatest cities watching some of the world's greatest artists, and she felt inspired.

She turned to grin at Jill by her side, who was staring off to the side, distracted. When she realised Alice was looking at her she snapped her attention back to the stage and slapped on a smile.

Alice nudged her. *You okay?* she signalled to Jill by pointing at her and then giving her a thumbs up, the music being too loud to hear over.

'Just thirsty,' Jill mouthed back.

Alice leant close to her ear and said loudly, 'Shall we go get some more water?'

'No,' Jill said, her dry breath on Alice's cheek. 'I'll just need to pee, and we have a good spot.'

They really did have a great spot, and the performances were so good, with the music reaching into Alice's soul and making her feel happy to be alive. Alice soaked it all in, wanting to remember every second. How all these phenomenal women were throwing dance moves and hitting the high notes in this torridity was commendable. The least Alice could do was sway against some people in the crowd to show her support.

During a break between tracks Alice dived into her bag to find her mini sun lotion stick. Where was it ... she pulled out her lipstick and a tissue, and noticed Jill beside her mopping her brow. She didn't look well.

'Jill?' she called over the elated screams of the crowd.

Jill's eyes focused on her. 'It's so hot,' she said, her voice quiet but her lips easy to read.

'Okay. Okay, I'm going to get you some water.' Alice craned over the heads of the people in front of her and tried to signal to one of the security guards. He wasn't seeing her, and she glanced back to Jill who had her forehead in her hands, being jostled by the people around her, slipping away from Alice like a plastic cup on the surface of the ocean. 'Jill,' she shouted back. 'Wait there, just wait one second.'

Alice pushed forward, waving both arms and shouting to get the attention of the security guard. She pushed and she shoved and at the exact moment the security guard spotted her, the band started up again and the crowd lunged forward as one.

'*Excuse me*,' Alice called out, her voice getting lost, as she tried to push her way through the ever-decreasing gaps between the bodies. '*I just need to get my friend some water, excuse me.*' But nobody was looking at her, all eyes were focused on the stage, and the jungle of people a tangle of limbs and sweat, elbows pushing and phones held high.

She edged closer to the railings, and she could see the security guard holding a bottle of water for her but he was distracted, his mouth clearly telling the crowd to *move back. Move back.* Alice paused and whirled back to meet Jill's eye one more time, trying to convey that someone was coming, water was coming, and Jill smiled at her.

The crowd lunged again and Alice felt something give way – the railing at the front – and she stumbled, tumbling, carried with the wave of people. Her leg sliced against something metal and she cried out, knocked to the ground, the lipstick that she'd forgotten she was even still clutching dropping under her hands, her palms dirtying.

Alice stood, wincing in pain, managing to extricate herself before the crush of people swallowed her up, and she looked for Jill. Their eyes met briefly, like a flash of sun on a moving wave, then she was gone.

Alice looked and looked, and she called Jill's name, but she was all at sea.

Chapter 6

'I heard there wasn't nearly enough water for everyone and that's what caused the panic.'

Whispered conversations dripped into Alice's consciousness from familiar voices and unfamiliar hospital staff during the twenty-four hours they kept her in after it happened.

'Where was security, though? They must have seen some warning signs that people were getting all hyped up.'

'I think it was just an act of God – nobody could have prevented that heatwave and people got desperate and claustrophobic and it was overcrowded.'

Speculating, wondering, gossiping, all cut with abstract phrases and acronyms that somehow related to her body and her health. Alice kept her eyes shut, letting the sleep and drugs wash her away.

'She was near the front I think, got out quickly and found her way to the first aid tent.'

'One of the lucky ones.'

'She keeps asking about a friend?'

It was raining again on the other side of the curtains – just like Britain had hoped for, had expected. *This* was a typical August day in Britain. Alice awoke to the gentle rhythm of the droplets against the glass. For a second she could make-believe she was in a spa, and this was a sound effects CD, and she was just coming to from a long and drowsy massage. But even with her eyes still closed, her face half-pressed into her pillow, her brain trying to back away from the thoughts she knew were reality, the fact remained.

Jill was gone.

She was dead, and it was Alice's fault.

When Ed Bright knocked on the door of his daughter's childhood bedroom a while later, with the trepidation of someone who'd been told by doctors and police professionals several times over the past week since it happened, 'avoid loud noises', she was already sitting up. Hunched, and staring at her fingers while they idly traced the floral pattern of her duvet cover, but upright.

'Hello, my love,' he soothed. 'Mind if I come and drink my cup of tea in here? I brought you one.'

It was a sweet turn of phrase, Alice noticed, her dad acting like she was doing him a favour by giving him company while he drank, rather than the other way around.

'Sure,' she replied, her voice croaky from days of rasping sobs. She patted the bed and Ed perched, getting up again a moment later to draw back one of the curtains, watching her for signs of this not being okay.

'Raining again,' he remarked, settling back down and blowing on his mug of brew.

'Why do you think I'm crying?' Alice smiled to show her dad it was a joke. Just a small one.

'Did you manage to go back to sleep?'

'Yeah, sorry again for last night. You and Mum must be exhausted.'

'We're absolutely fine.' He patted her shin ever so gently through the duvet.

Alice hadn't slept through the night for over a week now, ever since the concert. At the beginning her mind was switching off when she slept, fatigued by the rush of events, the information overload, and the tilting of her world. Instead she would come to in middle of the night and when she opened her eyes to the darkness a fear would consume her and she couldn't stop herself from crying out. When she started to sleep with the light on, the fears, the memories, knew exactly where she was, and they would creep into her dreams instead and find their way to her there. The result: crying out in her sleep instead.

Her parents seemed to take it in turns, like they'd done when she was a baby, to be the ones to get up and comfort their daughter, the feeling being that if two of them fussed around her it would be too overwhelming. Alice's pattern with her father was becoming that he would come into the room with his iPad and a hot chocolate, sit beside her on the bed and they'd watch old *Vicar of Dibley* episodes until she drifted back into – for the time being – a peaceful slumber.

'What are your plans today?' she asked him, as if it was just a normal day and plans mattered.

'Oh not much. Your mum wants to make a cake to take around to Jill's family ... We thought we'd go for a walk in a bit. Still good to get a bit of fresh air, even in the rain. Would you like to come?'

'To deliver the cake?' Alice couldn't even comprehend going to Jill's parents' house. The thought of being there, when their daughter was not, felt like she'd be mocking them.

'No, no,' her dad reassured, worried he'd gone and said the wrong thing. He didn't know how to navigate this. 'A separate walk. If your leg feels okay?'

Alice shook her head. 'No thanks, I'll stay here.'

'Are you sure? Why don't you take some painkillers and then see how you feel in a while?'

'No.'

'No painkillers?'

She shook her head. She had no right to numb her pain.

After the crush Alice had been considered 'one of the lucky ones'. Being so close to where the barriers broke she'd managed to release herself from the crowd fairly quickly. But she was disorientated and scared and she kept trying to get back into the throng to find Jill, to give her some water, until someone physically pulled her and dragged her to the first aid tent to stop the bleeding in her leg. She had no idea how long she'd been looking for Jill by that time, but she knew it would never, never feel like enough time. Jill was one of the six unlucky ones.

It hurt Alice to think about the concert itself in too much detail, or to analyse the sequence of events, because one thing was very clear to her: Jill was there because of her. She'd left Jill on her own. *She* was to blame for Jill's death.

'I don't like to see you hurting, my love,' Ed said, struggling for the words to show his daughter what he really meant.

Then don't look at me, she thought, unkindly, but managed to bite her tongue before she said it out loud. He was only trying to help.

Alice shuffled back down into the bed with care, wincing in pain, and pulled the covers up. She closed her eyes though she knew she wouldn't go back to sleep. 'I think I'm going to try and nap again,' she told her dad. 'Thank you for the tea.'

She heard him leave the room and pull the door to, but not closed, and she wished she could feel better quicker, for her parents' sake. But how could she pretend to feel okay when she couldn't even remember what okay felt like?

A day later, maybe two, Alice was pacing her bedroom, enjoying the ache it caused her leg. With each step she allowed the throb to vividly remind her not of the concert – she didn't allow herself to think of that – but not to forget to think about Jill, even for a second.

She picked up a pen from her windowsill and tapped it against her wound as she walked, an extra little sharp pain, an extra thing to fidget with.

The pen fell from her fingers and she cursed, crouching as best she could with her bad leg out to the side to pick it up. And within a microsecond she was back at the concert.

It was like a tableau she'd stepped into, where the world was frozen but she could see every detail of that second before it happened, painted in front of her in vivid, 4D surround sound. She was crouched to the ground, her hand pressed hard against her dropped lipstick, surrounded by legs and feet in outfits that had been planned and favourite shoes, that now danced as if they were on fire, looking for somewhere to step, looking for gaps to run into. Sweat and the scent of sticky, spilled soda rose from the ground and hovered in the air. Jill was behind her, half turned, a smile on her face and Alice cried because she knew what was coming. And she kept crying because she couldn't stop it and she wanted to shout out to Jill to move but she was frozen, they all were, frozen in a last moment that should never have happened.

Alice tried and tried to make a sound but all that came out was a strained, inaudible wail that went on and on.

Liz Bright was in the upstairs corridor when she heard the pacing stop, and had crept towards her daughter's door to listen, to see if it was appropriate to go in. When she heard the sound of her daughter cry out a few moments later her heart broke and she pushed her way in to find Alice crouched in a ball on the floor, her hand reaching statically for a pen, her eyes searching for something Liz couldn't see.

'Oh my love.' Liz rushed to her daughter's side and stroked her head, grasping her hand, saying her name over and over again. She didn't know if this was the right thing to do but every instinct told her to do anything to bring Alice back from the place she'd gone to.

Eventually Alice seemed to inhale again, her breaths coming thick and fast, her rapid eye movements becoming slower and her head lowered. The tears came, dropping from her in parallel to her entire body drooping into Liz's arms. 'Mum,' she said. 'I dropped my lipstick again.'

'It's okay, it was just a pen, you're safe, you're at home.'

Alice looked around. How could she be in her childhood bedroom when she was just *there*? 'It felt real, though. I saw her.'

'I know, but it's okay, I promise. I've got you.' And her mum didn't let go.

Later that same day, Alice ventured downstairs where her mum and dad were sitting at the kitchen table discussing something (probably her) in hushed tones.

Ed jumped up when he saw her. 'Hello love, how are you feeling?'

She shrugged. 'Okay.' She didn't feel okay, but she couldn't bear to tell them that a week ... ten days ... two weeks (how long had it been?) in and she felt exactly the same. Numb.

'Mum was telling me about your, um, episode this morning. I think we should ask the doctor to come back over, just for a talk.'

'I'm fine.'

Ed and Liz exchanged a glance. Ed opened his mouth

again but Alice shot in with the question which was the reason she'd come down in the first place.

'Where is Bear?'

'Bear?' her mum asked. 'One of your old teddy bears? I think they're all in the wardrobe—'

'No, Bear, the dog, Jill's dog. Is he okay?'

'Oh, the puppy,' Ed answered. 'The big puppy. He's fine. He's at Jill's mum and dad's.'

'How do you know?'

'I went over there the other day, just to see how they were,' Liz said, in an almost apologetic tone. 'I took some cake.'

'Oh yes, the cake,' said Alice. Liz and Ed got to keep a daughter, but at least Jill's parents had cake. 'How were they with you?'

'Fine. Very sad. I didn't stay long. Do you mind that I went?'

'No.' Alice wanted to know more. 'Did they say anything about me?'

'They asked how you were. I told them about your leg, and about how you were staying with us for a while.'

'Are they angry at me?'

'For not coming over? No, of course not,' Liz soothed.

'No, for . . .' Alice's voice cracked but she didn't have enough tears left in her at the moment. 'For being alive.'

Ed thumped a fist on the table, his own eyes prickling with tears, which was something Alice had never seen before. She had a flash thought about how if she had died he would have been doing this a lot.

'Ed . . .' said Liz.

'Alice, don't you ever say that or think that ever again,' he cried. 'I'm sorry, Liz, but I'm so angry that this stupid, stupid accident has … has … taken everything from so many people, and even the ones still here like our little Alice are having bad dreams and flashbacks and wondering if people wished they were dead.'

'Dad, I … '

'I'm sorry, love, I don't mean to get all worked up, I know it's not helping. Just please remember how important you are to all of us. Don't ever think anyone's angry.' He rubbed his eyes. 'Jill's mum and dad don't wish anything bad had happened to you – that wouldn't have saved their little girl.'

'But I asked her to come to the concert with me. She wouldn't have been there if it wasn't for me.'

Liz guided Alice to the table and placed a mug of tea in front of her. 'You just can't think like that.'

'But I do.'

'I know. I hope one day you won't.'

One day felt like a really long way away.

Chapter 7

Almost three weeks had passed since it happened, and at dawn Alice was back in her room, sitting up in bed, wondering why the sun had chosen today of all days to shine again. It seemed cruel.

Ed was nursing his cup of tea beside her, making small talk that she wasn't hearing.

'I guess I'd better have a shower.' Alice made a move to get up, lifting the duvet and glimpsing, before quickly looking away, the long, thin wound that would eventually scar, sweeping its way up her left leg. She stood and made it halfway to the door when she just stopped. Her shoulders sank, her head tipped and she stood in her pyjamas, hopeless. 'I don't want to go, Dad.'

Ed put his mug down on a book that had remained unopened on Alice's bedside table, and rushed to his daughter's side, enveloping her in his arms. His poor little girl. This poor, happy little thing going through something so very horrible, and as he kissed her straggled hair he thought, not for the first time, how at least he still got to hold her. It was heartbreaking, but his daughter was intact. He felt awful for even comparing himself to Jill's parents.

To Alice it was akin to being a small child again, unable to process anything beyond the walls of the past three weeks. And simultaneously it was as if her soul had aged twenty years overnight at having to face mortality. *I can't do it*, she repeated to herself. *I can't do it. She can't be gone.*

And then as quickly as they came, the tears retreated for now, like the watering can had just needed emptying again. She was back to empty, and she took a big breath. 'But I have to go, don't I?'

Ed stepped back. 'You don't have to, my love. You don't have to do anything. We've still got a lot of *Vicar of Dibley* episodes to watch.'

'But you think I should?'

'I think you should. I don't think it'll be easy; in fact I think you'll be in for a pretty lousy day, and I don't think you'll feel any better afterwards. But I think my Alice of the Future will be glad she went to her best friend's funeral.'

A little stabby thought crossed through her: *Jill won't have a future.* But he was right. 'Yeah. Okay. I really need that shower, though.' She smiled at her dad and left the room.

I don't have a best friend any more, she thought, as the hot water rushed onto her scalp. *I don't have my Jill. We had plans.*

She squeezed her eyes shut, rubbing a facial scrub into her forehead in slow circles. *This shower gel is mango scented. Jill and I had those mango mojitos in Vegas. She really liked them; I think she'd have liked this shower gel.*

I miss Jill. I wish we could switch places.

That wasn't true, though, and a little part of her was ashamed for wishing her life away at this time. If she had a wish, she'd wish for neither of them to be in the coffin. None of them to be in any of the coffins.

Alice wondered if any of the other victims' funerals were being held today. It was possible, but she probably would never know. She certainly wasn't about to scour the newspapers for grainy paparazzi shots and saccharine-soaked write-ups.

She lifted her face to the water, and it felt good. If only she could hide in here all day.

Alice was on the outside looking in. A spectator letting other people make the small talk around her, glancing at her occasionally with a morbid curiosity that pulled people's attention from poor Jill.

'Nobody's looking at you,' Bahira had whispered inside the church.

Alice had shuffled on the spot, her smart shoes pinching, her collar tight on her throat. Deep inside she knew Bahira was right, but with tissues squeezed tightly in both her hands she knew that if she fully let her guard down and accepted the reality that she was at Jill's funeral she didn't know if she'd ever come back out. It couldn't be real. The world wasn't that cruel.

The funeral was horrible but peaceful, and over quickly.

She'd clung to her friends, Bahira, Theresa and Kemi, silently pleading with them to not be angry at her for ever.

Alice now stood in the churchyard, under the newly appeared sunshine with Bahira, Kemi and Theresa, their faces looking like reflections of their younger selves, with their make-up minimal, their mascara wiped away onto tissues, their eyes tired. Inside the church hall was a small wake, but most guests were bringing their china cups of tepid tea back out into the open air. Theresa was telling a story they all knew, slowly and carefully, peppered with genuine smiles, about the holiday they'd all taken with Jill right after uni. Jill's many friends, from her many walks of life, stood in huddles all recounting their own memories.

'. . . And when we finally got on the boat, she said, "You can all call me the Codfather!"' Theresa paused and Bahira and Kemi chuckled. Alice realised a beat too late and then joined in too.

As Theresa, bless her soul, continued the story to fill the silence with a sliver of happiness, Alice's ears focused in on the conversation behind her. Jill's parents were talking to her brother.

'I spoke to Max, the man Bear came from, and he can't take him back,' Jill's mum was saying wearily. 'I mean, he was very sorry and said he would if we couldn't find anyone else, but he doesn't have the space to keep him.'

'He's a lovely dog. Jilly loved him so much already.' Jill's dad's voice cracked, which in turn cracked Alice's heart a bit more. Why were they talking about this here, now? Perhaps the mundanity of keeping organised helped keep reality at bay. Alice should try it sometime.

Jill's brother Sam, only in his early twenties and too young to be going through this, spoke with the quiet voice of someone who didn't know if they should be parent or child in this situation. 'I don't know how to help. I can't have pets at uni. I could take a year out maybe?'

'No, no you can't do that,' insisted his mum.

'Or I could come home every weekend to walk him, if you kept him, and I could look into finding someone to walk him on weekdays?'

Of course Jill's parents, her dad with his arthritis and her mum with her dodgy knee, wouldn't be able to raise a puppy, especially a big strong puppy that was, in Jill's words, going to grow into a grizzly. Alice felt silly for never thinking past the assumption that they would take on the dog, especially as they appeared more fragile than ever now.

Jill's mum sighed, her voice sounding defeated. 'I don't know what to do. Where to start. I just don't want to give him to someone we don't know, he was only with her a month but he was part of Jill.'

'I'll take Bear.' Alice left the conversation with her friends and turned around, the words falling from her lips, desperate to do anything that might contribute to the huge debt she owed her best friend's family. 'I'll take him. I'll look after him just like Jill would have. I went to the vet's and the puppy socialisation parties with her, I can help. Please let me help.'

*

43

While Jill's family exchanged a silent conversation with each other, which Alice didn't know whether to interpret as thinking about it or wonderment at how Alice could dare even to suggest it, Kemi appeared at her elbow.

'Alice, I don't think you have space for a dog,' she murmured.

'It will be fine. My flat is small, but he's only small ... at the moment, and I have the park minutes away for big walks.'

'I know you want to help, but you're so busy, Ali,' added Bahira. She turned to Jill's parents. 'Maybe I could have him for a while?' Even as she said it she sounded unconvinced.

'You have a dog already,' Alice said. 'I have no one. I'm alone.'

'What about work and things, though?' Bahira pressed, tugging Alice just out of earshot. 'Aren't you trying to get involved in more causes at the moment?'

'It's all just so unimportant,' Alice said, tiredly. 'I can't change anything, I can't stop anything, I can't even save my best friend!' The morning after it had happened Alice had woken up a different person. She'd given so much of herself to optimism, and without it she didn't really know who she was any more. She was crumbling, and she turned back to Jill's mum, dad and brother. 'Let me save Bear?'

Jill's mum shrugged, and then nodded, too overwhelmed to continue the conversation she'd started. Sam patted her arm, awkward but kind. Jill's dad cleared his throat. 'That would be very helpful, thank you, Alice. Even if it's just temporarily.'

Alice nodded, processing what she'd just done. 'How will I get him—'

'I have my car down here. I'll take you and him and his things back to London whenever you're ready,' Bahira interjected, pulling Alice away from the family, knowing the details didn't need to be decided right now.

'So,' said Alice when it was just the four of them again, nestled under the comforting leaves of an old oak tree in the churchyard. 'Anyone know how to raise a dog?'

Back at her home that evening, Alice was listening to her parents and her friends discussing her. They were all drinking tea and sitting around the living room, tired, emotionally worn, the different ages an inconsequential factor. It was like a board meeting being held at the very end of a very long day, where people occasionally remembered to include the person on the other end of the spider phone, which in this case was Alice.

'I'm just worried because it's a big responsibility for her. Literally. It just doesn't seem like a good time. She's still quite wary of things. Understandably,' Liz was saying, nodding encouragingly at Alice on the final word.

'My sister-in-law has a big dog,' Kemi said. 'And she's always saying how he makes her feel really safe. It could be that he helps her. You.'

Theresa nodded. 'And they do say dogs can help with shock and –' she whispered the next word, '– *trauma*.'

Liz looked to Ed. 'She's not had a dog before. It's a lot to learn.'

'I don't know if it's that much hard work,' Ed said. 'Jill already trained him up a fair amount, I remember Alice telling us.'

'But she doesn't want to leave the house at the moment. Maybe we should take him instead.'

'If I have a dog, I will leave the house,' Alice said without looking up from her tea. 'I promise. We can look after each other.'

'Where would you walk him around yours?' Bahira asked.

'The park is two minutes away. My street is quite quiet, too, so I can take him out for wees last thing at night.' Even as she said it, Alice found herself wondering if dogs could have litter trays.

'If having a dog is anything like having a kid, which it is, as I know because I have both,' said the ever-practical Bahira, 'it's a massive lifestyle change. You won't be able to go out and leave him for long. You'll need to find dog day care for if you have to go into the *Funny Pack* office. You have to take him out and walk him, twice a day, rain or shine.'

'I know all of this,' Alice said. 'I know it's not going to be easy, but I've made my decision and I've already told Jill's parents. I'm taking Bear. I need to do this.'

'It's not too late—' started Liz.

'Mum, I really do need to do this. I'm going to look after him.'

They all nodded, and then Bahira spoke up. 'Well, like I said earlier, if you want to come back with me tomorrow, you can. I'll drive you both. Otherwise just ring me when you're ready, no rush, and I'll come down and pick you up.'

'Thank you.' Alice sipped her tea.

Theresa sighed. 'I'm happy. I mean, it's been a horrible day, but I'm happy Bear is coming to live with you. It's like you get to keep hold of a little bit of Jill's heart.'

Chapter 8

'Good morning,' Ed said with surprise. 'You're up early.'

Alice walked into the kitchen dressed. It was nine a.m., so not early really, but considering the length of time she'd spent in bed over the past three weeks it was practically the crack of dawn. 'Where's Mum?'

'Here,' Liz answered, coming into the room and embracing her daughter. 'Going somewhere?'

'Actually, yes. I'm going to take Bahira up on the offer for a lift back up to London today.'

'Oh, honey, you don't have to go so soon, we can drive you back into town when you're ready, can't we Ed?'

'Of course we can.'

'I know, thank you, but I think I need to go for it. I remember Jill saying that puppies have about fifteen weeks before they stop learning things so easily, and he must be around that now. I think I need to get him home with me as soon as possible so he gets to know his new environment and any ground rules.'

It was funny, she was speaking like a convincing, functioning, human. Maybe this is how she would be from now on, a mask of a person. Because really, under the mask, she didn't think she'd ever be over it.

She smiled at her parents. 'Will you come up and stay, though, maybe next weekend? If you have no other plans? If you aren't sick of me?'

'Yes, any time,' Liz nodded.

'And if you wake up in the night and that pup is either making you more anxious or not making you feel better, you call us. Any time, it doesn't matter, we can come up and get you or come and stay, you don't have to be brave right through to the weekend.'

'Thanks, Dad.'

She'd called Jill's brother that morning. Her parents' landline number was forever etched into her memory bank from years of childhood phone calls to Jill almost every night to talk about TV shows or books or boys or uni choices. But it felt somehow invasive to call them on that directly, to have them pick up the phone without realising who was on the other end, and to give them no choice in whether to talk to her or not. So instead she called Sam, and asked him if she should take Bear today. He'd agreed, saying it would be a big help, actually, and the relief in his voice was enough to cement the deal for Alice. Bear was her responsibility from today, there was no going back. It was the least she could do to help. She owed this to Jill's family. She owed this to Jill.

*

As she and her mum approached Jill's family home to collect the puppy, Alice had thrown up at the end of their driveway. It came out of nowhere, and she didn't think anyone had seen, but she and her mum had sat on the pavement for at least ten minutes before making their way to the house.

'You don't have to do this, you know. You're going through enough, you don't have to be the one to take on a pet as well.' Her mum stroked her back as she said this.

Alice faced the concrete ground, her back hunched, her forehead sweating. 'I have to.'

Liz was silent for a few moments. 'Will you bring him back to our house then, and you can both stay there for a while?'

'No, I want to get him settled in his new home. It's not taking on Bear, that's not why I'm ...'

'I know.'

How could she go in there, into her family's personal space, without Jill? When she was the one who took Jill away? How could they ever forgive her?

'I don't want to see all the photos of her on the walls.'

'I know,' her mum soothed, lost for what to say.

Alice's breathing returned to the normal, numb breath she was getting used to, and she slowly rose, checking herself for traces of vomit. She nodded at her mother, and they slowly made their way up the driveway. Alice kept her eyes down, afraid to look up in case she couldn't stop herself looking towards the window in the top left-hand corner – Jill's child-hood bedroom.

Her mum knocked on the door, and the sound of scrambling feet on wood and crumpled ears being shaken out could be heard before the door had even opened.

When Sam pulled the door open, Bear scrabbled through and Alice exclaimed, 'Oh my gosh!', not believing how much he'd grown in the past month. 'Hello, you,' she said to him as he greeted her like a long-lost friend.

Bear circled her and bounced and waved his paws and beamed up at her, his eyes big and his tail wagging furiously. He sniffed briefly at her mum's knees before turning his attention back to Alice.

'Someone's pleased to see you,' Sam commented with a smile.

He remembers me. And she was surprised at how pleased she was to see him, this little tornado.

Alice crouched down and Bear nuzzled his head into her chest, his spindly tail still causing a tidal wave on the other side of the world. 'Hi, Bear, hi, do you want to come home with me?'

He leaned right into her face, his nostrils sniffing, and licked her nose.

'Is that a yes? We can keep each other company.' The three of them watched Bear as he stepped back from Alice and peered around her. He was still smiling, his tail was still wagging, but he seemed to be searching for the missing puzzle piece, and Alice knew what it was. 'She's not with me, I'm sorry.'

'Oh, honey,' Liz said, her heart breaking for her daughter.

'Why don't you both come in? It's cold out here,' said Sam.

He seemed grown up beyond his years now, with a seriousness to his voice that Alice didn't recognise.

Inside the hallway, Bear continued to look towards the door, as if he couldn't understand why Alice was here without Jill. And in all honesty, she still hadn't wrapped her head around it either.

Alice felt like a coward, but she stayed near the puppy, talking softly to him and keeping her eyes on him, while her mum spoke with Jill's family and followed them through the house gathering up Bear's belongings. It was only when all the bags were by the door, ready to be carried back down the driveway to Liz's car, that Alice stood and faced Jill's parents.

'I'm really sorry,' she said, her whole heart in those three words.

Jill's mum nodded. 'So are we.'

'I'm ... sorry,' she repeated.

'It's not your fault,' Jill's mum said, and pulled her into a hug, though it didn't feel the same as it used to. It felt more guarded. Did they know? Did they know that she'd been pleased when Jill had said she didn't want to lose their spots to get more water? Did they know that their daughter's supposed best friend put a good view at a concert over Jill's life?

'You've been such a good friend to Jill,' Jill's mum said, pulling back and revealing eyes that were pink and full of sorrow.

'She was the best friend in the whole world,' Alice whispered back. She took a breath and stepped backwards towards the door before the bile rose again. 'Please visit him whenever you want,' she said, the words sounding stiff in her own ears. 'Or I can bring him to you.'

Jill's mum nodded. 'Maybe sometime.'

She and Sam said goodbye to the puppy, Sam pushing his face into his fur for a long moment. Then Alice and Liz left, Alice holding Bear's lead, his bed and as many bags as she could manage, and Liz carrying the rest. Alice had refused any extra help, and Bear trotted down the driveway without looking back.

'Do you think he thinks we're taking him back to Jill?' Alice asked her mum.

'I think he's just a daft puppy looking forward to heading out on an adventure,' Liz answered.

The amount of stuff that Jill's parents had given her had filled the boot and the back seat of Liz's car, and then Bahira's car later that morning. On the journey back to London, Alice held Bear tightly on her lap, on red alert for anything that could cause her precious cargo – Jill's beloved puppy – any harm.

'How are you, B?' Alice asked her friend when Bear had stopped wriggling and dozed off.

'Good question,' Bahira answered, her eyes on the road. 'Very sad, quite pissed off and probably will have an enormous cry tonight when I get home, and everyone's in bed, and I let it all sink in.'

Alice nodded. She admired Bahira's strength and maturity and she nearly let the words all tumble out of her and admit how responsible she felt. But she'd lost a friend already, and the shameful, selfish part of her didn't want to risk losing another.

So instead she said, 'Call me if you need anything, won't you?' to which Bahira glanced away from the road quickly to give her a smile.

Chapter 9

Had Alice not volunteered to adopt a bear cub called Bear, she didn't know when she would have left her childhood home. Maybe she would have never returned to London, and to the real, cruel world. But her determination to give Bear a home again, some stability, meant she found herself back at her own front door only a day after the funeral. Only this time she was holding in her arms a wriggling fluff-bag.

Bear shifted in her arms, sitting his bum on her hands and his front paws on her shoulders, and licked at her face while she tried to pass instructions to Bahira.

'It's the key on the end, with the red dot ... that one ... that goes in the top lock ... it sometimes jams. Ugh, stop it, Bear. Flick the key to the right first then turn left, that's it. *Bear.*' She turned her head and the dog's tongue went in her ear instead.

Bahira laughed and eventually got the door open. Once all three of them were inside, with the door shut, Alice put Bear down. He stood for a moment on his little fat legs, before skittering through into her living room.

And now, here in her flat as he tottered from room to room, stuffing his nose into everything he could find, giving her belongings exploratory chews and peering under bits of furniture, Alice hoped with everything in her that he was finding it an adventure.

Bahira and she took turns going back and forth to the car and keeping the puppy in the house. They carted in a large, flat dog bed as big as a single mattress (way too big for this dog, surely?), food and water bowls plus one and a half *big* bags of food, mountains of practical things like towels and poop bags and pills prescribed by the vet, bagfuls of toys in crunchy, squeaky, ropey vibrancy, two harnesses, three leads, a metal crate ('though I think he refused to ever set even one paw in there' Jill's mum had said).

Once everything was inside, Bear nosed through it all, sticking his whole head into open bags and pulling things out onto the carpet.

'Shall I stay for a while and help you unpack?' asked Bahira.

'No, you head home to your family, we'll be fine.'

Alice bid Bahira goodbye, but in actual fact, she didn't know where to start. When she'd left this flat she'd had no idea she'd be bringing a dog back to live with her.

When she'd left this flat, Jill had still been alive. She hadn't been back here since before heading to the concert. Her make-up was still scattered on the mantelpiece under the mirror, the electric blue liquid liner she'd felt so Coachella wearing was just lying there, waiting for her to come home. And she could have so easily never come home.

If she'd never come home, would this make-up still be sitting here? Or would someone have cleared her flat by now, avoiding paying an extra month's rent, which in London wasn't cheap? And would each item she owned be carefully considered, or would things like this blue eyeliner, which had no meaning for anybody – it didn't even hold a place in Alice's heart – just be swept into the bin?

Alice picked up the eyeliner and dropped it into the bin.

Was Jill's house empty? Probably not – she had owned her house; there would be no rush.

Alice wondered if she should have offered to go over and help clear the house, but even thinking it caused a pain so deep in her heart that she couldn't imagine ever being able to find the strength to do that.

How horrible a friend she was to put her own pain over that of Jill's family, who also didn't want to clear their daughter's, their sister's, home where everything – *everything* – would remind them of her.

'I'm tired,' Alice said to Bear, looking at the mess in the living room. She was running on empty, and she couldn't, she just couldn't, face the pile of things quite yet. 'I just need an hour or two, okay?'

She pushed his bed up against the wall in the living room, threw a couple of toys on the floor, and filled a big bowl of water which she left in the kitchen. Then she went to her room, Bear sticking close behind her.

The clothes she'd left strewn on her bed – discarded

shorts from the morning of the concert, a top she'd nearly worn that day before changing her mind at the last minute, a couple of potential handbags that hadn't made the cut – had been folded neatly and placed on a chair, the bed cover neatened and the water glass from her nightstand washed and dried and put back upside down. Her dad had come into the city a few days after it happened to pack a rucksack full of her things. He'd packed a few clothes, pulled a book off her bookshelf – it was one she'd already read but it was a sweet thought – a tub of night cream, a hairbrush, a lip balm and a cuddly rabbit. He must have straightened it out for her.

'Bear, you're going to like my dad. He's kind.'

She climbed onto her bed and Bear trotted around the edge of it, looking for a way up. She watched him, assuming he'd just lie on the floor in a moment, but when he stretched his front paws up onto her mattress, wriggled his legs to try and haul himself up and whined at her, she helped him up.

'It's okay,' she said. 'You can come here with me. I promise I'll look after you now.'

Alice lay down on top of the covers, and Bear sank down right next to her, shuffling his back into her and going straight to sleep. She looked down at his tufty head, the colour of Bourneville chocolate but with flecks of burgundy, and a splash of white on the back of his neck. Above his eyes were two thumbprint sized 'eyebrows' in a rich amber colour that twitched when he opened an eye to see her peeping at him. His snout was white and freckled with dark brown and ginger dots, and still somewhat squashed in like an accordion. He stretched his legs, which also marbled from chocolate to caramel to the cream on his too-big paws, and his chest was a puff of pearly white fur.

She reached her fingers across and stroked his little head oh so gently, and he closed his eyes. 'You sleep now, puppy, I'm going to keep you safe.'

Chapter 10

It was strange having an extra thing in the house, something living and moving, that didn't stay where she left it like her familiar furniture or her art supplies. Later that afternoon, Alice kept getting a jolt in her heart when she was walking through her home, her muscle memory moving her around her belongings, before remembering to keep watch for where the puppy might be hanging out. His favourite activity seemed to be following her from room to room, so at least most of the time he was behind her feet, rather than in front of them.

As the summer darkness finally fell on London, Alice found the street noises deafening in a way she hadn't before. The sounds of cars, chatter, heels on pavements, distant lorry horns, all drifted through the cracks of her windows.

'It's so noisy here,' she muttered to Bear, who sat awkwardly, back legs splayed about, ropey tail strewn to the side and tongue lolling from his mouth. He tilted his head at her and belched, holding eye contact.

'Same to you!'

Well, it was probably time to try and sleep. Alice gathered her phone, her book that she still probably wouldn't read, a glass of water, some headache pills, and took them into her bedroom.

Bear followed close behind.

'No,' she said, ushering him back into the kitchen. 'You sleep in the kitchen, that's where you used to sleep.' She showed him the tiled floor, the water bowl, the soft rabbit toy she'd left out for him that Jill had bought. 'You like the cold floor. My bedroom has carpet.'

Bear popped his nose in and out of the water bowl and then walked past her and back towards her bedroom, stopping in the doorway to look around for her.

'Bear, you come back here. You're sleeping in the kitchen.'

There was a stand-off occurring, and Alice didn't quite know how to take this. 'Hey, I'm the boss here, come back and sleep in the kitchen.'

With that, the puppy broke eye contact with Alice and wandered off into her room.

Tears prickled her eyes and she blinked them back immediately. How ridiculous to feel emotional about such a thing when there are bigger problems in the world. She took a deep breath and followed the dog into the bedroom, picked him up, and carried him to the kitchen, where she put a chair on its side across the doorframe to block him in. He whinnied a little bit.

'I'm sorry, but you have to sleep in here. That's the rule.' Although, she wasn't sure whose rule she was quoting. Jill's perhaps? Would this furry little thing ever feel truly like he was hers?

Alice made her way back to her bedroom, loneliness and fear sensing an opportunity to come visiting. She ignored Bear's whines as she changed into her pyjamas.

She stopped brushing her teeth halfway through to shout, 'It'sh okay, Bear,' through a mouthful of foam, when he let out the first yelp.

She tried to ignore as the yelping got louder, lying in bed, staring at her ceiling.

It was when he woofed, a tiny cry of help from something thinking he was making a much braver sound than he was, that she jumped up and ran to him. He was fine, of course he was, he was just sat on the other side of the sideways chair, waiting for her. He stood when he saw her, and that stringy, ropey tail started flicking back and forth.

Alice knelt down. 'Are you lonely?'

Bear stared up at her.

'Do you miss her?'

He rested his chin on top of the chair frame.

'I miss her too,' Alice said, stroking the white patch on the top of his head. 'I'm going to try my hardest to give you a really nice life, just like she wanted. I'm going to take care of you, and make sure you're safe and happy. You're the top priority, now.'

Bear's eyes closed, his chin still resting on the chair, comforted by her voice and strokes. 'We have to help each other out a little, though – I'm new to this. Having you in my house is a huge learning curve, even after all the hours that Jill used to babble on to me about you. To start with, tell me why I should let you sleep in my room? I don't let men I don't know well sleep in my room.'

Bear got onto all fours, turned and ran to the stuffed rabbit and brought it back to her in his mouth, its ears dangling on the floor.

She couldn't help but smile. 'Is that for me? Is this a bribe?' She stood and reached her hand out and Bear backed away, bumping into the kitchen island, tail going wild. *Take it from me!* he seemed to be saying. *But you can't actually have it!*

'It's not playtime, it's bedtime.' But even as she said it Alice was moving the chair, putting it back upright. Bear bounced towards her, rabbit flailing, and pushed it into her shin, right on her wound. She winced and Bear dropped the rabbit, staring closely at her leg, sniffing her scabbed-over cut. He gave it a tentative lick, and then turned around, and sat his furry bum down on her foot, like a little bodyguard.

Alice thought in that moment that she might already love him a little bit. But just a very little bit. He was still proving to be a handful.

And that's how she found herself not only letting him follow her back to her bedroom, but also lifting him up onto her bed, where he wadged about for a while, walking up and down, pulling at the duvet cover with his tiny spikes of teeth, rolling on his back to see how his paws felt floating about in the air of her home. A few times he stepped on her, a heavy paw holding up eighteen kilograms, but she didn't mind.

'Shall we try and sleep, then?' she asked him.

He looked at her, then carried on shuffling about in circles, restless.

'Do you want to get down? Is the duvet too warm for you?' *I told you so.* 'I'm not turning the light off, if that's what the problem is. I sleep with the light on at the moment. I know it's very unreasonable but you're just going to have to put up with me being a bit weird for a bit, I think.'

He was watching her, like she had a little more explaining to do.

'Just give me time.'

Bear wandered up to her face, peered at her closely, exhaled at her through his nostrils, and climbed onto her pillow, curling himself around her head like a huge furry hat.

'You're sleeping there?' It was unconventional, and she prayed she didn't get kicked in the face, but she didn't exactly dislike it.

He sighed, a long, sleepy sigh. Alice kept firmly still, not wanting to disturb this funny visitor. He was finally settled, like he had all the time in the world for her.

It must have been morning. Alice was awake, her head foggy, the duvet pulled right over her, but through the fabric she could see the light in her room had changed from the stark orange of her bedside light, which had stayed on all night, to a more muted yellow, suggesting the sun was trying to break through the curtains.

She traced her finger up and down the wound on her leg, and a deep sadness settled over her as if the duvet itself was the weight of her sorrow. It had been a long first night alone, with tangled dreams of oppressive London skylines and her dry, thirsty throat closing to the point where she could no longer breathe. In her waking hours her first thought was always the guilt, her mind whispering at her again and again that she had caused this and that she'd live with it for ever.

She couldn't remember the last time she'd spent so long indoors, so long in bed. Just three weeks ago today she would have been up at dawn, running around, probably dreaming up cartoons that made light of a world she viewed through rose-tinted glasses. What had she even been working towards, trying to save the world when at any moment, any heartbeat could be someone's last?

The duvet shuffled near her feet, and then lifted an inch. A little black nose appeared, nostrils flaring, sniffing at Alice's toes. With a snort it disappeared again.

A moment later the nose reappeared, pushing a tennis ball in under the duvet, which rolled against Alice's feet, warm and gooey with dog dribble. The nose waited patiently, and Alice watched it follow the scent of the ball as she nudged it with her toes.

With a sigh, she gave in. There was one reason then, for her to still get up in the morning.

Even in the capital city the streets can be quiet on a Sunday morning if you leave early enough. Quiet was what Alice hoped for as she stepped out of her front door. She held

Bear's lead tightly, her baseball cap pulled low, wearing a bulky hoodie that wasn't really necessary in weather that still lingered with the threat of the heat that had come before it. Quiet and hidden and cold, that's all she wanted.

She'd taken Bear out yesterday afternoon, doing two circles of her block, walking close to the walls, her head down. She'd done the same in the evening, before it got dark, knowing he'd probably need a pre-night-time wee. But he needed a proper walk, and like it or not, she was the one who'd agreed to take him.

It was the same every time they left the house. Bear would get as far as the pavement and stop, looking up at her with big confused eyes and pulling back when she tried to coax him on. His little whine broke her heart over and over again because he just wanted them to wait for Jill. It was as if he remembered that he never used to walk without her, but couldn't remember that she didn't live here with them.

Then after a few minutes he would give in, and his slow walk would turn into a trot, and before long he was ahead of her, sniffing and snaffling against the ground.

This morning her heart thumped and she looked especially carefully before crossing the road. On the other side of her street, she stopped and looked back at the safety of her flat. Bear stood by her side, fidgeting, and that's when she saw the TRAVEL EUROPE THIS SUMMER advert on the side of the bus stop.

Their trip was off; of course it was. And at some point

she'd have to actually make all the cancellation under her cap she stared at the poster, all those hop memories and experiences that were paintings that wo never come to life now because Jill had left her. In tha moment an unexpected fizz of anger at Jill bubbled through the numbness.

Bear tugged on the lead.

'Just give me a minute,' Alice said to him. 'Please.'

So he sat on her foot and waited.

A lorry crept around the corner at the end of the street, and Alice didn't want the driver to see her. She moved her foot out from its warm cover and off they went, not stopping again until they'd entered the park, and there she remembered to breathe again.

The park was too big, too public, too open. Where would she hide with Bear if anything happened here? London wasn't the same city to her any more – it felt dangerous and overcrowded.

Feeling faint at thoughts of the park filling with people, she sat down on a bench and held her face in her hands, but Bear was having none of it. He stuck his nose between her hands and licked her cheeks.

'Let me guess, you had peanut butter for breakfast?' a voice said.

Alice's eyes flew open. She pushed her hands into Bear's fur, pulling him closer to her and looked up. In front of her stood a kind-looking woman with a dachshund, who was straining on his lead to get a sniff of Bear.

'Sorry, didn't mean to make you jump, but this one is

obsessed with peanut butter and he literally won't leave my face alone after I've eaten it. Bloody dogs!' The woman laughed and patted Bear with affection. 'What type of dog is this?'

Alice scrambled to find her words. 'Um, a Bernese Mountain Dog.'

'Oh, he's lovely, he looks like a little bear cub. How old?'

'Um, three months. Well, nearly four months.'

'Sweet. Come on then, Rufus, let's get you home. See you around.' And with that the woman smiled and walked away.

'Bye,' Alice called, embarrassed at her lack of sociability. 'Bye, Rufus,' she added to the dachshund.

Bear watched them go, sniffing at the air, curious to explore the smells of this new park. 'Let's walk then,' Alice said, pulling her cap back down a little lower.

'*Wow*, that's a cool dog,' a little boy said, stopping in his tracks in front of Alice and Bear. Alice stood stock still but managed a smile, and the boy's mum ushered him around them.

As they looped the park everybody wanted to say hi, or comment on Bear's markings, or say how cute he was, or ask to stroke him, or ask if he was a St Bernard. Alice was picking up speed, praying with each new person – was the park always this busy? – that they would leave her alone. How could people be walking around so carefree, talking about dogs and chatting to strangers, when only three weeks ago there was this tragedy in the city? When their friends or colleagues or commuter buddies had died? Why didn't they care? All she wanted to ask anybody who stopped her was, had they been there too?

Her senses on hyper vigilance, Alice sensed the man before she saw him.

Maybe she heard his running shoes on the grass, maybe she heard the faint music emitting from his headphones, but she gasped and stumbled to the side pulling Bear with her. She squeezed her eyes shut, and covered her head with her free arm.

The runner slowed to a stop after he passed her, pulling out his headphones and facing her. 'Hey,' he said, wiping sweat from his eyes. 'You okay?'

Alice opened her eyes, ashamed at her vulnerability. He was just out jogging. He was just a guy. Still, she struggled to form any words and reached her fingers into Bear's fur, breathing fast.

The man looked at her for a moment. 'Hey, boy,' he said to Bear. 'You looking after your owner?'

'Sorry,' Alice whispered.

'Don't apologise, I'm sorry if I scared you running up behind you. Sometimes I get so lost in my *Greatest Showman* soundtrack I forget about other people's personal space.'

Alice met his eyes, surprised, and laughed a little despite herself.

'I'm not actually joking,' he said, showing her his phone. 'Anyway, can I get you anything?'

'No,' she said, still feeling Bear's fur. 'Thank you, though. I'm just a bit . . . on edge.'

'I totally get it.'

Did he get it? Was he at the concert?

'Puppies are a pain in the arse but we get so protective over them. So I get it. At least he'll grow into a great body-guard for you. Take care of yourself.'

And with a wave and a smile, he jogged away, easy as that.

He didn't get it.

Back at the flat, Alice closed the door behind her with a sigh. She would have to face that again, and again, and again. Maybe she shouldn't have taken on the dog. Maybe they'd all been right.

Everyone in the park had been nice, she was aware of that. She was aware of the effect this silly great puppy had on people even before any of this had happened – she'd gone with Jill on her first outdoor walk with Bear and it had been exactly the same. People hadn't changed; she had.

Bear plodded through her flat like he owned the place after only one day, and went to have a drink. Alice stood in her living room, then wandered to the kitchen, then wandered to the bedroom. She wasn't sure what to do with herself. What would she normally be doing on a Sunday at home?

Making a cup of tea, she went back to her sofa and opened her laptop. Social media, her emails, it all seemed fruitless, a combination of a waste of effort and too much effort to even try. Closing her laptop, she hunkered down on the sofa, soon to be joined by Bear who was ready for a snooze, and she put the TV on for background noise.

She wasn't going to try, not today.

Chapter 11

As August took its last stretch before stepping into September, Alice and Bear kept each other company. She walked him as early as it was light, when most of the people out were joggers who still smiled at the cute puppy but tended not to stop. She wore headphones with no sound playing, and kept off the path to avoid people further, sticking to walking on the grass which she hadn't noticed was growing green again. To the outside world she looked deeply involved in a podcast, or an audiobook, or favourite tunes, but actually her ears were listening, alert. When she thought he'd had enough she'd scuttle them both back home, locking the doors behind her.

Alice ate a lot of toast and pasta, basic things she could buy in bulk from the small supermarket around the corner. She kept the curtains closed and her friends at bay. She wandered from room to room and watched a lot of TV, but never the news. She didn't want to draw, she didn't want to talk, she didn't want to think.

Bear slept when she slept and stuck to her side at all times, leaping when she stood, following her from room to room, keeping a close eye on her always. He seemed to hurt with a mild separation anxiety, and would bite her ankles or whine when she tried to leave the house, and so she did so less and less.

He desperately wanted to play every waking hour, bursting to life and full of bounce, and Alice struggled to find the energy to keep up. 'You do realise we apparently have to join the real world again at some point?' Alice asked him one time, after he'd knocked over her bowl of pasta by trying too hard to get at it. 'We probably can't both get a free pass for antisocial behaviour for ever.' But as she said it, a huge part of her closed its doors and battened down the hatches.

The knock on the door seemed so loud it made her jump, which made Bear woof in a way that surprised them both.

'It's just Mum and Dad. My mum and dad. It's okay,' Alice soothed, and Bear scampered towards the door (some guard dog). She nudged him aside to open the door and there were her parents, heads tilted in concern already. 'Hi.'

'Hello. honey.' Liz gave her a hug. The door was still open and Bear tried to make a leap for freedom but Ed caught him.

'Come in,' said Alice.

Usually if people came to stay, even her parents, she'd have spruced the place up, lit the odd scented candle, plumped the sofa cushions and had the kettle ready-boiled.

But as she led Ed and Liz into her living room she realised how stale it seemed.

'Sorry it's a bit of a mess, we're still getting used to … everything.'

'No problem at all, darling,' Liz said. 'I'll just pop the kettle on if that's okay with you.'

'We brought brownies,' Ed said, clutching a neat cardboard box from Waitrose. 'Mind if I have one with my cuppa?'

Bear's eyes were wide and he sniffed at the box. 'Sure,' Alice said. 'But don't give any to Bear.'

'Hard luck, matey, more for me. And your mum, of course,' Ed said, winking at his daughter and tucking in before Liz had even finished boiling the kettle.

'So how have you found it being back?' asked Liz. 'Have you been meeting up with any of your friends this week?'

'No, I've just been here.'

'Don't you have that exercise class on Tuesday nights you like? It would be a nice distraction to get back to doing something like that.'

Alice shook her head. 'I can't leave Bear on his own.'

'Oh, right.'

Her mum wasn't believing a word of it, and it irked Alice.

'So what's going on at home?' Alice asked.

'Not much,' Ed answered. 'It seems quite empty now you've gone again. I've fixed that leak in the bathroom.'

'Oh, that reminds me, while you're here can you just take a look at a shelf in my bathroom?'

'Of course, let's take a look now.'

It was all rather mundane, but each member of the family

was glad for some mundanity right now. All four of them shuffled down the corridor and into the tiny bathroom, while Alice pointed out a tilt that was appearing in her bathroom shelf. Ed pulled a pencil from his pocket and Liz helped by neatly stacking the items from the shelf on the nearby tallboy. It was only when they were all silent while Ed, tongue poking out to the side, was carefully drawing a pale line across the paintwork that Alice noticed her white noise machine – the dog – was no longer snuffling around her legs.

'Where's Bear?'

Her parents looked around, as if he might be hiding in this tiny space, and Alice left the bathroom and strode down the corridor. 'Oh *shit*!'

Bear was stretched, paws on the kitchen island, nose in the box of brownies. He jumped down, his tail wagging and his teeth full of gloopy chocolate.

'Shit!' Alice repeated, and her parents appeared.

'Oh no,' said Ed. 'I'm so sorry love, this is my fault.'

'No it isn't, I had no idea he could stretch all the way up there. Bugger, bugger, bugger.'

Liz looked in the box. 'He's finished the lot.'

'Bear, we were gone for two minutes!' Alice held her head for a moment. 'I need to take him to the vet, they say you need to get them there ASAP if they eat chocolate. It's toxic.'

Don't die, don't die, don't die. She couldn't handle it if anything happened to Bear, who had no idea he'd done anything wrong and was wagging his tail like the happiest dog alive.

'We'll go in our car,' said Liz, taking charge. 'Come on Ed, you find Bear's collar and lead and carry him to the car, Ali you get your things together and find the address for the vet.'

'I'm such an idiot, leaving them out,' Alice mumbled as she pulled on her trainers.

'I'm the idiot, love,' Ed said with sorrow.

'No you're not, he's my responsibility,' she replied sharply.

The three of them zoomed the five-minute drive to the vet's (as much as you can zoom anywhere in Greater London) and Alice's heart was thudding the whole time.

Bear was just pleased to be being taken somewhere new, so he bounded into the vet's like it was Disneyland.

'My dog, my puppy, my Bear just ate some chocolate brownies,' Alice babbled to the veterinary nurse behind the counter, who from the minute they raced through the door was leaning forward, cooing at Bear and handing him bone-shaped dog biscuits. 'We rushed straight over here.'

Alice was expecting a situation like on *Grey's Anatomy*. She thought sirens would wail, a trolley would appear, vets would be shouting about emergency surgery and people in scrubs would start running through the building.

Instead of freaking out, though, the nurse simply said, 'Whoopsie-daisy! I bet you loved them, didn't you, you naughty boy?' and called through to the vet. 'We have Bear Bright and he's got hold of some chocolate,' she said down the receiver, calm as anything. 'You'll be next in,' she told Alice with a smile, and went back to doting on Bear.

The clinic door opened and out stepped a kind-looking vet. 'Hello,' he said. 'I'm Peter. You must be Alice – we spoke on the phone?'

Alice nodded. She'd called her local vet's earlier in the week to register Bear and arrange a check-up. 'Is it okay that I brought him? I know he hasn't had his ... new patient appointment yet.' She had no idea what she was talking about.

'Yes, that's fine, I'll give him a little look over while you're in.' Peter ushered all of them through and Alice unclipped Bear's harness once the door was safely closed behind them.

'So he ate some brownies, eh?'

'It was my fault, I left them where he could reach them,' said Ed.

Peter laughed with kindness. 'Don't worry about it, owning a new dog is a learning curve. And this just happened?'

'Maybe fifteen minutes ago,' answered Liz.

'What were the ingredients of the brownies? Were they made of dark chocolate?'

Liz and Ed shrugged at each other. 'I don't know, they were Waitrose ones,' Liz said.

'Oh, very nice for you.' The vet ruffled Bear's ears, who was looking super pleased with himself. 'All righty, you did exactly the right thing bringing him in as soon as it happened. I'm just going to give him an injection and it's going to make him throw up rather a lot, I'm afraid. It'll basically clean out his stomach. Sound okay to you?'

'Yep,' answered Alice, sitting on the floor, her bad leg stretched out, and looking anxiously at Bear.

'He'll be absolutely fine,' Peter reassured her. 'After the injection we'll have about five minutes where he'll be completely normal, and that's when I'll give him a mini check-up. Then he'll get a bit droopy and dribbly, and his tail and ears will go a bit low, and then we'll have lots and lots and lots of sick and he'll feel very sorry for himself. And after he's done he'll still be a bit flopsy for a few hours. Maybe don't take him on any more walks today. But he'll start to perk back up again by this evening.'

'Okay,' Alice said, feeling rotten.

'Aaaand, there we go, all done,' said Peter, and Bear had barely noticed a needle being pressed into the squish of the back of his neck.

Alice spent the next five minutes watching him closely, watching for signs of waning, dreading the sickness coming but wanting the brownies out of his system. She'd only owned Bear for a week but she felt like she'd been a part of him all along, since the first time she'd gone with Jill to visit the three-week-old puppies.

True to the vet's word, Bear started to look less smiley after a few minutes. His ears flopped down and then his tail, and then he walked into Alice's open arms and rested his forehead against her tummy, as though saying, 'Mum, I don't feel well.'

And then came the vomit. So much vomit.

Peter chattered away to them all whilst at the same time putting fresh trays and towels out across the floor of the clinic, and Liz and Ed answered most of the questions while Alice stayed close to her pup. Eventually, when the tired thing seemed not to have anything left in him, the vet smiled.

'Okay, well done, everybody; that was an eventful first trip to the vet. Go gently on the food today. And you –' he booped Bear's nose, who looked at him sadly '– no more stealing brownies.'

Ed insisted on paying the bill, and the three of them returned to Alice's flat, with her holding Bear on her lap in the car.

Once inside, Bear skulked straight into the corner of Alice's living room – his living room – and lay down. Alice exhaled, and her mum appeared at her side.

'Jill would be very proud of how well you're doing looking after her dog, you know.'

'I just let him eat poison.'

'No you didn't, you just saved him. Believe me, as a mother – of a daughter, not a dog, granted – we can't stop bad things happening to the ones we look after. Okay? The most we can do is be there when they need us.'

Alice put the kettle on. 'Well, that's very Disney Channel of you.'

'Cheeky madam.' Liz laughed.

Ed, who'd been petting Bear, gently, walked into the kitchen. 'Those ended up being the most expensive brownies I ever bought,' he said. 'Shall I pop out and get some more?'

Chapter 12

When Monday came, and her parents had gone home, and she was back from Bear's morning walk, Alice made the decision to try and get back into work. She wasn't going to go into central London and attempt to work from the *Funny Pack* office. Instead she got out all of her art supplies and lined them up neatly on her desk. Then she refilled Bear's water and made a cup of tea. Then she had a quick shower. Then she sat down and got up again to load some washing.

There was a barrier up between her and her artwork. Her pen hovered over the paper and refused to make contact. Illustration usually came easy to her, but now it seemed like the hardest thing to climb out of her own head and enter the world of imagination that creativity needed. Alice just couldn't summon the optimism she usually painted onto the page. She couldn't create the humorous take on the world around her because she couldn't see the funny in it any more.

'Come on,' she whispered to the page. '*Come on.*'

She knew before she even got to this stage that it had gone. Her passions had evaporated and she didn't know if they'd ever come back. Alice sat for a long time thinking about this, and eventually picked up the phone to call the *Funny Pack* office.

She told them she needed more time out, even more than they'd already generously allowed her, and wouldn't be coming back in for a while. She asked them to work with another freelancer until further notice. She politely declined their offer to send her ideas, and compromised by saying she'd dig out some of her back stock and sell it to them if they were interested. When she hung up she was exhausted and turned to Bear, but he wasn't there. Rising from her seat, she followed the sound of snuffling, only to find him ripping one of her books to pieces in the next room.

'What are you doing that for?' she cried, wrangling the book away from him. 'Can I not take my eyes off you for a second?'

Alice went back to her desk and pulled out a large folder where she kept finished cartoons that, for a variety of reasons, she hadn't sold yet. She photographed them one by one to send over to *Funny Pack*.

Bear watched her. 'I always liked this one a lot,' she said, picking up one of the women dressed in superhero costumes. 'I guess I was waiting for the right circumstance to submit it. Now is the right circumstance, because otherwise we'll be on the street.'

It wasn't quite true. Alice had savings she wasn't planning on using on anything else now that her European adventure had evaporated, and her parents would always help her with rent if she asked, but she didn't like to take the risk of anything running out, and there were enough pictures here that, if they all sold at the usual *Funny Pack* pricing, could tide her over, at least for a while.

And now she could climb back into bed for the day.

Alice was getting lethargic. She knew it while she was walking the dog; she knew it from the sluggish feeling she got as the day went on; and she knew it from the state of her skin. Her body craved a good workout and some healthy food and water, but everything just seemed too much effort, especially since using her leg still smarted a little. It was easier to stay in and hide herself away.

Her muscles really showed weakness one afternoon, two and a half weeks into having Bear live with her, when he was off the lead, tearing around an enclosed part of the park while nobody else was in there, and he stumbled, tumbling down a bank, and yelped. Alice ran over to him where he hobbled in circles, whining.

'Stop moving, stop moving, puppy, let me see.' He leaned into her, his front left paw aloft.

Alice held it gently, looking for cuts or broken claws but there were none. 'I think you must have sprained it, if that's something dogs can do,' she said. 'You poor thing. Let's take you home.'

She stood, and Bear tried to follow, but he yelped and sat down again. It started to rain.

Alice could carry twenty kilograms of dog home. It was

a five-minute walk from here, maximum, and she used to be able to hold ten kilos on each side during the squat track at Body Pump. She scooped him up, grunting, while she straightened her legs.

Of course her body pump weights hadn't lolled about or tried to lick her face. They hadn't wriggled or tried to grab at leaves on trees with their mouth as they passed. There was also a reason she hadn't been doing twenty kilograms on the biceps track, because it was much, much harder, as she was finding out.

'Ohmygod,' she rasped, and had to pop him on the ground for the third time to shake out her arms, which were burning. The rain spattered in her eyes, but she could see her flat in sight at the end of the road. Bear sat next to her on the wet road, his paw still raised. 'Well, we can't just stay here. Come on.' She lifted him again and staggered the final distance, collapsing onto her hallway floor and releasing Bear who slunk straight to his bed for a grumpy snooze.

Alice looked at her phone to see a missed call from Bahira. She called back, still catching her breath.

'Hey, are you okay?' Bahira asked down the line.

'Is owning a puppy always this hard?' Alice answered.

'What did he do?'

'Fell over and hurt a paw; I just carried him home. He's also destroyed a book, chewed my furniture, had to be taken to the vet's after eating a box of brownies and won't leave me alone even for a minute, unless he's off doing something he shouldn't be.'

Bahira chuckled. 'Sounds about right, I'm afraid. It will

get easier, but not for a while. He's still learning his boundaries with you, and when he's learnt them he'll forget them all because by then he'll be a teenage pup.'

'Brilliant.'

'Look into puppy training, especially if he seems bored. I didn't know how much I needed it with our dog until we did it. And it's a nice thing for you both to do together, you know, out of the house ...'

'Good idea,' Alice concurred.

'I was just calling to see how things were going. Shall I come over?'

'No, it's okay,' Alice said quickly, feeling that twist of guilt again in her stomach. She breathed in, willing the fear and speculation to float away. 'But how are you? How are you feeling?'

'I'm coping,' Bahira said. 'It's weird not seeing Jill, though. It's just getting to the stage where it's been longer than usual not to have seen her, you know?'

'Yeah, I know.'

'The rest of us should meet up though, soon,' Bahira persisted.

'Sure.'

'Okay, I'll let you go, but let's keep in touch.'

It wasn't that Alice didn't like Bahira, or Kemi or Theresa. She liked them a lot. But she just wasn't ready to hang out with her friends without their heartbeat: Jill.

'Right, I'm taking you to puppy training,' Alice told Bear, as she nursed her wound which he'd just clamped onto with his spiky teeth. It had started with him nibbling her jumper when she'd reached to stroke him. He hadn't let go, and got all worked up, his nibbling getting harder and more persistent until she had to untangle herself from the mess and step away. He bounced up and tried to catch her with his teeth.

She picked up her laptop and sat on the sofa, annoyance streaming through her, her patience wearing down. 'You're making this harder. You're supposed to be on my side, but you're making everything so hard.'

Bear side-eyed her from the floor, his head tilted to the side and one of her soggy socks in his mouth.

'That's right, we're going to school. Both of us. You, to learn how to be a civilised member of society, and me to learn how to actually be a dog owner.' He pushed her with his paw while he pulled on her other sock, trying to remove it from her foot. 'I don't know, maybe you've always been secretly annoying. I think you put on the butter-wouldn't-melt face just for visitors.'

Alice typed 'dog training classes London' into Google, and clicked on the first link that came up, opening the vibrant yellow and purple page of the Dogs Trust. '"Dog School London,"' she read aloud. '"Teaches owners how to give their dogs skills for happy lives." Did you hear that Bear? Do you think they might have some skills for me to learn too?' She continued flicking around the site, finding useful snippets about good places for dog walks, tips on recall off the lead, profiles of the trainers, all things that kept her mind occupied, if just for a little while.

'It's a five-week course,' she whispered to Bear, who had

settled his head down on her foot now and was drifting to sleep, his too-long legs stretched out in front of him and his nostrils twitching softly. 'Five weeks until we're all better.'

She knew she was talking rubbish, but as she clicked on the 'enquire now' button and filled in details about herself and Bear, she felt a sense of purpose. Something to aim towards, for Bear's sake, beyond just being. Just surviving.

Alice didn't even realise until later that night, while she was lying awake, that she'd just made a plan. A plan that involved leaving the house and being around other people. Well, how about that?

Chapter 13

The following Tuesday evening, Alice pulled up into the crunchy gravel car park outside the green-painted Dogs Trust buildings. She was running late because it was only as she was about to leave the house that she'd realised she should wear something other than the dog-walking clothes she'd lived in for the past month.

'Come on then,' she said, unclipping Bear so he could jump from the car, the hurt paw a distant memory in his chunky little head. She gathered in her arms all the things she'd been asked to bring – treats, a blanket favoured by the dog, a toy, and some food stuffed in one of the rubbery butt-plug-looking chew toys.

She took a breath, her eyes automatically doing a dynamic risk assessment of the grounds. Bear pulled at his harness, desperate to get inside, like he knew this was All About Him. 'Stop pulling,' she hissed. 'You're going to embarrass me before we've even started.'

He ignored her of course and got as far as the door in record speed, and pushed his nose against the glass, tail wagging.

'Well, hello,' said a woman in a purple Dogs Trust T-shirt who opened the door, addressing Bear. 'You're a big boy, you must be Bear.'

He, of course, jumped up on his hind legs and embraced the woman, showing Alice up further.

'Oh thank you so much,' the woman said. 'I can see we have a very friendly one on our hands.'

Alice nodded. 'So we need help with the jumping up and the pulling, please. He just wants to meet and be best friends with everyone.' *The opposite of me.*

'No problem, he'll be a very polite young man by the end of these five weeks. Come in, come in. I'm Geraldine.'

Alice and Bear were led to a chair with a bowl of water next to it, set up at the end of the room. Alongside their section were four identical set-ups, each separated by a low, Dogs Trust divider.

Geraldine explained to Alice that there was plenty of time, and three other dogs and their humans would be coming along today, and each family was to take a seat in their own space and put the dog's blanket down beside them, and try and get their pups to settle.

'Lie down,' Alice asked of Bear, who ignored her and tried to walk around his section on as wide a berth as his lead and harness would allow him. 'Bear, come here, lie down.'

He stopped and looked at her. *What's in it for me?*

Alice glanced at Geraldine, who was facing the other way,

heading back towards the main entrance, so she pulled a treat from her pocket – one of the bacon flavour ones she knew Bear really liked – and bribed him back over to her.

He skipped back over and snaffled it from her hands, even making a move to lie down, until his head whipped around to the door.

'INCOMING!' someone bellowed, chuckling, and in raced an eager dog with dark fur, long white legs and big pointy ears on an extendable lead, followed by a large, jolly man. Both looked as if they could have shared a can of Red Bull on their way over here, with the dog bouncing straight over her barrier and tangling herself around a bemused Bear, and her owner pink and smiling and jogging after her.

'Evening,' he said. 'This is Pearl! She never runs out of energy, but I tell you, she's improved my fitness levels no end. I have to run to keep up with her, but I have been known to pick her up and carry her on her walks sometimes when I don't have it in me – don't tell my wife.' He winked. 'I'm Barry, by the way.'

'Hello,' Alice answered, freeing Bear who was happily bopping Pearl on the back with his paw while she kept wriggling her bum at him like a woman who knew what she wanted. 'I'm Alice; this is Bear.'

'He's a big boy. That's a proper dog. Pam, look at this proper dog,' he called to a woman – his wife, Alice presumed – who was struggling through the door with Pearl's full bed and a huge bag of toys and treats, as though she was moving her into the Dogs Trust centre for the next five weeks.

'Ooh, look at him!' Pam said. 'Pearl, he'd make a lovely boyfriend for you, very manly.'

'What type o' dog is he?' asked Barry. 'A St Bernard?'

'A Bernese Mountain Dog.'

'A Burmese Mountain Dog, eh? Where's he from, then, Burma? Must be hot for his kind over there.'

'Actually from Bern, in Switzerland. Bernese,' said Alice. She then felt rude for correcting him, so asked, 'How about Pearl, what type of doggie is she?'

'Switzerland!' piped up Pam. 'Lovely, we went there for our honeymoon. Lots of mountains, there.'

'Beautiful place. Pearl's a bit of Collie, bit of Pointer, lot of pain in the backside,' said Barry affectionately.

The thing Alice was learning about dog owners was that their worlds often revolved around their beloved hounds. Not necessarily all the time, but when they met other dog owners their pooches were a constant source of conversation, knowledge-swapping and anecdotes. Nobody asked personal questions. Nobody was talking about the state of the world. Nobody discussed trauma and inner demons. It was all about the dogs, and Alice liked it.

As the room filled with more puppies and people, and the dogs went berserk trying to be best friends with everyone in the room, Alice settled into her corner and relished the anonymity.

Geraldine in her purple T-shirt positioned herself at the front of the room and talked them all through the format of the next five weeks. Pearl, in the section next to hers, was paying no attention to Geraldine and staring at Barry pleadingly, piercing woofs escaping as she tried to make him throw an imaginary tennis ball. Bear sat beside Alice, craning his neck to watch her.

'Does anyone ever feel close to tears?' Geraldine asked, and Alice snapped back to attention. 'Does anyone ever let those tears flow?'

Barry and Pam chuckled next door.

'That's quite normal. Dogs can be bloomin' annoying. But the thing to remember is, they aren't trying to be annoying, they just don't understand our world. Imagine if one of your friends came over and wanted a cup of tea, but wouldn't tell you in English, wouldn't point it out, wouldn't give you any hints apart from playing an elaborate game of 'hot or cold'. That's what it's like for puppies. They'll learn words and learn to associate them with certain things, but they don't know what they mean just because you say them louder and louder. It takes patience and repetition, and a lot more patience. Don't you wish sometimes people had more patience with you?'

Alice reached down and stroked the top of Bear's head with her fingertips, and he tipped his nose right to the ceiling, his eyes sparkling. *Thanks for being patient with me*, she told him, silently.

It was beginning to get dark by the time Alice and Bear left their first training session that evening. 'Autumn is really here, puppy,' she told him as she led them both to the car.

She'd never been afraid of the dark, and on the outskirts of London it wasn't ever really going to be dark, but an urgency to get back home into her bright nook of a flat washed over her.

With Bear in the back seat, lying down and sleepy, she sat for a moment trying to shake away the nasty feelings that were creeping into her consciousness. 'Go away,' she whispered. 'Go away, I've had a nice evening.'

Alice plugged in her phone and found a playlist of soft late night moods, and for the first time since the concert she allowed music to flood her ears, providing an intoxicating distraction that meant before she knew it she was pulling out of the car park and making her way home.

She focused on the road and on the beat of the music reverberating around the car. She was coping. It wasn't easy but she was out, and she was driving, and it was dark, and she was so lonely but then Bear's nose poked through the gap between the seats and rested on her shoulder.

Maybe she wasn't completely alone. She leant her cheek on him.

Chapter 14

From then on the weekly training sessions became the linchpin of Alice and Bear's routine. She settled into a life of being only with him, and was glad to be left alone. She didn't go back into the *Funny Pack* office, and instead they bought all her drawings, perhaps out of pity.

When she took Bear for his twice-daily walks, she saw increasingly familiar faces, but she continued to wear her earphones without any sound, and they seemed to accept that this quiet girl with the big puppy didn't want to talk.

She spoke to her mum and dad on the phone regularly enough, but mainly about Bear and what he'd been doing that week. She avoided questions about herself.

She slept a lot but never felt rested, and ate a lot but never felt satisfied. Her time with Bear was the only thing that made her feel happy, like when he was practising his growls or chasing his own tail around her living room, or had climbed onto the sofa and snuggled his furry back into her, and they fell asleep, spooning. In bed he would keep her warm by lying right up against her, calming her night tears, and he was very nearly able to scrabble up onto the mattress himself, rather than place his front paws up and wait for her to come and lift his bottom.

Bear was growing and Alice found herself daily telling him, with complete honesty and awe, how big he was getting. The tufty black streamers on his ears were beginning to flow, his nose was longer and stronger, like a concertina that had popped out, and it now proudly displayed all of his black and orange freckles. His tail had popped like a firework and had changed from a white-tipped rope to a plush, cloudy plume. The sharp pins of his teeth were falling out and making room for great white gnashers. He was leaning more, and had become interested in feet and the backs of knees. He was changing quickly, and filling up what little space there was in the flat.

And every week their outing came around, and Alice would pack up his 'school' bag, he would be on his best behaviour for an hour, and then they would drive home to music in companionable silence.

'He's definitely improving and being a bit more structured, but he can still be naughty and restless when it's just him and me,' Alice said to her mum after four sessions. 'It feels good to be doing something towards making him better and happier and more settled.'

Alice's mum 'mm-hmm'ed down the line. 'And have you thought any more about maybe seeing someone yourself?'

'What, about Bear?'

'No, like a doctor or a therapist, perhaps.'

'I don't need to see anyone, Mum, I just need to get this dog more settled and then everything will be fine.'

'Mm-hmmmmmm ...'

Alice steered the conversation back to Bear's training. 'We just need to keep practising, that's all. We have homework to do. And everyone there loves him.' Even when he was being a pain, Alice felt pride with how instantly Bear could make people fall in love with him, and he always reciprocated. He was just like Jill in some ways.

'So just one more week left?' her mum asked.

'Yep, one more session and then he'll be perfect,' Alice joked.

'Maybe it would be nice to plan in something else for once it finishes, you know, to keep you motivated to leave the house.'

'Mum ...'

'*Liz*,' Alice heard her dad say in the background.

'I just think it's been good for you having a bit of routine back. How about trying to go into the office again, just once a week?'

'I can't leave him on his own. I don't need to go into the office, I can't, I'm not ...' Alice ran out of words. She wasn't ready yet. She wished she was, she wished she felt better, but she also wished Jill wasn't dead, and she wished she could go back in time, and she really wished she wasn't having this conversation.

'I didn't want to upset you, it was just an idea.' Liz wavered, and then her dad came on the line.

'Your mum's not trying to upset you, love,' he said.

'I know, I'm just not ready.'

'That's okay, there's no rush, she just . . . ' he paused, as if waiting for her mum to leave the room. When he spoke again he was quieter. 'She just wants you to be okay. She thinks all the time about how she could have lost her little girl, we both do. But we don't mean to put any pressure on you. We'll wait.'

Alice was watching Bear, and thinking, did he always take up that much space on her sofa? He was luxuriating on the cushions, his ears dangling over the edge, and when he caught her watching him his mouth opened in a big, tongue-lolling smile. Despite everything, Bear certainly brought a little laughter back into her life.

The doorbell rang and Bear rolled off the sofa.

'Who's this?' she murmured to him, assuming it would be the postman, and he pushed through to go to the door with her, causing her to bump and edge her way around him.

'Oh! Hi!' Alice stood at her door and faced Bahira, Theresa and Kemi. Bear appeared, her tone of voice arousing the curiosity in him, and he nudged and bumped into her calves from behind, desperate to see who it was. 'What are you guys doing here?'

'We're here to visit you,' said Bahira, with her usual practicality. 'Like it or not.'

'Oh. Well, come in?' Alice opened the door wider, excruciatingly aware of her dog-walking clothes (which really were now just her 'clothes'), her messy hair, her lack of make-up.

'Holy mackerel!' Theresa exclaimed on entering the

corridor. 'Alice, put the light on, this puppy can't be as big as I think he is.'

'Sorry, it is a little dark in here.' Alice shuffled past them to flick on the hall light, then led them into the living room and threw some empty crisp packets in the nearest bin. She gathered up a few used mugs and glasses.

'Mind if I open the curtains?' Kemi asked, carefully.

'Of course,' Alice replied, keeping her eyes on the mugs in her hand. 'It just keeps the flat cooler for Bear if the curtains are closed, that's all.'

'Oh, sure,' Kemi said, but Alice caught her glance at Bahira.

'I can't believe you all came over here. It's Saturday. Don't you take Zara swimming on a Saturday, Bahira? And Kem, you're training for that half marathon next weekend, aren't you?'

'You remembered!' grinned Kemi.

'Sorry I don't reply much in the group WhatsApp. I do lurk there, though, and keep up with the conversation.'

'I can run tomorrow.' Kemi waved her hand, dismissing both her training, but also Alice's embarrassment at dropping out of touch. 'Now, let's have a cuppa.'

'Ooh, I'd love a cuppa,' said Theresa, who was snuggling into Bear, much to his delight.

Alice glanced at the clock. 'Did you guys want lunch or anything?'

'Sure,' replied Bahira. 'What do you have?'

Alice walked them all to her boxy little kitchen, Bear scrambling to be first, and she ran her fingers through his fur like a comfort blanket. 'I have crisps, fish fingers, some frozen pizzas, potato waffles . . . All the beige food you could want,' she joked.

'Pizza sounds good to me,' Theresa said. 'We brought a load of goodies as well.' She opened one of the plastic bags they were carrying and dumped a load of fruit and vegetables on to the side. What an odd gift to bring over. 'I'll make a side salad.'

'How long can you stay for?' Alice asked.

Bahira faced her. 'The rest of the day. Your mum didn't think you'd have any plans, and we never see you any more.'

'You spoke to my mum?'

'Who do you think suggested we bring vegetables?' Bahira picked up a red pepper and waved it in the air.

'Okay,' Alice said, feeling a little helpless in her own home. 'I'm just going to get changed. Back in a minute.'

She left the three of them in her kitchen and raced to her bedroom. Bear loyally followed her in and she shut the door behind them both, holding back the tears that were forming, though she didn't know why. Was she happy they were there? Worried about what they'd say? Sad to be having to put on a show? Or just a little overwhelmed?

Alice walked back out of her room, deflated. She hadn't changed, she didn't have the strength to put a mask on. Bear stayed close by her side.

Theresa looked up from the salad, and Bahira and Kemi turned. Alice opened her mouth but no words came out.

Bahira stepped forward first and wrapped her arms around Alice, closely followed by Kemi and Theresa.

'I'm just having a bad day,' Alice whispered.

'We know,' said Bahira.

'Do you ever, since it happened, just feel like you'll never be back to you ever again?'

They all agreed, every one of them, and then they stood like that for a long while, until Bear pushed his nose in between their legs.

Theresa laughed, betraying a sniffle. 'You're doing a good job raising this big handsome man. Jill would be really happy.'

'Please look after yourself, though,' Bahira said softly into Alice's ear. 'You're a shadow at the moment.'

'I'm not good company. I don't have the energy,' Alice replied. She didn't mean it unkindly, she just couldn't bring herself to subtext her feelings.

'If there was one thing Jill was famous for, it was being someone who stayed checked in with all her friends, especially you. So if you won't let us be here for you, we'll be here for her.'

Alice nodded and let Kemi lead her into the living room and the two of them silently cleaned up bottles and wrappers. Bahira and Theresa walked in shortly afterwards with salad and pizzas and when Alice went to retreat to the sofa, Theresa steered her to eat at the table. Bear couldn't believe his eyes and didn't quite know what to do with himself with them all sitting with their plates so far away from him.

'How's it been training Bear? Is he a handful?' Theresa asked, bending her hand down to stroke him again.

'Yes,' Alice answered. 'We've been going to puppy training classes, though.'

'That's good, good for you!' exclaimed Kemi, as though Alice had just told her she was partaking in nightly speed dating.

'Thanks. He's definitely learning to be a bit better behaved. He's quite needy and gets a bit anxious if I have to be away from him, so I'm pretty much with him twenty-four-seven. I guess I should leave him more, but well, I don't want to.' Alice shrugged.

Kemi chomped on a piece of pizza. 'Do what you want. As long as he's happy and you're happy, you know, relatively speaking, you can choose to raise him however you like.'

The rest of the visit went by more easily than Alice expected, with conversation kept light and small-talky, but Alice kept thinking about what Kemi had said. As long as she was happy and as long as Bear was happy . . .

'Don't become a stranger, okay?' Bahira said when the three of them were leaving Alice's flat a while after lunch. 'And call if you need anything.'

'I will. And the same to you. Thanks for coming,' Alice said, meaning it. 'And thanks for the vegetables.'

'Our pleasure.'

When she closed the door she faced Bear, thoughtfully. So if neither of them fitted that criteria, about being happy, maybe it was time she did something about it?

Chapter 15

Alice watched Bear a lot over the next couple of days. She watched him stare out of the window, lie down only to get up and move somewhere else a short while later, walk up to her with hope in his eyes and an endless stream of toys he wanted her to play with, bump into her furniture and curl himself awkwardly around doorways.

'We're like birds trapped in a cage, you and me,' she told him on the Tuesday afternoon before his last puppy training class. 'Only we're not two budgies, we're two bloomin' great barn owls.'

Bear signed with resignation.

'I'm just sad all the time, and you didn't sign up for that, did you? You should have a big, happy home and lots of space and light and freedom to grow into those silly great paws. Because you're still growing, you're going to get bigger and bigger and it's not fair to keep you here. I'm sorry. I'm sorry.'

She was tired, and didn't have any fight left in her. Bear

climbed up next to her on the sofa, uninvited, and nudged his strong nose under her arm until it lifted over him. He pushed his face super-close to hers and licked her face, which was gross but also a little bit comforting.

'Are you being a therapy dog now?' she choked, a small laugh escaping. 'That's nice of you but I'm a lost cause. I don't want to have to be strong any more.'

She'd once been a big fan of change and adventure. If she could find that spirit again, surely that would be better than giving up?

'I think I need to leave London.'

'Leave?' Alice's mum looked up from gazing proudly at Bear's dog school graduation certificate that he'd been given the night before.

'We don't *fit* here any more,' Alice explained, pouring them both a cup of tea.

Liz, who was visiting for the night, put down the certificate. 'Do you think you'll be happier somewhere else?'

Alice shrugged. 'I think I need to try.'

'I think moving is a very good idea, but I'm worried you'll feel the same just . . . somewhere else. I wish you'd find some help, just to talk things through.'

Alice sat down with her tea and tried to formulate her words. 'Even if I do go to see a counsellor or someone, at some point, I need something to change, for me and for this puppy. I'm not taking care of either of us properly.'

'A therapist could help you with that.'

'But moving is what I want to do *now*. Bear is getting way

too big for this flat, it's not fair on him, and what's the point in spending loads of money trying to get something bigger in London? I'm hardly living the London life any more. Besides, being here everything leads back to ... everything just hurts, all the time.'

Liz sipped her tea and stretched her arm out to squeeze Alice's shoulder. 'We certainly don't want that. Where would you like to move to?'

'Now, that I haven't figured out yet. Somewhere very different to here.' Alice paused for a while, wanting to elaborate, but not even sure what she meant herself. Eventually she opened up. 'I can't not think about the concert. I can't stand the heat, or the noise, or the crowds. And I know it's October now and the heatwave has gone but I just feel so boxed in, everywhere, outside or inside and the thought of so many people and cars and crowds just make me ... I can't breathe any more. I feel like I was wearing rose-tinted glasses and they've been smashed to smithereens. And I don't want to be like that. I don't *want* to want to hide away.'

'You're definitely not yourself. We miss the old Alice.'

'I don't feel anything close to the girl I was three months ago. I just feel like I need to change something, and I don't think I can change anything while I'm in this environment.'

'Tell me your dream environment,' Liz prompted. 'Somewhere quiet?'

Alice thought. 'Quiet, light, lots of space for Bear. Somewhere *cold*.'

'Maybe you should start by taking a trip?' Liz brightened.

'A break might do you good. We can look after this big Bear for a week or two.'

'I can't leave him,' Alice said automatically. 'What if he thinks he's been ... abandoned again?'

'You *can* leave him,' her mum said with care. 'But it's up to you. Maybe take a trip with him, that could be fun!'

'Where do you want to go, Bear? I bet you'd appreciate going somewhere chilly. He's so glad it's autumn,' Alice told her mum.

'I bet he is, he's a winter Bear.'

Inspiration struck Alice, a sparkle in the back of her mind that lit like an optical fibre flickering to life inside her, and she couldn't believe she hadn't thought about this before.

Alice turned to Bear who was sitting on the floor patiently, happy that these two were chatting above him, everyone staying where he could see them. His mouth hung open in a smile, big eyes trailing from Alice to her mum, pleased to be close by and included. 'How about I take you to Switzerland, to the Bernese Oberland and up a mountain?'

'Ooh, now that sounds like a tonic,' said Liz.

'Shall we take you back to Switzerland and leave you there?' Alice joked, running her fingers through the thick fuzz of his chest. Bear lifted and paw and plonked it heavily across her arm. 'I mean ... you would probably quite like a visit to your home country. You could visit all your relations.'

'Switzerland wouldn't be too hard to drive to,' Liz nudged.

'I know,' Alice answered. 'It was going to be the last stop on Jill and my trip.'

'And it won't be too cold yet – your dad and I went there around this time of year when we were first married.'

'I have a friend who lives in Switzerland – Vanessa. We were going to visit her while we were out there, and she was fine having a dog to stay in her house.' Alice was thinking out loud, still playing with Bear's fur.

'Why don't you call her?'

'I think I'll email. I don't want to put her on the spot.' Alice reached for her laptop. 'I'll just check what the rules are about driving through the Chunnel with pets . . . I know you can do it, but it was Jill who looked into all that before. Hey, look.' She had already distracted herself googling Bernese Mountain Dogs in Switzerland and her screen had filled with images of happy pups twinning with her own, standing tummy-deep in the snow, or proudly atop hills. 'Imagine if it snowed while we were out there. Bear, you would *love* the snow, it'll be like a big cold blanket for you.'

As Alice chattered away to the dog, lost in the happy distraction of research, her mother made an excuse to leave the room. Something about grabbing a jumper from the bedroom. As she left, Alice shot her big smile – it was nice having her mum around.

A few minutes later, Bear walked out after her, stopping in the corridor and looking between the bedroom and back at Alice on the sofa. 'I know, Bear, the herd has separated,' said Alice, getting up to go and find her mum. She wanted to tell her the good news: that not only could dogs travel in your car through the Eurotunnel, but that it only took thirty-five minutes, and that there was an exercise area in the departure terminal with free poop bags!

She followed Bear into the corridor and stopped when she heard her mum on the phone in the bedroom, speaking in hushed tones.

'She's making plans, Ed,' she was whispering, pride and pleasure in her tone. '... Yes, plans for things to do ... A holiday first, and also moving house at some point, but something for her to dig her teeth into, beyond the upcoming week.' Alice listened to her mother breathe more lightly, a sunbeam in her voice. 'It's fantastic, like seeing a bit of her old self back again.'

There was no turning back now.

Chapter 16

Alice scuttled back to her laptop to email Vanessa and ask about visiting before her mum caught her listening.

> Hi Vanessa, how are you? Sorry to contact you again out of nowhere, and thanks for your kind message about Jill. I miss her a lot, and I know she would have loved to have visited you in Switzerland.
>
> If the offer is still open, I wondered if I could still come after all, with the dog, who I've adopted? We're thinking of getting out of London for a week or two, and climbing up a mountain might be just what we need.

A reply came back almost instantly.

Yes yes yes! the email said. Only I have an idea to share with you. Can you give me a phone this evening?

'Hi, Vanessa?'

'Alice! How are you doing?' cried the voice on the end of the line, a voice Alice hadn't heard for close to ten years, but which still had the bounce she was familiar with, the melodic accent when Vanessa spoke in English. 'I am so sorry to hear about what happened, I can't believe you were involved in such a horrible thing, and Jill . . . oh Jill . . . I want to hug you.'

'Thanks,' Alice said. 'Hopefully we can do that soon. How are you?'

'I'm okay, but listen, I really think you need to come to Switzerland because we will look after you and your doggie. I think you should come longer than a couple of weeks. Your email sounded so sad.'

'Sorry . . .'

'Don't apologise, you're so British, lovely Alice. You are allowed to be sad. But if you're sad in Switzerland we can make you better. Mountain air, lots of cheese, sexy snowboarders . . . eh? Come on!'

Alice laughed. 'It does sound good, but we can't impose on you more than a couple of weeks. This dog is getting bigger by the day.'

'I love him already! But here's the thing, I actually have a . . . what would you call it . . . an ulterior motive. See, I really want to see you and spend loads of time with you and your hunky dog, but I'm like, two weeks away from starting a new job – I'm going to be travelling around the country leading chocolate and cheese tours for tourists. I'll be on the road really the whole of the winter season.'

Alice's heart sunk a little. 'Oh that's okay, maybe another time?'

'No, you don't understand. I still think you should come. You could have my house while I'm away. Stay for the whole winter – your Bear will love it, there will be so much snow for him. I'd be popping back every couple of weeks for a few days, so we can have lots of mini get-togethers instead. What do you think?'

What did she think? A million things, to be honest, all at once. She couldn't just move abroad for a whole season. Certainly not to Switzerland; she didn't even speak the language. What language did they even speak where Vanessa lived now? She remembered that Vanessa spoke Swiss German, but did everyone else in her ... village? No, no, she couldn't leave her parents, or her friends, or her work.

But throughout all these thoughts there was a ripple of excitement building in her, because actually, she *could* leave, that's what she wanted, she'd even said so out loud to her mum. And she *could* move abroad – plenty of people did – and she would have done it in a heartbeat before all of this happened.

Could she do this now?

'Helloooooo, are you still there Alice?' Vanessa sang out.

Alice laughed. 'Sorry, I was lost in thought. I don't know ... my job ...'

'You are not freelance any more?'

'Yes, sort of, I mean yes ... I just don't think I can.'

'You can escape how you feel at the moment. You *can* escape.'

Those three words. They shifted something in Alice and she looked over at Bear, snoozing, squished into the space between her sofa and her coffee table. He needed more than this. He needed fresh air, space, something different to look at.

'You're sure you wouldn't mind us living in your house? You don't mind dog fur everywhere?'

'Why would I call you up and offer this if I minded, you silly Brit?' Vanessa laughed. 'You would be doing me a favour. And you two will love my house and my neighbours and you will make a lot of friends and eat a lot of food and have a lot of adventures, okay? Okay. Settled, yes?'

Alice had two options. She stayed put, hiding from the world, or she escaped into it. She chose safe but sad, or she chose happy. She knew what Jill would have wanted her to do, and before she let herself consider it any further she said, 'Yes.'

The next two weeks were a blur. Alice poured all her energies into preparing for their big trip. Visits to the vet, pet passport application, packing lists, calls to Vanessa, numerous online shopping orders for snow wear, and giving notice on her flat seemed only the tip of the iceberg. It was during her first attempt at boxing up her belongings that she intended to store at her parents, and tidying parts of her apartment, that Alice noticed just how slack she'd become with cleaning.

Great furballs hunkered into corners, surfaces were dusty, mirrors and windows were grimy and the smell of dog hung in the air. The only parts of the house that seemed well maintained were those that directly affected the dog, as if her own living space hadn't mattered to her.

Alice was clearing out her bathroom cupboards, and was about to throw a half-used bottle of Neal's Yard bubble bath into the bin, when she stopped herself. Maybe it would be nice to have a bath for a change. The house was chilly because she had all the windows open for Bear, and the thought of encasing herself in warm water seemed indulgent, yes, but like something she could allow herself to do.

She pushed the cardboard box she was packing aside and threw on the taps. If she didn't do it now this bubble bath would probably end up in the bin after all. Then she pulled a couple of other just-packed, not-used-in-months things back out of the box – a body scrub, a face mask, a *razor*.

As the bath ran she pottered back down the corridor to find Bear, and was glad to see he was still snoozing away beneath one of the open windows.

Alice helped herself to a glass of wine and returned to the bathroom, dropping her clothes on the floor and sliding into the warmth. She closed her eyes and breathed.

Sometimes you just know when you're being watched. Cracking her eyes back open she faced Bear's nose, centimetres from her own, stretching over the side of the bath. His chest fur dangled over the edge and was speckled with bubbles.

'Now I know for a fact you don't want to get in this bath,' she told him. 'I was left with scars last time we bathed together.'

Bear rested his chin on the lip of the bath and continued to stare at her.

'I mean they were very tiny scars compared with this big

mutha,' she lifted her leg a little to show him. 'But still. I don't want any more.'

He backed away a little and whined.

'Hey, it's okay.' Alice reached her hand out of the bath towards him and he came forward again to lick at it. 'I don't mind having baths, they're only bad when they're happening to you.'

He whined again and turned in the small space, bumping the door, and then looked back at her, willing her to come with him.

'It's okay,' she repeated. 'It's okay that you can't get to me. I'm fine.'

Bear signed and sat down on the floor, staring into the bathroom and panting. This slightly killed the mood, but she continued nonetheless, keeping up the chatter to comfort him.

'Look, this body scrub is lime flavour,' she babbled, explaining every step she was taking. 'It smells yummy.' Lifting her leg from the water again she very carefully ran the scrub over the length of her wound, treating it with attention she hadn't really bestowed upon it until now. She spent a long time running her hand back and forth over it, long after the scrub had washed away. By this point Bear had flopped into a lying position, but his eyes were still open and watching her.

Alice shampooed her hair and then dipped her head back into the bath. She knew bath water wouldn't really clean it properly, but whatever. Sinking her ears below the surface she closed her eyes and imagined a world where everything was silent again. Not just silent from outside noise, but from the internal noise, the memories, the worries.

Something pressed firmly against her forehead and she shot out of the water to see Bear back leaning over the bath, his spongy nose damp. He woofed, as if angry at her for scaring him like that. 'All right, I'll get out.' Alice pulled the plug and shuffled out of the bath and into a towel before Bear could completely dry her skin with his tongue. They bumped past each other going out of the bathroom. 'Let's hope Vanessa's bathroom is more spacious, huh?'

A card arrived the following morning, the day before she was due to move out. It was marked first class, somebody trying to get something to her before it was too late.

Alice opened the card in her nearly empty flat, giving the envelope to Bear to rip into shreds. She put her hand over her mouth when she realised it was from Jill's parents.

Dear Alice,

Your mum and dad told us about your trip, and we wanted to wish you safe and happy travels. We're so grateful to you taking on Jill's beloved dog and taking such good care of him, and she often spoke about how much she wanted him to see Switzerland and 'get completely covered in snow'.

We also wanted to give you something, and we've left it so late so that you have no time to give it back. Please find enclosed a cheque. Jill put aside some savings during her last few months especially for the trip you and she planned

to take. She was so excited about that trip, and we want
you to take that money to put towards living costs out
there. We really owe you so much more for all of the
expense I'm sure Bear has cost you (your mum also told
us about those brownies!) and if you ever need anything
please let us know. You've been like a second daughter to
us for all of Jill's life, and that doesn't need to stop.

Please have a wonderful time, send photos, and enjoy
this adventure on behalf of Jill.

Much love xxx

Alice was floored. They didn't need to do this, she didn't deserve this kindness. But what a lovely, warm gesture it was. She would use the money wisely, and take their letter with her.

It was time to say some goodbyes.

Alice wrote a letter in return to Jill's parents, thanking them and promising to fulfil their daughter's dreams while she was out there. She called each of her friends in turn and had short, but sweet, conversations, promising she'd see them soon. Her parents were the hardest to leave, a deep worry that came from knowing the worst could always happen tucking itself inside of her, something she knew she'd carry with her now whether she was three or three thousand miles away.

But it was the cusp of November, and she'd be back to visit for Christmas in less than two months. She knew she needed this.

She was leaving today. The belongings that she knew she wouldn't need had been taken to her parents' house, and her flat was all but cleared out, apart from a few things from her dresser still to pack in a bag which she was taking with her.

'It's so strange to see this place so empty,' she said to Bear, who was licking at the skirting boards. 'Turns out partially furnished instead of fully furnished would have given you lots more room.'

Alice pulled open her sock drawer and tipped the contents onto the floor. Something she'd all but forgotten rolled out and across the floor.

Reaching forward, Alice picked up the lipstick with two fingers. The cap was scratched from that time she'd run over it with the hoover last year. The label was faded from having rubbed against the inside of her handbag every day since she'd first bought it. The sliver of a crack from where the lid met the base was lined with the soil that had permeated everything during the crush. Why had she clung on to this like it was important? What strange things people did when they didn't know what to do.

She couldn't help herself. She placed it in her left hand and closed her fingers around the lipstick, waiting with a sick fascination to see if the nightmare images would return, eclipsing her view of her current reality. But they didn't.

Instead, Bear got up from his spot on the floor and wandered over to see what she was looking at that wasn't him. He grabbed a pair of bundled socks in his mouth, but dropped them soon enough to snuffle his nose against her closed fist until she agreed to open it.

'This lipstick was my favourite lipstick in the world for a long time,' she told him, letting him sniff it with curiosity. 'I used to wear it every day. And I had it with me the day we lost your mum. Your other mum.'

Bear sat down to listen, so she continued. 'They said I was still holding this when I was looking for her. Clutching hold of it, like it was important – temporary paralysis or something. Isn't that silly? It's a lipstick. It's just a lipstick.' Alice took a big breath. 'Why did I hold onto this, and not her?'

Stretching his neck forward, Bear picked up the lipstick from her hand using his teeth, and dropped it onto the carpet, watching it roll. He pushed it with his nose and it rolled off under her dresser. Bear looked pleased with himself for removing the memory.

Alice fished the lipstick back out, though. It was either coming with them or going in the bin, there was no other option now. She put it back inside a sock, and put the sock into her suitcase, even though she might never wear the shade again. She was leaving today, and her baggage was coming along with her.

She took a final look at the four walls of her bedroom, memories floating inside her head. 'I hope I'm going to miss this place someday.'

Chapter 17

'Just hold on a minute, Bear, I know I put them in here somewhere,' Alice said, one hand holding Bear's lead, the other deep in between the stack of bags, dog paraphernalia and snacks that filled the boot of her car.

Bear was straining to get at a discarded crisp on the ground inside the Eurotunnel terminal, his paws sliding on the lacquered flooring. Finally she pulled out a handful of poop bags. 'Just in case,' she said to him, and shut and locked the car, taking Bear for a bit of exercise before they made the crossing and left England behind them.

'Look, a St Bernard,' someone cried not far away.

They'd only been driving for two hours so far, Islington to Folkestone being relatively easy, but Alice was relieved at how chilled Bear had been in the car. Much more so than she, who had needed to pull in twice for drive-thru Starbucks to calm her nerves and stop herself from turning around and going straight back to her parents' house.

After a vigorous run about a lovely big dog exercise area, Alice went to the pet reception, where Bear couldn't have been made to feel more welcome. Then it was back in the car, drive the car into the Shuttle, and thirty-five minutes later they'd be in France. How easy it was to run away. She could almost feel the Channel breeze calling her off this little island.

'So this is the plan,' she told Bear an hour later, who seemed no more interested in urban Calais than he had been in urban Folkestone. He raised his orange eyebrows at her from the back seat, where he lay hunkered down in his travel hammock. She smoothed the map out on the passenger seat, just in case she needed to see the bigger picture. 'I've put into the satnav the whole route from here to Vanessa's house, which is nearly ten hours of driving time. We can't do that all in one day, so we'll spread it over two, depending on how you get on. Let's get going and see how far we get before you become restless, okay?'

Bear yawned and closed his eyes, looking as comfy as if he were back in her now empty flat, squished between the sofa and coffee table.

'When we start to get bored of driving, I'll find a nice place for us to spend the night.' She was talking to herself now (was she always?) as she pulled the car away from the Eurotunnel terminal and began winding her way through Calais, thinking carefully over the rules of French roads and reminding herself to drive on the right.

As city turned to suburbs which turned to countryside,

Alice relaxed into the seat, a freeness tingling through the back of her neck and down her spine. It felt good to be making a change. She hadn't felt brave for a while, and now finally she was doing something to survive, and to live.

'You know,' she said to Bear, peeping at him in the rear-view mirror. He opened an eye and looked towards her. 'Your mum, your first mum, always wanted to take you on a road trip to Switzerland. She talked about it before you even lived with her. I was going to go with her. So this was always written in your stars.'

He stretched comfortably and closed his eyes again.

For the next couple of hours, Alice let her mind drift as she followed long French motorways. For the first time in what felt like a long while she found she was thinking ahead instead of back. Picturing what was to come instead of what had been. She imagined Bear's little (big) paws dipping into snow for the first time. She thought about how clean the mountain air would seem compared to London. She pictured all the cheese in Switzerland oozing deliciously into her belly.

Bear was getting shuffly in the back and let out a whine, so she pulled off at the next exit to let him out for a wee. But he didn't seem to need to go, and instead hung close to her and refused any water.

'Did you just need to stretch your legs a little? Shall we get back in and carry on now?'

They climbed back in the car, but Alice had only been back on the road for ten minutes when Bear whined again, and then promptly threw up all over his bed on the back seat.

'Oh no, oh Bear, you poor thing, please don't lie down in it, please please please.'

Alice pulled off again and using a mixture of poop bags, wet wipes and dog towels, cleaned the sick up as best she could, only for the same thing to happen again shortly after they resumed their journey.

'Well, one thing I didn't factor in was you getting car sick.'

She stopped the car again, cleaned up, and this time lay a big towel over the whole bed. She got out her phone.

'We haven't covered as much ground as I'd hoped today, but we've got all day tomorrow. Shall we call that it and then set off early in the morning? I'll be more prepared for puppukage tomorrow, just in case.'

Alice looked on the Airbnb app for nearby pet-friendly accommodation. 'Where even are we?' she asked aloud.

GPS told her she was not far from a little village in the Champagne region. 'I'm not adverse to that,' she told Bear, and clicked onto a listing that seemed reasonably priced. 'What do you think of this – a private room with a *salle de bain* inside a chateau! Fancy staying in a castle tonight, Bear? Will that suit you and your dodgy stomach?' The advantage of a castle, along with it being quite interesting and hopefully laced with free champagne, was that it would hopefully be cold, which would suit Bear to a tee if he was currently a bit hot and uncomfortable.

It was decided. The chateau, divided into apartments, with bricks the colour of champagne itself, shuttered windows and two spiky turrets, had an instant book feature, which was perfect for a girl and her dog wanting to check in within the next twenty minutes. She booked it without another thought, and then drove slowly down the lanes towards the address, hoping not to disturb Bear's stomach any further.

'Look at this, Bear,' she said as they pulled up.

In the low afternoon sunlight it was even more beautiful than the photos had suggested, surrounded by tall trees and the quiet you can only seem to find on grand estates in the countryside.

Bear hopped out of the car and as Alice was just thinking how quiet it was and how the air was fragranced with distant wood burning, Bear ran straight to the middle of the lawn for a poop. Alice chased after him, bag in hand, peeping up at the chateau windows for disapproving guests.

'Thanks for that,' she said to him, leading him to the front of the house. The door creaked pleasingly and she was surprised to see a reception on the inside, where she checked in as if it were a hotel. The host, an attractive man with extremely tight trousers and a touchy-feely attitude with her dog, showed them to their room.

'Here you go,' he said with a rich accent. 'This is for you.' He produced a small welcome basket out of nowhere for Alice, containing macarons and madeleines, and a tiny bottle of champagne. 'And this is for you.' He crouched down and gave Bear a thousand kisses, plus his own welcome basket of star-shaped dog biscuits.

'Thank you so much,' said Alice, and bid the man a *bon nuit*. She realised there was no restaurant on site, nor for a few miles, and she didn't want to get back in the car, so that evening she and Bear forced themselves to relax for the night. She gave Bear his pre-packed meal while she munched away on biscuits and champagne, and they whiled away the hours watching French TV together without knowing what was going on. Then they slept, with Bear below the large single-paned window and Alice with several layers on. It was good training for the mountain, she thought, as the champagne bubbles floated about in her until she drifted to dreamland.

Chapter 18

The following morning the weather had turned, and a low, damp fog hung over the north-east of France. Alice wanted to get going early, so she gave Bear just a tiny amount of breakfast.

He glowered at her.

'Well, I'm sorry, mister, but after yesterday's performance I'm not risking you in my car on a full stomach. For both our sakes. I'll top you up when we stop for loo breaks.'

They said *au revoir* to the chateau and joined the motorway again that would take them down through France and into Switzerland. It was slow-going, the visibility causing everyone, not least Alice, to crawl along. That, combined with the extra hours of driving she'd have to be putting in today, caused Alice to keep one eye on the road, and one on the clock.

Thankfully, Bear seemed to be getting on much better today, stomach-wise, and seemed almost in a huff when

Alice pulled over on the outskirts of a small village to give him a water break.

'We don't have long, okay? Out you get,' she encouraged him, and he sighed and eventually jumped from the car and sniffed at the small bowl of water she'd put out.

It was now midday, although the sky was the same thick, ash-grey it had been all morning, with not a trace of sunshine breaking through the clouds. They were still crawling through rural France, and it would be at least a couple of hours if not more by the time they hit the Swiss border.

Alice called Vanessa.

Vanessa answered on the first ring. 'Hi Alice, how is your journey?'

'Slow and foggy,' answered Alice, while Bear raised his nose to the damp sky.

'Foggy? It's very beautiful here on our mountain today – how far away are you?'

'We're still in France because we didn't get as far as I would have liked yesterday.'

'How come?'

'Turns out this puppy gets car sick.'

'Oh, poor little Bear! So how far away are you?'

'That's why I'm calling. I don't think I'll be at yours until maybe late afternoon. What time are you leaving?'

Vanessa paused, making calculations in her head. 'Really the latest I can be leaving is late afternoon. Five, *maybe* six at the very very latest. After I've been on the train down the mountain, it will take me two hours and a bit to get to Zurich and I really can't get there too late – I have to be up to welcome arriving guests at seven in the morning tomorrow.'

'No, I completely understand, I don't want to hold you up, and I definitely want to get there before dark. What time is sunset in Switzerland at the moment?'

'Six-thirty, more or less.'

A thread of anxiety gnawed at Alice. 'How would you feel about leaving me your keys somewhere? I know that's a lot to ask, but ...'

'I don't mind doing that, but I was hoping to give you an enormous hug and meet your Bear, and show you around my home.'

'I know, I hope I can make it in time.'

'Okay, look,' said Vanessa decisively, 'get back in the car and get going, and call me again later to let me know how you're getting on. Maybe give me a phone call when you make it through the border. *If* you make it over the border.' Vanessa's laugh tinkled down the phone, a sound that brought memories of eating strange South American snacks in thirty different hotel rooms with her and Jill, gossiping about the other people on the tour, howling with laughter at the characters they were sprinkling their lives with.

The memory was holding on to Alice, and she let it, even after she'd hung up, and even as she was back curling around these French roads. It soothed her.

But even so, when she finally rounded the corner on a road curtained by pine trees, to see the modest cream buildings of the French/Swiss border control, she was relieved.

It was four o'clock in the afternoon, and by the time she'd passed through the customs checks it was half past.

Alice pulled over again and ripped open a packet of cookies, taking the last drink from her flask of coffee that she'd refilled before leaving the chateau. She chomped down on a cookie and faced facts. She wasn't going to catch Vanessa before she left. She was also possibly not going to make it to Mürren before dark. She took her phone out.

'Hi, Vanessa, I'm in Switzerland!'

'Ahhh, welcome home,' Vanessa cried, which lightened Alice's heart. *Home.* She looked around for a moment.

'I don't think you should wait for me to arrive,' she admitted.

'Yeah, I think you're right,' Vanessa agreed. 'I'm so sorry I won't be here when you get to my house – *our house* – but I'm going to make it all cosy for you and leave you many instructions.'

'Thank you. I mean, it might be really smooth-sailing from here, maybe I might just catch you?'

'Smooth sailing? You are getting a boat somewhere?'

'No, sorry, it's a phrase. I mean the weather is better than it was, and if the roads stay clear ... '

'Yeah, but you remember what I told you about Mürren being car-free, right?' Vanessa cautioned.

Alice hesitated. She remembered *something* about that. 'Yes ... ' she ventured.

'You forgot, huh?' There was that carefree laugh again. 'I bet you packed all of your kitchen sink, yes?'

125

'Maybe.' Alice glanced in through the rear windscreen at the boot full of clobber. Then she glanced at her dog, who took up nearly as much room. 'Just remind me of the details of where I should park?'

'Okay, you pay attention, all right? Don't get distracted like that time in Brazil when you were so in love with that boy with the long sleeves you nearly joined the wrong tour.'

Alice laughed, the sound surprising her. 'He did have lovely sleeves, and lovely fingers.'

'Focus, woman. So drive your car to Lauterbrunnen, park up, and then go to the station. It's really clearly sign-posted and so simple to use. You need to take a cableway to Grütschalp and then change to this cute little electric train. Then my chalet is steps away from the train station in Mürren. Simple!'

Alice gulped. 'Two separate journeys?' With a dog, with all her stuff, to a place she didn't know, in the dark. Maybe she should just find another dog-friendly hotel for the night.

'Yes. And this is important. There are two ways to get up to Mürren, but you have to park at Lauterbrunnen, because that way the station is so so close to the house. If you park at Stechelberg and take up that cableway you will have a ten, maybe a fifteen minute walk with all of your things when you arrive. That station is the other side of Mürren. Okay?'

'Lauterbrunnen. Not ... Stet – Stetchenblog.'

'Stechelberg.' Vanessa paused. 'You can handle it. But if you're worried, just take from your car the things you really need for the night and go back and get the rest in the morn-ing. And my house has plenty of food and drink and warm sweaters you can borrow, so don't worry about weighing yourself down with any of that.'

I can handle it. She had to bloomin' well handle it. She'd made this choice and she really didn't want Bear to have to face another long day of driving tomorrow. She would get there tonight, or at least get as close as she damned well could.

'Seriously,' Vanessa said. 'I know you have been through tougher things than this. I know it.' She let her words sink in. 'Now get back in the car, and get over here. I have a bottle of brandy waiting to warm you up from the inside.'

'Thanks, Vanessa.'

'Don't mention it. Just drive. And we will catch up properly in a couple of weeks when I'm back for the weekend, okay?'

'Okay.' Alice hung up and Bear pulled her towards the open door of a small general store beside the road. Bear was so nosy – he always wanted to investigate any open door – but this time it wasn't such a bad idea.

Stopping at the entrance, Alice attempted to tie up Bear to a bicycle rack outside, but he tried to scramble into her lap and pulled until he rasped when she moved away from him. 'I know, you don't know where we are, but I'll be two minutes.'

Bear continued to whine, until the shopkeeper, an elderly woman with a severe face, barked, 'Eh!'

Alice looked up at the woman, who gestured towards Bear, and then gestured into the shop. Alice didn't know what she meant, and after a little more gesturing the woman said, 'In! In!'

'In here? Dog in shop?' Alice asked, clumsily.

She untied Bear, keeping her eye on the shopkeeper in case this was *so* not what she'd meant, but the minute Bear's big feet were sliding through the door her face went from fierce to full of joy. Her cheeks pinked and she held her arms wide and Bear swung into her, twirling in circles and licking her face.

The woman babbled at him in affectionate Swiss French while Alice collected an armful of water, snacks and other provisions in case they got stuck anywhere between now and Mürren, and kept an eye on her Bear. It was like he was right at home.

'Beautiful Bernie,' the shopkeeper enthused as she rung up Alice's items. 'Beautiful, beautiful.' She then watched, waving, as the two of them returned to the car.

But Bear wasn't ready to leave his new friend. Or at least, he wasn't ready to have to get back in the car again.

'Come on, up you get,' Alice coaxed him. 'Up. Come on. Up. Up. Bear, up.' She stood holding the car door open and gesturing inside but to no avail. Tapping the seat and throwing in treats didn't help either. Bear stayed stock-still, staring at her.

She scooped her arms around his waist and tried to lift him, letting out a guttural moan. 'Jesus Christ, you're a heavy thing now.' She managed to raise his front paws up to the seat but he dabbed at her cheeks with his nose, sniffing and snuffling and blocking her vision. The moment she let go, he put his paws back down.

'Come on, just a couple more hours, then we'll be there.

I know it's boring and uncomfortable – it is for me too.' She rolled her shoulders. 'Do you feel sick again?'

They stared at each other for a moment until Bear whined and tried to back away from the vehicle.

'Oh Bear, please, please get in the car. I'm sorry.'

Alice was so focused on trying to nudge her increasingly anxious dog back into the car that she didn't even notice the old woman from the shop appear until she'd flung open the opposite door and stuck her round face through.

'*BOO-BOO-BOO-BOO!*' She made delighted, chirping sounds towards Bear until he turned and peered into the car, stepping forward for a better look. On seeing the shopkeeper he took a flying leap straight into the back seat, tail wagging, and nestling his face against hers again.

Alice rolled her eyes. Honestly, one minute he can't bear to leave her side, the next minute he's having a holiday romance with a stranger.

She closed the door on her side, placed her shopping in the passenger footwell and returned to the driver's seat, thanking the lady.

The shopkeeper gestured for Alice to open the back window, and once Alice had leant over and clipped Bear in, she did so. The two had a final snog through the open window, and Alice hit the road again with a grateful wave.

She closed the window and looked at Bear in the rear-view mirror. 'Sorry to pull you away from your new girlfriend.'

He sighed and lay down on the back seat in a huff.

'Half an hour in Switzerland and you're already doing some kissing. I think you're going to be okay here.'

They wove through the roads of Switzerland, skirting the edges of the city of Bern, and on towards the mountains. The sun sank lower, making the clouds before it turn from white to steel blue. The air grew colder, and Alice had a decision to make. Stop now and find a hotel that would accept her and her dog, or face the night sky and the mountain roads for the final thirty kilometres.

I know you've been through tougher things than this. Vanessa's words rang in her ears. It was true. And although she'd driven home from the dog school lessons in the dark over the past couple of months, there was far less light pollution in the Swiss Alps than there was in London. It was time to learn to face the dark again.

It was far beyond dusk now, the roads, landscape and sky all paling into shades of indigo. The mountain passes were hard to see and the roads twisty. Flakes of snow kissed the windscreen, seeming to head straight for her, sending her windscreen wipers into overdrive.

'Shit,' Alice whispered, the anxious feeling gnawing against her stomach. 'It's okay, Bear, nearly there.' She stretched an arm back between the seats and ruffled her fingers through his soft fur, her stress levels immediately reducing a little. He responded by giving her hand a lick. He was okay. He was doing better than her.

Why oh why hadn't she planned this out better? She should have left England a day earlier. She should have made two overnight stops after all so she was driving up the mountain pass during bright morning light. Granted, she hadn't known she'd hit the delays but still, she felt stupid for putting herself and Bear in this situation.

There is no 'situation' yet, she reminded herself, trying to pull herself back from thinking the worst-case scenario. Soon they'd reach Lauterbrunnen, the village at the foot of the mountain where they had to leave the car and board a cable car with their belongings to travel the last stretch to Mürren. Really soon, according to the satnav.

'We're just fifteen minutes away,' she said into the car. 'Fifteen minutes, please wait for us, cable car. Please don't do your last run until we get there.'

She leant forward in the seat. It was okay. If the cable car was gone, they could stay the night somewhere in Lauterbrunnen, it wouldn't be a problem. But the dark felt heavy and unfamiliar, when she'd been making an effort only to exist in the light for the past few months.

She sucked in the air as the road took another barely visible left, and slowed down further, the destination drifting that much further from her grasp.

Chapter 19

'I might give you some of Vanessa's brandy too, if we ever get there,' Alice murmured to the dog as she crawled the car forward. She followed the tail lights of a car up ahead, and in the darkness could see the shape of mountains looming above her.

It took everything she had not to think about the concert crush. Which meant the thoughts and memories were there, clamouring and clawing to get in and distract her from the road. She focused on Bear's consistent panting, calm and comfortable.

Eventually a street lamp appeared, and then another, and another, and when a large sign appeared pointing towards a multi-storey car park, with a picture of a cable car with 'Mürren' written beside it, she exhaled with relief. The road widened and sloped-roofed buildings lit from within popped up on either side, a large canvas of happy skiers strung high over the road.

Alice indicated left towards the car park, saying, 'I think we're here, Bear!' *We made it!*

In the back seat he sat up and yawned, shaking out his ears.

But there was a man beside the entrance to the car park who seemed to be turning people away. Alice opened her car window, a blast of freezing air entering their warm pod, and asked, 'Excuse me, we're looking for parking to go up to Mürren?'

The man, wrapped up in thick clothing, the tip of his nose bright pink, replied, 'For Mürren, keep going to Stechelberg and get the cableway up the mountain.'

'Keep going? We can't park and go up from here?' No, no, no, this wasn't the plan. They were *here*.

'No because the car park is full. There is a renovations taking place so it is only half of the size right now. Stechelberg is six kilometres that way.'

'But Stetchenblog—'

'Stechelberg,' he corrected.

'It's the wrong . . . ' She faltered. He couldn't do anything about that, and a couple of cars were now indicating to try and come in after her. So Alice nodded a thanks to the man and reversed, making her way back to the main road. She drove in silence, watching the comforting lights of Lauterbrunnen recede and the darkness welcome her back.

Six kilometres may seem to stretch long like elastic after nightfall, but in reality the lights had started to appear again after ten minutes. Dotted beside the road, one after another, were simple, illuminated Christmas shapes taking her into Stechelberg. A bell, then a tree, then a star, and before she knew it the road took her off to an open-air car park with a large building – the cable car station – at the end.

Alice pulled into an empty space between two other cars, very very carefully as the car park wasn't gritted and she was driving over an inch or two of snow now. And she switched the engine off.

'*Now* we've made it, Bear,' she said, and both the dog and the car heaved a sigh of relief.

Alice rolled her stiff shoulders as her stomach growled. It felt so good to know she wouldn't be needing to climb back into this cramped vehicle for some time, and the few other people pottering about the car park reassured her that the cableway was still running.

She opened the door and *whoosh*, the cold air hit her. Wow, the wind chill in the mountains was real. She grabbed for her coat and for Bear's lead, and he was about to hop out of the car when he came to a standstill, peering over the edge of the car onto the ground below.

Alice blew upwards, trying to warm the tip of her nose. 'Come on, what's wrong?'

He stared down and she adjusted to try and make more room for him to get out. As her boot slipped just a little on the ice, she realised what he was staring at. 'Bear! Your first experience of snow! Look.' She scooped a handful into her glove and held it to his face. He pressed his nose into it and left it there a while. 'Do you like the cold? There'll be plenty more of this over the next few months. Are you going to have a go at walking on it?'

She gave his lead a small, very gentle tug, and Bear stepped down, lifting his paws high as if it could be three feet deep. He toddled forwards, dragging his nose into the snow as he walked, weaving this way and that, listening to the sound it made under his paws. He tried leaping in the air and watched it powder-poof around him, and he tried licking it off the back of the car while he waited for Alice to gather their belongings and take them to the cableway station.

Alice worked fast, her fingers freezing, and pulled out his bed, her handbag, one of her suitcases, the bag with his food and toys and a food bag. She surveyed the pile of belongings. Because of Bear, she would only have one hand at her disposal, and this was *way* too much to haul up a mountain.

'What do we not need tonight?' she asked him.

Bear stuck his head in the bag of his stuff. He was telling her that if nothing else, this bag was essential.

'Maybe we don't need your bed,' she mused. 'You slept all over the place in our old house, so I'm sure you can do without it for one night. Don't look at me like that – it's huge. If I take your bed I can't carry your food and toys as well.'

He snorted through his nose and rested his chin on the lip of the boot, resigned.

She put the bed back in the car, for now.

'I guess I don't need everything in this suitcase.' Alice opened up the case on the car park ground, revealing her carefully packed winter clothing and toiletries. *Jesus*, it was cold. No time for keeping things neat. She pulled out a

135

handful of clothing and underwear and threw it back in the boot, making a gap big enough to stuff her handbag into.

'Okay, that's two-in-one. We'll leave my food bag, since Vanessa said we could eat her stuff. Don't judge me, Bear, you eat my food all the time, and we'll replace anything we use up. As for your bag . . . ' She pulled out seven bright dog toys in various textures, sizes and colours. 'Pick just two favourites for tonight.'

Bear snuffled along the line of toys, settling on a balled-up rope that had seen better days, and a lump of hard wood that he liked to chew on. Alice returned them to his bag, which was now closable, and balanced it on top of her suitcase, the bag handles strung over the suitcase's own extended top handle.

'I think we can manage this lot.' She closed the boot, locked the car, and stopped. More specifically, Bear stopped. He sat down and refused to move.

'Bear, come on, it's cold, let's get in the cable car.'

He whined back at the car.

'Are you kidding me? You couldn't wait to see the back of it earlier!' Alice tried to pull him but instead he lay his tummy down in the snow, not breaking eye contact. 'Oh my God, are you actually lying down to stop me from moving you? Bear, we can't stay here. What's the problem?'

Nothing. Nothing but a fixed stare and a big sigh.

She opened the back of the car again to fetch a bag of his treats she knew was in there somewhere, something she could use as a bribe, and Bear leapt up, pushed his head around her and clutched his bed with his teeth.

'Don't eat that, it's your bed,' cried Alice. But Bear was already pulling it out of the car. She wrestled with him to try and stuff it back in, but he wasn't letting go. 'You are so stubborn. Come on, I can't carry that as well, we'll get it in the morning.' She waved a treat under his nostrils, which he ignored.

'I am *not* carrying these bags, and you, and that whopping great bed tonight. I'm tired, and it's dark, and we don't know where we're going. I'm not doing it.'

Five minutes later, Alice was trying to hold her temper as she carried her bags, the dog lead, and the whopping great bed to the exit of the car park. Bear skipped along next to her, pleased with himself for getting his own way.

At the entrance to the station, Alice put down the bed that was wedged precariously under her lead-wielding arm and studied a map and a timetable before giving up and making her way to the counter, leaving everything but the dog in a heap by some stairs.

'Hello,' she said to the lady manning the enclosed ticket booth, wrapped in a thick black jacket. 'We need to go to Mürren?'

'Do you ski?' the lady asked.

'Not really,' answered Alice.

'If you want I will give you return ticket with pass to use the cable cars and chairlifts as much as you wish?'

'Actually, I just want a one-way. I have to collect some more things from my car tomorrow, but other than that I'm not coming back down.'

'Oh okay!' The lady pressed a few buttons and Bear

balanced on his back legs to put his paws up on the counter, the nosy thing. 'Hello,' the lady addressed him. 'You are moving to the mountain too?'

Alice nodded. 'We're here for the winter.'

'Wonderful. You will love it very much.'

The lady pointed Alice and Bear up the stairs to the waiting area, under a large sign that read, *Gimmelwald-Mürren-Birg-Schilthorn*. To reach the very top of the mountain, the Schilthorn, you needed to take four different cable cars. Alice dragged their belongings up the steps, hoping the change at Gimmelwald wouldn't take long. She needed a wee.

They had about twenty-five minutes to wait (twenty-three minutes, to be precise, and from what she'd heard of Swiss rail travel, precise was how it would be running) and the waiting area was deserted. The cold air crept in through the wooden-panelled walls, and she could see her and Bear's breath billowing in front of their noses. The lights were stark and large black and white images of the mountains acted as decoration alongside a Nescafé hot drinks dispenser and a vending machine containing interesting Swiss nibbles.

'*Ovomaltine*,' she whispered aloud, reading an orange-wrappered chocolate bar. Was that the same as Ovaltine? Did they have Ovaltine chocolate here?

She led Bear to a large window and peered outside, straining to see if she could make out a cable car approaching from the heavens. Bear jumped up, paws on the window, which she probably shouldn't let him do but he was a nice hugging height when he was all stretched tall like this.

Outside was the inky outline of the Eiger, one of the most impressive mountains in the Bernese Alps. Barely visible at this time of night, it was almost impossible to imagine the scale.

'Wait until you see it in daylight,' said an accented man's voice, and Alice turned to see a cableway worker sweeping the clean floor of the terminal. 'You are just visiting, yes?'

'Sort of, we're staying a while.'

'Showing your handsome dog where he is from?' The man bent down to say hi to Bear.

'Yep,' said Alice. 'It's really quiet around here, though, I was expecting more tourists.'

'The snow it came earlier than expected this year. All the holiday companies will be trying to pull in their staff and start the ski season as soon as they can. You will have a lot of company up there in no time.' He smiled and went back to work.

Alice turned back to the window and snuggled into Bear. 'Until then it's just me and you, okay? Shall we go up the mountain?'

Chapter 20

Two very immaculate and very on-time modes of public transport later, with the easiest change ever (a hop across the platform at Gimmelwald where the next cable car was ready and waiting), they were officially in Mürren, and the doors would be opening in three ... two ... one ...

Alice heaved and pulled all of their belongings, including Bear himself, out of the door of the cable car, her heart racing in case she couldn't do it in time. She needn't have worried; the cable car operator, her only companion as they'd drifted the slow, dark, journey up the mountain, seemed in no rush to head back down again.

They emerged into a large, modern building, not that dissimilar to a small UK train station, with some waiting areas, an information desk and a (closed) newsagents-slash-café-slash-gift shop. A cold breeze seeped in through the large automatic doors, and Alice took a moment to rearrange her belongings and dig her phone out of her coat pocket.

She flipped open the map app which was preloaded with directions to Vanessa's chalet, and turned on the spot a few times, getting her bearings.

'Okay, Bear. It's an easy route but it's going to take about thirteen minutes to walk it. And then we'll be finally at our new home.' She was so tired. Tired of travelling, tired of worrying. But she was so nearly there, so she picked herself and her bags up, now balancing her phone in the cup of her glove also, and they exited together into Mürren.

When she stepped outside, something very small in Alice changed. The streets, lost under a thick white blanket, were quiet, and the snow without footprints. All the chalets seemed empty and lightless, but for pretty fairy lights arranged under roofs, and strings of LED snowflakes framing the path overhead. Only the street lights hummed, and when she looked up she saw fine snowflakes falling past the glow.

It was a different world and it filled her eyes and heart, a million miles from the too-wet or too-hot streets of London where in every footstep she felt the deep echo of the ones that Jill left no more. Here her footprints felt like they were hers and hers alone.

Alice held Bear's lead tightly as she trudged and dragged and hunched ever forward, the ending an unfamiliar distance away. Her dog pulled her in zigzags, investigating the new smells, sticking his whole head into snowdrifts, flinging clumps of it up with his nose. Her heart burned and her breath was short from the altitude, and her body sweated under her thick snow jacket.

The walk was difficult and slow, but all of that hardship wasn't even registering as Alice was completely in the moment, drinking it all in. She'd never seen so much snow. It was easily a foot, maybe two-foot deep on top of all of the sloped chalet roofs. It swept up the sides of wooden walls and slept upon windowsills. To her right those mountains, grey against the silken black sky, loomed like friends watching over her as she and her dog made their lonely journey.

Eventually she reached the other train station, and she knew she was near. She veered to the left and followed the slope of the hill up, panting, checking the map on her phone, bumping into Bear, hearing the snap and crackle of her shoulder muscles as they worked to pull the loaded suitcase those last few steps.

And there it was – Vanessa's front door. The chalet lights had been left on inside and it was like a glowing lighthouse welcoming her safe passage home. She took a moment to look back at the mountain and the village behind her, and catch her breath.

Alice found the key, right where Vanessa had said it would be underneath a wooden bear cub statue perched on the decking, and opened the door. A fat sprinkling of snow fell from the doorframe onto her head, but she didn't mind, she'd made it. Entering the chalet, she dumped her bags, set Bear free from his lead, and closed her door behind her, sinking to the ground and leaning her aching back against it.

She took in the surroundings, while Bear scurried in and out of her vision, nosing around every corner and every room in the house.

From her viewpoint on the floor, Alice found herself in a large, open-plan living room straight out of an Abercrombie & Fitch winter commercial. Ashy cedar-wood walls and a high, sloped ceiling surrounded her. A snuggly-looking jade corner sofa wrapped around a wood burner which, though unlit, was still emitting a festive, smoky scent into the air. Slung over various parts of the sofa and armchairs were a zillion blankets – tartan ones, faux fur, fleece. Behind the sofa was a long dining table, and behind that, the kitchen area. To her left was a staircase leading to the second level (*she was living in a real house!*) and to her right floor-to-ceiling windows that looked out onto darkness sprinkled with a line of street lights, presumably where she'd just traipsed.

'We live here now,' she told Bear. 'Sort of, for a while at least.'

Bear stopped and looked at her, his big triangle ears pointing forwards. He bounced on the spot, ready to play a game now he was free of the car and the lead.

'In a minute, and I'll get you some dinner soon, too. And some water. I just need one minute.' She let her eyelids close, her head propping back against the door.

She heard him before she felt him, that impending pant, those padding paws. And splat, the wet-sponge-like nose prodded her cheek. *Wake up, lady,* Bear seemed to be saying. *Don't you know it's play/dinner/exploring time?*

'Okay.' Alice sighed, standing and running her fingers through his ears. Even when he was annoying she still couldn't resist him.

Alice reached down and untied her boots, Bear batting at

her feet, stepping over her legs and chewing on the laces as she did so. She kicked them off and left them on the floor, which would be fatal to the shoes if she left them too long, and hauled herself back up to pad towards the kitchen. She filled Bear's water and food bowl, placing them for now by the back door.

Alice trailed her fingers over the counter tops that she would make breakfasts and dinners on, the mugs she would drink morning coffee from, the clock she'd glance at to see the time from all the way over in the living room. She perched on a bar stool at the kitchen island, and imagined herself treating it like her own, sitting with one leg curled under her, her art materials spread out on the surface of the island.

Hmm.

'How long do you think it will take for us to feel like this is more *home* than *holiday home*, Bear?' she asked aloud. 'We'll be here for about six months. Even with Vanessa coming back and forth we're bound to get comfy, right?'

He finished his food and took a long, loud, slurp of water.

'Maybe not, like, our-own-London-flat-comfy, if you know what I mean. But, happy-comfy. Fresh surroundings-comfy. Let the daylight in-comfy.'

Bear wandered over to her and flopped down on the ground by her feet, his own tired, heavy body thudding, and his eyes were closed in contentment within moments.

'Well, I'm glad you're already there,' said Alice, and she stretched across the island to reach a notepad with a letter scrawled on the open page.

Sali Alice!

I am so sorry we didn't see each other before I had to leave. This weather! We haven't had this much snow this early for a really long time, so I just couldn't leave it any longer before I set off. I hope you and Bear didn't arrive too late. Text me when you are home, okay? I need to know my soft British visitors are safe!

I don't know what food and drink you like so I just bought some things for now but there's a little shop in the village – you'll find it. Look to your right – I leave some house instructions for you, plus a leaflet about good walking trails so you + dog can explore. I also leave him some dog treats because I love him so much already.

You can think of me tomorrow morning starting my first tour group! I will feed them cheese for breakfast, which you tourists always find funny. I will see you for lots of wine and kisses and talking in 2 weeks, I'll let you know exact date I'll be back as soon as possible.

Kisses for now,
Vanessa xxx

There was a kindness in Vanessa that echoed that of Jill. The type of kindness that made her willing to give her home over to Alice, who really was no more than a memory to her. This is just the type of thing her best friend would have done, and that thought filled Alice with warmth.

Like a candle flame, it was flickering, and it was delicate, but Alice was finding that thoughts of Jill that a few weeks ago would have brought darkness were now bringing light.

Chapter 21

Alice woke early the next morning, the first day of November, with the air in the guest bedroom biting. Her thin PJs, used to only having to withstand the warm flat nestled between floors and walls of other flats, were not proving their worth. It was only when she sat and pulled at the thick, furry blanket at the end of the bed that she realised it wasn't that early after all – it was nearly eight.

Alice wrapped herself in the blanket. Did she even wake up in the night? She couldn't have slept right through … could she? It had been months since she'd been able to do that. It must have been the quiet up here in the mountains.

Across the room, on cue, Bear let out his low, moo-like groan and stretched and opened his eyes to peep at her. Seeing her sitting up he got to his feet and did an impressive downward dog followed by a loud shake that ran from his flappy ears through to the tip of his plume of a tail.

'Good morning,' Alice said to him. 'I didn't even hear

you thumping about in the night – did you sleep all the way through as well?'

Her bladder twanged to tell her that yes, she did sleep all the way through, and please could she get up now, thank you.

Bear followed her to the en suite bathroom and watched her wee. She yawned as she did her business. 'We're going to go for a big walk in a minute, mister. You must be desperate for a run-around. We'll just have some breakfast first and take a look at how to warm the house up a little.'

When she was done, she dragged two jumpers from her suitcase and, shivering, headed down the stairs, Bear thumping down in front of her. At the bottom, she stopped in her tracks.

'Bloody hell!'

Light. Natural light filled her space in a way it hadn't in months. The vista she faced, framed in all its glory by the floor-to-ceiling windows in the living room, was magnificent. The pale dawn sky basked proudly behind the jagged mountain range that rose on the other side of the valley, the white peaks of the Eiger, Mönch and Jungfrau painted golden on the very tips from the rising sun. Sleeping before her and back along the length of the village that sat halfway up the mountain was a sweep of chocolate-box chalets, their sloped roofs each under a duvet of snow. Pine trees popped up from the ground in all directions, like Christmas trees on holiday.

Despite the temperature, Alice opened the side door and stepped out on to a wide balcony. Bear followed, and leant against her left leg, keeping her scar warm. She'd been hiding in a box, cramped and too small, and darkened by the little windows and narrow London street with its engulfing buildings. And now it was as if the box had been torn open and she had all the light and space she didn't know she needed.

Alice could see for miles. She could breathe deep lungfuls of cold air, and she wanted to. The sky seemed huge, the snowy pathways seemed endless. Bear could run anywhere. She could run anywhere.

She ran her fingers through Bear's fur, a million miles away from home, and one step closer to feeling normal again.

'Change of plans. Shall we go for a walk first?' Alice suggested, a few minutes later. Bear jumped to attention, his tail wagging, and he beamed up at her. 'Don't look at me like that, I know it's usually you telling me it's time to go. But I quite fancy exploring, and I've also got a craving for something warm and sweet for brekkie, if we can find a bakery.'

She clung on tight as another optical fibre inside her lit up, similar to the one that had sparked her into coming on this trip in the first place. The ones that were pulsing messages to her to *choose happy*. It was such a small change, the want for something tasty for breakfast, rather than just 'whatever there was'.

They padded back inside and up the stairs, Bear pushing to walk in front of her and stopping every few steps to check he was going the right way. In the bedroom, Alice emptied the contents of her suitcase out onto the floor (she could put it away later, she had all the time in the world!) and Bear leapt on a pair of ski socks to skitter about with while she got dressed. She pulled on thick tights, a cosy knitted jumper dress with a thermal vest underneath, some ski socks – not the ones currently getting slobbered over – and her new Roxy snow boots and snow jacket. She even gave her scar a caring little touch with her finger before it disappeared into her tights. It was part of her, after all.

'Come on then, sock thief,' she said to Bear, and descended the stairs like a Michelin man. Alice found her hat and gloves on the table, loaded up with dog treats, poop bags, Swiss francs and good spirits, and popped Bear's collar and lead on him.

The moment she opened the front door a crack, Bear's nose was through it, shoving his way into the shallow snow-drift that had settled in front of Vanessa's home overnight. He sunk his snout into the powdery cold, picking his paws one at a time through the flakes. It crunched underfoot as Alice navigated spinning on the spot, performing a Tonya Harding-impressive triple axel as she held Bear's lead, locked the door and pulled out her phone to snap a photo or five.

The sun was fully up over the mountains now, making the snow glitter and the sky a bright glacial blue. Clean, cool air kissed the tip of her nose as she made her way carefully down the hill. She'd never seen so much snow. It seemed even bigger, even thicker and even whiter than she'd appreciated last night, with huge piles of it forming walls around the pathways, and weighing down the branches of the trees.

The chalets they passed revealed their pretty details in

the morning light – exteriors made of chocolate- or amber-coloured wood, window shutters painted in greens and reds, balconies with delicate carvings and long, sturdy icicles that draped themselves from corners or dangled from awnings.

Some properties had lazy smoke circling out through chimneys, and soft lighting behind curtains, suggesting she and her puppy weren't the only souls in the village after all. The quiet hotels and closed restaurants had well-maintained foot walks leading to the front doors, with densely packed snow on their paths; they looked close to opening for the season.

Bear was bouncing and sniffing and pronking next to her, taking bites out of the snowdrifts and holding his tongue under dripping icicles, so Alice tentatively let him off the lead. He scampered in zigzags in front of her, never straying far, but desperate to smell and taste everything in this new place.

'Don't run off, okay? I'm trusting you to stay nearby. And don't run into anyone's house. And don't eat yellow snow.'

They walked on, retracing her steps from last night, only this time she became aware of all these details she hadn't noticed about the village – a big ice rink to her right, a cute café to her left, a funicular railway, the tracks posture-perfect up against the mountain. Chairlifts and cables stood still and quiet, enjoying their rest before the tourists arrived.

'Oh look, Bear!' As they rounded the corner, Alice spotted the open doors and bright lights of a Coop supermarket beckoning.

This time, Bear was happy to be tied outside, so long as he could sit right in the doorway of the store facing outwards, sniffing the air, toes wiggling in the snow and beaming up at the sunshine and blue sky.

Full, narrow aisles with overflowing baskets of produce and racks of unfamiliar food tempted Alice with every step. She followed the sweet smell of baked goods until she found what she was looking for and stocked up on mini loaves and sugary pastries. She then backtracked and loaded her basket with fruits and vegetables, finally found the milk and then stood staring at the entire wall of sausages and cold meat, wondering where the bacon was.

'Bacon ... bacon ... bacon ...' Alice mumbled, searching past packets of cured hams and ginormous bratwurst. She picked up a small packet of pancetta and was about to put that in her basket when a woman in ski boots, with a pink nose and ski poles under her arm, tapped her on the shoulder.

'Bacon?' she asked with a grin and an accent.

'Yes,' replied Alice, unsure what the question was that was being asked.

The lady shifted the poles to her other arm and rummaged between the packets of meat until she produced what looked like a larger pack of what Alice was already holding, and thrust it towards her. She tapped the chilled rashers and smiled. 'Bacon.'

'Thank you,' said Alice, warmed by this kindness. 'Thank you so much.'

The woman grinned and walked off, her ski boots

clump-clump-clumping and a loaf of brioche swinging from her gloved hand. Alice weaved her way to the cash register, grabbing en route a bag of Ovomaltine powder and a big orange-packaged bag of Ovomaltine biscuits to try. As she paid she watched the bacon woman exit the store, give Bear a passing pat on the head, and then click her skis back on her feet and take off down the hill, bread bag flying on the breeze behind her. What a way to commute.

Alice took a satisfied breath. She could see herself living here. Right now she felt very *happy-comfy*.

Later that morning, the two of them were ensconced back in the chalet, with Alice pottering around unpacking her belongings. She'd made a record-time zip back to the car after dumping her shopping, praying the whole way down the mountain and back up again that Bear wouldn't be destroying Vanessa's beautiful Alpine home. *'My' home?* She tested out the thought.

When she'd returned, pink-cheeked from the cold air combined with sweat from walking hastily up the hill with lots of bags and a big snow jacket on, she laughed out loud to see Bear hadn't budged an inch, and remained in a peaceful slumber beside the large window in the living room.

He had raised his head when she came in, got up, shook himself out and pottered over to stick his head in one of the bags, just in case food was hiding in there.

Now she was in the guest room – *her room* – surveying her 'warm clothes' spread out on the floor. She said to Bear, 'I'm going to have to go shopping soon. A few jumpers and

152

leggings from H&M really aren't going to hold out for a full winter wonderland.'

Bear wandered over to her, grabbed a sock in his mouth again and bounced out of the room before she could stop him.

Shopping was low on the priority list. Vanessa had insisted she make this place feel like home, and Alice's heart longed for a place to at least imagine as her own. She would start with the guest bedroom.

It was already a travel-brochure dream, decorated in amber woodwork, pastel linens and cosy homeware. But Alice took a particular shine to the window seat. It was small and you had to sit in it with your knees bent, but because of the slope of the hill below the chalet, if felt like you were looking out atop the world. She ran her fingers over the wood and pictured the addition of some fairy lights, some warm socks, a book, a mug of tea and her dog beside her, and this little nook would feel like a cave – a place where she could keep an eye on the world but feel enclosed, and safe.

So that was the plan for that little space. Now to spread herself around the chalet a bit more.

Alice carried her laptop, books and art materials downstairs, and put them carefully onto a spare shelf in the living room. She was hardly likely to feel inspired to draw an amusing feminist cartoon while she was in Switzerland, but maybe she'd have a go at a snowy scene or something, for a change.

'Look how Instagramable this place is,' she said to Bear as he chewed her sock and watched her make a coffee. 'I mean the view, of course, but all the wood panelling on the walls, the blankets, the snow piling on the balcony. It would be a very hygge post.'

Alice hadn't touched social media since the concert, almost three months earlier. Maybe she should just check in. But as she opened her phone and navigated to the various sites, a sense of foreboding trickled over her. She was about to jump back down a rabbit hole that felt at odds with her serene surroundings, and a warning bell went off. Nope, this was a new beginning – she wanted to forget all about the real world while she was out here.

So instead, Alice took a quick photo of her mug of coffee resting on the ledge of the balcony, the mountains in the background and, ignoring all other notifications, posted the photo to Instagram and asked the app to sync it to her Facebook and Twitter accounts too. 'Taking time out,' her caption read. 'See you on the other side.'

No hashtags. She didn't want to be 'found'.

The sun was lowering in the sky when Alice got back from taking Bear on his afternoon walk through the deep snow. He was becoming quite the pro now, still lifting his legs as high as he could with each step, but moving with a happy, confident lack of gracefulness that was causing Alice's phone to overheat from taking too many photos.

Back at the chalet, peeling off her wet gloves and woollen hat, she noticed the temperature inside wasn't about to help her dry out. 'Brr, it's cold in here, isn't it?' she said to Bear, who had realised his nose was all wet from the snow and was rubbing it on the rug in front of the unlit wood burner.

Without taking off any more layers, Alice flicked the kettle on and leafed through Vanessa's house instructions for details on the heating. They were minimal, to say the least: 'If you get cold, put on the wood burner. Logs outside. Matches in kitchen drawer.'

She'd never felt so London.

'Okay, well, I'm in charge so I need to keep us from getting pneumonia. Wait here,' she told Bear. 'I'm going outside to get firewood.'

The gloves went back on, and back out into the snow she went. She trudged almost the entire circumference of the house, falling twice into the sloping snowdrift, before coming back around to a tiny shed that was almost like a small outside loo. Maybe it had been once, the door was old and creaking enough on its hinges. Inside was an axe and some thick chunks of tree trunk.

With a sigh, and an image of a nice brandy by a warm fire concentrated in her mind, she picked up the axe and rolled one of the sections of wood outside, hoping a few minutes in the snow wouldn't be enough to dampen it.

Alice bent at the knees to pick up the axe and twinged at the heaviness, the movement sending a small shockwave of pain down the length of her scar. Through gritted teeth she swung it hard.

Boof. The axe nestled into the wood like a knife on an avocado stone. She was going to need to try a little harder.

Thud. Her second try took all her strength and yet still the axe head was only half submerged.

Alice struggled until it became free again and felt her

frustration building. Ignoring the pain in her leg she put her whole back into it, and . . .

Crack. Ish. A section the size of a rib-eye steak broke off and Alice grabbed it out of the snow. It was a start.

She chipped away at the wood, feeling it in her leg the whole time, but whereas the scar usually made her feel weak, out here in nature, chopping wood to keep her and her boy warm, she felt like it was a battle wound, a reminder that she was a warrior and was living for both herself and her best friend. She had some of the power back.

With about half of the lump of wood in jagged kindling, Alice knew she needed a couple of big logs if she wanted the wood burner to last more than half an hour. So with her biggest swing yet, she brought the axe down with a strength she didn't know she had, a roar emitting from her throat, and she fell forwards as the blade plunged into the wood. Her scar landed hard in the snow, her hands stinging inside her gloves from the hot weight meeting the cold impact. She fought to catch her breath, but when she looked up to see a split through the centre of the wood, needing only a wiggled release of the blade to break it in half, she grinned.

Alice walked back into the cabin with a well-needed dose of confident swagger, and when she'd lit that damned wood burner – which really wasn't difficult, she'd done the hard part – she poured herself that much-anticipated brandy.

Chapter 22

It was Monday when Alice and Bear had arrived in Switzerland, and by Friday she was feeling as self-sufficient as Leonardo DiCaprio in *The Revenant*. Chopping wood, building fires, taking heavy-booted walks in the snow to get food . . . well, that was probably where the similarity ended, but even so, she was feeling very at one with nature. Very few people talked to her, because very few people were really around, and those who did were kind and polite and then rushed on with their own business of readying their village for the winter season. She wasn't having to answer to anybody or field difficult questions. She didn't need to keep the curtains closed because there were no longer tall, windowed buildings opposite looking into hers. She had space.

Bear was happy. He liked the wide rooms and cool flooring that Vanessa's home offered, and he liked exploring the snow-drifts and wood piles for new, outdoorsy smells and tastes.

Alice's nook in her room was complete. She'd found a

small box of clear fairy lights at the Coop and strung them around the window pane. She'd also bought a soft fleece blanket for herself, and a stack of second-hand books that had sat on a wire trolley in the corner of the store asking for charity donations. They were a lovely mix of escapist fiction, with battered covers and yellowed pages. They were perfect.

By early evening her stomach growled and she couldn't stop thinking about sausages. On her way back from the Coop earlier she'd passed an inn, not far from her chalet, with all the lights on and someone hanging Christmas decorations in the window. The Eiger Guesthouse, nestled under the wing of the Hotel Eiger, was calling her.

Alice gathered herself up, popped on Bear's collar and picked a book from her new bookshelf. 'I bet you think I can't read, because I've never picked up a book in front of you,' she said to Bear, who stood by the door, ready to go anywhere she was willing to take him. 'But before you came along I was quite a bookworm.' Well, not before *him* but before ... it. She hadn't picked up a novel for ages. She held up the book and studied the cover, which displayed a man and woman with big eighties hair, embracing in a way that looked like her neck and back might snap in half. 'Okay, we'll start with this one. Come on.'

Down from her chalet, and round the corner, the Eiger Guesthouse seemed to be welcoming them in from the cold with a soft glow, a cleared pathway and candles alight on every table behind the window. Alice pulled open the heavy door and peered inside, hoping that they had at least one table in a dog-friendly zone.

A woman rushed by, the same woman who had been putting the Christmas decorations in the window earlier, and came to a skidding halt at the sight of Alice and Bear. 'Come in, come in!' she cried. Bear took no encouraging and pulled Alice into the warmth of the pub. Wooden panelling lined the interior, with red-cushioned benches facing little individual tables. The walls were brimming with old black and white photos of people skiing and sledding, and James Bond movie posters. On the bar was a basket with packets of crisps and mini Toblerones to purchase. As well as candles, each table boasted a bottle of the 'wine of the week', just there to tempt you, and on the windowsills behind were big glass jars filled with corks.

While the woman, clearly the Eiger Guesthouse's manager, snuggled with Bear, who was up on his hind legs with his paws on her shoulders, she simultaneously called instructions in Swiss German to the various waiters and bar staff about the two tables being occupied. 'Okay. My name is Ema. Are you ready for some food?' she asked Alice all of a sudden, like an old friend.

'I really am, yes please,' Alice replied.

She was led to a table by the window, and the next-door table was pushed aside to make room for Bear's bulk. She was given a menu and a biscuit for her dog, and then Ema had zoomed away again.

Alice took a moment to turn and look out of the window behind her. Snow had gathered around the edge of the glass and the snowflake lights she'd seen on her first night were sparkling above. She was very cosy indeed.

159

'What would you like to drink?' asked Ema, reappearing.

'Oh um,' Alice opened the menu and flicked the pages quickly. 'I think ... a beer. Yes, just a light beer of some kind.'

Ema flicked the page for her to the appropriate place. 'A blonde beer?'

'Okay.'

'You want small or large?'

'Large,' Alice found herself saying, suddenly craving some gulps of cold bubbles.

'Good girl!' Ema cried and disappeared again, calling her order to the barman, who moments later walked over with a large glass beer tankard with a handle, and the brand 'Cardinal Blonde' emblazoned on the side.

Alice felt like a regular, even on her first night here. There was something so safe and so immediately welcoming about the Guesthouse, but also about Mürren that ... now it may have been the sweet, bubbly beer she was gulping talking ... but she had an overwhelming feeling of homeliness. Being here was like a hug for her soul.

Alice ordered a second beer, much to the manager's delight, and the 'Oberland Rosti', a local speciality. What came was an iron skillet filled with a huge boomerang of sausage smothered in thick onion gravy, and a buttery pile of rosti potato with a hint of rosemary.

Bear rested his chin on the table until she cut him a piece of the bratwurst. Then, once he'd sunk to the floor and stretched his big legs out for a cosy snooze, she picked up her book.

Alice had barely read two lines when she looked up again at the dog.

'Are we happy here, Bear?'

He opened his eyes and beamed at her, his tail starting to wag against the table leg because she was looking at him.

She smiled and went back to page one. It was nice to have a friend.

The following afternoon, Alice was reading her book, Bear slept on her feet, and the only sound in the world was the soft crackle from the fireplace. The book was actually rather good, lots of sexy bits and also a very intriguing story about a doctor who was secretly a duchess but her devious colleague found out and was trying to steal her priceless ruby. Sex kept getting in the way, like it does.

But outside this fantasy land, even before she could hear a thing, Bear became alert to a distant sound. He raised his head, eyes trained on the door. Then he raised himself further, propped up on one elbow like he was Lionel Richie shooting an album cover.

'You okay, hun?' Alice asked, putting down the book.

Bear glanced at her and whined, unsure why his peace was being disturbed.

Finally Alice heard some voices, laughing, moving closer towards the chalet. She stroked Bear's head. 'Hey, it's okay, it just means we might be getting some neighbours. We're not living in a zombie apocalypse after all. Maybe the ski season is starting – *Bear*!'

He'd jumped up and was facing the door, growling a low rumble, a sound akin to distant thunder.

The voices got closer and Alice's heart quickened as they came right up to the door. Bear let out a deep woof, on red alert. He stood between Alice and the entrance and woofed again, and again, shoulders hunched and ears forward, and even though she still thought of him as a puppy – at six months old with slightly-too-long back legs that he hadn't grown into yet – looking at him now she realised he was probably the size of a fully grown 'normal' dog. He looked quite tough.

Bear glanced back at Alice before facing the door again, warning the strangers, *Get away!*, but the voices didn't break, they just continued past and then Alice heard the sound of locks and boots being stamped at the neighbouring chalet.

She crouched down and got Bear's attention, who turned, tail wagging, now he'd rid the world of danger, and licked at Alice's face. 'They were going next door, nothing to worry about,' she said, when she could get her words out without the risk of being kissed. 'But thanks for saving me.'

Alice returned to the sofa and tried to focus on her book, but her eyes kept being pulled to the side window. Something was different out there on the mountain, but she couldn't put her finger on what. She read the same sentence three more times before she realised it was movement. The ski lift: it had been activated. She couldn't see anyone on the slopes yet, so she guessed it was a pre-season lift warm-up, if they did such a thing.

She watched it, mesmerised by the slow, methodical movement. From here it looked like it would make no noise at all, like it was just existing in its own space, up and down.

There was a loud knock on the door and Alice started, not quite knowing what to do with herself. Who would be visiting her? What was 'hello' in Swiss German? Why hadn't she wiped off yesterday's crusty mascara yet?

Bear, who didn't seem to regard this knock as a threat, was already waiting by the door, and when she went to open it his nose pushed its way through before she had a chance to grab him.

'Bear!' she cried, just as the man behind the door whooped at the sight of a big Bernese Mountain Dog bouncing out and into the snow. The man turned as Bear circled him, tail going at the rate of knots, jumping up to hug him.

'Down, Bear, down, come back in here, I'm so sorry,' she was saying, but the man was laughing loudly and hugging and petting her dog like they were old friends.

Bear eventually jumped down and legged it back into the house, wanting to show it off to the mystery visitor.

The man brushed the snow off his coat that Bear had kindly just painted him with. '*Vanessa, du hesch e Hund*? Oh!' He looked up and saw that she was not Vanessa. 'Sorry, *ich heisse* Marco ... are you English?'

'Yes, do I look English?'

'Yes.' He laughed. Marco was tall, maybe a touch older than her, with a smiley, open face and sandy hair a similar colour to his lightly sun-kissed cheeks. He was wearing a thick ski jacket and salopettes, and his accent when he spoke English reminded her of Vanessa's – sing-song and welcoming as he effortlessly pronounced his words. 'I am Marco, I'm so sorry for disturbing you and this amazing dog.' He ruffled Bear's ears, who'd returned to the door to find out why his new best friend hadn't come inside to play yet. 'I was just coming to say hi to Vanessa; she doesn't live here any more?'

'No, she does, I'm a friend of hers and I'm house-sitting for her over the winter. She has a job as a tour guide, going all over Switzerland. She'll be back for a few days in a couple of weeks.'

'Oh, that's cool. You are here all winter? I just arrived next door! We are new neighbours!'

Bear squeezed his way in between Marco's legs and just stood there, his front facing out into Mürren and his bum in the house, and the act suddenly made Alice aware she was letting all the heat escape.

'Would you like to come in and have a cup of tea?' She couldn't have sounded more British if she'd tried, but inviting someone in just for the social aspect was a bit alien to her these days.

'Sure, I'm not interrupting you, no? Wow, I forgot how nice this view is, huh?' He beamed at the living-room window.

'I'm Alice, by the way, and this is Bear,' she said, making her way to the kitchen, wondering just how close Marco and Vanessa had been. 'Do you actually drink tea, or would you prefer a coffee? I think I saw some instant coffee in here.'

'Tea sounds fun, thank you. So you're really here for the whole season. When did you arrive in Mürren?'

'A week ago. Apart from some new friends in the Coop and the Guesthouse, you're nearly the first sign of life.'

'It's quiet out of season, right? My housemates are ski instructors and I'm a paramedic on the mountain rescue helicopters. We're usually some of the first people here, not including the residents, like Vanessa.'

'You do mountain rescue?' Alice asked as she pottered about the kitchen, her thoughts brewing just like the tea.

'Yes, I do it all year around but during peak season we can do up to twenty-five rescues a day, so they call on extra staff to be positioned in the mountain resorts. I always come to Mürren because this is where my brother and his wife – two of my housemates – always come to teach. We always rent the chalet next door, it's home for half the year. I love it here.'

Twenty-five rescues a day? What must it be like to know you're having such an influence on people's lives? She wanted to know everything, she wanted to tell him about Jill and ask him if there was anything she could have done, but now wasn't the time. 'I love it here, too,' she answered, simply.

'Hey, you should come for dinner tonight over at ours!'

'Oh no, you've just arrived, I'm sure you don't need me getting in the way. Besides, I can't leave Bear.'

'No, you bring Bear, he will be a big hit, everyone will love him. In fact, send Bear over, you can stay home!' he boomed and she found herself laughing along. Marco was warm and easy-going in a way she always used to be when trying to connect with new people. 'I am just making a joke. Come on, you are the new Vanessa, it would be amazing to have you there and we can all get to know each other. Please come. It's only going to be pasta or pizza or something but we'll have wine. Or tea if you prefer.'

Alice handed him a mug and he sat down on the sofa after asking, 'May I sit here?' politely. Bear sat beside him, his new pal.

'Okay, thank you, that would be very nice,' Alice agreed, already wondering how early she could come back here. Marco seemed very nice, and she wanted to get to know him, but a whole group of ski instructors? It just seemed like it might be a party crowd and she really hoped her quiet mountain retreat wasn't going to end up as loud as London.

And then he said, with warmth and genuineness, 'It's so nice to meet people from other countries. Thank you for choosing Switzerland!' and she felt like the biggest party pooper for thinking such grumpy-old-woman thoughts.

'Thank you for having me,' she said, laughing.

'What do you do in England? Or are you working out here? If you don't mind me asking.'

'I'm a cartoonist, mainly. I draw political, satirical, feminist or just funny illustrations for magazines and online publications and stuff.'

'Wow, that's a good job! Have you published in anything I would know over here in Switzerland?'

'I did have a cartoon printed in the *New Yorker* once, that was probably my crowning glory.' She felt the little surge of pride for herself that always came with that memory.

Marco whooped. 'The *New Yorker*, that is incredible, that is such a big deal, your mum and dad must have been like, wow, everybody look at our daughter.' He said all of this without a hint of sarcasm or effort to play cool his enthusiasm.

'They were pretty pleased. My dad carried a copy around with him and kept showing people for a while.'

'Do you have a copy here?'

'No.' Well, actually, she did, but it was among all her other art supplies, tucked away on the shelf. She glanced at it. Maybe at some point she would show him.

'I hope I can see some of your cartoons while you're here,' Marco continued. 'Do you ever draw your dog?'

'I haven't yet, actually, but he would make a good subject!'

'In the snow you would only need three colours – white, black and orange.'

Alice laughed, and Marco ruffled Bear's ears again, causing him to loll his head back appreciatively. 'You know, my brother and I used to have these dogs when we were growing up. I remember most a big lady Berner we had called Martha.'

'Good name!'

'Oh yes, she used to follow us around every room but if we tried to follow her anywhere she would stop dead and refuse to move. Like, don't follow me, go away! We loved Martha ... Did you know these white spots on the back of their necks are called "Swiss Kisses"?' he looked at Alice.

'No I didn't, but that's cute. I'm always burying my face into that bit and kissing it, whether he likes it or not.'

'I bet he loves it.' Marco scrunched softly behind Bear's ears for a moment, who closed his eyes in bliss. 'I know you

167

were all cosy and relaxed over here, but can we pop next door so I can show my brother your dog? Please?' Marco looked so hopeful, and Bear wasn't about to leave his side, so Alice agreed and they stepped out into the snow and trudged the few steps further up the hill.

'Everybody, look!' Marco called to the house as he flung open his chalet's door and pushed Bear's bottom inside. Bear took off, excited by the squeals of delight from within, his paws slip-sliding on the wood and his ears bouncing. And just as thrilled as he was to meet these new people, they seemed equally thrilled to meet him. Three people of a similar age to Alice descended into the living space like moths to a flame. In no time, Bear was in the middle of the circle, waggy-tailed, making sure everyone got a heavy lean here and a paw to hold there, and a big shining smile for each of them.

'Come in, come in, it's your turn next.' Marco grinned at Alice. He held her mittened hand for her as she balanced just inside the front door, tapping her heels against the frame to try and remove the bulk of the snow from her boots before she came inside. This simple gesture of help, where nothing was meant but kindness, saw another optical fibre flicker to life.

When Alice was fully inside, the sound of the chalet door closing caused Bear to break free from the group and bound back to her, squashing his head into her legs for a moment, before hurling himself around and back to the others. *Look at all my new friends!* he seemed to be saying.

'Hello,' Alice waved, unsure whether to attempt any Swiss

168

German, but her mind going blank. 'Sorry about my crazy dog, he's still a puppy and he loves meeting people.'

There was a chorus of 'hellos' and 'this dog is so cool!'s and then Marco said, 'This is Alice and Bear; they have done in Vanessa and stolen her home.'

Alice laughed and explained, 'We're living in Vanessa's house for the winter – she's an old friend of mine – because she's just got a new job leading people on cheese and chocolate tours of Switzerland.'

'Sweet job, well done Vanessa!' said the only woman of the group, with a New Zealand accent and ice-blonde braids, stepping forward with a final ruffle of Bear's soft head. She stuck out her hand. 'Hey, I'm Lola. Not a showgirl. Are you an instructor too?'

'Oh no, I've actually never been skiing.'

'Well, keep it that way, honey, and stick with me. Because boarding is best and skiing is . . . ' She blew a raspberry and made a thumbs down motion, causing the other housemates to erupt into a volcano of good-natured insults to hurl at each other. Lola's laugh was contagious, and Alice was mesmerised by how in sync this whole group was. Were they all family?

'Anyway, anyway,' Lola continued, shushing the group. Bear sat in front of her and looked up, causing her to laugh. 'It's nice to meet you. You're living here for the whole season?'

'Yep.' Alice inhaled. Yes, she was, though it was hard to wrap her head around the fact that she actually lived here now, albeit temporarily.

'That's great, looking forward to getting to know you. If

you need anything, just say the word, we've all been coming here for years now.'

'We've basically never grown up.' A man, similar in height to Marco but of a stockier build, and with the same open face, leant over and kissed both her cheeks before slinging an arm around Lola. 'Hello Alice, I'm Noah.'

'Noah is my big brother,' Marco said with a sweet pride. 'And Lola is his wife, so she is my sister now, sort of.'

'Ah, when did you get married?' Alice asked. They were a good-looking couple. They looked like the type of couple that would have a cool Instagram and adopt huskies and do loads of adrenaline-pumping activities before having fantastic athletic sex, stopping only to go and get more beer. Maybe she should stop reading that book.

'In the summer just gone,' Lola replied. 'Well, the winter. It was in New Zealand in July at this place called The Ledge near Queenstown, which is where we live for half the year.'

'We basically follow the snow backwards and forwards from her country to mine.'

'The wedding was *insane*,' continued Lola.

Noah cut in. 'Insane.'

'At this place – The Ledge – you are literally on this flat rock near the top of a mountain, in the snow, with these beautiful views and you have to get there by helicopter. Thank Christ it was a nice day, eh?'

'Imagine if it had rained, oh my God!' Noah laughed.

'It really was – wow!' Marco interjected. 'I was very lucky to be there as best man. Just two witnesses allowed.'

'Well, we needed you there in case either of us fell off the cliff,' said Lola.

'I was not invited.' The last man in the house stepped forward and greeted Alice. 'I'm David.'

'We will renew our vows just for you,' Noah said, patting him on the back.

'Are you also related to ... someone?' Alice asked.

'No, Marco and I are old friends. We served together in the military.'

'How long were you in the army?' She turned to Marco.

'About a year,' he replied in that easy-going voice. 'It's mandatory in Switzerland, everybody is conscripted. You don't have that in England, do you?'

'No, nothing like that. How did you find it?'

'Alice, I'm so sorry to interrupt,' David said. 'Marco, we have to get going to HQ. Were you going to come with us to get the lift passes?'

'Oh shit, you're right!' Marco replied, and Noah and Lola jumped to attention too. Alice noted how polite they were to talk to each other in English with her around. Or maybe it was for Lola's sake. Either way, it was nice. Marco turned to Alice. 'These guys have to go and check in with the ski school to say, "Hey, we've arrived, hello, put us on your payroll please, and give me a lift pass thank you." I usually go with them just to make myself all ready for the season.'

'Of course, go, go. Come on Bear. Bear, head out of the bin.'

'You'll join us for dinner tonight, right?'

The others all chorused in welcoming agreement.

171

'I would need to bring him, though.' She pointed at the puppy, who still hadn't removed his head. 'I haven't really left him alone here yet for more than an hour.' *Here, or anywhere.*

'Yes of course, we're all family now, this winter.'

Somewhere, Alice felt like Jill would have smiled at that.

Chapter 23

That evening, Alice took a while deciding what to wear. Not because she was trying to impress, but because she was out of the habit of going anywhere in the evenings except to take Bear for a wee.

'I just don't know if I have small talk in me,' she said to the dog, who looked up at her from where he was sprawled on the floor. 'I've only really chatted to you for a few months, and it's very one sided.'

He yawned, like he was bored of her too, and she chuckled. 'Okay, let's go.' She pulled on her coat, picked up a bottle of wine she'd bought at the Coop, and they made their way out into the night air.

The snow was thick underfoot, and hardened on the very top by the cold air and lack of fresh powder from the day. Her breath was pluming in front of her face, and she held Bear tightly as they walked back up towards the neighbouring house. Before she knocked on the door she took a moment and looked back at the mountains in the gloom, the stars and moon hovering over them and casting pale light on their rugged surfaces.

She hoped tonight went well. She hoped they didn't ask her too many questions, she'd much rather sit back and listen to them talk. She hoped she could come home early.

When David opened the door she was greeted with the warmth of an old friend. There was no stuffy, stilted small talk, no awkward tour of the house, no questioning 'What can I do to help?' Instead she was swept straight in through their living room to the open-plan kitchen, where the radio was playing, a glass of wine had already been poured for her, and a conversation about the Harry Potter movies was mid-flow.

'Hey, Alice,' cried Lola. 'Could you chop up these onions for me? Drink up, drink up. Bear, you want a carrot? I'm just saying, in the later movies Draco was hot.'

'We went with pasta!' explained Marco, who appeared to be head chef for the evening, but everyone was helping out with their own jobs, cooking and chopping and sautéing and boiling. It felt very equal, and even Bear wanted to be in on the action so settled with his carrot right in the middle of the kitchen floor.

Noah edged around the dog, shifting his chopping board to the left with no bother. 'But the character was an asshole. All that eyebrow-raising.'

'He wasn't an asshole, he was misunderstood,' Lola countered.

'Like you, Noah,' added Marco, and chuckled.

'What do you think, Alice? Draco Malfoy, yay or nay?'

'Neville Longbottom for life,' she answered, and everyone cheered. Alice laughed. This was so easy, to laugh and feel part of the friendship group, and be normal, but Jill was still dead.

The thought hit her like lightning, sobering her immediately, but she kept her mask in place. It was okay to have a night off from feeling crap, she told herself, finishing with the onions and gulping down her wine.

'So when does the season actually start here?' Alice asked. 'I saw the lift running but nobody seemed to be on the slopes yet.'

'It's about a week from now,' answered David, topping her up. 'But you'll start to see people out there from tomorrow or the next day. Instructors getting in a few runs before all the tourists turn up.'

'It's so amazing up in the mountains when the runs are really clear,' Marco enthused. 'You feel on top of the world.'

'Did you say you've never been skiing or snowboarding before?' asked Lola, and Alice shook her head. 'You're going to have a go while you're here, though, right?'

'Um ...'

'Ah mate, you have to. I'll take you out, we'll make a day of it.'

Marco drained the pasta. 'She is a really fun instructor, and you will only break like, three bones maximum.'

Lola swiped him with a tea towel and as a group they continued cooking up the hearty dinner. For Alice, it felt nice to not be in charge. She'd been a dog mum for three months and was always making the decisions and figuring it out, but this evening she was relaxing into the position of guest. And she felt most relaxed because she wasn't made to feel like a guest, she was made to feel like family.

At the table, with the rich aromas of tomato sauce, red wine and garlic baguettes, and the soundtrack of Bear snuffling his way around the table seeing who would likely be most susceptible to his puppy dog eyes, Marco asked, 'Alice, how do you know Vanessa?'

'We met travelling, years ago now, just after university. Another friend and I took a trip around the world and we were on a tour of South America with Vanessa. She was travelling alone, so the three of us ended up hanging out together for a couple of months. We've always kept in touch but I haven't seen her in person since then. Vanessa's really nice, though, the type of person who you don't feel like you've drifted apart from.'

'Yeah, David thinks so too.' Marco snuck a look at his friend.

'Okay okay, yes, it is the worst kept secret in Switzerland that Vanessa is my dream wife,' David answered. 'Everybody knows this.'

'Except for her.' added Marco.

Noah snuck a piece of pasta for Bear. 'Well, you say that, but maybe this is why she's gone for all of winter, yes?'

David laughed, good-naturedly. 'This could be true.'

'Where did you go in South America?' Lola asked.

It was hard for Alice to think about her year travelling without thinking about Jill, but she couldn't stay silent, and as topics went, something that happened ten years ago would be easier to talk about than something that happened three months ago. She would just keep it factual. She wouldn't think about things like how Jill had spilled her can of cola inside her sleeping bag on the night bus right at the start of a twelve-hour journey across Peru, causing them both to erupt into tear-inducing laughter every time they nearly, finally, were drifting off to sleep. She gulped, pushing that thought and any others like it back.

'We went from Peru, through Bolivia and into Brazil, ending in Rio. It was amazing. The whole trip was just, well, probably the best year of my life.'

In Rio, Jill had coaxed them both into joining a volleyball game on Copacabana beach, their big British bottoms bouncing happily among the toned, be-thonged Brazilian butts. She had made friends so easily.

'It was actually my friend Jill who saw that Vanessa was about to eat breakfast alone the first morning of the tour.' She said her name, she couldn't help it, and although it made her heart skip and a lump form in her tummy, it wasn't entirely awful. She tried it again. 'Jill went straight over to her, made some joke about *dulce de leche*, and next thing we knew Vanessa was sharing our room most nights, with her single room being used as the ... staging area when we were getting ready to go out.' That wasn't quite true. The single room was the room they used if any of them met a holiday romance, but that was between Vanessa, Alice and Jill, she thought with a smile that came onto her face unexpectedly.

'We've known Vanessa for, what, three, four years now?'

Marco posed the question to the group. 'As long as we've known her she's lived alone here, really independent. We're here like a pack of puppies and she's travelling the world on her own, having adventures on her own. It's actually really admirable, you know?'

The others agreed, and David said, 'She's always seemed so good at putting herself out there and going for what she wants to do. Living her life. It's cool.'

'You seem really like her,' Lola said, topping up Alice's wine.

'Oh no, I'm not very adventurous or brave.' Well, that wasn't strictly true. Somewhere, sometime ago, she was pretty adventurous and open to trying new things.

Lola shrugged. 'You came out here on your own, with a dog, to live in a new country for six months. I think that's cool as.'

'Vanessa should be back next weekend, just for a couple of days,' Alice said. 'I bet she's looking forward to seeing you all. When do you all start work?'

Noah and Lola searched each other's faces, as if the answers were in there somewhere. Alice thought not for the first time how connected the two of them seemed, so interwoven, the threads of their lives were tight together.

Noah answered first. 'Probably next weekend. It sounds crazy, but there's no official "start" day, it's just when the tourists come. The ski lift will have been operating from today because all the instructors and the mountain rescue crews need to warm up and check on the surroundings.'

Lola nodded. 'It's likely our first lesson bookings will

be next weekend, but we might be called upon for ad-hoc private lessons before then, if anyone arrives early. Oh, you know what we should try and do this week?' She clapped her hands which made Bear jump to attention. Lola laughed and stroked the top of his head. 'Let's go to the hot springs, before all the tourists arrive.'

The others all agreed heartily, and Lola added, 'You too, Alice.'

'Where are the hot springs?' she asked, saddened that her first reaction, in the privacy of her own mind, was to try and think up an excuse not to.

'It's a little bit of a drive, but there's this gorgeous great big hotel with these different thermal pools dotted outside, it's absolutely luscious. I know the owner from way back when we worked together at a hot springs joint in New Zealand, and he'll let us in before they're officially open, if I ask him.'

'Alice, these pools are so warm it's like a hug from a Bernese Mountain Dog,' Marco enthused, his eyes sparkling. 'Seriously, you should come along.'

It all just sounded very sociable, Alice told herself. But then, was that actually a problem, or was she just telling herself it was a problem? 'What do you wear in a thermal pool?' she asked, realising it was a stupid question as soon as she'd asked it, but she was buying time.

'Just your swimmies,' Lola answered.

Alice thought of her leg and its war wound and the questions it would raise. 'I think I'll have to give it a miss, I don't know anyone else here that could look after Bear.'

'Well, let me talk to my friend first, eh? See what day he

can open up for us. It might be that one of us won't be able to make it anyway, or maybe my mate could look after him at the hotel.' Lola glanced at Alice while she got up to make a pot of coffee. 'Your choice though, of course,' she added, a gentleness in her voice. 'Whatever you want to do.'

What she wanted to do was be brave. She wanted to force the constant voices out of her head and step back into the world, scars and all. Maybe she just needed to go for it, to dip into the water, one toe at a time.

Chapter 24

Two mornings later, Alice was leaving the chalet to take Bear for his morning walk. She was chattering away to him like she usually did, unaware that Mürren was coming to life in front of her. It was only when somebody whooshed past her on a pair of skis, wearing a hot-pink onesie ski suit, that she looked up.

The vista was like the opening shot of an old Hollywood movie – big wide mountain landscapes and vibrant techni-coloured people gliding and whizzing and laughing as they sprinkled themselves against the white snow. The ski lift was flowing up and down the mountain, relaxed in the morning sun, and the doors of the shops and restaurants in the village were open wide.

'Alice,' Marco called, leaning out of his house wearing just salopettes and a T-shirt.

Bear turned and saw him, dragging Alice with him to his door.

'Where did all these people come from?' she asked, noticing his toned arms and wondering how they weren't more goosepimpled.

'This is nothing, all these people are just resort staff and some early birds. Wait until the weekend!'

'Marco, *huustür*!' a voice shouted from within.

'Oops.' Marco chuckled and stepped out into the snow, shutting the door behind him. He was wearing boots at least, but Alice couldn't stop thinking about how cold those bare arms must be. 'That was my brother. I always leave doors open and let the cold in.'

'Are you not cold now? Not very very freezing? Because we're on a mountain at the moment, you know.'

'No, I'm fine, I just wanted to catch you quickly. And if I get cold –' he turned to Bear, '– I'll catch *you*.' Marco reached his arms down and wrapped them around Bear's warm body. Bear responded by tilting his head back and trying to lick up Marco's nose.

Alice caught herself smiling at Marco. Their new friend.

'Anyway,' Marco said, standing and wiping his face. Bear settled down, sitting his bottom on Marco's feet. 'What are you doing today?'

'Oh, well …' She wasn't sure 'finishing my racy novel' was going to cut it.

'Because Lola managed to get the thermal springs guy to open up for us, we can go this morning.'

'Right, wow, but I have Bear to look after.'

'Well, David can't come today, he has a private lesson booked at eleven o'clock. It is just a one-hour taster lesson, but it's a client who is very rich and David is hoping it'll lead to more! So he says he'll look after Bear for you, just drop him over at ours when you're ready. He'll be okay for an hour while David is out, right?'

'Um . . .' She didn't know. She didn't know if Bear would be okay in a different house, with a new person. She didn't know if he'd miss her or whine for her. She didn't know if David would dog-nap him and she'd never see these big brown eyes again. 'Um . . .'

Marco's excited voice softened. 'Hey, I promise he's in good hands with David. I promise.'

She believed him. But she still didn't know if she was ready to be in her swimmies in front of these virtual strangers.

'I shouldn't be putting you on the spot,' he said. 'My bad! Why don't you have a think about this, and if you want to, come by with Bear a little before ten. Okay?'

'Okay,' she replied.

Marco opened the door to duck back inside, but leaned back out at the last minute and poked at her arm through the fabric of her snow coat. 'Lovely warm water giving you a hug,' he persuaded in his sing-song voice. 'Hot chocolate in the pool . . .'

Alice laughed, and from inside the house Noah shouted, '*Huustür*!'

Alice continued down the slope, her mind arguing with itself. *I know I don't have to go. I don't have to do anything.*

Bear paused to make some yellow snow and Alice looked

183

at the snowshoe train that threaded off into the trees to her left. She should do that at some point. *Shouldn't I go for it, if even the smallest part of me wants to?*

They turned right instead and walked the long way around the lower part of the village, the mountain range across the valley on one side of her and Mürren sweeping upwards on the other. Her footsteps made creaking, squeaking sounds in the snow, that were drowned out momentarily when a small golf-cart thing, the only vehicle she'd seen in the village, zoomed by, the name of one of the hotels stencilled on the side. Inside the cart were two men clutching skis and laughing their heads off.

What's my problem? This is a fun thing to do with nice people, and if they stare at my scar that says more about them than it does about me.

As the walk drew to a close and Alice was walking back up the last stretch to her chalet, she couldn't shake the desire to build on this new friendship. She was lonely, and that part of her was winning over the fearful part. She looked at the chalet beyond hers and it was clear how much she needed this.

Back inside she stamped the snow off the soles of her boots and rubbed Bear's legs with a towel and said to him: 'I want to go today, Bear. But what about you? We've only been here a week. No, I shouldn't leave you with a stranger. I can't explain to you that I'll be back soon and that it's all going to be okay; you won't know that I haven't gone for ever. I should stay.'

Bear sank down on to the ground, sensing he was settling in for the long haul.

'But if I don't go I'm not choosing happy. I'm just waiting around, and what am I waiting for? I'm allowed to do nice things.' But even as she tried to persuade herself it was true, her voice wavered, thinking about Jill.

She would go. It scared her, and made her feel vulnerable as hell, and she didn't know how she would explain her scar. But if she could be around these nice people for a few hours, without her comfort blanket, then maybe she could handle ... who knows what else?

She didn't know how to say it out loud, because 'I'm glad I came' wouldn't have expressed the deep, emotional gratitude she was feeling now for the comfort of this warm, enveloping water. The pools were large and calm, and after arriving at the hotel Alice had changed into her costume and raced outside so quickly she'd already been bathing a full two minutes before the others began appearing.

It really did feel like a hug, but one where she could still open her arms wide and tilt her face to the sun, and breathe.

Alice kept her relaxed, eyes closed, body turned away position while the others got into the water, in an unconscious message that she'd like them to offer the same respect to her when she got out.

'Alice, you look like some serene ethereal being,' said Lola, her voice warm, as she glided past Alice. 'Isn't this gorgeous?'

'It's ... exactly what I needed,' Alice replied.

Lola made an 'mmmm' sound as she tilted her hair back into the pool. 'Me too. People love coming here after they've had a few days on the slopes because it feels so good on the muscles, but I like to come here at the start of the season, before anything, as close as possible to my arrival date. It just washes away the real world, you know?'

'Yeah, I do know.'

'I have a problem sometimes with anxiety, and when I'm in cities I feel really pressured and claustrophobic – sorry Alice, do you mind me telling you this?' Lola stopped swishing her hair in the water and looked Alice right in the eye, her mascara running. 'I know you live in London – I hope you don't think I'm being insulting?'

'Not at all, I think it's nice that you're telling me.' That didn't feel quite like the right turn of phrase, but Alice was distracted by how open and honest this woman was with her, and how at ease she seemed.

'All right, tell me to shut it though, if you're thinking "Christ she talks about herself a lot". Anyway, so I feel like that and it's all a bit blah, and then I like to come here and do this; watch, come and do this with me.'

Lola swam to the edge of the pool, so there was only the natural stone edge of the pool separating them from the view of the Bernese Alps, in all their splendour. Once there she crouched, so just her nose and eyes were above the water, and she blinked at Alice until she did the same. Lola then motioned for them both to turn and face the view.

Alice wasn't sure what they were doing, but she went along with it, and soon realised this was the point: they were doing nothing except letting time elapse.

After a few minutes Lola lifted her head. 'Doing that

makes me feel cleansed and not anxious any more. It reminds me it's okay, I'm here, and there's a big sky and loads of room for everyone.' She laughed. 'Bet you think I'm bonkers.'

'Not at all.' Alice returned her laugh.

'You guys,' Marco interrupted them. 'Alice, what do you think?'

'I think I want to stay here all winter.'

'Yay, you like it! We're going to move up to the second pool, it's basically the same thing but a little tiny bit warmer. Are you coming?'

'Sure!' Lola answered, and all three of them were already standing and making their way up the steps.

Alice looked around for her towel but it was on the other side of the pool. She swam towards it, the water drifting past her like warm silk, and climbed out, wrapping it around her waist to cover her legs completely. By this time, the rest of them were already wading into the next pool, whooping with delight at the temperature, which was only a few degrees warmer than the previous, but made all the more delicious because of the brief interlude back in the snow.

Alice reached the edge of the pool, and hesitated, self-conscious. They weren't staring up at her, in fact both Lola and Noah were already floating on their backs with their eyes closed. But she still felt exposed and open to scrutiny in a way she hadn't felt since she'd lain in the hospital bed.

No one's looking, she told herself, *do it now*.

She dropped the towel, leaving it messily on the side of the pool where it would probably get very damp and very cold, very quickly. And rushed down the steps. Marco looked up and straight at her left leg.

'Hey, that's a big scar!' he commented, eyes wide. 'You fought off a shark or something?'

Lola's eyes flew open. 'Marco, you idiot, don't you know not to ever comment on a woman's body when she's in a swimsuit? You've embarrassed her!'

Alice crouched into the water, the warmth lapping around her ears sounding like a reassuring voice, and the thought crossed through her that actually she didn't care what she looked like in a swimsuit any more. Life felt too short to be worrying about tiger stripes of cellulite or the violet patterns of thread veins. The only reason she didn't want her body on show was because with the scar came questions. And with questions came memories that pick-axed their way through her calm shell of protection.

'Oh no, Alice, I'm so sorry, I absolutely did not mean to embarrass you.'

'You didn't, it's fine,' she said to him, and smiled at Lola. 'It's really fine.'

Lola closed her eyes and went back to lying on her back, and they were all silent for a couple of minutes. Then Lola asked, 'How'd you get the scar, though?' She peeped one eye over at Alice.

'Lo, oh my God,' said Noah.

'It's okay,' Alice answered. 'Well . . . '

She took a breath, and took a moment. She sunk herself down so the water covered all but the top of her head, from her nose up, and looked at her surroundings. She looked at the warm mist circling the surface of the pool. She looked at the snow, marked with footprints, surrounding the pools. She looked to the distance, at the Bernese Alps that were bigger than any of this. She was ready. Alice lifted her chin out of the water.

'Did any of you see on the news the crush at the outdoor concert in London back in August?' The words sounded too blunt and factual, like she was reading from a news bulletin. But if she scratched beyond the surface, to the layers of memories that protected the feeling of hot skin on skin, the terrifying sounds, the disaster movie images and tinny taste, she wasn't sure she'd be able to tell her story out loud. Not yet. 'Well, I was there.'

'You were there, at the concert?' Noah whistled. 'I bet that was really scary.'

'I've had better weekends.' Alice smiled.

'Did you see much of what happened?' asked Lola. Alice knew from experience this meant, 'did you see anyone die?' and she didn't blame her, it was natural to want to hear first-hand experiences.

'Sort of. It all happened really quickly so I only remember ... certain elements. But I was near the front so I was very nearly sucked into it all. And ... ' She gestured to her leg. 'This happened because I fell against one of the broken railings.'

They floated in silence for a few moments, while everybody weighed up what they should or shouldn't ask. Alice waited, methodically moving her hands in sweeping circles beneath the surface of the water. She was okay now. Talking about it was okay. She was a million miles away.

189

Marco moved a little closer, rippling her circles with his torso. He raised his hand from the water and brushed his sandy hair, darkened by the wetness, from his forehead, causing it to spike up in the cold air. He looked straight at Alice, eyes soft and caring, like he really wanted her to answer his question honestly. 'Were you all right?'

The question was loaded and could have a million paths that led to it. And so her honest answer was, 'No.'

'*Are* you all right?'

She hesitated, and moved her eyes from the soft furrows of his water-dropleted brow down so they locked with his, fusing this connection with this near-stranger. 'No.'

Lola's arms descended on her, pulling her into an Amazonian embrace, wet flesh knocking together and icy hair against her cheek. It was oddly comforting. 'I am so sorry that happened to you. What a dickhead life can be sometimes.'

'That's very true,' Alice replied. 'Thanks.'

Lola kissed her quickly on the hair, at the side of her head, an action they both found a little odd, but it seemed appropriate at the time, and she floated a short distance away, knowing not to push the subject any more, for now.

Marco's fingers found hers under the water and he held them, only briefly, but in a way that made her feel less alone. And then he too gave her space.

Alice lay back and breathed in, slowly, filling her lungs with mountain air, and allowed her arms to drift sideways and her legs to rise to the surface. Her eyes were closed but she knew her scar would be visible, wet and glinting against the sunshine, and she thought of Marco's face when he'd seen it. Big, curious eyes, an openness to wanting to know more, no judgements, no shock or disgust. She smiled because he reminded her of when Bear came to the door of the bathroom and stared up at her in the shower. Bear never cared what she looked like, he just liked how she looked and wanted to know more about her.

She focused on the feeling of the warm, velvet water on the length of her scar, unhidden and unashamed, and let it have a little of the self-care that maybe it deserved.

Chapter 25

On Saturday morning, Alice was awake and curled in her nook hours before the sun rose. She'd had a bad night, her demons finding her all the way up here in the mountains of Switzerland, scratching away at her protective surface. By four a.m. Alice couldn't lie down any more, feeling like the weight of her memories was crushing her, so she'd got up and wrapped herself in her blanket, under an amber pool of fairy lights, keeping watch out of her window for any trespassers.

By six a.m. Alice sighed in frustration with herself, shifting her weight, and Bear blinked up at her before going back to sleep.

Vanessa was arriving today. She would get to Mürren mid-morning and be gone by the same time on Sunday; it was a whistle-stop tour back to her home.

Vanessa was going to want to talk about Jill.

Alice didn't want to talk about Jill. She hadn't told her new neighbours about Jill yet, more than a passing mention – they didn't know about her being at the incident as well. She hadn't hung out with Vanessa before without Jill around. And why the hell did Jill have to be the web that held everything together?

She was spiralling again, the worry and the imagined conversations of the past and future twisting and poking at her brain.

Also, *also*, today was the 'big day' that everybody kept talking about, the day Mürren was going to be overtaken by happy, noisy holidaymakers. Though the night was still very present, yellow lights were starting to be switched on down at the Hotel Eiger and the Alpin Palace opposite it. The low moon was showing off the streaks of snow on the mountains. Occasional sounds of boots crunching through unbroken snow were lifting towards her nook.

Stop. Alice instructed her mind to stop wallowing, and stepped down from the window seat. She walked down the stairs, keeping her footsteps as quiet as possible as if that would preserve her peace and quiet for just a little longer, but then Bear thundered past her to be first to the bottom. He stopped in his tracks and waited for her, not knowing where they were going.

'I'm going to make a cup of tea,' she told him. 'You want a cup of tea?'

Alice busied herself for the next couple of hours with tidying up the house (though it was fairly tidy anyway) and doing a few chores. She was still lost in herself though when she walked Bear through the deep snow at the back of the village, where it was always shaded by the chalets and mountains so the sun never reached it. Even this weekend it was quiet.

She looked up and saw Marco behind his house, stabbing a long metal stick into the deep snowdrift that had piled up. She watched him for a moment, and then made a decision.

'Marco?' she called.

He saw her, waved and propped the stick against his chalet. 'Hello, good morning, neighbours!'

'Hey, so, Vanessa's coming home today, as you know.' Alice was speaking fast, wringing her hands together like her body was trying to tie knots around her to save her from speaking out loud.

'Oh yeah, cool.'

'Yeah. But listen, can I tell you something?'

'Of course.' Marco pulled off his gloves and wiped the trickle of sweat off his forehead, ready to give Alice his full attention.

'I just wanted to tell you, tell *someone*. I wanted to say something about Vanessa and me and my friend Jill. It's just that Vanessa might mention what happened and I didn't want it to be awkward if we were all hanging out together.'

'I am intrigued.' Marco smiled.

'Ugh, I'm not making a lot of sense. I've only known you guys for like, a week, so you probably don't even care, but you know the other day at the spa when I told you about how I got the scar on my leg?'

He nodded and edged closer to her, as if wanting to put a hand on her shoulder but stopping because he didn't know if it was appropriate. 'Yes.'

'And you asked if I was all right?'

'Yes.'

'Well, the reason I said no is because ... is because ...'
This was so hard to say aloud. This was why she didn't want
to see a counsellor, or go to therapy, or sit in a support group
sharing stories of death and shared misery. 'Because I lost
my best friend that night. Jill. Jill died.'

Marco dropped any respectful distance and pulled her
into a hug, hidden behind the chalet, in the snow up to their
knees, and for the first time since tossing and turning her
way through the night she felt a frisson of relief.

'Sorry, I just thought Vanessa would probably bring her
up and I'm probably over-thinking things,' she said into
his jacket.

'Don't apologise. This is really shit for you.'

'Well, yeah. It's been a tough few months.'

'I bet. And I know raising a big Bernese Bear isn't easy,
on top of that.'

'Bear was actually Jill's dog originally, I adopted him after
she ... you know.'

'You saved him.'

'Well, I couldn't save her.'

Marco hesitated, seeming to weigh up whether to say his
next thought out loud. 'You know, in my job I am always trying
to save lives. And I can't always do it. It can be a pretty heavy
weight on you and make you very sad when that happens. But
sometimes the person, or the situation, or the conditions, or
the accident mean that it's out of your control. You just have to
know you did everything possible and be peaceful with that.'

'How do you ever know if you did everything possible?'

'I don't know. You just have to trust yourself. Be kind to yourself.'

Alice looked up at him. He got it. She felt a sparkle connect between them and she didn't know if he felt it too, or if it was her body desperate to hang on to the closeness of another person, but she felt it as clear as the cold mountain air, as big as the blue sky above and the peak of the Eiger, but as delicate as the snowflakes that hugged their calves.

She moved in for another hug, uninvited but needed, and they were silent for a moment, while she tried to organise her chaotic thoughts.

From her position scrunched against his chest, she looked at the stick he'd been using, now seeing it was an extendable aluminium rod with bright flashes of colour at various intervals, and a measurement running up the length of it. 'What's that?'

Marco turned his head to see what she was looking at. 'That's my penis ruler.'

Alice felt a big bubble of laughter break through her, bringing her back to reality, and a real warm fondness flooded her veins for this man.

'Just kidding,' he grinned, sheepishly. 'It's an avalanche probe. Look.' Marco removed his arms from around Alice and stepped through the snow to retrieve the probe, then showed her how it collapsed and extended. 'This spiky end goes in the snow, and you measure how deep it is really quickly, if you're in a rescue situation. It's part of an avalanche kit I left here last year, and I was just testing out all the bits of equipment to make sure nothing was broken or rusted.'

'Wow. Should I have an avalanche kit?'

'You said you've never been skiing or snowboarding before, right?'

Alice shook her head.

'You probably don't need one, at least not at the moment. It's definitely essential if you're going off-piste, but maybe learn on-piste first.'

'Okay.' She hadn't really made any plans to try skiing or snowboarding, which seemed silly now that she thought about spending six months in a ski resort. Maybe she'd look into that.

'Vanessa probably has some of the kit in her chalet, actually, maybe ask her this weekend. Just in case you go snowshoeing in the backcountry or something.'

'That is actually something I'd like to do!' Yes, plodding around a vast, empty, flat vista strapped to a pair of tennis rackets was up her street, and she was quite serious about that. Bear could come along to that. Although she'd probably steer clear of anywhere avalanchey. 'Do you do a lot of off-piste skiing?'

Now the conversation had lightened, the two of them, plus Bear, whose fur was becoming crystallised with chunks of wet snow, ambled back around the side of the chalet, chatting.

'You mean outside the job? I do some,' said Marco. 'But with Air-Glaciers it's often a requirement, because many of the rescues involve the chopter dropping you somewhere on the mountain away from the normal runs. They have all the equipment if we get a call-out, but I like to keep my own set nearby in case of an emergency.'

'So you've saved people who've been caught in avalanches?'

'That, and other situations. All sorts of things can happen up a mountain when you mix snow, ice, freezing temperatures, confident holidaymakers and a little too much après-ski mulled wine.'

She mulled that over. 'I think I'd like to hear more about it sometime.'

'Are you interested in joining the team?' he smiled.

'Not quite, just interested in general.' But there was something comforting to her, at this stage in her life, about listening to stories of people being saved.

Marco was about to answer when the two of them heard a loud squeal.

Chapter 26

'ALICE!'

Alice looked up to see Vanessa coming up the slope, looking exactly the same as she had all those years ago. Not *exactly* the same – her hair was darker, her cheekbones more pronounced and her skin sun-blushed and peppered with freckles. She'd grown sleeker and more put-together, but her warm, megawatt smile shone through.

Vanessa's hair was pulled back and she wore leather snow boots, thick leggings and a bright white snow jacket. With the mountain vista behind her and the backpack on her back, she could have been a picture postcard from their past, and that was … brilliant. Vanessa hurried forward, skilfully skipping over the snow like a pro.

She threw her arms around Alice, causing Bear to shuffle excitedly around them both, tangling them in his lead, his tail going wild. 'Alice, I missed you. Welcome to Switzerland!'

'I missed you too,' Alice said into the fur of her jacket, holding tight, not wanting to let go of this connection to her and Jill's backstory. 'Welcome home, to you!'

'You look exactly the same.' Vanessa pulled back and admired Alice's face. 'No wait, not quite – you don't wear the red lipstick any more?'

'Good memory!'

'You always had that lipstick on, even when we were very drunk I could pick you out of a crowd because of that shade,' she laughed.

Alice smiled. 'I haven't worn it for a while.'

Vanessa let it drop and turned to Marco, who was waiting patiently to embrace his old friend. 'Marc, so happy you are back, you've been making Alice feel welcome, right?'

'I hope so,' he replied, stealing a look at Alice. 'How is the new job?'

'Oh, it's wonderful, but I will be the size of a chalet by Christmas. Wow, all this cheese!'

They laughed, and Alice appreciated again what a kind touch it was that Swiss people spoke to each other in English in front of her.

'And this must be the famous Bear, come home to the hills of Switzerland?' Vanessa crouched down and made Bear's day by covering him in kisses until he wrapped himself in circles and leaned against her, pushing her into the snow.

Once Alice had managed to extract Bear, and Vanessa, they bid goodbye to Marco and went towards their own chalet. Alice looked over her shoulder and caught his eye as he did the same, in the doorway of his place. She mouthed, 'Thank you,' and he smiled.

Inside, Vanessa went straight for the kettle, dumping her things on the floor. After she'd filled it and flicked it, she came back over to Alice and took her hands. 'How are you?'

'Better for being here,' Alice answered honestly. 'I can't thank you enough, Vanessa, for being so kind and letting me stay. Please say the minute you want your house back to yourself?'

'Hush, I am so pleased you are here,' said Vanessa. 'But I am so sorry you're going through this, and I'm so sorry for the loss of Jill.'

Her directness was refreshing, and somehow it opened the door for Alice to talk with the same blunt openness. 'Thank you,' she said. 'I miss her a lot.'

Vanessa poured them both a coffee without asking, handing one to Alice, and leading them to the sofa where she propped her feet under her and slung her arms back on the cushion, right at home.

Alice watched her. It felt so odd having Vanessa here in the chalet, moving around with the ease and knowledge that Alice was still getting used to. She wondered if she'd ever feel that at home in a house that would never be hers.

'How's your leg?' Vanessa asked.

'Pretty much fine now,' Alice answered, sipping on the sweet black coffee which wasn't how she'd usually take it, but she drank it with gratitude. 'I have a lovely long scar forming that I'll show you at some point, and it can ache a bit with too much physical exercise, so I haven't really done a lot apart from dog walking for the last few months, but it's really nothing. Really, nothing.'

'Have you been suffering since it happened?'

'Suffering?'

'Emotionally,' Vanessa clarified. 'The whole thing must have been terrifying, and losing a close friend on top of that. You've had therapy, yes?'

'No, I don't think I'm bad enough to see a therapist. I didn't actually see or remember much, it all happened so quickly and I was pretty disorientated. I have these little flashbacks but it's all just final moments, just really seeing Jill for the last time.'

'You have flashbacks of the crush you were caught up in, but you don't think that's bad enough to warrant visiting a therapist? Alice, I went to see a therapist because I was going through a ... what's the word in English when you're told you can't come to work any more?'

'Fired?'

'No, not as bad, when it isn't your fault.'

'Redundancy?'

'*Redundancy* situation, thank you, and I couldn't cope with the transition. Have you been taking care of yourself?'

Alice thought of the junk food and the lack of daylight and the personal hygiene failings before coming to Switzerland. She laughed. 'No.'

'Hmm.' Vanessa frowned at her, but didn't push it any further for now. 'Well, I hope being here for the winter will help, even if it can't heal, okay?'

Alice nodded, keen to change the topic for now. 'Tell me about your new job.'

'Oh, it's *great*,' Vanessa enthused, stretching out her legs and wriggling her toes. Beside the sofa, where he lay near his new friend Vanessa, Bear looked up to check if he should come over and chew her feet. He decided against it and lay down again with a contented sigh. 'I was worried I wouldn't get such a good tour guide job again, and although this one means I'm away from home almost all the time, it's a really fun tour, with the added bonus of having a wonderful old friend waiting for me on my weekends off.'

'How have your guests been so far?'

'Really lovely. You can't imagine a happier group of people than those who have come on holiday to celebrate chocolate and cheese.'

'That *is* the dream combo. Do you remember our tour guide for the Bolivian salt flats?' Alice surprised herself by bringing up this memory.

'Of course.' Vanessa chuckled. 'He was always telling Jill she was "sweet like chocolate" and she gave him an educational about how chocolate wasn't naturally sweet, and neither was she, and if he didn't stop objectifying her she would give him a taste of just how bitter she could be.'

'All while holding up a piece of paper with his head office phone number on.'

'She was so great,' Vanessa laughed.

'She was.' They sat in silence for a moment while Alice drank her coffee and thought about the good times with Jill and Vanessa in South America, and Vanessa seemed to be doing the same.

'So you've met my winter neighbours,' Vanessa commented.

'I have; they've been very welcoming. They've been looking forward to seeing you, though, I think they were all a little disappointed to find me behind the door.'

'I don't think that's true,' Vanessa replied, and drained the last of her drink. 'What do you think of Marco? He's nice, right?'

'He's really nice. He's the first one I met, actually, because he came over to see you. Did you know he and Noah used to have Bernese Mountain Dogs growing up?'

'Oh yeah, I think I knew that.'

'They've all been so kind, the brothers, David, and Lola's really cool.'

Vanessa nodded. 'She's so cool, I really like her.'

'They've had me over for dinner, and they took me to the hot springs earlier in the week.'

'Ahh, you went to Lola's friend's hotel? I'm so glad. Did you like it?'

'I loved it, it was ...' she thought about Lola's words, back when they were nose-deep in the warm water. 'It was just what I needed. I think they'd like to hang out with you tonight, if you want to?'

Vanessa shook her head. 'I'll go over for a coffee later, or maybe we can all have brunch together. I see those guys every six months. Tonight I want to catch up with you, over wine, and talk about the last ten years. Everything we haven't fitted into emails.'

That was nice. Alice propped her feet under her, mirroring Vanessa. 'Thank you again for letting me stay in your house.'

'Thank *you*. You're doing me a favour, like I said before. I hope you're making yourself at home?'

'I am, sort of. I'm getting there. I learned how to chop wood.'

'Why?' Vanessa laughed.

'For the wood burner.'

'Did you use all the wood under the awning already?'

Alice blinked. 'What wood under what awning?'

'There's like, two months' worth of logs in a storage box just outside the house.'

'Oh. Well, there's still two months' worth because I hacked up one of the sections of tree trunk in your shed. I hope that was okay?'

Vanessa looked puzzled. 'Sure, I didn't even know it was in there. How did you break it up?'

'With your axe.'

'I have an axe?'

They were going around in circles, and Alice asked, 'How do *you* normally chop up your logs?'

'I go to the Coop.'

'You go to the Coop,' Alice repeated. 'Where I'm now guessing they sell bags of logs.'

'Big bags. They deliver too.'

'Of course they do.' Alice couldn't help but laugh. 'You know, Jill always used to say I was one for finding solutions to problems that didn't exist.'

'But you know, knowing how to swing an axe is a good skill. Maybe you could teach me sometime.'

'I wouldn't add it to my CV just yet. Hey, I was just speaking to Marco about his mountain rescue team. Do you have an avalanche kit?'

'I have some stuff somewhere.' Vanessa waved her arm in the general direction of some storage. 'If it's anywhere it'll be in one of the cupboards by the door. That's where I keep any emergency stuff, if you need it. Torches, first aid, bring the axe in if you want.'

'Ha ha. It must be pretty amazing to work on a mountain rescue helicopter, though. Don't you think?'

'Like Marco does?'

'Imagine spending your days flying above the world and helping save people's lives.'

Vanessa shrugged. 'I don't know, I think there's a lot more to it than that. It's probably quite dangerous, and I know Marco can be called out on emergency even if he's not on shift. But you're right, it's pretty nice what he does, huh?' she continued, breaking Alice from her thoughts.

'He's really nice.'

'Another coffee?' Vanessa got up and Alice watched her walk back to the kitchen, running her hand fondly along the cedar-wood wall as she went. Bear followed, but kept looking back at Alice to check she hadn't gone anywhere.

'Have you and Marco got ... history?' Alice asked.

'*History?*' Vanessa teased.

'Like, you know, spare-room-in-South-America "history"?' Alice was just making casual chit-chat.

'No,' Vanessa said. 'I just think he's a really nice guy. He has a good heart and a kind soul. I think he could make someone really happy one day. Or maybe help a someone sad get back to being a happy person again.'

'He makes Bear happy,' said Alice, brushing off Vanessa's loaded answer. 'As do you, clearly.'

'Well, he is making me very happy too.' Vanessa stroked his head, which he tilted back in bliss. Then she looked back at Alice. 'You know you can have any of them over here while I'm gone, don't you? I mean it when I say I want you to feel at home. Invite them over as a group, they've all hung out here so many times in the past, or individually . . . '

'I'll bear that in mind,' said Alice, getting up and taking her coffee from Vanessa. 'Now, before we do anything else, take me on a belated house tour so I know if there are any other whole cupboards full of logs that don't need chopping.'

As Vanessa led her and Bear from room to room, mostly pointing out things Alice had already discovered, she found her thoughts drifting to Jill again, as they so often did. And if she relaxed, and gave into the thoughts, she could almost picture her here, with the two of them, as if it were those heady backpacking days once again. It was nice.

Chapter 27

'I've never been on a ski lift before,' Alice confided to Lola, as they stood outside the Mürren Ski School office, at the bottom of the baby slope.

It was a week since Vanessa's visit, which had been short but oh-so-sweet, and Alice had been thinking a lot about her surroundings. The more she stood at her windows looking out the more she itched to be living in it, like there were shadow puppets of a past Alice that wanted to break through the screen.

The village was bubbling with holidaymakers now, decked out in brightly coloured snowsuits or geometric salopettes and ski jackets, dragging skis taller than them or rental snowboards criss-crossed on the bottom with the signs of fun had by previous visitors. But still it felt calm, with a peaceful, chilled vibe. Alice adjusted her goggles, glad to have taken Lola's advice and hired polarised ones, as the bright sun bounced off the snow.

'Well, I'm not surprised you've not been on a ski lift, not having been on a snowboard or set of skis before, either,' replied Lola. 'But we're not going high to begin with. In fact we don't even hit the lift unless we go up another level, so don't panic. We're going up that baby slope for now.'

A toddler whooshed down the incline in front of her, fat little legs and arms making a tiny stick figure in the padded onesie she wore. She drifted to a stop and fell face first into the snow.

Lola laughed at Alice's panicked face. 'She's fine.' As predicted, the little girl pushed herself up, giggling her head off. 'That'll be you in a minute.'

'The whooshing or the falling on my face?'

'Both.'

'Let's go then.' Alice picked up her board and started up the slope, her boots feeling heavy and alien on her feet, but making a satisfying stomping sound in the snow.

'That's the spirit,' said Lola, 'Except we're not going anywhere yet.'

'Oh.' Alice stopped.

'First of all we're gonna strap our leading foot into our snowboards. Your front foot, Alice.'

Alice bent over and fiddled with the ridged straps. It took a few goes before she managed to pull them tight instead of just unclipping them over and over again, but finally her 'leading' foot was locked in.

'Great,' said Lola. 'Now follow me; we're just going to walk a tiny bit up this slope and then practise putting our other foot up on the board and gliding down. Real slow.'

Alice stepped forward and smacked the board into the back of her calf. She took another step and landed the board flat, and it started to take off down the almost flat slope, causing her to hop rapidly in a circle until she fell to the ground.

'It's okay, this is the hardest bit,' Lola lied. 'Is your leg hurting at all, though? Shout if you want to stop.'

'No, it's okay, my sore leg is the other one, the one safely strapped in.' Alice struggled back to her feet and managed to, very slowly, shuffle her way towards Lola. Jesus, this was tough on the calf muscles.

They spent the next ten minutes learning how to take your loose foot up onto the board and let gravity bring you a couple of metres towards the ground again. Lola told Alice to keep her arms straight and let the curve of the slope take her. Take her it did. She fell each time.

'It's time to go to the top,' Lola said.

'To the top of the mountain?'

'The top of the baby slope. We're going to use the rope tow.' Lola made her way towards a slow-moving rope that ran up the centre of the beginners' zone and beckoned to Alice to follow, which she did, clumsily. 'So just grab hold of the rope and swing your foot up on to the board. I'll meet you at the top.'

It was easier said than done, and Alice wobbled and stumbled and clung her way until she was level with Lola, at which point she wobbled and stumbled her way towards her, the awkward snowboard still dangling from one foot. By the time she'd reached Lola and sat down, her hair was frizzing out under her helmet, her hands were sweating inside her gloves and her body was tired.

She tried telling herself it was the bulk of her clothing, the stiff angle of her boots that didn't allow her ankles to move, the drag of the edge of the snowboard in the snow, but actually it was highly likely worsened by her lack of physical activity over the past few months.

Lola, on the other hand, had glided up as if she were on a travellator to first class.

But that was okay. Alice was taking a step forward for getting her fitness back. That was the best she could do.

'Sit,' said Lola, and Alice obeyed gladly, the snow cold but dry through her thick salopettes. 'Now, here's where ski school really starts. Lesson one. Look around and feel gratitude for your surroundings.'

It was such an unexpectedly to-the-point command that Alice found herself doing so before even thinking it through. Her eyes swept over the jagged outlines of the mountains before her, the streaks of white snow weaving through grey rock and dark green trees, the bright open sky, the bustle of the village, the sloped roofs of Mürren. She found her home for the season among the rooftops and smiled, wondering what Bear was up to with Noah. She felt Lola's eyes watching her. 'It's beautiful.'

'It is, but I want you to look beyond the *look*, and I want you to feel it. Don't look at me, it doesn't matter what I'm doing.'

'I don't think I understand.'

'I just think you deserve to have a moment here, on top

of the world, with nature and fresh air and no mad puppy to look out for and feel grateful for being alive.'

Alice was about to protest, but before she could Lola continued, her voice softer.

'I know it sounds callous, honouring the dead doesn't mean you should stop living. Be grateful to be here, right now, *because* your friend can't be. See the world for her. Have experiences for her. Build a future because she won't get one and I bet she'd be pissed at you if she thought you were in any way throwing away yours.'

Alice inhaled. She wasn't expecting this today, and she wasn't sure how she felt about Lola bringing it up like she knew anything about what she was going through.

They sat in silence for several minutes, Lola's words sinking in through Alice's toughened skin, until Lola said: 'I know none of this is my place to say, but I kinda know what I'm talking about. I lost both my mum and my dad to cancer in the same year, and yeah, they'd lived much longer lives than your poor mate, but they were still full of health and happiness before it happened. The difference was they had a bit of time before they passed to tell me what they wanted me to do, whereas I think you've been dealing with this blind.'

Alice nodded. She had refused help, outside her family and friends, and what a pressure to put on them; they weren't grief counsellors.

'Everyone's different, and I was never lucky enough to know your friend, but my parents told me I had to bloody well grab everything I wanted from life, and be present in everything I do. And my mum told me that doing that didn't mean I was forgetting her, it just meant she would go in peace knowing I was going to live the life she always wanted for me.' Now it was Lola's turn to take a deep breath of the frosty air and she briefly closed her eyes, her face to the sun and a small smile on her lips. When she opened her eyes again she said, 'And my mum was a professor who had the smarts, so don't go telling me she didn't know what she was talking about. Now, no more crying until you fall over, okay?'

Alice laughed, wiping off her misted goggles. 'Deal.'

'Are you ready for Lesson Two?'

'Does Lesson Two take place on an emotional roller-coaster, too?'

'No, lesson two is clipping ourselves into our boards.'

'Oh okay, actual snowboarding.'

'Of course. We're not out here to talk about your dead friend and my dead parents all day.' Lola smiled and squeezed Alice's shoulder, and through the lenses, Alice held her gaze for a moment in a thank you. Another optical fibre lit up and connected.

Lola spent a while demonstrating how Alice should pull the hard plastic straps as tight as they could go, and then how to get out of them again.

'Are you ready?' she asked.

'Are you cold?' Alice stalled, looking at Lola who was considerably less bundled than she was, wearing just salopettes and a long-sleeved base layer, which was pushed up to her elbows.

'Are you procrastinating?' Lola stood on her own board

and curved through the snow with a gentle whoosh sound, similar to a pencil on paper, to stand in front of Alice, and she held out her hands.

Alice's soundtrack consisted of heavy thuds of landing in the snow, and now was no different. Even standing took three goes. Finally she reached up and clasped her gloved hands into Lola's and allowed herself to be pulled to standing. She wobbled. 'Woah, it feels weird to be nailed to a board.' She instinctively leant her bum back, feeling like if she let her weight come forward they would both tumble back down to the ski school office.

'It sure does. But I'm going to be holding on to you all the way down, okay?'

'All the way down? You're sure?'

'Yes, Alice, I promise.' Lola held her gaze. 'Just keep holding my hands and move with me.'

'You won't let go?'

'You're safe.'

'Okay, let's move.'

'We are moving.' Lola smiled and Alice broke eye contact with a gasp, to notice for the first time the vista behind Lola's head drifting to the right.

Alice felt a bubble of happiness pop out in the form of a laugh. 'How are we doing this, I'm not moving?'

'I'm moving us just by leaning my weight a little.' They came to a stop. They'd drifted all the way across the wide baby slope in a lazy diagonal. 'Now you're going to take us back to the other side again.'

'Back up to where we started?'

'Back to that side, but we'll keep travelling *down* the hill. Snowboarding uphill is more Lesson Twenty-kinda stuff.'

'I think you're joking about that,' said Alice. 'So how do I move us?'

'Lean to the left . . . with your whole body . . . a little more, and keep your weight in the direction you want to go. I know every instinct is trying to tell you to lean back.'

Alice stared at the ground, the compressed, bumpy snow of the slope, and tried to force her body to do as Lola said.

'Flatten your board just a little more . . .'

'Flat? But won't I fall forward?'

'No, because I'm holding you. But also because you're only going to do it for a second to get going, then you're going to shift your weight back a little so the edge of the board is just carving into the snow, creating a tiny platform for you.'

Alice was holding Lola's hands and staring at the soft ground beneath her board. 'Like this?'

'You tell me.'

Looking up, Alice cried, 'We're moving! I'm doing that!'

'You sure are,' said Lola. 'You show this mountain who's boss.'

'I am, and I'll show it.' Alice couldn't keep the dopey grin off her face. It was crazy to feel such a sense of achievement, but she was actually proud of herself.

As they neared the side again, Lola said, 'Now, whenever you feel ready, I want you to shift us to going back to the right without stopping.'

'I can't—' Alice stopped herself. 'Yes, I can do that. Let's do it now. What do I do?'

'That's my girl. Just simply start leaning to the right, remembering to come a little forward on your board to help you make that forty-five degree angle.'

'*Woooooooooo!*' Alice loved the feeling of navigating the mountain. She loved the feeling of her nose getting cold, her fingers squished against Lola's, her hair sticking to her face under her helmet. She might have run away from the real world, but if she was going to fall into Wonderland, this winter version was making her feel like she'd made the right choice.

Before she knew it, they'd traversed down to the bottom of the baby slope, and the little toddler girl had giggled her way past them twice, without a care in the world.

'Thank you,' she said to Lola, her smiling, patient instructor who had stuck by her side, just like she'd promised. 'For all of this.' She spread her arms wide, feeling gratitude, just like she'd been instructed, but in this moment to this woman who had forced her to open her heart a little today.

'You have nothing to thank me for yet.' Lola smiled. 'Thank me at the end of the day, if you don't want to smack me over the head with your board. Right, take your back foot out of your bindings, and let's go again.'

The pair unclipped and Alice pulled her foot from the board, already walking with a gait. She subconsciously reached down and held her thigh as they walked, feeling her scar ache deep inside.

Lola caught what she was doing and asked, 'How's that leg? Still okay?'

Alice enjoyed the ache, her painful reminder, her second

shadow. The day the ache left would be the day she'd stop thinking about Jill, surely, so it was reassuring to have it there with her. 'I'm doing well,' she answered.

'Let's go, champ,' Lola answered. 'And this time, I might let you go it alone.'

Off they went back up the baby slope. *Baby steps*, thought Alice.

Chapter 28

Today, Alice had watched the sun drift all the way across the sky. It had been a long time since she'd spent the whole day outside, the last time being summer in London, oppressively hot and crammed with people jostling for space on every pavement and in every pub garden. It couldn't have been further removed from the snow-covered Swiss Alps.

Her cheeks were blushed pink with mild sunburn. Her lips had chapped in the cold. Her head thumped from smacking down onto the slopes at speed a few too many times. Her muscles ached with exhaustion. Her hair was a mess. Her tummy growled. She'd experienced every emotion, from embarrassment, annoyance and frustration to pride, but as she and Lola finally arrived back at the chalets late in the afternoon, she was awash with tired relaxation.

'Are you looking forward to seeing that big Bear?' Lola asked.

'Oh yeah.' Alice laughed. 'I might fall asleep using his furry tummy as a pillow.'

'Hey, no sleeping yet, you forget about après-ski.'

'I don't think I have the energy to go back out.'

'Oh God, we're not going out. The best thing about a day on the slopes is sitting back and looking at the mountain you just conquered with a big mug of mulled wine.'

That did sound tempting. More than tempting.

'You go on in,' said Lola. 'We're going to make the most of that massive balcony of Vanessa's. We've got a couple of bottles of Glühwein at ours so I'll go and grab them and come back. You say hi to your doggie and then get all the blankets you can find and take them outside. And no showering – bad hair and stinking socks are all part of the experience.'

Alice hadn't even opened the door when a freckled snout was trying to crowbar its way through. 'Hello,' she said, laughing. When she managed to get the door open and slip inside, Bear turned into a pogo stick, boinging up on his back legs to kiss her face, twirling in circles, running around the living room, his tail wagging, and Alice sank to the ground to get covered in licks and gnaws. How amazing to have someone so pleased to see you after only one day apart. 'I love you, you funny dog,' she said.

'He loves you, a lot,' said Noah, coming in from the balcony with his laptop under his arm, rolling his shoulders back. 'That's one happy puppy.'

Alice stood. 'Thank you for looking after him today. Was he much trouble?'

'Are you kidding? I should be thanking you! I got all

my writing done, with this view, and in the company of a real dude.'

He sounded so like Marco when he pronounced Americanisms, and Alice smiled. 'Talking of the view, your wife is on her way back over here for the evening.'

'Let me guess, she's bringing the Glühwein?'

'Spot on! Will you stay and have some? I can make dinner – it's the least I can do to thank you both.'

At that moment the door opened and in burst Lola holding two bottles of wine, and bobbing behind her were David and Marco. 'No way are you cooking dinner,' said Lola. 'I've brought reinforcements.'

'Hey!' Marco greeted her with a huge grin and plonked the chips and dips he was carrying down on the side, to wrap her in a big tall hug. He too was clad in salopettes and a base layer that highlighted his toned stomach. His cheeks were slightly sun-pinked also, and he had the faint outline of ski goggles framing his eyes.

Alice could get used to being welcomed home by such happy beings.

David also kissed Alice quickly on the cheek before heading straight to the kitchen to put down the heavy load of cheeses, meats and pastries he was carrying. 'Skiing is hungry work. We basically brought over our fridge, is that okay?'

'Sure,' said Alice, and popped the oven on. Her contribution would be to cook up the whole stack of pizzas she'd bought. Lola was already pouring the mulled wine into a pan, Marco was rolling about with Bear, and Noah had popped back to their house to put his laptop away and grab a few extra blankets.

Alice loaded her arms with the blankets from Vanessa's living room, and stepped back out into the cold to arrange them across the chairs. She closed the balcony door behind her to keep the heat in, and as the sun dipped behind the mountains, she turned and looked at the warm scene inside the house. *Be present*, Lola had suggested. So Alice took a moment and let it seep into her soul.

The sky had darkened to a soft navy, the mountains phantoms in the foreground. The five of them lounged on the balcony, warm wine their elixir, calories truly replenished. Bear lay on the wood, his fur ruffling, happy in the cold breeze, snoring gently.

Marco and Alice shared the bench, leaning into each other in companionable silence, sipping from their glasses. Two thick blankets were pulled over both of them, and as they started to slip, Marco pulled them up over Alice's shoulders and said, 'Hey guys? Did you realise it's December in just over a week?'

Noah squeezed Lola, who sat on his lap snuggled into the same chair. '*Schöni Fäschttäg!*'

'This means "Merry Christmas",' Marco explained.

Alice tried tying her tongue around the words but it took a few attempts and Bear moo-stretched to tell them they were all being too loud. 'What are you all doing over Christmas? Will you be working it?'

'The lovebirds have Christmas off this year,' Marco said as Lola wobbled on Noah's lap, reaching for more wine.

'It's true,' she said. 'We're heading back to Noah's folks in Lucerne for Christmas – we get four long days to drink and eat and be merry.'

'Us lonely hearts have to stay and work,' said Marco.

'We are the unloved ones,' David agreed, and Marco laughed.

'You can't pop home for Christmas at all?' Alice asked. 'But you're so close.'

David shrugged. 'Actually, I have the week after New Year's off so I'm going home then.'

'It's okay, I take the Christmas shifts every other year, and I don't mind,' said Marco. 'My mountain rescue crew, they are like family as well. We go through so much together and spend so much time together. And Noah and Lola are bringing my parents back with them after Christmas to stay here for a few days, so that will be really cool. My mum is cool, you will really like her I think, Alice.' Marco beamed with pride.

'She will really like you,' murmured Noah, and Lola gave him a subtle nudge that Alice noticed.

'Are you going to be around, Alice?' she asked her.

'No, I think I'm heading home for a few days. I'll have been away for nearly two months by then, so I'll be missing my mum and dad. They're pretty cool, too.' Not seeing her folks for a couple of months wasn't that unusual for Alice, but she'd grown more reliant on them, more keen to make the most of them, during this year, and she spoke to them on the phone several times a week. Still though, England remained a black cloud for her, and she liked hiding in the protective casing of her Swiss snow globe.

'Will you take Bear with you?' Lola asked.

'I assume so. I guess I'd better factor in a couple of extra days of driving time – it's too long to make him sit in the car all the way from here to the UK in one day.'

'I will look after him,' said Marco. 'Leave him here with me.'

Alice turned to face him. 'I can't do that, you'll be working.'

'Yeah, but between me and David we can sort shifts so we're never leaving him alone for more than a couple of hours at a time. We are very powerful and important here.' He puffed his chest up, making her laugh. 'David, you would be okay with this, right? You are no Scrooge?'

'You offer me the chance to spend Christmas with someone else instead of just you and your ugly Christmas jumper? Yes please. Very yes please.'

'No, no, I can't ask you to look after him for several days. I just can't.' Alice looked at Bear, splatted out on the decking, his nose between the banisters to get maximum cold air. He made her smile all the time – maybe the question wasn't could she leave him with them, maybe it was could she *leave him*.

'Okay, maybe think about it for a bit, but we would love to have him, he is family now. And then you can fly and it means you will be back quicker.' Under the blanket, secret from the gaze of the other three, Marco leaned into Alice a little closer.

She smiled. She would think about it. 'So just how ugly is this Christmas sweater?'

Noah, David and Lola groaned in unison. 'It's so ugly,'

David laughed. 'But he loves it and it comes out every Christmas.'

'My mum made it for me when I was a teenager. I told you she was cool. It's woollen and way too baggy, I don't know, she must have used eighty balls of wool. And it has a reindeer on the front.'

'Only it doesn't look anything like a reindeer,' Noah interrupted. 'It looks like a cat with big whiskers and pointy ears, but also with these thin branches for antlers, and a red pom pom nose.'

'It's beautiful,' confirmed Marco. 'Lola, you have a mission this Christmas to find Noah's jumper. It will be somewhere in that house.'

'No, no, I burnt it many years ago,' said Noah.

'He wouldn't have done that, it is there. Check the floorboards.'

Lola chuckled. 'Will do.'

Marco settled back against the bench, a happy smile on his face, and observed the now inky sky. 'I am so happy I can nearly wear my Christmas sweater.'

The temperature had dropped further and there was a definite frost in the air, like the menthol from a strong mouthwash. But no snow drifted down, and Alice had a thought. 'I think it's a really clear night, shall I flick off the lights so we can see the stars?'

That was met with a unanimous chorus of yeses, and the group rose sleepily from their seats, keeping themselves wrapped in their blankets, and moved to the edge of the balcony while Alice leant inside the door and switched off

224

the lights from inside the chalet, plus the balcony lamp. Warm gold was replaced with instant blackness, but a second later their eyes adjusted to the panoramic dome of silver star glitter above them. Alice had never seen a sky so clear. The Milky Way was visible, Orion's Belt, the Dippers. Well, probably lots of other constellations but that was the extent of the ones she knew.

God, it was big out there. Bigger than her and her problems, bigger than the concert, bigger than divided opinions and shifting blames. The depth of the universe made her feel incredibly small, but not insignificant. Life was always forming histories and she was part of that. Alice still wanted to make her mark, something deep inside her wanted to remind her of that.

I was here, Jill. Alice was present and living. *I am here.*

Chapter 29

Her day on the slopes, and the night under the stars that followed it, had uncovered something in Alice. Like a pebble hidden under the sand, a small grain of hope was making itself known. Hope that maybe life could get better again.

She was afraid to admit it out loud, or to put too much pressure on it, in case it burrowed its way further down. And she was weak without it; she didn't have the energy to force it to grow quicker than it could. It was nearly four months after the incident; who knew how many more months it would take?

But today was the first of December, and she had less than one month before she went home.

'Hi, Mum, it's me,' Alice said on the phone that morning. 'Happy Christmas month.'

'Hello, sweetheart!' Liz cried. *'Ed? Ed? Alice is on the phone!* How are you this morning?'

'Quite good, thanks, I went snowboarding a few days ago for the first time.'

'Oh that's brilliant, it must feel nice to get those muscles moving again? Did it feel nice?'

'It felt awful for a couple of days because I was so achy!'

'Oh,' Liz replied.

Her mum sounded so deflated that Alice clarified, 'But good achy. Yes, it was nice to get a bit of exercise.'

'Was your leg all right?'

'It was okay. So I'll see you in a little over three weeks because I'm going to come home for Christmas.' Alice injected more brightness into her voice, ramping up the festive spirit.

'Goodie!' Liz cried. '*She's definitely coming home at Christmas, Ed!*'

'Shall I turn the heating on now?' Ed shouted in the background, guffawing at his own joke.

'I'm looking forward to it,' Alice stated.

'Oh, so are we. How are you feeling now? In general?'

Liz and Ed waited with baited breath, and Alice could hear the expectancy in their voices. She was pretty honest with her parents usually, and it wasn't that she wanted to lie to them now, but the desire to prevent someone else from suffering, or worrying about her, was strong. Her parents were rocks but they were only human, and they so desperately wanted their daughter back to the happy girl they knew she could be that they were unwittingly trying to help her to the finish line via any means possible.

'Coming out here was definitely a good move,' she answered honestly. And then, 'I feel a lot better.'

At least she intended to by the time she went home.

*

227

Outside the windows of Alice's Swiss chalet, fat flakes of snow drifted down, and inside Dean Martin sang through a compilation of Christmas classics quietly in the background while she made herself a morning coffee and thought about the phone call with her parents. Bear snoozed beside her feet, and she could almost imagine in this idyllic scene that she wasn't broken any more.

The decision was made now. She had three weeks to sort herself out, no time to dwell.

Alice hovered in the centre of the living room, standing on a ledge. She looked up the stairs towards her bedroom, looking for that craving in her to go back to bed, draw the curtains, give into the dark until this was all over. Then she looked at the window, the view, the possibilities, the Christmassy scene and the light, and she knew if she could just stay in that, distract herself with festive traditions and making new, happy memories, maybe she could cling onto that grain of hope. Maybe she could fake it until she could make it.

And with that, a candle flame of an idea fizzed to life. The more she thought about it, the bigger it grew.

Alice pulled on her snow boots and kissed Bear's head, saying to him, 'Bear, be good, I'm popping next door.'

She left the chalet and trampled a path in the deep white powder between hers and Marco's, and rapped on the door.

He answered almost immediately, his eyes warm like the fireplace. 'Hello, you. I was just about to make some lunch before heading down to base in Lauterbrunnen for my shift. You want some?'

'No thanks. I'm glad you're home, though. How's your morning going?'

'Good. I was working late last night so this morning I slept in and then have been just doing chores, you know.'

'Do lots of people need rescuing in the middle of the night?'

He gestured for her to come in and he closed the door behind her. She noticed one of his Air-Glaciers sweatshirts slung, crumpled, over the arm of the sofa. It looked big and warm, and she felt cosy just looking at it.

'No, and we can't fly the helicopters too close to the mountains and the cables in the dark, it's too dangerous,' Marco continued. 'But one guy yesterday was stuck on one of the faces after he got lost hiking, and then the cloud came in so we had no visibility. It was just about dusk before we finally airlifted him out, and then we took him to base to treat him before delivering him to hospital. It was a late night because of the paperwork and cleaning up the equipment. Anyway, I am "blah blah blah".' He motioned talking too much with his hands. 'How is your morning?'

'I like to hear about it, it's interesting,' said Alice. 'And my morning is … well, I've been making some decisions. That's why I'm here.'

'Oh that's cool,' he said with interest, and touched the small of her back to indicate she could take a seat at the bar. He poured her a cup of tea and pushed a box of gingerbread cookies towards her. Her Swiss friends loved assuming their British visitor always wanted a warm drink. It was a sweet gesture.

Ask for what you want, she thought, watching his tall form moving around the kitchen, strong arms, soft face, sleep-tousled hair, slim waist. She would like him to hold her again, but that wasn't what she was here for today.

'Marco, can I take you up on the offer of looking after Bear over Christmas?'

He turned, a big smile on his face. 'Of course! David and I would be honoured.'

'You'll take care of him, though, right? I haven't left him with anyone since I took him in. He's ... everything to me now.'

'I will take so much care of him, you can trust me.'

She thought they could. He was kind – they all were – and Bear was so comfortable with him. 'I don't want to put him through the long car journey again, but I think I have to go home. If I fly I can go on Christmas Eve and be back on Boxing Day.'

'Take as long as you want. I'll be here, with him. And David.'

'Where is David? I should check it's okay with him too.'

'He's still on the slopes. It's just me here at the moment.'

'Oh.' Oh. The silence probably only lasted a moment but thanks to the snow against the window, the wood of the cabin, the warm air in the kitchen, she could have been in the opening shot of a Christmas number one music video.

Marco broke the spell by noticing the time. 'Oh shit, I

have to make my way down the mountain to work soon. What are you doing for the rest of the day?'

Alice stood, thanked him again, and used it as an excuse to give him a quick hug around the waist before leaving. 'Today I am finding ways to get my life back.'

Chapter 30

Back in her chalet, Alice sat on the floor with Bear, who looked up from where he was lying and gave her one of his paws.

'Thank you,' she said. 'Now listen. I love your company so much. But I think we both need to learn how to be on our own a little bit more.'

He peered at her.

'I don't mean for long. I'm not going to leave you for long, but I think it'll do us both good if we get used to spending a bit of time just in our own company.' Alice didn't really want this – she would spend all her time with Bear if she could, he was her comfort blanket. But she didn't want him to grow up with separation anxiety, scared of being left alone in the house and wondering if his family was ever coming home. And she'd committed to being apart from him for a period in just over three weeks. This was for his own good.

There was a café that she passed whenever she walked through Mürren that kept catching her eye – Café LIV, which sat snuggled in the bottom corner of a chocolate-brown chalet, under green and white awning. Outside sat a couple of wrought-iron chairs, with faux-fur rugs draped over them and snow piling on their arms. When Alice looked through the window the inside always seemed warm and inviting, like looking into the house of a happy family at Christmas time.

Today Alice would go in.

She bid goodbye to Bear, who already had two feet on the bottom stair waiting for her to leave so he could go upstairs and sleep on her bed and, dressed in her warmest clothing and her big woollen hat, she stepped out once again into the falling snow.

Over the familiar white pathways through Mürren she trudged, head down and blinking eyelashes against the big, blobby flakes that dampened patches of her hair that poked out from under her hat and hood. The clouds hung low, but there was still a freshness in the air that moistened her skin and seeped into her lungs as she breathed. Stomp, stomp, stomp up the slope past the Alpine Sports Centre and the ice rink, which was empty of holidaymakers today. Stomp, slide, stomp through the shortcut between two chalets, the snow piling against their sides.

And there was the café, looking more inviting than ever in this weather.

Alice opened the door and stepped into the warmth. Small pine tables dotted the floor and a long bench covered in grey and sage green cushions lined the two windowed walls. The counter brimmed with homemade cakes and tray bakes, with a sprinkle of fairy lights hanging from the ceiling above. Chalk boards advertising daily specials and shelves loaded with baskets displaying local crafts for sale decorated the internal walls.

The soft, bluesy voice of Sarah Vaughan played in the background. The foreground was a gentle buzz of chatter rising from the tables, the cash register chinging and the noise of steam puffing from the coffee machine behind the counter.

Alice hung her wet ski jacket on a peg by the door and picked her way to an empty table in the corner by the window to put down her gloves and hat. The sweet smell of cakes led her back to the counter where a smiling gentleman asked her in English what he could get her.

'Um ...' she glanced back around the café, a sanctuary from the snow but with a wonderful view, and felt instantly at ease. She'd like to stay a while. 'Please may I start with your nachos special? Then one of these.' Alice pointed at a flat-topped cupcake with a pool of baby-pink icing sinking into the bun.

'Nachos and a vanilla plumcake, of course. Would you like a beer with that? It's just an extra two francs with the nachos.'

'Sure,' Alice replied. She had nowhere to be this afternoon.

The man waved away her credit card. 'You can pay at the end. I'll bring your beer over to you shortly.'

Alice took her seat and gazed out of the window, where

a snowcat was edging back and forth, its big rubber tracks creating a pathway between mounds of snow, and her mind wandered.

Alice needed something to do. She'd been thinking it for a week or so but the thought had crystallised in her mind this morning. She needed to feel normal again, to do something that meant she was pushing forward. Specifically there was a longing in her for passing, fleeting interactions with the outside world that could help rebuild her, brick by brick, while she practised being alive even though Jill was not.

Her beer arrived, cold and bitter, the perfect accompaniment to the sweetcorn and tomato salsa topping on her nachos, which came shortly after. She ate slowly, allowing her surroundings to seep into her, and outside the window the sun broke through a crack in the clouds. It danced on the snowflakes, which had relaxed into gentle silver glitter falling from the sky.

With the same hesitant, careful slow motion as the snow outside, Alice reached into her cross-body bag and pulled out the thin, six-by-four sketchbook and pencil that she carried everywhere but hadn't taken out in months. In her eyeline, leaning her head back against a window, sat a customer with a coffee in her hand and her eyes closed in bliss. She had ski goggles pushed onto her forehead and hair that stuck out in carefree tendrils around them. She looked as contented as a cat, and Alice created a postcard-sized sketch of her using a few simple lines.

It felt good to flex her drawing fingers again. Pulling

out the page and leaving it to one side, she next doodled the window and the scene outside. And then the counter covered in cakes. And then the snowcat, only she made the driver a cat, and smiled.

The man from behind the counter appeared and reached for her nachos bowl. 'All done? Do you want a coffee to go with your cake?'

'Oh yes please, a coffee with cream, please,' Alice replied.

He tilted his head and looked at her drawings. 'These are nice – you just did these?'

'I did. They're very rough, though. I'm an artist back home but it's . . . been a while.'

Off he went to make her coffee, and the woman from her sketch stood up and rolled her shoulders, ready to head back out into the cold.

'Excuse me,' Alice said, catching her attention.

The woman turned and pointed at herself with a questioning look.

'I drew a picture of you,' said Alice. 'I hope you don't mind.' She held out the sketch, giving it to the woman.

The woman took it and looked surprised, then pleased. 'I have no money for this,' she said in a strong accent, sounding apologetic.

'No, no, you can keep it, if you want it.'

The woman looked confused so Alice tried to clarify across the language barrier. 'You looked happy. For you.'

'I take?'

'Yes.'

The woman wrapped the drawing carefully in a napkin

and tucked it inside her ski jacket. 'Thank you. Thank you very much.'

Alice smiled and the music inside Café LIV changed to Nina Simone singing 'Here Comes the Sun'. The piano tinkles accented the tinkle of teaspoons against coffee cups and Nina's sweet voice twirled like spinning sugar above their heads. Alice let in a little more of the sun. Today she'd made someone happy.

'Excuse me,' she asked the waiter when he returned with her coffee. 'The crafts you sell here in the café – can anyone sign up somewhere to sell their goods?'

'Are you thinking of selling your drawings?'

'Maybe not these, they're so rough. But I could bring in some others to show you?'

'Sure, bring them by sometime. If they fit with our vibe we can certainly make some room on the shelf for you. In my experience, tourists prefer to buy things that they can either use, like those woollen headbands, or something small and inexpensive they can take home that will remind them of their trip, like our Café LIV mugs.'

'Small and local, got it. I have some ideas in mind.'

'You're the lady with the Berner, aren't you?'

'Yes!' Alice beamed with pride at the mention of her famous Bear.

'There's a good subject, right there.'

He left her alone, and she tucked into her plumcake. The cake was sweet and tangy, with a delicate sugary crust and the silkiest cream cheese frosting that dribbled down over the sponge when she stuck her fork in.

Making plans, being out on her own, enjoying the big outdoors again. She was a big step forward from the person she'd been back in London, and she was proud of herself. Alice was climbing her mountains.

Chapter 31

Alice pulled her art supplies down off the shelf, where they'd sat, untouched, since she'd arrived in Mürren. Now, the day after she'd had her 'me-time' in the café, she spread her belongings on the table, unsure where to begin, until Bear appeared out of the corner of her eye. Looking over, he was stood facing her, tail up in its big, fluffy question mark, and bright, happy eyes. In his mouth was one of her snow boots.

Look what somebody left for me! he seemed to be saying.

Alice chuckled – her bad, she forgot to put them out of the way.

After extracting the boot and stowing it back where it was supposed to be, by the door, but this time a little more hidden behind the coats, she returned to her sketch pad. And three minutes later, there he was again.

She looked up. He had the boot back in his mouth.

He looked so funny, this tufty great puppy, bigger than

239

most full-grown dogs, holding a whopping great boot that nearly touched the floor.

'You just have to be the centre of attention,' she said, grabbing her pad and a pen from the pile.

She spent a couple of minutes drawing a quick cartoon of Bear and her boot. She added a line of snow on the ground and some fat snowflakes, and scrawled 'Kisses from Switzerland' in the top corner. She always included a little cartoon of some kind with her Christmas cards to her parents, and they'd like this one.

Stepping away from the table she went to Bear, ready to take the boot off him, but this time he wasn't going to give up his gift so easily. He growled and swung his tail and boinged on the spot, waving the boot from her grasp. She laughed, despite herself. 'Bear, drop it, that's my boot, I don't have warm furry feet like you so I need that back.'

He pushed his front low to ground with his bottom in the air, growled again and sprung up, the boot swinging back and donking him on the head. It didn't stop him for a second, though.

'You never take yourself too seriously, do you?' Alice said to him. 'I think you're going to be just the subject I need.'

Alice remembered a TED Talk she'd listened to once where someone had said that actually you can trick your brain by faking it until you *believe* it. Alice had lost her friend, but had also completely lost herself along the way, and it was just possible that she was beginning to find herself again.

The peace that came with starting with a blank page and

sweeping shapes and colours, careful lines and just the right level of detail, was something that had always soothed her soul. It helped her make sense of the world.

By lunchtime, she'd created several rough sketches and had a list that trailed two pages of A4 of possible cartoon ideas – funny positions Bear lay in, amusing situations he'd got himself into since she'd had him, his first experiences in the snow, his life in the mountains. She could almost visualise the story of his life coming together through the eyes of her pen. Additionally she'd listed some of her favourite views, venues and experiences since coming to Mürren. She planned to take a mixed portfolio of ten finished drawings to the café within the next couple of days to see what they thought.

'Look, Bear,' she said, and he looked up. 'These are of you. These will keep us busy until I go back to England, won't they?'

She was walking in the air, Aled Jones style. 'December is going well so far, Bear,' she said, and her energy clearly transferred to him because he leapt up and put his giant paws on her shoulders so she could hug him. 'When did you get so huge? Are we growing together now?'

'I need some lunch,' she said aloud. 'And I fancy something thick and warm and hearty, and I don't think we should stay in here all afternoon, because we have to keep on growing. You want to come with me to the Eiger Guesthouse?'

Back out she went into the snow, this time with her walking furry blanket in tow, and they set off (carefully) down the slope into the village. It was heaving, the visibility being not great on the slopes, and everybody had given up skiing in favour of the sweet aromas of fondue emanating from restaurant doorways.

Alice and Bear made it to the Guesthouse and before Bear had even stuck his nose in the open doorway to sniff the air, the super-friendly manager Ema came rushing over to embrace him and shower him with dog treats, welcoming them both. She bustled Alice to a great table by the window in the corner, with space for Bear to settle down, should he ever decide to do so. At that moment he was far more interested in craning towards the other tables laden with delicious food.

'Cardinal Blonde?' Ema asked, already walking away to fetch a menu for her.

'Urm, sure!' replied Alice. Why not?

A waiter returned with her drink and she asked him, 'What would you recommend?'

'For you, or for my new favourite dog?' he replied. 'I love these dogs. I'm from Germany and we don't have as many of these as here in the Bernese Oberland, obviously. Now I see them loads and I love love *love* them.' To Bear he added, 'You can help yourself to every person's plate in this restaurant, yes you can, yes you can.'

A few people on nearby tables smiled politely but shifted their plates away.

'Anyway,' he continued. 'Recommendations. Hmm. You look like you want to warm up. How about this?'

He pointed to a sausage dish similar to the one she'd had last time. 'Actually, I might go for a pizza,' she replied, looking at the array of delicious toppings. 'The Pizza 007 sounds good. What's the link with James Bond and Mürren? I feel like I see a lot of Bond stuff around.'

'You don't know?' Ema cried, stopping en route past, a hot fondue in her hand. *'On Her Majesty's Secret Service* was filmed at the top of the Schilthorn mountain just behind us. At Piz Gloria. It is a claim to fame, even though it was fifty years ago.'

'Ohhhh,' Alice replied. 'I haven't seen that one.'

'Watch it as soon as you can,' instructed Ema, and carried on with her fondue.

The waiter took Alice's menu. 'A Pizza 007 for you.' Then he leaned in and whispered, 'And can he eat sausages?'

'Yes,' she whispered back.

'Okay, I bring him one.' He tapped his nose like they were the secret agents, and scurried off to the kitchen.

Her pizza arrived, with a small, fat sausage on the side as promised for Bear, and Alice tucked in, savouring the garlicky, bacony flavours. She looked out of the window as she munched away, Bear doing the same, contentedly watching the world go by. Occasional thoughts would drift in, questioning how the world carried on after atrocities like the one she had witnessed, and yet it did. But she wanted to be glad of the fact, not to resent it.

She picked up her glass of beer that she'd agreed to on impulse, because what better way to start the Christmas season on such a snowy day, and cheersed the faint reflection of herself in the glass, whispering, 'To the world.'

*

It hadn't all been light since coming to Switzerland, and it certainly wasn't for Alice over the next two weeks. She kept hold of her hope tightly, but there were days, and nights, that felt more like thick mud than powder-light snow.

Going back to England played on her mind and her emotions, looming in the ever-decreasing distance. *Come back*, it would say to her. *Come back, close the curtains, lie down and don't get up.*

But she kept her promise to herself about pushing herself forward, and every day when the thoughts and worries threatened to smother her from within, that would be the moment she'd bury them deep and take herself out and onto the mountain.

After her snowboarding lesson with Lola, Alice had – with the rose-tinted glasses of someone whose physical aches had subsided – decided it felt good to have her body feel strong and used again. She knew her leg injury might cause her pain, but she needed it. If it went away, it was like it had all been erased. She didn't want to let her skills go to waste, so she bought a lift pass for the season, and bought some of Lola's old equipment off her, and vowed that every day she would practise for an hour.

She wasn't really fussed about being a pro snowboarder. Which was lucky because she was pretty awful at the moment. But it gave her something to think about. It presented opportunities for shared smiles with strangers during a pause in the sunshine. It let her skin see the sunshine and her heart beat faster. And slowly, slowly, with each day that passed, Alice got stronger. She fell less, and stood up tall more and more.

And she'd found something else to do, something festive, just for her and her Bear. Every day on their evening walk, they went off to find the day's Advent window. She'd discovered this Mürren tradition by chance on the third day of December, passing a house with a beautifully decorated window including a giant sparkling '3'. Every day was a different house, and anyone was invited to come along and take a look, and enjoy an *apéro* – a drink and a small bite to eat and a chat with a local resident. With every *apéro* she felt more at home.

Café LIV had accepted her drawings, and Alice worked daily creating more, adding festive touches to draw in the pre-Christmas customers. The calendar edged ever closer towards the big day, and she treated herself with dog hugs, random books, warm teas while sitting in her nook, a chat with her friends next door. One morning, after a restless night, she had to really drag herself out of the door for Bear's walk, so when she was out she bought some ingredients at the Coop and her treat, or her distraction, was to bake some *Basler Brunsli* – traditional Swiss Christmas cookies – from a recipe she'd found online. As the day at the thermal springs had told her over a month before, it was okay to have a little self-care, just as it was okay to feel really crap about everything. She didn't do a great job on the cookies, and Marco, Noah and David all politely spat theirs out into napkins and promised to show her how it was done sometime. But nevertheless, she persisted.

Chapter 32

On the fourteenth of December, Alice was busy on the internet researching Swiss festivities for her illustrations when she saw something that caught her eye. How far was Zurich from here? A couple of hours?

Vanessa's tours started and ended in Zurich. She often had a free evening when one ended and before the next one began, but it wasn't worth her coming all the way back to Mürren. If Alice could combine what she'd just spotted with a visit to Vanessa, then why not?

Five minutes later, following a quick text conversation with her tour guide friend who was currently sitting at the front of the bus on her way into the deliciously named town of Gruyères, Alice was crunching to the neighbouring chalet and rapping on the door.

'Bear and I are going on a road trip tomorrow afternoon. Does anyone want to go to Zurich with us? We're going to see the Singing Christmas Tree.'

Marco, Noah and David all cheered heartily, and Lola laughed. 'The *what*?'

'Have I never taken you to see the Singing Christmas Tree?' Noah asked her.

'No, I would remember that.'

'It's a Swiss Christmas tradition,' Alice answered. 'Apparently. It's a big Christmas tree-shaped structure that choirs stand on in rows and sing festive carols and songs. And there's a Christmas market there as well. It looks really special all lit up with twinkly lights and glowing stars.'

'It sounds mad but amazing. I'm in,' said Lola. 'Are you staying over? Zurich's a couple of hours away.'

'Yeah. I didn't want to drive back late in the dark. Vanessa's got the night off tomorrow and the Airbnb she stays in between tours is dog-friendly. I was going to see if we could both stay with her, so I can see if you guys can all crash there too?'

'Find out the address; maybe we can get an Airbnb in the same building. Or at least *we* can.' Lola motioned to herself and Noah. 'It would be nice to not have these two under the same roof for twenty-four hours.'

'I have a regular group lesson at eleven o'clock in the morning on the Friday, but Thursday afternoons are private bookings so I will block it out as unavailable,' said David. He looked up at Marco from his phone calendar. 'I have nothing in tomorrow after 12.30. If that's okay with you?'

'I have a day off tomorrow and then am on the late shift on Friday,' Marco replied. 'Besides, how could I deny you a night under tinsel stars with Vanessa?'

'Okay, let's do this then.' She'd made a plan! 'Do any of you have a car we could take? I can take one, maybe two people in mine with us. Or I can try and take all of you if we can persuade Bear to sit in the boot.'

'We can take our car,' Noah answered. 'I don't think that dog will fit in the boot.'

Alice was relieved. She'd never tried putting Bear in the boot before, but she knew *she* wouldn't fancy a two-hour journey in there. 'So we can all go! This is really lovely.' And she meant it.

By the time the morning rolled around, the plans were all set. They'd take two cars, Noah and Lola's, and Alice and Bear's, and Marco and David would join one car each. They'd leave after lunch, arrive in Zurich mid-afternoon, meet Vanessa at her Airbnb and check Noah and Lola into theirs, in the same building, then head out to experience the famed Singing Tree and the *Weihnachtsmärkt* – the Christmas market.

Bear was on his best behaviour all the way down the cableway to the car park at Stechelberg – sitting when told, not pulling on his lead, giving a paw whether people knew they needed it or not, and sticking very closely beside Marco.

'You are my shadow today, right?' Marco said, stroking him behind the ears, and Bear gazed at him in adoration, leaning into his hand.

'I think you better go in the car with Alice today,' remarked David, heading for the other car beside Lola. 'I don't think Bear will let you out of his sight.'

'It's me and you, buddy!' Marco grinned at Bear as the three of them crunched carefully over the icy tarmac to Alice's car.

The car was covered in a layer of snow and ice and Alice had to wriggle the handle for a minute or two before the back door would open and she could guide Bear inside and clip him in to his hammock.

'You jump in, I'm just going to scrape the ice off,' she told Marco.

'No way, I will help!' he cried, and as she made a start with the ice scraper, he used his credit card to push great sweeps of powder from the windows.

Alice stole a glance at Marco from the other side of the car, at his muscles working hard and his arms flecked with snowflakes.

It was tough going – the ice was thick and hard – and by the time the two met over the front windscreen, they both had sweating foreheads, despite the frosted fingertips. Eventually Alice hopped in the driver's seat, with Marco next to her in the passenger side.

'Brr, feels like we've climbed into a fridge!' she remarked, turning on the engine and upping the front heaters. She was pleased to find the car started, having not driven it in over a month. Then again, it had often sat for long periods on its lonesome in London. 'Thanks for your help. Let's just wait a few minutes for the car to get herself ready.'

Alice was rubbing her hands together, her finger joints cramped and cold, when Marco reached over and cupped her hands in his. 'It's okay, trust me, I am a paramedic,' he joked.

'Is this what you do to patients up mountains?' she asked.

'Well,' he said, still holding her hands firmly in his, thawing them out. 'If we were up a mountain I would actually be wrapping you up in a tight bundle and putting heat pads under your jacket. But I think that is more third date territory for us, yes?'

Alice knew he was joking, he was just being kind, funny Marco, but huddled in their little car with only the noise of the engine running and snow framing the glass on all sides of them, she felt like she already was wrapped in a bundle with him. And she liked it.

But they should get going. She broke free and put the Airbnb address into the satnav. 'I hope you're wearing a lot of layers, because we can't keep the car too hot or this one will start whining.' As it was, Bear was already snoozing, stretched out on the back seat, happy to be with company.

'I will be just fine. I'm very happy to be chauffeur driven all the way to Zurich! I have brought car snacks.' He pulled out some cookies and a flask of coffee that she could already smell. 'And a car playlist, if that's okay?'

'What's on the playlist?' Alice pictured some obscure Euro-rock filling her car for two hours, but Marco plugged in his phone and out of the speakers came the soft, warming sounds of the Rat Pack singing Christmas classics.

'This is nice,' she said, driving out of the car park into the snow-lined lanes, settling back and enjoying the feel of independence that came with being on the road, combined with the solidarity of company.

'I really like this album,' Marco replied, tapping away on his leg.

Alice nodded, and even Bear stuck his nose between the seats and sighed with comfort.

'Did you always want a dog, before you took him on?' asked Marco.

'No.' Alice laughed. 'I actually distinctly remember thinking Jill was mad getting a puppy. I thought he would take over her whole life . . . ' She paused, not meaning it to sound so poignant. 'But he did, in the best way. She only had him a month but she loved him so much already. He was all she spoke about; her phone was filled with photos of him. And now I'm the same!' Alice's pre-Bear existence seemed so distant now.

'Was it hard, having a dog this big while you lived in the city? Because I remember even as young puppies how chunky they are.'

'Well, Jill lived further out of London than me, and she had a big house and garden, so for her space had never been an issue. For me, I lived in a tiny flat which felt more tiny the bigger he got. Have you seen *Alice in Wonderland*, the Disney version?'

'I don't know. Maybe. I think so, when I was small.'

'There's a scene where Alice starts growing and growing and fills every room of the house to the point her arms and legs are poking out of windows and her head through the roof. Bear was kind of like that.'

'Filling up your whole life,' suggested Marco.

Right when it was feeling kind of empty. 'Plus the walking routes were limited where I lived. So yes, it was hard, hence why I moved here.'

'I never asked – what made you pick Switzerland over just, you know, the English countryside?'

It was such a big question that Alice didn't quite know where to start, so she started with where Bear had started. 'Jill always wanted a Bernese. She said they had expressive eyebrows, and she liked that in a person, she thought it showed soul.' Alice chuckled at the memory. 'So even before we picked him up she was researching everything about his home country, planning to bring him here on holiday, so excited about the future with her new pal. When everything happened and I took him in, going away on a trip was the last thing on my mind. I just wanted to stay indoors and sheltered, then it felt like I had control.'

'That makes sense,' said Marco. 'With a holiday there's the expectation that you will be having the best time every minute of the day.'

'Exactly. But, as you said, he got bigger, I got ... to be honest ... grosser, and it was time for a big change. I was only going to come on a short holiday and tie it in with seeing Vanessa, but then, well, you know the rest.'

They were silent for a while, the road gliding under the shade of the mountains, the sky a bright blue overhead. And then Alice added, 'To Bear, she was everything, and she was taken from him. So I want to make sure I'm doing what she would have wanted – giving him the best life I can. I know, I know, he's just a dog, but he was *her* dog.'

'You're doing a great job, he seems very happy.' Marco leaned his arm back to stroke Bear's nose, who caught his sleeve in his mouth and held on tightly, even as he started to close his eyes to sleep again.

'Thanks,' said Alice. 'I hope he's happy. I don't think I'm great company for him a lot of the time. But we're trying, aren't we, mister?' She glanced back at the daft doggo.

As Frank Sinatra's smooth voice started singing 'Have Yourself a Merry Little Christmas', Marco left her alone to her thoughts for a while. She thought of Jill and how happy she would probably be seeing Bear out here enjoying the snow. This little Bear, who didn't know what was going on or why Jill had left, but he did seem happy, and that was the best Christmas gift she could give to her best friend now.

'You're a good listener, you know,' she said to Marco, reaching out to touch his arm, briefly, wanting contact. He beamed. 'You're quite similar to Bear.'

'I am honoured!'

'You just … my parents, mine and Jill's other friends, even Vanessa are a little too close to everything. I'm not okay yet, that feels like a *long* way off, but you just listen and don't … I don't know …' She trailed off, not really sure what she was trying to say.

'Have you spoken to anyone, like a professional, if you don't mind me asking?'

'No,' she said quickly. 'No. I know everyone says I should but I just can't yet. You may have noticed, I've firmly got my head in the sand, or the snow, at the moment.'

'What do you mean?'

'I just don't want help right now.' She shook her head. 'I'm not in denial, I'm just, what's the word – disconnected?'

'Like you just want to shut the world out and, what's a good word … wallow?'

'Exactly. So I went to the extreme and ran away to the mountains!'

'Hmm.' Marco turned and gazed out of the window.

'What are you thinking?' Alice asked.

'I was thinking, in my expert medical opinion as a paramedic, that when you were hiding in your flat in London you were running away. I think when you came here that was your first step to coming back home.'

At that point, Bear sat up, yawned, and rested his chin on her shoulder, making Alice laugh. She didn't know what to think about Marco's insight at that point, but when he handed her half a squidgy cookie he'd just split, she took it, meeting his eye for a second, and smiled.

'What about you?' she asked through a mouthful of chocolate chips. 'You had a dog growing up. Do you want one now you're an adult? Take mine if you like, he's a handful,' she joked.

'I'm an adult?! I would love your dog, he's a real dude. But yeah, any dog would be great. I'd like a St Bernard; you see them around here a lot. We should actually explore the Oberland more. Maybe when you're back after Christmas, I can take you to visit the museum where the most famous St Bernard in Switzerland lives.'

'What makes him so famous?'

'When he was alive he saved the lives of over forty people that he rescued from the mountains. He was called Barry, and he is my hero.'

'Is that why you joined a mountain rescue crew? To be like Barry?'

'I'm sure a therapist would say something like that.'

'So he's not alive now?'

'Oh no.' Marco shook his head. 'He died in 1814, but his body is preserved.'

'Okay . . .'

'I will take you, we'll make a date of it.'

'It sounds very romantic,' she quipped back, and wondered how they kept straying to the topic of romance today, and she saw Marco smile from the corner of her eye. 'Maybe we won't bring Bear, though, he might find it a little confusing that a dog doesn't want to play with him. So you want your very own Barry one day?'

Marco cracked into another cookie to share. 'Oh yeah. At least one. I want to train him to do mountain rescues also, and come with me on my treks. I have the best job in the whole world.'

'What do you love about it?' She enjoyed hearing him speak passionately about things, be it dogs, the mountains, or even Christmas sweaters. He had that sing-song accent combined with the type of voice you could hear a smile behind. She was so used to her own inner commentary, which had become so monotonous, that he was a gust of mountain-fresh air.

'Don't get me wrong, it's not easy,' he was saying. 'It's

hard work and you can be going out in horrible conditions, and the hope that's pinned on you to save a loved one can be overwhelming. But I feel like if I can be there helping, doing what I can, and I'm lucky enough to have the skills to do so, then why wouldn't I?'

'Why wouldn't you?' she echoed.

'You want a coffee?' Marco asked, reaching for the flask.

'Actually, can we have a short burst of cold air first? I feel like I want to blow away a couple of cobwebs.'

'Sure!'

Alice reached for the car stereo and turned the volume up on Sammy Davis Jr's 'Jingle Bells', and pressed the button for all four car windows to lower. They were driving alongside a lake and traffic was quiet, so she slowed the car down and breathed in the frosty breeze.

'Wow, it's fresh out there, huh?' Marco called over the noise of the wind.

Bear was in heaven. He whole big face was framed in the open window, his nose visible in Alice's rear-view mirror. His eyes were closed against the sun and the cold air spread its fingers through the streamers of his ears. His nostrils pulsed, and every few seconds he'd have to bring his big tongue into his mouth to moisten it again.

'He is happy, isn't he?' she said to Marco, who reached back and stroked Bear's side as he leaned in pleasure towards the side door.

'He's living his best life,' Marco agreed. 'And are you happy? Or at least, as happy as you can be?'

Alice smiled at him, then leaned her head towards the

window, took a final gulp of air, and then closed them, making sure Bear's snout was back inside. She kept her eyes on the road but in her mind all she could see was Marco's face. 'Yes.' She breathed in. 'Okay, let's have that coffee.'

Chapter 33

Another hour and several long stretches of tunnels that scooped their way underneath the Alps later, and Alice, Marco and Bear were navigating their way through the streets of Zurich to find Vanessa's apartment. They drove beside the river, alongside medieval buildings and pretty bridges. Alice craned her neck to look up, searching for the right block of flats, and Marco directed her with the confidence of someone who'd been here a thousand times.

When they arrived they found the other three already there in Vanessa's apartment, Lola and Noah having checked in down the hallway, and David trying to play it cool, when it was all he could do to stop himself staring at Vanessa.

'This is so nice,' Vanessa enthused, greeting each of her final three visitors with a warm embrace. 'I like having visitors! It gets lonely on these tours.'

'Lonely, even with all the people you're showing around?' asked Marco.

'I think it's possible to be at your loneliest when there are lots of people around,' Alice said as she took her shoes off, without stopping to think what she was saying.

She looked up to see them watching her. Wow, what a Christmas Spirit she was.

'Exactly,' said Vanessa, stepping in. 'It's gorgeous to have you all to stay because I don't have to host. We're equal.'

'So let me start off by making a drink for everyone,' said David, moving over to the kettle.

'Oh David, you've had a long journey, I'll do that,' Vanessa countered, but David just touched her arm and stood in front of the kettle. 'You're letting us stay here, Lola and Alice drove, this is the least I can do.'

They smiled at each other and Alice caught Lola's eye, noticing the sweet contact.

After a drink, a sit down, and a chance for Bear to sniff everything in the apartment, the group were ready to head out towards the Tree and the market.

It was already darkening when they set off, their breath foggy in the clear air despite it being several degrees warmer than up in the Alps. The group, led by Vanessa, weaved their way through the medieval streets of the old town until the amber lights formed a glow in the sky above, and they knew they were nearly there.

Alice sniffed the air, mirroring Bear who walked next to her, and smelled the cloves and cinnamon of mulled wine stalls. Bear pulled in small zigzags, exploring the streets and snuffling up fallen crumbs of gingerbread cookies. The streets were busy, the sky was dark, but somehow

259

Alice – although with a sharpened mind, always it seemed, for any potential threat – was calm. Although Switzerland was proving to have light and dark times, she was certain she was experiencing more happiness than fear in this place. Seeing more light than dark.

'There it is!' Lola was the first to spot the Tree, tall and central, immediately obvious when they came into the square. It was a tiered pyramid stage, seven rows high, consumed by pine branches and silvery waterfall fairy lights that hung down like icicles. Shuffling on each tier was a line of people, dressed in red hats and scarves and long forest-green coats, holding song books. Excited chatter from the crowd, and the soon-to-be-singers filled the air, until loud speakers projected a burst of merry music. The choir took a breath, and ...

DECK the halls with boughs of holly ...

The joyous music reminded Alice of the Christmases of her past and all of the happy traditions that surrounded them. This was her dad's favourite Christmas song. He liked to draw out the first 'DECK' for as long as possible, and then pull his family into a big bear hug. He was funny. She was lost in the music, with Bear sitting on her feet with his back to her, just happy to have all of them around him in a semi-circle.

'FA LA LA LA LAAAAA, LA LA LA LA!' sang Vanessa, Marco, David and Noah at the top of their voices, along with the rest of the crowd. Alice met Lola's eyes and they chuckled, Bear bouncing up at the sudden noise.

'TIS the season to be jolly ...

Marco grabbed Alice's hand and raised it into the air with his. 'FA LA LA LA LAAAAA, LA LA LA LA!'

Alice sneaked a look at her new friends. She would miss them at Christmas, all of them, and that was unlike her. She'd only known them a month, and maybe they were just rebound friends, but she felt like she was expanding her comfort zone, and for the first time, other people were part of it.

The song finished, the choir shuffled, the crowd clapped, and Bear lay on the ground and started licking fallen food scraps.

'Fröhliche Weihnacht überall!'

'Oh,' said Alice as they started up again, and saw Vanessa, Marco, David and Noah look at each other in joy, their faces drenched in nostalgia.

Three songs later it seemed like the perfect time to top up with some Glühwein. They made their way through the crowd, away from the Tree, and strolled along the line of little huts that made up the Christmas market.

They drank the hot, sweet wine out of Christmas tree-shaped souvenir mugs, they nibbled on Swiss festive cookies and Austrian-imported cheeses and hams, Alice bought some delicate wood-carved ornaments for her parents, and they talked. There was a simple ease in the air which waltzed with their Christmas spirits, and Alice felt the same.

'Shall we make a picture?' asked Vanessa, pulling out her phone. It was late, and they were all suitably merry, safe in the cocoon of warm feelings and friendship as they looked out across the Limmat river, curling its way from Lake Zurich into the city.

They huddled together as a group, and Alice grinned a genuine grin into the camera. *Make a picture.* She liked that phrase, it sounded nicer than *taking* a picture. Like instead you were making memories that you could hold onto.

'And now we go around and tell our Christmas wishes.'

There was a collective moan and Lola said, 'Man, Marco you are so lame, nobody wants to be all profound, we've had too much Glühwein. Or maybe not enough.'

'No, no, I'm not talking about Big Wishes, or Big Life Dreams, I mean actual Christmas wishes, for this Christmas, something you would be very happy to receive, or have happen.'

'You go first, little brother,' said Noah. 'What is your Christmas wish?'

Marco gazed at the water, thinking. Alice watched his eyes scan the lights opposite, his mind dreaming. Eventually he did his funny chuckle. 'It's quite hard, huh?'

'I'll go,' said Vanessa, and David stood a little straighter to listen, his own Christmas wish written all over his face. 'I wish for happy customers on Christmas Day. I want to love this job, but if anyone complains or is upset about something on Christmas Day that would hurt. I want to enjoy the day too.'

The group nodded in unison – the ski instructors in particular were well aware how disheartening it could be when a customer forgets it's your one Christmas Day of the year too, even if you're working it.

'My Christmas wish,' Noah spoke up, 'is that my

wife just once consumes some Swiss chocolate that isn't Toblerone.'

Lola laughed. 'My Christmas wish is for you to shut your damned mouth.' She shut it for him by planting a big kiss on his lips, in a very Kodak moment in front of the lights of the city. 'Alice?' she asked when she broke free.

'My Christmas wish is for my parents to believe I'm okay,' Alice said carefully.

'When you head home you mean?' Lola asked.

'Yep. They've been worried, for months now, I'd like to make them believe I'm ... better.'

'Do *you* believe it?'

Alice shrugged at Lola. 'One wish at a time.'

'I have thought of a Christmas wish,' Marco announced. 'I wish for Alice's parents to be happy for Alice too.' He took her hand in his, their big coat sleeves causing the action to be out of sight of the others, and squeezed it, whispering. 'Let's pool our wishes, huh, double-stuff it so it really comes true.'

'Okay,' she whispered back, touched, but they didn't let go of each other and that became all Alice could think about, even when attention moved to David.

'My Christmas wish,' he said, looking a little glum, a little worn, with the warm pink tinge of someone who's made merry with a little too much mulled wine. He sighed and looked at Vanessa, who pretended not to notice and looked out across the river. David sighed again. 'Is to burn Marco's Christmas jumper.'

There were cries of *No!* and *Never!* and then Lola

said, 'And finally Bear? What's your Christmas wish this year?'

Bear looked up at her at the sound of his name, and then walked head first into Alice, burying his face in her legs, giving her access to his ears to stroke. Alice laughed and crouched down, wrapping her arms around his stocky body and pushing her face into his softer-than-soft fur. 'I love you so much, Big Bear!' she exclaimed, meaning it with all her heart.

Lola grinned and it turned into a large yawn, which was closely followed by Vanessa, and when David slurred something about finding a pub Marco said to the group, 'I hate to be Mr Party Pooper but David and I have to get up early in the morning to get back over to Mürren. Which means our designated drivers do as well, sorry. Unless you want to stay on and visit with Vanessa, Alice, and the two of us can go in Noah's car?'

'I would love that,' said Vanessa, 'But I'm working tomorrow as well. I'll be back over for New Year's, though.'

They walked back through the darkened streets, each humming variations of the festive music they'd heard throughout the evening. Bear was tired, Alice could tell, so hopefully he'd sleep well tonight and maybe also in the car tomorrow.

She stopped while Bear had a lazy wee, not bothering to lift a leg but instead just squatting like he used to as a smaller puppy.

Lola turned to look for her and then hung back. 'So was it as good as you hoped?' she asked, falling into step with Alice.

'The Singing Tree? Yes, I actually loved it. I'd forgotten my own fondness for quirky traditions and festivities. What did you think?'

'I think if I could sing like any one of them I'd climb up the nearest tree and belt one out too. When they sang "Halo", oh my God.'

'Mmm . . . ' Alice agreed. She was tired.

'And the Mariah cover was also great, but more importantly, what's going on with you and my brother-in-law?'

That woke her up a little bit. 'Nothing,' Alice hissed, aware of Marco only a few steps ahead.

'Yeah, but also something, right?'

Alice touched Lola's arm to hold her back a little, Bear slowing beside her. 'I don't know,' she confessed. 'I'm not out here for holiday romance or anything like that. I don't mean to be leading him on.'

'Don't you like him?'

'Yes, but . . . I can't be mushy and sweet and going on dates at the moment. I'm not in a good place.'

'He knows that, you know,' Lola pointed out.

'I just don't know what to feel. And Jill's not here to help me with the answers. No offence, it's just that you're a little biased.'

'Okay, let me ask you something.' Lola started walking again but they kept their pace slow. 'If Jill was here, and you weren't, and she'd been lonely and sad but had a shot at letting someone in and maybe being happy, what would you tell her?'

Oh, Jill. Alice couldn't form the words to answer because

they clung in her throat, as if they knew they could never be spoken to Jill, not really.

Lola rubbed a hand on her back. 'It's okay, you don't need to say, I think I can guess. But maybe you should treat yourself like you would your best friend. Be nice to Alice, she's had a tough few months.'

Chapter 34

Alice slept in fits and bursts that night. Vanessa's rented apartment had a spare box room with a sofa bed, which she and Bear took, and David and Marco took a sofa each in the living room. She slept with the window open, which meant the tip of her nose, sticking out above the duvet, was icy but Bear was happy, as opposed to shuffling and panting and trying to get out of the door all night.

She spent a long time thinking about her journey over the past few months, and at two a.m. she was following an internet rabbit hole, reading about a thing called the change curve, based on a 1960s method of describing the emotional stages of grief, developed by a Swiss-American psychiatrist. She'd certainly been through the shock, anger, maybe a little denial. There was a chance she was on her way out, struggling up the hill towards the light, challenging herself and accepting what had happened, but did she actually feel like that, or was she just fooling herself into thinking she could be normal?

She didn't let herself see what the last stage was supposed to be. She didn't want to know yet what the last page of her supposed story was.

'I was awake a lot of last night,' Alice told David in the car on the way home. He and Marco had switched on the way back, and though it was always the plan, Alice suspected that Marco thought she might need some space.

David was slumped in the seat, staying very still, his eyes half closed but not asleep. He was the vision of a hangover.

'Are you feeling okay?' David asked, as if worried she'd ask him to take over in the driver's seat.

'Oh, I'm fine to drive. I'm actually glad to have set off early today, it's going to be nice to get home and maybe go back to bed for a bit.' She glanced at him. 'Not that you can do that, sorry.'

'I think I will have just enough time to make a big rosti breakfast when we get back; that will fix me.'

They continued the drive in silence for a while, no music today, the only sound being Bear's snoring from the back seat. Overhead, blobby clouds dotted the aqua morning sky like plump snowmen who'd floated away. The large lakes beside the highway, Lakes Lucerne and Brienz, had been sprinkled with glitter made of sunshine.

'It's Christmas in just over a week,' she said after a while, as much to herself as to David.

'A week, huh?'

'Yep. This time next week, it'll be Christmas Eve tomorrow, and I'll be flying home.'

'Are you looking forward to it?'

'Yes and no. I'm looking forward to seeing my parents – yesterday helped actually, I'm feeling a lot more Christmas spirit thanks to all those singers.'

'And all that Glühwein.'

'Yeah, you must have a *lot* of Christmas spirit in you right now!'

David cracked a smile and reached for a can of Coke he'd bought before they set off.

'Vanessa seems to be really happy in her new job, doesn't she?' Alice asked. How cruel she was to bring up Vanessa when he was hungover and trapped in her car, she thought, but didn't let it stop her.

David's eyes opened a little wider. 'For sure, it sounds like she really enjoys it.'

'She's working at Christmas, but coming home for a couple of days at New Year, is that right?'

'I think she said this.'

'Hmm. Hey, just out of interest, is mistletoe a thing in Switzerland?'

David looked at her, a smirk creeping onto his face. She kept her eyes on the road, impassive and innocent.

'Why, do you want to hang some between you and Marco?' he countered.

Touché.

David yawned and reached an arm back to stroke Bear. 'So you think I should go for it with Vanessa, do you?'

'She hasn't said anything to me, and I may have known her a long time but I probably don't know her nearly as well as you do, *but*, I mean ... '

'She doesn't seem repulsed by me?'

Alice laughed. 'Well, you have to start somewhere. I don't know, I'm nobody to give romantic advice, I've been happily single for years and I'm too much of a mess to do anything about my own love life at the moment, but part of what I was thinking about last night was not letting things pass you by. If you want something, or someone, you should probably go for it because who knows what's around the corner.'

'It is true.'

'I'm still learning the theory rather than the practice, though.'

'You'll get there.'

He said it so easily that Alice found herself believing him, and believing in herself.

'He likes to watch you when you eat, but he'll sit down if you tell him to. He'll just carry on staring at you after he does.' It was Christmas Eve, dawn only just breaking over the little village, which meant the view was still soaked in pre-night, post-morning blue. Alice was talking Marco and David through Bear's long list of quirks, care instructions and anything else she could think of to delay leaving for the airport. 'I leave lots of bowls of water around for him, including one downstairs at night even though he'll probably want to sleep up in one of your rooms with you. Is that okay?'

'Yes, that's fine,' said Marco, who was in the eye-watering

Christmas jumper and yet still snuggling close to Bear's warm fur. There was something about the softness of Bear's coat that demanded to be constantly touched. He was a true comfort blanket.

'He might actually jump on your bed in the middle of the night, which is a surprising way to wake up, but then he'll just want to flop down next to you. Well, on you. It's nice, but you can tell him to get off if he's at all annoying.'

'Marco will enjoy the company,' David joked.

'We're going to be just fine,' Marco said, his voice confident and reassuring. 'We'll have a very merry Christmas. Do you think he likes my Christmas sweater?'

'I think he loves it,' Alice answered. 'Thank you both again for doing this. I feel bad leaving you with him when you should be relaxing.'

Marco stood up and put his hands on her shoulders. 'Don't feel bad. Take a break, visit your parents. We are so happy to be looking after a big Bernese, you have no idea.'

'Will you let me know that he's okay?'

'I'll send you a thousand photos a day.'

'Do you think he'll miss me?'

'He's going to miss you a lot,' Marco replied, looking into her eyes. 'So much, but it's Christmas Eve, and you fly back on Boxing Day. He'll cope without you for two nights.'

'We're going to keep him completely distracted and occupied,' David said, as Marco picked up her bag for her.

Alice knelt down and nuzzled into Bear, who stood in front of her pressing his huge furry head into her chest while she rubbed behind his ears. 'Have a very merry Christmas,

Bear. I'll be back in two sleeps. I hope you have a brilliant time with the other boys.'

Bear lifted his head and beamed at her, his big brown eyes looking right into hers with such wide innocence. She stroked his cheeks, marbled with white and rust fur, and he stretched his head forward to sniff her face as close as he could get. Finally he pulled his head back, and wrapped a wet mouth around her arm which was his version of a Swiss kiss.

Tears threatened the back of Alice's eyes when she stood and waved goodbye to the dog. *How ridiculous*, she tried to tell herself.

David produced a dog biscuit from his pocket and Bear's attention was pulled away. He stood on his hind legs, his paws on David's shoulders, to eat it from his hands. Marco, and Alice, then left the chalet.

Out on the snow they crunched their way towards the station. After the Zurich trip she'd managed to park back at Lauterbrunnen, so she didn't have far to go this morning. 'You don't need to carry my bag down there if you want to get back,' Alice said.

'It's my pleasure,' he answered. 'I wanted to check how you were really feeling.'

'It's silly . . . he's just not been on his own at night since I took him in. I hope he sleeps okay.'

'Him, or you?'

'A little of both,' she confessed.

'Is there anything else on your mind?' They kept walking while Alice thought about how to answer his question.

272

'Here I'm in a snow globe. Back in England I feel exposed.'

'I understand that. Is there anything about going back you are looking forward to, that you can focus on?'

'I really want to see my parents, and I'm looking forward to the familiarity and traditions. Those things just keep getting gnawed away at by that feeling of going back to the place that on the other hand brought so much misery.' They reached the station. 'I am such a Debbie Downer. Sorry. Merry Christmas Eve, Marco.'

'You are no downer, you are human. I don't have the answers, but I hope your journey goes well, and I hope you enjoy your family, and I hope you come back on Boxing Day feeling better.'

'I am so rubbish. I'm moaning about seeing my family and you don't even get to see yours until after the big day.'

'Not at all. Merry Christmas, Alice.'

'Merry Christmas, Marco. Thank you for everything.'

Alice reached up to hug him and they held each other a moment longer than necessary. *Take care of my Bear*, she was trying to tell him through her arms. *He's all I have.* And when they pulled back she kissed his cheek which was stubbly and warm. Everything about Marco was warm.

But still they held on, perhaps just for a couple of seconds, but long enough for the lightest snowflake of a kiss to pass between each other's lips. It was so fleeting it was almost hard to be sure it really happened, but Alice stepped back and into the train without another word, and they waved at each other through the window, both a little surprised.

Her heart tugged when she boarded the train and it

pulled away. Could she do this? But as it made its way further from Mürren, crawling down the mountain and edging her closer to home, her phone tinkled.

She'd received a gift through iTunes. She opened it with curiosity, and smiled a grateful smile. *A Rat Pack Christmas* had been gifted to her, along with a note from Marco: 'Maybe this will help get you in the Christmas spirit, or at least distract you from sad thoughts and remind you of us up here in the snow, missing you, and looking forward to you coming (to your second) home. Love, Marc and Bear xx.'

'Merry Christmas, Marco,' she whispered again, looking through the glass and up the mountain she would soon be back to climb.

Chapter 35

Alice watched the seatbelt sign, waiting for it to be switched off, as the plane crawled its way to a stop. Beyond the oval window, the weather was a stereotypical English December – pale grey clouds covering the sky like a duvet without a cover, a wet ground even when it wasn't raining, a coldness hanging around in the air that felt like it could be the same cold that had nipped at Dickens's nose.

Finally the sign pinged and the illumination disappeared, and the passengers were home for the holidays. There was a scramble to be the first to pull their bags and duty-free presents and coats and scarves from the overhead lockers in order to stand awkwardly in the aisle.

Alice stayed put, resisting London for as long as possible, but grabbed for her phone and flicked it off airplane mode. She waited for news from Marco, anxious to know Bear was okay, and if he was going to mention their kiss. Sure enough, true to his word, her phone tinkled with not one but two 'pupdates' in the form of photos. One showed Bear peering at a snowman, out on a walk, and the other was a selfie of Marco with his arm around a very relaxed-looking dog. Alice smiled.

'Cute family,' a woman standing in the aisle commented. 'Merry Christmas to you all.'

'Thanks, you too,' said Alice, without bothering to correct her. He hadn't mentioned what had happened, but maybe that was for the best for now. She had other things to think about over the next couple of days, aside from this mountain rescuer's warm lips and kind eyes.

It was strange to be back in the UK. Walking through Heathrow Airport felt so familiar and yet so distant from the life she'd led for the past two months. Spaces seemed cramped, people seemed busy, signs seemed too big and intimidating, and she felt alone without her dog at her side. She kept her thoughts busy through passport control by letting bubbles of happy holiday memories foam inside her, little things that reminded her of comfortable familiarities she could enjoy again. She wanted to make her parents smoked salmon on toast for Christmas breakfast. She wanted to find Quality Street hidden inside the big, real Christmas tree. She wanted to wake up in her childhood bedroom again and remember it for the many Christmas mornings that had sparkled through her life before now, and not for the three weeks she'd spent under the duvet in there following Jill's death.

As soon as she spotted her mum and dad in the arrivals hall, waiting beside a huge lit-up ribbon Christmas tree, her mum in her favourite plaid Christmas scarf and her dad tucking into a Toblerone, unaware of his daughter approaching, England reminded her where home is.

A rush of comfort took over and she picked up her step, bag bashing against her leg. She stumbled into the arms of her mum and dad, tight squeezes cramping necks.

'Whoopsie,' murmured Ed, brushing a chocolate smudge he'd created from her shoulder.

'Merry Christmas, love,' said Liz. 'It's good to have you back.'

'We've missed you, poppet,' her dad added.

'Oh, I've missed you two,' Alice replied, all the pent-up anxiety she'd built between leaving Mürren and arriving in London rushing away. 'Merry Christmas!'

As they walked towards the train station, Alice's mum and dad chattered on about the weather and the turkey they'd bought and the Christmas TV they'd been watching and the village decorations. Alice listened with one ear, while thinking how strange it was that this didn't feel that strange. She'd anticipated cowering her way through the airport, the familiar black fear looming behind her, pushing her forward when she wasn't ready, mocking her because it was the time of year where she had to pretend to be happy.

So how come she actually felt happy?

Not *over*joyed, but joyed.

'Righty-ho, it's just gone one-thirty, anyone for a late lunch?' Liz asked with a false brightness that automatically made Alice suspicious. 'Your dad and I thought we'd all pop to Regent Street first before going home, see the Christmas lights that everyone's talking about this year, go and see the toys in Hamleys like we used to, have a big hot chocolate somewhere. What do you think?'

'You mean, go into the centre of London rather than just go home?'

'Yes, Regent Street. You always liked Regent Street.'

'But it'll be crowded.' *Anything could happen.*

Liz and Ed glanced at each other and Ed shook his head, just a tiny movement, but Alice saw it and said, 'Well, we can give it a go.'

'We don't have to,' Liz answered, worry on her face like she'd crossed a line. 'It was a bad idea, let's go home.'

They would have a much happier Christmas if they thought their daughter was okay, and wasn't permanently damaged. She wanted to give that to them.

'Nope, it'll be nice to go to Hamleys again, it's been years. Maybe I could find a present for Bear there, like a ball or a stuffed toy.' Alice slapped on a smile and forced the ringing in her ears to be drowned out by her inner voice singing Rat Pack Christmas songs as loud as it could.

'How is that big bear?' Ed asked as the three of them made their way to the train platform. 'Bet he likes the snow.'

'Oh, he loves it,' Alice enthused, and she found herself chattering about him and his adventures all the way along the Piccadilly Line until they found themselves nearing the Piccadilly Circus stop, on the south end of Regent Street. It wasn't until they joined the bustle towards the ticket gates that it even occurred to Alice that she'd just done her first Underground journey since before the incident.

Tourists and last-minute shoppers bumped into her and stopped in front of her. It wasn't easy: Alice concentrated on breathing and counting the seconds until she would emerge outside, following the stream of people like a trapped fish not wanting to tangle itself in netting further. Her mouth grew dry and she kept her eyes down, holding tendrils of her parents' clothing, possibly without them even noticing, but not wanting them to end up beyond her reach. Like Jill had been.

The daylight burst through as they ascended the steps, and before she did anything Alice lifted her face to the sky and breathed. It was the same sky she would have been looking up at in Switzerland, she just had to remember that, and find stillness in that thought.

She lowered her eyes. 'Oh, wow!'

Floating above the road, strung between the parallel sweep of Portland stone buildings that made up Regent Street, were vast, glowing angels, their bodies and wings made of a mesh of wire and tiny lights. They hovered, as if guarding the shoppers below within the blankets of their intertwining costumes. It was the best light show she'd seen on Regent Street, after many years of coming here, and it wasn't even dark yet.

'This is beautiful,' she said to her parents.

Liz looked so pleased. 'We thought you'd like it. We'd seen photos of it in the paper. It's quite calming, isn't it?'

'Yeah,' Alice agreed. Despite everything that had happened, she had to admit that there were some things about London you just couldn't beat.

They stood, looking up for a long moment until Alice became aware of how the cold air must be feeling to her parents, so she tore her eyes away. She was ready to battle her way through the crowd, expecting to need her guard up for the barrage of hostile, busy, suspicious people.

It was busy, yes, but the atmosphere was jolly. Shoppers were smiling and hauling their great bags of last-minute shopping, Christmas music floated out of every shop along with a puff of warm air, visitors leaned and stood on tiptoes and waited patiently for their turn to get close to the window displays of the big stores to take photos.

These people weren't scared, nor were they full of hate. This wasn't the image she'd been cultivating in her mind, born of her own demons. But *this* was London. Resilient, not resentful. Strong enough to let happiness in. The London she had loved hadn't gone away; she had.

'Here we are. Remember when we used to bring you here as a child every Christmas?' Ed asked, coming to a stop outside Hamleys, the huge toy shop that was the world's oldest, and a London institution.

As there had always been, a couple of toy demonstrators dressed in the signature red coats were in front of the store, whirling colourful playthings and keeping up an ongoing chatter to welcome in customers, who all dutifully made their way in through the vast open doors.

It was madness, but a happy madness that Alice remembered so well, and because of that it made her feel safe.

The three of them entered the store and, without any real

purpose, were swept along until they found themselves in the soft toy department, where a cuddly dog caught Alice's eye.

'Look, a Bear! Not a *bear* bear, a My Bear!' She held up the stuffed Bernese Mountain Dog, its orange-thumbprint eyebrows, white nose and feet and flash of Swiss kiss on the back of his neck so familiar. 'I have to get this, a Christmas present for that puppy when I get back.'

'I'll buy that for you, love,' said Ed, reaching for the soft toy.

'That's all right, Dad, I've got this.'

'No, let me,' he smiled.

Liz walked past them to look at some classic Hamleys teddy bears and whispered, 'Let him do this, you're still his little girl.'

Ed looked pleased with himself as he headed to the till, leaving his wife and daughter to mosey around the Harry Potter displays.

'Is Dad okay?' Alice asked.

'Yes, he's fine, we both are, I just know he's been thinking a lot about what happened to Jill, and what would have happened if . . . you know.'

Alice nodded, full of sadness for her dad's aching heart. 'Do you see Jill's parents around much?'

'Sometimes. We've been over a couple of times. They always ask after you.'

'How do they seem?' To be honest, Alice didn't really want to know the answer to any of this, but she still felt compelled to ask. She could well imagine how Jill's mum and dad, and her brother, seemed – sad, angry, broken, bitter.

'They're … coping,' Liz replied. 'But they walk a little slower now, talk a little less. Sam has been coming back a lot and helping them with things. They ask after Bear as well, and I've shown them some of the photos you've been sending me, of the two of you in the snow.'

Alice wondered how they felt seeing her off having a jolly holiday with their daughter's dog.

Her mum put an arm around her, pulling her back to the present. 'They were happy to see them. They seem happy that you're looking after him so well, in a place Jill talked a lot about taking him. They aren't angry, Ali, I promise you. And they wouldn't have any reason to be.'

'But—'

'It's Christmas, my love. I hope you can give yourself the gift of a break.'

At that moment Ed reappeared clasping a Hamleys bag with the Bernese Mountain Dog toy inside. 'Merry Christmas to you and Bear,' he said, as jolly as Santa.

'Thank you.' Alice hugged him, feeling like she was ten years old again. 'Do any of you fancy eating soon? I've got a sudden hankering for a pie and mash, though it's more like an early dinner than a late lunch now. My treat.'

'Well, our treat,' Liz corrected. 'I doubt you have a lot of dosh this Christmas.' She smiled as she said it, and Alice thought, *it actually feels good to be home.*

Two hours later they were finishing the last morsels of mince pie and hot chocolate from their table at the Queens Head pub near Piccadilly Circus, tummies full, just like they should be at Christmas time. Liz and Ed had told her all about their past couple of months: the Halloween trick or treaters they'd had for the first time, and that they'd had to give out all of Liz's supply of KitKats because they hadn't had any other sweets in; the village fireworks on bonfire night which had been a complete washout but fun nonetheless; and how Ed had only finished his Christmas shopping two days earlier. In return, Alice told them about seeing Vanessa again, trying snowboarding for the first time, and her new friends. She felt herself smiling as she talked about them, especially as she enthused about how helpful Marco had been, and pressed her lips together, remembering.

'He sounds like a very nice chap,' Liz said, stealing a glance at Ed who nodded, a little embarrassed by the conversation. 'It sounds like you've made some lovely close friends there. Will you see Bahira, Theresa and Kemi while you're back?'

'No, I don't really have time,' Alice answered. In actual fact she probably could have squeezed in a drink at the pub if any of them were around this evening, but ... maybe she'd just give them a quick ring; they were probably all busy with their own families. Still, she felt a knot of guilt at not following through on her promise to keep in touch more.

'You're flying back on Boxing Day, is that right?' asked Ed. 'Do you have to leave so soon?'

'Ed ...' Liz cautioned.

'I do. Marco and David are being very kind looking after my huffing great dog for me, and he isn't easy, and they need to work.'

283

Ed nodded.

'Maybe you could both come out and visit me in the New Year?' Alice continued, keen to keep the mood light and the belief going that everything was fine. 'Mum, you'd love the outdoor hot springs they have out there. They'll even let you have a glass of bubbly while you sit in them.'

'Well, that sounds very nice, we'll look into that, won't we, Ed? Are you sure Vanessa wouldn't mind yet more people staying in her home?'

'No, she wouldn't mind at all, she's said I can have visitors.'

'Okay, we'll take a look at that then.' Liz stood and brushed stray mince pie crumbs from her long coat. 'Now, who's ready to go home and light the fire?'

'Oh, I am!' Alice said. 'I'm very good at lighting fires now.'

Christmas Eve after dark was a magical time, hope and anticipation radiating through the illuminated trees in windows, and on the faces of those you passed as you rushed home to wait for the last sleep before the big day.

Inside the Bright household, Liz and Ed had made the family home as warm as a hug and full of familiar traditions. The tree was decorated with a lifetime of collected ornaments – the miniature Empire State Building Alice had brought her parents back from a trip to New York, the faded gold and red bauble Ed and Liz had bought on their honeymoon in Norway, the strange clay snowman Alice had made in primary school which would have been better suited as a Halloween ornament, to be quite honest.

As Alice touched the various items from her history she

284

thought, *I made it*. She was home for Christmas, and she was happy to be here, and that's all she could have asked for.

Liz appeared at her side with a glass of Baileys for her. 'It's good to see you smiling again.'

Alice took the Baileys. 'One of my new friends, Lola, told me a while ago to have gratitude for life. We were at the top of the mountain at the time – well, the top of the baby slope – so I think she was partially trying to pep talk me into zooming downhill on a snowboard. Anyway, it was good advice and I'm trying hard to follow it.'

Ed appeared with a plate full of piping-hot cocktail sausages in a sweet sticky glaze. 'I know it's an odd pre-dinner appetiser, but I couldn't help myself.' He grinned. 'Lovely fire you've lit there, Alice, how'd you learn to do that?'

'It all started with an axe ... '

In bed that night, Alice turned off the light. Her mum had put a mini Christmas tree on her bedroom windowsill with some tiny fairy lights laced around it, and it reminded her of her nook glowing away in Switzerland. It gave her the confidence to embrace the still comfort that came with darkness (just not pitch-black darkness).

She watched the numbers on her projector clock tick closer to midnight on the ceiling.

''Twas the night before Christmas, when all through the house, not a creature was stirring, not even a mouse,' she whispered. 'Three ... two ... one.'

It was Christmas Day. Alice pulled from under her pillow a photo that she'd dug out earlier that evening. It was of her and Jill, dressed in matching Mrs Claus outfits, from way back when they'd got Christmas jobs behind the bar at the local pub and had felt the place needed some Christmas spirit. In the photo, Jill was posing like she was in a festive-themed pin-up calendar, while Alice, with her signature red lipstick, was laughing with her face pushed back creating a hundred double chins. It was an awful photo of her but she'd always loved it – Jill being carefree and effortlessly spur-of-the-moment, Alice finding the funny in everything. Even before she was drawing her tongue-in-cheek cartoons and having them published as far as New York City, she'd always had that element to her personality. She hoped she could get it back one day. It was part of the reason Jill had loved her, so she used to say.

'Merry Christmas, Jilly,' Alice said to the photo, illuminated only by the tiny glow from her Christmas tree, and gave it a kiss. She tucked her best friend back underneath her pillow, keeping her safe.

She reached for her phone.

Schöni Fäschttäg! she wrote in a text and hit send.

Marco replied almost immediately. *Merry Christmas to you! Merry Christmas to Bear also – is everything going okay?*

He's lying on my bed, snoring and kicking me in the face. So yes, all is calm, all is bright, we are having a lovely time. It's just gone midnight with you, right?

Alice looked at the clock and thought for a moment. *Argh, it's one a.m. in Switzerland, isn't it? I forgot! Did I wake you?*

No. David wanted to watch the Die Hard *movies this evening – those are his favourite Christmas movies. We only went to bed recently. How is home?*

Good. Relaxing, surprisingly. Thank you for the music you sent me – it really helped.

Anytime.

I'll let you get some sleep, she wrote. *Night night, both of you.*

Marco took a few minutes to reply. She kept seeing the three dots of somebody composing a message appear and disappear. Finally it came through. *Miss you.*

He followed it quickly with a gif of a Bernese puppy bouncing in the snow wearing a Santa hat, and a kiss.

A kiss. Was this just a bit of fun? Was a bit of fun what she desperately, down in her core, needed? Maybe it could be so much more.

Alice snuggled down under her covers and thought about all the things she was grateful for, until the fairy lights on her miniature tree began to swim in front of her eyes, and they eventually closed.

Christmas Day was as it should be; a day of harmony and of family, and for her parents' sake Alice tucked thoughts of Jill away into her memory box just for today.

Her parents gifted her with thoughtful items she could take back to Switzerland with her – thick, cosy socks, a new set of drawing pencils, a sweet necklace with a silver snowflake and some of her mum's home-baked biscuits. In return she gave them wooden handicrafts and candles she'd bought at the Christmas market in Zurich, a bottle of the yummiest Glühwein which she'd managed to pick up in Geneva airport at the duty free, and a framed photo of her and Bear on their balcony in Mürren.

After feasting on the biggest turkey probably ever bought for three people, even more pigs in blankets and a fat bowlful of Christmas pudding, the family retired to the sofas to rub their tummies and watch the Queen's Speech.

Alice reached down to rest a hand on Bear's body only to remember with a start that he wasn't there. How nice it would be to have his heavy lean against her body right now. She was surprised how much she missed him. She'd been with him daily for four months so she probably needed a break, but she felt the loss more than she expected. Maybe because of the other losses she'd suffered this year, it felt more heightened.

'You all right, love?' Ed asked, looking over and stifling a burp.

'Just missing Bear,' she replied. *And Marco*, she thought, surprising herself, not intending to have even been thinking of him. 'It's very silly.'

'No it's not, he's your companion,' said Liz. 'And you miss him just like we miss you.'

'Mmm ... ' Alice closed her eyes, just for a moment, the warmth of the fire, the heaviness of her food and the midday glasses of port and wine settling inside her head.

A few minutes later, Liz and Ed exchanged a glance and whispered, 'Merry Christmas' to each other. Ed turned the TV off, Liz crept over and draped a blanket on her daughter and they both reached for their books. But neither read the words in front of them. Instead their eyes kept trailing back to Alice's face, peaceful sleep behind her eyes, her skin looking brighter, her breathing more controlled. They knew she was trying to put on a front of getting better for them, but in this moment they could see she really was.

Before you could say 'January sales' it was Boxing Day and Alice was back at Heathrow Airport. Ed and Liz had filled her bag with homemade treats to keep her going and the kind presents they'd given her. They promised that they would visit soon and reminded her that she could come home any time, even if just for a couple of days.

Alice felt bad leaving them, and she'd truly enjoyed herself far more than she thought she would. But the thought of wrapping herself around her big soft Bear again was almost pulling her to the plane like a magnet.

Up on the departures board her gate was announced, and although there was no rush to board (the gate wouldn't actually open for another half hour) she took the opportunity to say her goodbyes.

'I'd better make tracks, security can sometimes take yonks,' she said.

'Okay, honey, well – thank you again for coming.' Liz gave her yet another hug, but that was fine with Alice.

'Thank you for a perfect Christmas,' Alice replied. 'See you soon, okay?'

'Text us when you get back to Vanessa's and send us a picture of Bear,' said her dad. 'Let me know if he likes his toy from Hamleys.'

'I will,' Alice promised. 'Love you both a lot. Bye bye.' She waved and walked through security, turning back to wave once again before she had to go out of sight. How lucky she was to have them.

After passing through security she stopped at one of the departure terminal bars for one last drink of Baileys. She drank, and people-watched, and it dawned on her as she looked around at the people dragging their ski equipment, the WHSmith with piles of cosy hardbacks on tables by the door, the duty-free sales assistants with their tinsel-garnished uniforms, that she was looking at everything through different eyes than when she had arrived two sleeps ago. Then it had felt cramped and busy and too hectic in comparison to peaceful Mürren. Now she didn't feel that, and she wondered if it had all been in her head before, that she hadn't been allowing herself to see the happiness because she was so convinced it would be the opposite.

Alice checked the time on her phone, picked up her bag and knocked back the remaining slug of Baileys, crunching on an ice cube just like Bear would have done.

Chapter 36

If running on snow didn't make Alice want to pass out from the effort, she would have run all the way up the slope from the train station to her chalet. Her face was stretched into a smile just thinking about seeing Bear again – it felt nice to enjoy missing someone.

She went straight to Marco's door without even stopping by Vanessa's first to drop her things off, and through the frosted glass panel she saw a white nose appear, peering up at her.

'Hi, Bear!' she cried, as she knocked on the door, and she saw the white tip of his tail begin to wag furiously. Then the unmistakable tall form of Marco appeared, and he pulled the door open as wide as he could with Bear trying to stuff his snout through to get to her.

The second Marco had wrested the door wide enough, Bear burst through and plummeted into Alice, spinning in circles, licking her face and bashing her in the eye with his plume of a tail. She fell back into the snow, giggling. 'Hello, you! Hello! Happy Christmas!'

'He's going to eat you for his Christmas lunch!' Marco exclaimed, and reached a strong hand down to help her up.

'Hello to you too,' she said, finally detangled, and gave him a hug which Bear joined in with, eliminating the possibility of a welcome-home kiss, for now.

'Welcome back. Come in and have a coffee.' He led them all inside, Bear weaving in and out and through Alice's legs, unable to take his sparkling eyes off her. 'He's so pleased to see you!'

'I'm pleased to see him, too. I missed him a lot.'

'How was your journey?'

'It was good, easy, much easier than a fifteen-hour drive with a dog in the back. I have you to thank for that, and David.'

'I'll pass that on – David's on the slopes at the moment. He was supposed to teach a group of friends a Christmas Day lesson yesterday but they cancelled because they got too drunk at the Christmas Eve après-ski party in the village, so he's taking them today instead.'

Alice took a seat at their kitchen counter while Marco made some big mugs of coffee. 'So how did everything go?' she asked. 'Did you two, you three, manage to have a happy Christmas?'

'Oh we had a great time. We watched a lot of movies, which Bear liked because he could sleep by our feet. We ate a lot, which Bear liked, because of food. We played in the snow. Look.' Marco pointed out of the window to where two snowmen and a snowdog had been constructed.

'That's Bear's spare collar!' she laughed. 'And that's your Christmas jumper!'

Marco pointed them out one by one. 'That one is "Christmas Day-vid", wearing David's spare goggles, that's "Happy Christ-Marc" in my jumper, and the dog is "Santa Paws". Everybody helped, although Bear peed against Santa Paws version one, so we had to build an extra layer of snow-fur around him.'

'It looks like you had a lot of fun.'

'We did. One lady went past on her skis and said what a lovely modern family we made.'

Alice laughed. 'And when do your actual family arrive?' She sipped her coffee – it was perfect.

'Tomorrow. You'll come over and meet them, yes?'

'If you want me to?' Of course Alice wanted to, but this felt a little like a meet-the-parents situation.

'Absolutely. Sorry, though, if they give more attention to Bear than you. They will love you, but they will *love* your dog.'

'I'm used to that by now. Oh!' She pulled out her phone. 'I promised I'd text my folks when I got back. Excuse me a mo.' She sent a quick message, and then went to her bag and pulled out the Bernese soft toy, holding it out to Bear whose eyes widened. He put his mouth around it very delicately, raised his tail high in the air and went skipping around the kitchen, pleased as punch with his new pal. 'My dad bought that for him,' she explained.

Alice tried to take a photo of Bear with the toy but he was too busy leaping about. In the end she had to enlist the help of Marco.

'Bear, come here, come here,' he called, and Bear wandered over to Marco and sat on his feet, the teddy in his mouth, and Alice snapped a picture while Marco was grinning down at him. She sent that to her mum. *One happy Bear*, she wrote. *And one Marco.*

Her mum replied, *Very nice!* which Alice found enigmatic. And then another message followed, saying *Glad you're back safely. Bear looks well and Dad is pleased he likes the toy. Your friend Marco is pleasing on the eye, isn't he?*

Alice hid the screen of her phone in case Marco had spotted that. How embarrassing.

'Okay, I'd better take this one home. Thank you for the coffee, but more importantly, thank you for looking after him. I really appreciate it. Going home felt easier knowing he was safely back here with you.'

'Any time.' Marco smiled.

'You're . . . ' She stopped herself, not really knowing what she wanted to say out loud. 'You're a very nice man.' Well, that sounded awkward. Nice one, Alice.

'Thank you. You are a nice woman. And you are a nice dog.'

'Good. Well, now that's established, see you in a bit. And thank you again.' She made her way to the door, picking up her things.

'Do you want a hand with your stuff?'

'No, it's fine. Although maybe you could carry Bear's things over for me?'

'It's going to feel quiet at our house without him snuffling around,' Marco remarked as they walked together over the snow, which felt thicker and more powdery than it had when she'd left.

'Feel free to come and drink some of my coffee if you need a bit of noise again,' Alice replied.

'Okay, thanks.' He put the things down just inside the door and the two of them met eyes for a moment, dopey smiles on their faces. He reached over and squeezed her mittened hand, and then turned and walked back to his house.

Alice closed her door and exhaled. She faced Bear. 'So?' she asked. 'You were my market researcher. Is the mountain air just making me dizzy or are you as smitten as I am?'

The following morning, Alice was in flow, sketching cartoons of Bear building snow dogs, when cheery noises arose from next door. She peeped out of the window to see Noah and Lola returned, along with two older people that must have been Noah and Marco's parents. Cases and coats and gifts were being passed through the front door, with cries in both Swiss-German and English of 'Merry Christmas' and 'Happy New Year', nobody quite sure which should be said in the interim period between the two dates.

Bear stood by the front door, waiting to be let out to meet these potential new best friends.

'Let's give them a little time to settle in and spend some time with their son before you go barging in and steal everyone's thunder,' Alice said to him.

He looked at her, huffed, and sat down, but still faced the door.

She loved that view of him – his big, rectangle of a back,

neck as wide as shoulders, head as thick as neck, with his ears squared forwards, listening, his Swiss kiss a handsome detail. She picked up a new sheet of paper and sketched this view of him too.

It felt good to draw again. There were some subjects that didn't translate well in cartoon form – either it wasn't appropriate or their naturally animated selves couldn't translate on the page. But Bear's quirks, his tufts of fur, his expressions and his silliness worked well.

Bear came back towards the table and flumped down, lying on her feet, covering both with a heavy warmth. 'Remember when you used to be so small that you'd only be able to lie on one of my feet?' she asked him. Not that he had ever been what a normal dog owner would call 'small'.

She reached for her phone and scrolled back through countless photos from the past four months, stopping occasionally at particularly amusing ones in order to transfer them into cartoon form. It was only when her tummy let out such a growl that Bear jumped up that she realised how long she'd sat there, and how many little cartoons she'd drawn.

Alice went to the kitchen and picked up the Tupperware box of homemade mince pies her mum had packed her off with, all decorated with pastry stars and edible gold glitter spray. She had an idea.

'Fancy stretching your legs a bit, Mr Bear?' she asked, pulling on her snow boots and a big scarf. She tucked the tub under her arm and took Bear next door.

Lola answered the knock, throwing the door wide open

and her arms around Alice. 'Merry Christmas!' she cried. Bear charged in without waiting for an invitation, leaving snowy, wet paw prints across their wooden floors. Not that any of them minded – indoor snow was par for the course for ski instructors.

'Come in. Noah's folks are here, you gotta meet them. Oh, your dog already has.'

In the living room, Bear was already desperately stretching his neck forwards trying to lick at Noah and Marco's mum's chin, while their dad was picking up scattered pieces of a Cluedo board from the floor, Bear's tail sweeping it for any remains.

'Did Bear do that?' Alice cried, mortified. 'Bear, down, come here. I'm so sorry.'

Marco's dad looked up, the same happy smile as his son. 'Hallo! Don't apologise, I was not playing well, this is the perfect result.'

Marco's mum wrenched herself away and stood up, crossing to Alice. 'So this tornado is Bear, and you must be Alice? We are hearing a lot about you this year.'

'Hi,' Alice replied, a little shyly. 'Sorry about the game. And the licking.'

'Not at all, he is so like our old dogs. Oh, Patrick, let's get more dogs, yes?'

'Sure!' said Marco's dad.

'Such wonderful dogs. Don't they make lovely companions?' his mum continued. 'When he was growing up, Marco was often pretending he was one of our Bernese dogs. For maybe six months he would describe himself as the brother of Hund-Hund, our first Bernese, and he is walking around on all four feet and begging for treats.'

'Mum!' Marco exclaimed, coming in from the kitchen. 'I was only, maybe, five,' he explained to a snickering Alice and Lola. 'And it was your fault – you kept telling me I had exactly the same personality as the dog. I got confused.'

'*Hund* is dog, right?' asked Lola. 'So your first dog was called Dog-Dog?'

'Your husband named him,' Patrick said. 'Don't let him name your first born, okay?'

Noah rolled his eyes. 'Alice, meet my dad Patrick, and my mum Sonja.'

'Hello,' she replied. 'I brought some mince pies over that my mum made back in England. I wondered if anyone would like one?'

This was met with high approval, so Alice moved to the kitchen to heat a plate of them up in the microwave. Marco went with her and put on the kettle.

'So these are traditional British mince pies, huh?' he asked, pouring out seven mugs of steaming teas and coffees.

'Sure are. You want one?' Alice replied.

'Definitely, please.'

'Alice, we are now talking about traditional Swiss food,' Sonja was saying, while Bear nestled up to her. 'I will make a fondue tonight. Are you liking cheese?'

'I am,' she replied.

'Excellent, you will join us.'

It didn't sound like a question, but Alice still looked at

the actual house hosts – Lola, Noah, Marco and David – for confirmation. They all nodded without question.

'I've not made fondue before,' said Alice. 'Could I help?'

'Of course! Food is always better when everyone is in the kitchen and all the wine is open. Noah, Marco, I know your fridge will not have all I need. Please go to the Coop for kirsch and nutmeg? Do you already have the cheeses, garlic and white wine?'

'We have Emmental and Gruyère,' said Lola, peering into the fridge, along with Bear. 'Will that do?'

'Hmm. Buy Reblochon at the shop too, that will do.'

'I have white wine, and a garlic bulb,' Alice offered.

'We have both of those two,' Lola said.

'You my dear are the perfect accompaniment to this evening just as you are,' Sonja said as a way of reply. 'It's settled then. Tonight, seven o'clock, we feast.' Sonja was definitely a woman used to taking charge. 'And it's the holidays, let's dress up in our best sparkle.'

'Mum, this is a ski resort, I don't think we all have sparkles with us,' said Marco.

'Ah, darling, sparkles are not about the clothes on your back, they are about how you carry yourself.' She clapped her hands. 'Tonight we fondue and sparkle.'

Alice surveyed her meagre wardrobe, wondering if any of her clothes, entirely made for comfort and cosiness, could pass for a sparkling 'dressed up' occasion. Her thermal polo neck was a nice electric blue ... but who was she kidding? It was still a thermal polo neck.

Well, it was the best she had, so on it went, with some black jeans and her snow boots. She found a scrap of tinsel, which she wove around Bear's collar, and was about to head next door when she thought of one more thing. Something she used to wear all the time, that when she put it on she felt immediately dressed up and ready to face the world. That made her feel stronger, more confident and more powerful.

Taking the red lipstick from its hiding place in her drawer, she held it in her hand for a moment, waiting to see if another flashback would come. But she was okay. She took off the cap and hovered it over her lips. She was okay. And even when Alice had smoothed it on, pressed her lips together, and smiled at herself in the mirror, she was okay.

'Hello,' she said to herself. 'You took your time coming back.'

She opened the door, not bothering to put Bear on the lead. He seemed to know that no lead meant they were only going next door, and so out he hopped, straight into a snowdrift, and ploughed his way towards Marco's home.

Alice tapped on the door and then opened it, hearing the music and laughter and chatter from the outside. 'Hello?' she said, and Bear pushed his way past her and skittered straight into the kitchen.

'Alice, thank God.' Sonja appeared at the kitchen door. 'Come quick, we must start the fondue before these people drink all of the white wine.'

Marco appeared beside his mother, holding two glasses of wine, one half drunk, one new, presumably for Alice. He stopped in his tracks when he saw her. 'Wow.'

'Wow nothing,' Alice said, self-consciously.

'I like your lips. Urm. Your lipstick.'

Sonja rolled her eyes and beckoned her in. Inside the kitchen was steamy and busy, with all six of them already pottering about grating cheese and nutmeg, and wiping garlic cloves around the insides of two giant cast-iron pans.

'Alice, you are in charge of alcohol, because these can't be trusted,' Sonja said, plonking a bottle of kirsch brandy in front of her, and grabbing the white wine bottle from Patrick's hand. 'We need . . . let's say two big glasses of wine in the pans, one in each, and then can you start them simmering, please. Bigger glasses than that. A little more. To the very top of the glass and tip straight in, good girl. When that's up to heat, we stir in the Emmental – oh no!'

They all turned to the Emmental, or more specifically the lack of it.

'*Bear*!' He turned to look at Alice, his paws on the counter, his nose right in the cheese, and grinned. For him, it was like Christmas all over again! 'I am so so sorry, I'll run down to the shop now and get some more. Bear, why are you so naughty when we're around other people?'

Sonja waved it off. 'We have more Emmental. Who can resist it, yes Bear?'

'Sorry sorry sorry,' said Noah, running into the kitchen. 'I had to use the bathroom, too much wine, I left my station of guarding the cheese.'

'Your mum is very kind,' Alice said to Marco in a low voice, as he passed her to get to the fridge.

'Just to the people she likes,' he said, and lightly touched her arm, his eyes flicking to her lips again.

Once all three cheeses were in and had been stirred by Marco until they were super-smooth, Alice was asked to add the kirsch and the nutmeg. Lola and David were chopping chunks of bread and boiled potato, Noah was setting the table and Patrick was topping up everybody's wine.

'It's snowing again,' Alice remarked, seeing fat flakes pass by the window as she carried one of the pans to the table. She gazed out at the dark sky, and Bear came and joined her. 'I know I've been here for two months but there's still something magical about seeing the snow fall, at least to me. It makes everything clean and ready to start again.'

It had been a squeeze fitting five plus Bear around the dining table, but seven plus Bear was very cosy indeed. Alice sat at one corner, so she could try and keep Bear next to her lest he leap up onto the table and devour an entire pan of cheese. Beside her was Marco, then David, and opposite David sat Sonja, then Patrick, then Noah and Lola, opposite Alice. The two pans were positioned evenly, but everyone huddled even closer together to get nearer to a pan with their dipping implements.

'This smells so delicious, Sonja,' Lola gushed, taking a huge sniff of the pan, and everyone '*Mmm*'ed in agreement.

Sonja waved them away. 'Bon appétit!'

Alice spiked a chunk of bread onto her long fondue fork and dunked it into the bubbling cheese. It smelt rich, the garlic and nutmeg aromas popping through the tangs of cheese and alcohol. She blew, and then put the warm forkful in her mouth, and had to stop herself from falling of her chair.

'Thish ish shoooo good,' she enthused, her mouth sticky and happy. 'Marco, your mum is amazing. Have you tried this?'

'Many times, but it never gets old.' He scoffed his own chunk. The whole table started devouring the meal, the wine a perfect accompaniment, and even Bear settled down, realising his tummy had probably had enough cheese for now, and that maybe he should snooze it off.

'So Alice, you are staying in Vanessa's chalet, yes?' Sonja asked.

'Yes, for the whole winter, but she's coming back and forth because she's working for a tour company near Zurich for the season. She'll actually be back in a couple of days because she has New Year's off.'

Sonja nodded and turned to the man opposite her. 'And David, that's perfect for you, will you finally take the opportunity to give her a kiss?'

Lola whooped with laughter, dropping a lump of hot bread and cheese on her lap.

'Mum!' Marco cried. 'You are the worst person sometimes.'

'What? I think he needs a little encouragement. It took your father five years to ask me to date. In the meantime I met, married, and divorced someone else just to keep me occupied.'

'She's joking,' Noah clarified to the table. 'Aren't you?'

'Yes, yes, it's a joke, but the point is ...' She waved

her fondue fork around a few times, trying to think of the right words. 'What do they say in England, Alice? ... Grow a pair.'

'Oh my God,' Marco said.

Lola was still laughing her head off and Patrick was helping himself to more wine, having given up long ago trying to curb his wife's meddling.

'Don't "oh my God" me or I start on you next.' Sonja winked at Marco.

Noah stepped in. 'Mother. Nobody is asking for your help. Drink more wine and, you know, shut up.' He was laughing as he said it, though.

'I'm just saying, New Year's Eve, I can see three girls and three boys and you're all young and attractive so you all might as well ... '

Alice stepped in. 'Grow a pair?'

'Exactly.' Sonja beamed. 'Now Alice, how have you found living in Switzerland? Tell me all about the things you've done.'

'Oh, I feel really at home, especially because these guys have been so welcoming. It's such a beautiful country. Um, we went into Zurich a couple of weeks ago to see the Singing Christmas Tree ... ' As Alice prattled on about the Christmas market and the beautiful lights, she was acutely aware of Marco's arm pressed up against hers. He almost seemed to be leaning into her, like Bear would do, in a protective but also really comfortable kind of way.

After the meal was done and their bellies were full, a tiredness washed over Alice, as if the past few days and the

304

lead up to the festive period had caught up with her. She stifled a yawn and after being refused point blank on her offer to help clean up, she thanked Marco's parents and the others and she and Bear took their leave.

Seeing everybody else plodding about, overstuffed and distracted, Marco slipped out of the door with Alice to walk her the few steps home.

'So, that is my mum,' he said, laughing as they stepped into the frosty night air. The snow was still falling, a gentle breeze picking up the flakes and dancing them around the sky. It was beautiful, like a Christmas card, the mountains vast and indigo under the blanket of night, the snow thickening on the roofs of the buildings that sloped down into the village, and golden lights glowing out of windows.

'She's nice,' Alice said as they stepped through the snow, leaving deep footprints.

'She's mad.'

'We're all a little mad, I think it makes us interesting. Seriously though, the whole evening was nice. I meant what I said about feeling very welcomed here.'

They stopped outside her chalet and Bear took a moment to throw clumps of snow in the air using his snout, searching for the best spot for an end-of-night wee.

Marco shrugged. 'It feels like you've always been here. It wouldn't feel the same without you now.'

She breathed out, slow, her breath icy, and saw him shiver. 'Do you want to come in?'

Marco faced her, matching her breath, the world seeming to still and wait for his answer. He smiled. 'I'd better not.' He tilted his head back to his own house, indicating his house guests. Then he added, 'Not tonight.'

'Okay,' Alice replied, relieved that the intensity had passed, disappointed it had to end.

Marco inhaled deeply and wrapped her in his arms. 'Goodnight, Alice,' he said to the top of her head.

'Goodnight, Marco,' she said into his chest.

She closed the door behind her and Bear and went straight up to her nook, where she climbed in and gazed at the inky view, hopeful about what might come later.

Chapter 37

It was the thirty-first of December, the end of the year, and New Year's Eve, finally. It was past eleven and Alice stood with Lola and Vanessa on Vanessa's balcony, flutes filled with bubbles in their gloved hands, looking at the stars above and the rest of the Mürren celebrations below. They wore gold paper hats that Alice had found in the Coop, and inside the boys, including Bear, were taking polaroid photos with comedy New Year's props and glasses that Vanessa had brought back with her.

'This is so beautiful,' Lola breathed. 'I love your house, Vanessa.'

'It's literally the nicest place I've ever lived in,' Alice agreed.

'My house is your house, both of you, you know that.' Vanessa had been adamant she wanted to host New Year's, despite hosting them all in Zurich only a few weeks back. 'From my balcony you can see all the other houses with all the other people on their balconies, and it makes the celebrations that much richer to be able to toast the neighbours,' she had said. 'From next door you just look at the back of my house.'

'Goodbye, past,' Lola said into the night sky.

'Yes, good riddance to this year. Hello future,' added Alice to the mountain peaks. 'I've got a lot of hope pinned on you, don't let me down.'

Lola cheersed her. 'I think next year will be kind to you. You've got another four months here, with us, and that's a good start. Your pup is only going to get bigger, which is cool, and it means even more of him to love. You've got a guy in there who's besotted with you, and I don't see you complaining . . . '

Alice tried to bat the comment away but Lola went on, moving past the subject quickly.

'And you're going to keep recovering, keep making it through each day a little better than the day before.'

'You're very sweet. I hope for that as well. I just need to be a bit braver next year.'

'Does that mean you're going to try and take on a red run with your snowboard?' Lola asked.

'Yes,' said Alice, and laughed. 'I suppose it does. But braver in everything. I used to have less fear because I could always see the funny side of things, or if not funny I always had hope and could think, "Well, of course this is just a blip." I had hope in humanity. Then I lost it all – I lost the will to try, and so then I lost hope, and I lost myself. If I could have one thing next year, it would be to be brave enough to get up and try again.'

'I want to be brave too,' said Vanessa. 'I doubt myself too much after redundancy, like I will not be good enough again. Shut up, Vanessa!'

'Yes, shut up Vanessa indeed,' Alice said, heartily. 'You are so good at what you do, don't you dare tell yourself otherwise.'

'I won't. In your words, hello future!'

'Wait wait wait, I want to be brave as well,' Lola added.

'You have more bravery in your little finger than anyone I know,' said Alice. 'I think you don't have blood, just pure adrenaline.'

'I am pretty brave,' she agreed with a laugh. 'Even so, it's a scary world out there, no harm in always working on the warrior queen within.'

The three women raised their glasses.

Maybe it was the alcohol, maybe it was the stars, maybe it was the end of the toughest year of her life, but in that moment it felt like everything stilled, and Jill was by her side.

'*I like your new friends,*' Alice imagined her saying.

Alice turned her face from the others as if she were looking at the view, when actually she was looking at the spot on the balcony where Jill stood, in her mind. She gave a small nod.

'*Do they make you feel less lonely?*'

Alice let a single tear fall from her eye, trailing down her cheek, finding its way over her skin ever so gently. She nodded again.

'*You should be happy. And you were right – I would always want you to choose adventure.*'

Her heart ached with the pain of missing Jill. She opened her mouth, wanting to say out loud how much she wanted to see her again, how much she missed her, how sorry she was, but no words came out.

'*Remember what they told you, that I felt almost no pain. Your face was the last thing I saw when I looked up. What a send-off.*'

In her mind Jill smiled the smile that Alice knew so well, then shivered; she'd never liked the cold.

'*I have to go. But there's a lot of love here for you, not least from Bear. Enjoy it.*'

Alice sank her head down on her arms, which rested on the wood of the balcony. She cried, and two sets of hands placed themselves on her back, Vanessa and Lola soothing her.

'*Happy New Year,*' Jill said in her ear, and was gone.

Alice took a deep breath and stood back up, wiping her eyes. 'Sorry, I couldn't stop that coming out.'

'Don't apologise,' said Vanessa. 'Can I get you anything?'

She shook her head. 'It's okay. It's gone now, and it's okay.'

At that moment, the bells in both of Mürren's churches began tinkling happily. The balcony door opened and Marco stepped out, his face happy, with Bear budging his way past him, smiling up at Alice. The sight of them was just the tonic she needed.

'This is the ringing out of the old year,' he explained, peering into the darkness. 'This is how we say goodbye to everything that happened over the past twelve months.' He then looked over and spotted Alice's pink eyes under the lamplight. 'Should we come back?'

'No, no,' said Alice, beckoning them all out. 'It's nearly midnight, come on out.'

He stepped over and without a care for the raised eyebrows or unsubtle nudges, put an arm around Alice and pulled her close. She returned the hug, holding him around the waist and looking out at the mountains, enjoying his warmth. Moments later, her shins were nudged with the heavy lump of Bear sitting and leaning against her.

'Here it comes,' said David, and sure enough the church bells went silent for a moment, until just one started chiming the countdown to the new year.

'Ten . . . nine . . . eight . . . '

Warrior women, that's what Lola had called the three of them. As they all counted down, Alice stood a little taller and met the eyes of her sisters.

'Seven . . . six . . . five . . . '

She put more power behind her voice with every number.

'Four . . . three . . . two . . . '

Brave . . . Strong . . . Happy . . .

'*Happy New Year!*' they cried in unison, and Alice was brave. She reached up and took Marco's cheeks between her gloves and pulled him into her. They kissed, and it was full of life, just like she needed.

His hands touched her hips, pulling her a little closer, and she felt his mouth curve into a smile against hers. They broke apart only a moment later, but a dizzy pleasure remained, unmasked, on her whole body, and before they moved away to wish a happy new year to the others, Marco caught her eye and beamed, stroking a hand over her hair, his fingers causing tingles down her neck.

Someone grabbed her arm. It was Lola, pulling Alice into an embrace. 'Happy New Year, future sister-in-law!' she shrieked.

'Look over there,' said Noah in a loud whisper. He pointed to David and Vanessa, kissing in the corner. 'I think we've lost them to the night.'

Alice grinned, and as the church bells regained their happy chorus, and the merry bunch took each other's hands, she was ready to be lost to the night.

Chapter 38

'Good morning,' Alice rasped with the croaky voice that comes from singing too loudly and hydrating too little. She turned and handed a coffee to the sleepy head who had just walked into the kitchen.

'*Guete Morge*,' replied Vanessa, taking a seat at the table, and holding the coffee cup as if it was keeping her upright.

'Happy New Year!'

'Indeed. Where is your man?'

'At home,' Alice answered. 'There's only one man allowed to sleep in my bed, whether I like it or not, eh, mister?' she said to Bear, and his tail wagged in agreement. 'Where's yours?'

Vanessa collapsed onto her hands and chuckled. 'Ohh, I am a wicked witch when I have champagne in me. Alice, where were you to keep me sensible?'

'I could never keep you sensible. Don't you remember the night of a thousand caipirinhas?'

'"Just two drinks then home to bed",' Vanessa quoted.

'"We have an early bus in the morning." Did we even go to bed in the end?'

'No, we went straight from dancing on the tables to the hotel lobby at six a.m. It was Jill's fault, I think.' Vanessa winked.

'Yep, all Jill's fault.'

Vanessa slurped her coffee. 'I did tell him, though, I said I don't know what I want yet, so we could only kiss if he understood that. I said, I don't want to lead you on.'

'What did David say?'

'Mmm, something about, how about we get a kiss in before you decide you might not want me. I shouldn't have let it happen, but the stars and the drink, and the blahblahblah.'

'It was New Year, don't beat yourself up. I'm sure he'll understand if you don't want to take things any further.'

Vanessa leant across the table and whispered, 'He is upstairs, though.'

'What?!'

'I'm kidding, relax. What are you doing today?'

'Walking the grizzly bear, then going back to sleep. You?'

'I should talk to David. He heads home for a week today. You want to do something with me later?'

'I want to do *nothing* with you later.' Alice yawned.

'Let's lie under blankets and watch bad movies all day.'

'Now that's a good start to the year.'

When Alice and Bear returned from their walk, Vanessa was already lying on the sofa under two faux-fur blankets. Bear bounded straight over and rested his chin on her, his nose centimetres from her face, sniffing.

Vanessa reached a hand out and stroked his head. 'I just talked to David,' she said.

'What happened?' Alice pulled off her gloves, scarf, coat, salopettes, boots and down to her soft PJs that she was still wearing underneath, and joined Vanessa on the other side of the sofa.

'I said I was sorry for letting it happen, it wasn't an intention to lead him on, I just got caught in the moment. He said he was sorry if I'd felt in any way pressured. I said no I wasn't, and actually I quite liked it, but our lives are quite far from each other. He said I was right. I said, fight for me, man. Then we kissed some more. Then I realised I still had some alcohol in me, so I said goodbye, let's talk when you get home, and I came back here and threw up.'

'You threw up? Are you okay?'

'Yeah it was from all the champagne, not from him.'

'Shall I light the fire?'

'I was hoping you'd say that.' Vanessa grinned and pulled the covers up to her chin.

Alice pottered about, placing logs into the burner along with a little kindling, and when it was going she went into the kitchen and made two coffees – black and sweet like Vanessa liked – and grabbed a big bag of crisps left over from last night, then cosied back down on the sofa.

They lay in comfortable silence, watching the fire, the soft crackling filling any need for chitchat.

'So when are you next seeing Marco?' Vanessa asked through a mouthful of crisps, after a while.

'I'm not sure. I remember him saying he has a pretty busy

week this week because he swapped some shifts around when his parents visited. But hopefully we'll get to hang out a little.'

'How do you feel about last night?'

Alice thought about it. 'Alive ... if that's the right word. Like, I'm just so ready to live again, and I'm not saying I'm there yet, and certainly not that kissing Marco has fixed me in any way, but I'm beginning to see how I want my future to be again, and I don't want to waste time or play games. If I like someone, I want to spend time with them. Stepping into a new year helped, somehow.'

'In other words ...'

'In other words I'm going to go for it.'

'Yaaaay!' Vanessa said and lifted her coffee cup in a 'cheers' motion. 'Now, how do you fancy watching the cheesiest movies we can find on Netflix?'

'Yes please, the more fondue-like the better.'

Alice and her friend settled in for the long haul, enjoying the simple pleasure of escaping.

Marco called around late that afternoon, and Alice hauled herself off the sofa and rolled her shoulders. They were on their third romcom and Vanessa had fallen asleep twice.

'Hello, you two,' he greeted her and Bear. 'Hello Vanessa,' he called as she got up and pottered upstairs for a bath.

'Hey you,' Alice answered.

'So about last night ...' Marco looked at her a little shyly, a little happily.

'About last night ...'

'I had a really nice time.'

In answer, Alice ran her hands around his waist and tilted her chin up to kiss him. It was warm, like everything else about his heart, soul and body. Even before the incident, Alice's comfort zone had been small. Now it was expanding, and he, Bear and the others were firmly on the inside. She was at peace.

'How was your day?' she asked, leaning against him lazily.

'It was intense. We took the chopter right up the other side of the Mönch to rescue this guy who'd fallen fifteen metres into a crevasse.'

'Fifteen metres? How does that happen?'

'The problem is if there's wind that blows the powder or the conditions are bad you can just not see them until you're *whoosh* ... in them.'

'Was he okay?'

'Nothing more than a dislocated shoulder. And a little cold. Crazy.'

Alice exhaled. 'Yeah, my day was super active as well.' she gestured to the sofa.

'This is really late notice, but what are you and Bear doing tomorrow?'

'I don't know. Why?'

Marco looked excited. 'One of the other paramedics wants to swap shifts, so I unexpectedly have the whole day free. I know the rest of the week is going to be mad so I thought we could go and do something fun.'

'I'd like that a lot!' Alice said. Vanessa was heading off at the crack of dawn, and deciding how she was going to put her life back together could wait another day. 'Did you have something in mind, or are we brainstorming?'

'Is there anything touristy you'd like me to take you to do?'

Alice thought for a moment before an obvious thought struck her in the head. 'Ooh, have you been up to Piz Gloria, at the top of the Schilthorn?'

'Sure, many of the ski runs go from there or from Birg, the cable car stop between Mürren and the Schilthorn. You know what I've never done, though? All of the James Bond things.'

Alice was ecstatic. 'So you've never done the James Bond brunch?'

Marco laughed. 'Nope.'

She changed tack. 'Do you want to watch a movie this evening?' As if she hadn't watched enough today.

'Okay . . . '

'Have you ever seen *On Her Majesty's Secret Service*?'

Marco had seen that particular Bond before (she was pretty sure it was the most frowned-upon thing to admit you hadn't done if you were a Mürren resident) but that was lucky, because he was fast asleep a third of the way in. He was shattered, and she couldn't blame him. But while he napped on her sofa in front of the wood burner, Bear stretched out beside him, and Alice sat on the floor resting against Marco's legs, she was enthralled. This was the Best Film she had Ever Seen. It had glorious 1960s fembots with big hair and winged eyeliner, cutting one-liners and extravagant, death-defying chase scenes. And it was set right here! There was

318

the Mürren ski lift! There was the top of the mountain ranges she now knew so well! She couldn't wait to get up to Piz Gloria in the morning and see it in all its 007 glory.

After a particularly dramatic scene where a scantily clad Bond girl was being brainwashed about her chicken allergy in her sleep (seriously), Alice turned her head and grinned at her two snoozing boys through a mouthful of popcorn.

Jill would have loved this movie just as much as she did. *I think she would have liked you, too*, Alice thought, peeping at Marco's peaceful, handsome face.

Chapter 39

On the morning of the second of January, a well-rested Marco and an overexcited Alice were waiting for the next cable car to take them up to Blofeld's lair itself at Piz Gloria. Waiting with them, stuffed between the barriers that angled people into the carriage, was a crowd of people in full ski regalia, of all colours, the fabric rustling against itself with every movement. Heads were covered with helmets with chunky goggles atop, the glass marbled with brightly tinted polarised lenses. Skis and boards and poles rested upright in arms and boots clonk-clonked while people shifted their weight, dripping snowy clumps onto the wet floor.

Alice was still feeling the intoxication of New Year's hope running through her blood and she looked up at Marco from where she was squeezed in next to him. 'So you come up here and ski down, like these people?'

'Sometimes. Most people get off at Birg, the stop in between us and Bond World, but you can ski from both.'

'Could *I* ski from both?'

He smiled, as if struggling for words that didn't sound condescending. 'Well, perhaps one day. It is black runs from the Schilthorn, but from Birg you could do blue and red runs and keep coming back on the cable cars.'

'Okay. Maybe one day. I'm still definitely a blue run woman at the moment.'

'You have three weeks to get really good and then you could enter the Inferno.'

She frowned at him. 'The what?'

Marco pointed to a TV monitor near the queue which showed a promotional video for what looked like a huge ski race inspired by the devil.

'That's happening here?' Alice asked.

'In the last week of January. The Inferno. Every year, it's the biggest event in Mürren. Thousands of people come to ski in the race or watch and it's really fast and really dangerous!'

Alice hesitated. 'Thousands of people, all here at the same time?'

'Yes, it's crazy, but very fun. You'll start to see over the next two weeks they will start to put wooden devil masks beside pathways to show the route, and all the shops and hotels decorate their windows with devils and fire.'

'Have you ever done it?'

'Once.' Marco laughed. 'I crashed and had to drop out about halfway down.'

'Were you okay?'

'Yes, but everyone is going so fast so if one person wipes

out it's like dominoes. My brother has entered a few times. He's pretty good.'

'I don't think I'll enter this year,' Alice joked, but her attention kept pulling back to the TV monitor showing the huge crowd of people. She shook the thought from her head. Totally different place, totally different crowd. *Don't think about it right now.*

'I wonder if Bear's asleep on my bed right now,' she said, changing the subject. 'I took him for a big walk first thing this morning to tire him out. I hope he doesn't mind me being gone for the whole morning.'

'He'll be fine, and I bet he is loving having the chalet to himself. Oh, here comes the cable car.'

They shuffled in, and Alice squeezed her way next to the window on one side. The cable car swept out of the station and into the sunshine, which beamed warm rays into the Perspex box they were crammed into. It glided up, up, up, almost stroking the face of the mountain, whose pine trees poked upwards to meet the sun, and whose snow was glistening and untouched other than by the neat lines of hoof prints left by mountain goats.

Whoosh! Far below them a lone skier appeared, carving elegant trails through the untouched snow, a flash of electric blue ski suit against the pure white. 'They've come from Birg, practising their off piste,' Marco explained.

At Birg, the majority of the winter sporters departed. Just a few remained, along with those without equipment who were looking for some secret service fun. Alice snuck a look at the faces of two women around her age chatting in

322

Italian, their skis battered and loved, their lift passes dangling, crumpled, from plastic wallets on their jacket sleeves, and their cheeks freckled and suntanned. Alice's own face had picked up a hint of colour in the winter sun since she'd started 'hitting the slopes' in December. She loved each new freckle, and each hint of a goggle line that appeared, as if they were little medals.

On the cable car went, up to kiss the glorious blue sky above, leaving the lower peaks behind it. At Piz Gloria they were nearly three thousand metres above sea level and the panorama of the Swiss skyline that it presented was ...

Well. When Alice stepped out of the cable car and exited the station onto the viewing deck, she didn't have any words. The mountain tops stretched before her, behind her, all around her, and she was on top of the world. There was the Eiger, the Jungfrau and the Mönch, and what felt like a hundred other craggy points decorated in blankets of white and flecks of grey stone.

'What do you think?' Marco asked, putting an arm around her to keep her warm.

'It's very big,' Alice replied, not doing it justice. 'Puts life into perspective up here.'

He was quiet, and she realised she kind of wanted to cry, but something about Mother Earth was telling her to be brave, and be present. Also, it was extremely cold up here and there was a good chance that if she cried the tears would freeze on her cheeks.

Alice took a big inhalation of the fresh mountain air and took Marco's hand, and they spent the next twenty minutes strolling along the viewing deck, taking photos with some strategically placed Bond cut-outs, and making each other laugh with their 007 poses.

She was just wondering if her eyelashes were frosting over when her stomach gave a deep growl. 'Shall we go inside and have our brunch?'

'Good idea,' said Marco, whose brows definitely had a frozen look about them.

'I'm just going to nip to the loo,' Alice said when they entered the Piz Gloria building that housed the restaurant and the Bond World exhibit. She was wondering if a Swiss German man had any idea what 'nip to the loo' meant when she realised to her delight that the door to the toilets said 'Bond girls'. It got better. Inside, the cubicle doors were decorated with Bond silhouettes at various stages of him being shot at. And then the most amazing thing happened when she sat down to pee.

The cubicle went dark and above her head the ceiling panel turned into a multicoloured light show. Then the voice from the movie – the brainwashing voice *from the movie* – boomed out to tell her that her chicken allergy was cured! It was the most surreal experience, and Alice could not stop giggling on her toilet seat. Then just to fully send her over the edge, when she pressed the flush the sound effect of a dramatic shoot out blasted out of the speakers.

Alice emerged from the loos still laughing, and took a while explaining it all to Marco. She mopped at her eyes as they made their way up the steps to the restaurant and said,

'Who knew that a toilet with showmanship would get me laughing like that again? Wow, look at this!'

'It's just like in the movie!' Marco replied, taking in the revolving, 360-degree panoramic restaurant.

'Weren't you asleep by this point?'

'I woke up sometimes, usually when you were gasping or clapping.'

'Did I do that during the movie?'

'Oh yes, you were very in the zone.'

The two of them were led to a table right beside the window, where they could see all the mountain peaks moving very slowly beyond the glass. The restaurant was fairly quiet, which gave a relaxed, date-like feel to the situation. Alice gazed at the surroundings, fully absorbed in memories of the movie the night before, and she kept pointing out details to Marco about what was the same, and what had changed.

'Look, look,' she said, pointing to a TV screen that played on loop one of the scenes filmed right where they were sitting. 'Isn't this cool?'

'It is cool,' Marco agreed. 'Why have I never been here before?'

'I want to come here every day. Shall we get some drinks?'

It was an all-you-can-eat brunch buffet and you were allowed to stay for two rotations of the restaurant, so ninety minutes in total. 'Hey look, free Prosecco!' Marco said. 'You want some, Bond girl?'

'I'm going to make mine a Buck's Fizz, because it feels more in keeping with the movie,' Alice answered.

'What is Buck's Fizz?'

'Orange juice and champagne. It's very nineteen-sixties. You want one?'

'Okay.'

Back at the table, and loaded up with their fizz, coffee, Ovomaltine, croissants, rosti, sausages, yogurt, cheeses and all sorts of things to give them a tummy ache, Alice looked at Marco.

'I liked meeting your family the other day.'

Marco sipped his Buck's Fizz and didn't seem to enjoy the taste all that much. 'They really liked meeting you. I'm sorry my mum is quite a big personality!'

'She was lovely. You and Noah are lovely and very kind, so I wasn't really expecting any different.'

'If you make her fondue for anyone she'll want to see pictures.'

'Your parents must be pleased that their sons spend so much time together. Have you always been close?'

'Yes, we are very close. I like him a lot, he's a funny guy and a good brother. I miss him when he goes to New Zealand over the summer but he always comes back to hang out with me.' He laughed. 'You don't have any brothers or sisters, is that right?'

Alice shook her head. 'No siblings, just me. I'd known Jill since school so she was, in a way, the closest I had to a sister, I guess.'

'Are you still friends with anyone else from your school?'

'I'm still really close with our other friends from university – Bahira, Kemi and Theresa.' Her gut twisted a little and the claws of guilt tap-tapped at her while she tried to justify to herself why she'd pushed them away over the past few months. 'Jill and I just always got each other, we always lived not that far from each other, we'd be the first people either of us would call for anything.'

Oh God. It had just occurred to her that Jill wouldn't ever come to her wedding, that Jill wouldn't even have a wedding. It was a silly, insignificant thought to have right now, but it sucker punched her. Guilt seized the opportunity to wedge further into her mind the fact that she was pushing her other friends away as well. Alice turned to the view and breathed in and out, in and out, and waited until the worst of the thoughts tired and wandered off.

'Saying goodbye is very hard,' Marco said when she came back to the here and now.

'What does it feel like to save a life?' she asked in return.

'You mean in my job?' He thought about it for a moment, his gaze on the mountains outside, and she watched as his eyes, reflecting the sunlight, flickered over their peaks while he thought. 'It is amazing to know you've helped. You feel proud, and emotional, and often very tired. But you also feel humble because whichever way it goes, you have always done the best you can. Whatever the result, you do not control life, you could not stop the person from doing this thing, or stop nature from behaving how she wants. I love what I do, and when the day is ending and the helicopter is flying over these valleys I just always have hope that tomorrow will be another successful day. That is a strange answer to your question, right?'

'Not strange, honest.'

Alice drank the last of her Ovomaltine. His words were comforting to hear.

She pulled the folded Piz Gloria guide out from her pocket and spread it out on the table, moving aside their empty dishes. 'Now. To avoid risking you thinking this is the worst date ever, I suggest we head downstairs soon to the Bond museum and forget about all of the death in the world for the time being.'

Marco smiled. 'That sounds like a very good plan.'

When they stood to leave the restaurant he took her hand like they'd been walking that way for years. Down the winding staircase they went and into a darkened series of rooms dedicated to the filming of *On Her Majesty's Secret Service*. Marco pointed out behind-the-scenes photos from around Mürren and Alice read aloud facts. When they turned a corner to see a life-size helicopter set up in front of a large simulation screen to mimic a scene from the movie where Bond is flying over the Alps to Piz Gloria, Alice hopped inside.

She sat in front of the control panel in the dark, with Marco beside her, sweeping images of soaring above tree-peppered mountain tops before her eyes. 'Is this what it's like to be you?' she asked him.

'A little bit.' He grinned. 'I'm not always in the front with the pilot, it depends how many of us are out on a rescue mission.'

'Amazing, though ... to be able to get up above the world every working day.' They sat for a few minutes and Alice relaxed into the sensation of flying like a bird. She breathed in and out, in and out, and eventually rested her head on Marco's shoulder. He put an arm around her and pulled her closer to him, fusing their connection.

'This is definitely not the worst date ever,' he murmured.

The pale light from the video screen reflected on his face in the dark and she looked at this man with whom she felt so comfortable now. She didn't know what they'd become, she wouldn't be living in the same country as him come summertime, but at a time she needed a new friend he'd become more than that.

Alice leant closer to kiss him. And that was when a third head poked into the helicopter cabin and said something in abrasive German.

Marco pulled away from her and said, 'I think we're causing a queue.'

They hopped out into the dark to see a line of four people waiting for their turn, and gave a bashful wave of apology.

They emerged from the Bond World museum and back out into the brightly lit gift shop.

'I think that's it. Do you want to head back down the mountain?' Marco asked.

'Actually –' Alice checked the time '– do you want to make one more stop?'

'I can't believe you wanted to do this,' Marco yelled over the wind that whistled through the valley and licked the side of the mountains.

'I thought it would be funny,' Alice called back. 'I don't

remember why!' Even as she said it though she let out a burst of laughter that was carried away from her.

They stood on a wire rope, surrounded by a protective net, that clung to the side of the mountain face at Birg. The Thrill Walk, as it was called, wound around a section of the mountain and let you stand against the vertical walls and admire the sheer drop below you.

They walked on, whooping and laughing and daring each other to look down. 'Let's make a picture!' she cried, and as they posed with fearful faces in front of the dramatic backdrop, they made a memory also.

It was a ridiculous situation, really, standing on the side of a mountain with the wind in your hair and a sheer drop below you. But Alice – the old Alice, who saw the funny in everything – was having so much fun. She felt brave. Alice was alive.

Chapter 40

Alice returned home that afternoon buzzing. She *wanted* to be brave again. She *wanted* to celebrate the good, despite the bad. She wanted to rise up stronger.

'You're a clingy Bear, aren't you?' Alice said to her shadow, after she'd warmed up in the shower. He padded about after her, watching her every move and giving her his paw every time she tried to pass him, in case she went out without him again. 'No need to worry, it's me and you for the rest of the day today. No more going out, apart from your walk, no more house guests. Just me and my dog. Okay?'

Alice looked at her phone and saw a voicemail message.

'Happy New Year!' cried three voices in unison down the phone. 'Ali, it's Bahira, Kem and T'rees, and we miss having you here.'

It was Bahira talking now, and Alice smiled at the familiar sound of her voice.

'Listen, we missed you at Christmas, your mum said you

were back but for a really short time, so we were *think*ing . . . '
Bahira paused, and Theresa took the opportunity to shout
into the receiver, in her girlish voice, 'We want to come and
see you in Switzerland!'

Alice's face fell. But . . . this was her hideout.

Bahira continued. 'It's a madhouse over here in my home
and I can't bloody wait for back to school so I can have some
peace and quiet. We were wondering, the first week back
at work in January is always quiet for all three of us, so how
would it suit you if we all flew over next Tuesday for, what
did we say, two, three nights?' There was a short discussion
before Bahira said: 'Two or three nights, depending on flight
times and prices. It's been way too long and your mum said
you're doing really well and that your friend is happy for you
to have visitors come and stay, so let us know as soon as you
can if that would work out for you, timing wise, and we'll
make the arrangements.'

Alice hung up the phone.

She was making good steps forward, she was on the
upward climb now, on her way out of the valley of darkness, but there was something about being pushed, even by
well-meaning friends, that made her lose her footing and
stumble back.

'I thought you were being brave,' she scolded herself.
'They're your friends, of course you should say yes.'

Alice couldn't seem to focus her mind over the next couple
of days. She was building quite a collection of illustrations
to sell at the café, and an idea was forming under the surface

about making a whole portfolio of cartoons that documented Bear's early life to send to a publishing house. But something in her resisted, refusing to think any more about the future until she stopped running away from the past. Alice's thoughts kept drifting back to her friends from the UK coming out to visit her. She wanted to be okay about it, to be excited, but the pressure and the expectations made her want to hammer a slat of wood across the door with every day it drew closer.

'Knock, knock.' Lola appeared at the entrance to her chalet. 'Oh sorry, you're working.'

'Barely,' Alice replied. 'I could use a distraction from myself actually. Do you want a cup of tea?'

'Sure, thanks. Hey, man.' Lola came into the chalet and crouched to greet Bear, whose tail wagged on the floor but he couldn't quite be bothered to get up. Lola took off her gloves and hat and sat down at the table. 'Sorry, I just tramped snow through your living room.'

'Considering we bat that exact line back and forth to each other almost daily, don't worry about it. I thought you guys all had a really intense week this week? I wasn't expecting to see much of any of you.'

'Yeah, my eleven a.m. sprained her ankle so I've got an unexpected hour free.'

'Ouch, sorry to hear that.'

'I'm not! Are these all cartoons to sell here?' Lola sat at the table and picked up a couple of Alice's Bear pictures, treating them with care.

Alice finished making the drinks and carried them back

to the table. 'Some of them. I was thinking maybe of sending off a bunch of the dog ones to a few publishers back in the UK. I'm not really sure if anyone will be interested, but I'm beginning to run out of savings so I'm hoping someone might. I need to get the whole collection done and put together before I know the best approach to take, but today I am just not feeling it.'

'Ugh, hate days like that. What's this one of?' Lola picked up a sheet of paper with darker ink and harder lines than the others, and scrutinised it.

'Oh that's nothing, just a doodle from this morning.'

'Is that little person in the corner supposed to be you?'

Alice leaned over to look at the drawing. It didn't mean much, really, it was just a quick sketch of her old living room back in her London flat. The curtains were closed so the walls were dark. It was a pretty grim drawing really, she was just trying to keep her pen moving, but with all of the thoughts of Kemi, Theresa and Bahira visiting the memory of those three months after the concert and before Switzerland kept returning.

'Yeah, that's me hiding out in my flat. It's really just junk.'

'It's powerful. This is how you felt after the concert, huh?'

'Something like that.'

'Do you still feel like that?'

'Not here,' Alice said, honestly. 'It feels really different here, but then more time has passed and I'm much further away from the situation. It's like two different worlds.'

'That are about to collide when your friends visit,' Lola summed up.

Alice took a long drink of tea. 'What if they want to talk about Jill all the time?'

'You talk about her with us. Would it be such a bad thing?'

'But none of you knew her. They all knew her, almost as well as I did, and they'll be able to bring up memories, anecdotes, conjure her up at any moment and I won't be able to control it.'

'You could ask them not to speak about her?'

'It's not even just the things they say, though. It'll be … Theresa wearing earrings that Jill gave her, or Kemi saying an expression that Jill used to say that we've all long forgotten who said first. It's looking at the three of them and not seeing the fourth.'

Lola sighed, feeling bad for her friend. 'I know, it must be painful. But tell them that; they're your friends and it's okay for them to know you're still sad. I think they'll be really impressed, though – I can see you're trying and you're getting there, and I think your friends will too. I'm sure they'll notice a big difference in you.'

Alice thought about this and then said, with a half-smile, 'What if they think I'm *too* better and have forgotten all about Jill?'

'Woman!' Lola threw her hands in the air. 'Anybody ever told you that you overthink things? Listen, why don't you tell them about your new boyfriend? That's a sure fire way to get the conversation moving in another direction.'

Alice laughed. 'He's not my boyfriend.'

'Really. What is he then? Your companion? Your lobster? Your *lover*?'

'He's just my . . . Marco.'

'Yeah, yeah. Right, I'm gonna run next door and grab some nosh before hitting the slopes again. Thanks for the cuppa, and good luck with the drawing.'

After Lola had gone, Alice sat back in front of her sketch pads, but still her thoughts couldn't focus on things doggie. Bear had been her primary focus – her reason for getting out of bed, her trigger to move to Switzerland, the thing she felt lost without over Christmas – ever since the incident. Now it felt like the other part of her, the part that remembered who *she* was and what had happened to *her*, had opened a door and peeped out.

Alice let her out.

Chapter 41

It was an emotional few days, raw and personal, and everything inside Alice came out on the pages of her sketch pads. Many times she wanted to stop, but she was determined to persevere, allowing herself the release.

Her mind and her heart were laid out on those pages, and the result was a beautiful collage of heartbreaking and heart-warming illustrations. She drew her memories of the crush, sometimes in vivid detail, sometimes in vague darkness. She drew the months of isolation, even when people (or animals) were around. She drew the funeral and the way the sunlight glinted on her friends' make-up-free faces. She drew Switzerland and the stars and the mountains and how tiny she felt against them, but then drew them again with her getting bigger. She drew Marco's profile. She drew the Hamleys window. She drew her nook. She drew her journey.

By the end she was exhausted, and she slept so deeply and

for so long that it wasn't until Bear leapt on the bed at nine o'clock the following morning, needing to be taken out for a wee, that she emerged back into the world.

Wrapping herself in her snow jacket and snow boots over the top of her pyjamas, she stepped outside into the snow, the sun bright and already zooming into the sky. Bear jumped into the snow and legged it to the side of the house where he cocked his leg and weed for a jolly long time.

'Good morning,' she heard behind her, and turned to see Marco, geared up and heading out to work.

Alice smiled. She felt dozy but clear-headed, crumpled but fine with it. 'Morning,' she said back.

Marco went in for a kiss but she stopped him. 'For your own safety, I would save it for later. I've just woken up.'

'Well, I'm glad you slept okay. I can't wait to get to bed this evening, it's been a long week.'

'Everything okay?' she asked.

'Just so busy, non-stop, you know? We had a really hard rescue which finally finished this morning. It took a couple of days and it didn't work out.'

'I'm so sorry.'

'Me too.' Marco nodded, the weight of the world on his shoulders right now.

'Are you working tomorrow?'

'No, not at the moment.' He rolled his shoulders. 'How's your week been?'

Alice breathed. 'Intense. In a different way to yours, of course. I've been drawing again. Have you ever heard of expressive writing therapy?'

He shook his head.

'Well, anyway, I've been sketching out my thoughts and memories from the past few months, a bit like I used to do for work, hopefully will do again one day, but super-forcing the spotlight on myself. How is that dog still having a wee?'

Marco laughed. 'So how do you feel after having done it?'

'I feel like somebody's gone into my head and given it a good sweep up. They've left the pile of rubbish in there, but it's cleaner and more ordered. You must think I'm such a headcase.'

'I don't at all,' he replied. 'Can I see them?'

'No. At the moment they're just for me. I hope you understand. I might show them or use them someday, but right now they're a bit . . . '

'Personal?'

'Yeah.'

'Fair enough.'

'So you'd better get going,' she said, now that Bear had finally finished. 'Feel free to come over later if you want to talk, have some wine and fall asleep on the sofa.'

'I will definitely do that.' Marco leant over and kissed her on the cheek. 'What are you going to do today?'

She rolled her neck and breathed in the fresh air. 'I think I might go snowshoeing. And then tomorrow I'm going to take you to lunch before my friends arrive.'

He laughed, delighted. 'Okay then. Have a great day, both of you.'

'And you.'

Alice went back inside still floating on a sleepy cloud. Maybe she'd take a cup of tea back to bed first.

Alice had been sitting in the snow for five minutes trying to get some bastard snowshoes on her feet. She was at the start of the Chänelegg Trail, a 3.6-kilometre round trip that was supposed to be one of *the* things to do in the region, and frankly, she was embarrassed not to have done it yet. But not as embarrassed as she was to still be here, freezing her butt cheeks off, knackered without even having gone anywhere.

'Oh for ...' Alice mumbled, and pulled her ski gloves off her hands using her teeth, using the smallness of her bare fingers to wipe the snow away from the bindings of the tennis racquet-like platforms she was supposed to wear. 'Jesus, it's cold,' she remarked to Bear, who was lounging on his back, legs apart, like a holidaymaker under a scorchio sun. 'Why are there so many straps?'

Eventually everything seemed to be in place. Her gloves were back on, although it would be a while before her fingers thawed, and she hauled herself to standing.

The trail began near her chalet, where the village ended and the slope lifted upwards into the woods. On this bright, late Sunday morning, though the sky was clear blue and the sun high in the sky, she seemed to be the only one partaking in this activity.

It was awkward to start with, the back of the snowshoes clacking together and the path narrow, causing her to keep stepping on her own feet.

'Hey look, Bear,' she said, bringing her knees up high to

step straight down into the thick snow. 'I look like you when we first arrived in Switzerland, remember?'

Before long, the chalets of Mürren were behind them, and they faced Alpine forests. Bear was in heaven, off the lead, running and pronking and rolling in the snow, messing it all up and gobbling great mouthfuls in lieu of having a drink. He stuck close to Alice, her furry friend, the two of them enjoying each other's company.

It was a steep ascent through the thick trees, the sun silking between the branches and causing the colour of the snow to vary from indigo to bright white depending on where the sunlight and the shadows hit it. Alice tried Bear's trick of eating snow to hydrate herself, but the powder was so fine it just disintegrated to barely a drop when it hit the warmth of her mouth.

'This is very hard work,' she said aloud to Bear, her brow sweating and her thighs and calves already beginning to ache. She jammed her poles in and out of the snow before her, trying to keep a little of the weight off her bad leg, and that helped a bit.

All of a sudden the treeline ended and the two of them stepped out at the bottom of a plain of thick, untouched snow and a clear sky.

Alice inhaled, stopping to take in her surroundings and catch her breath. 'It's just beautiful,' she said. 'We could take on the world from up here, couldn't we, Bear?'

He stopped and leaned against her legs, catching his own breath.

She wanted to point this out to her friends. She was

looking forward to showing them this place that was healing her. She took another deep breath, smiled into the sun and, energised, continued up the last bit of slope to the top of the hill, creating a cavernous trail upwards.

'I think,' she panted to Bear, each creaking, crunching step a labour of love, 'we're going to be okay. I really do. We have more good days than bad days now, huh? Oh my gosh!'

The view at the top was breathtaking – a winter vista of the Bernese Alps stretched proudly in panorama, the north faces reaching into the sky in splendour. Blue and white, and forest green, and Alice drank it in.

She was about to whoop at the top of her voice before she remembered about avalanches, so instead she crouched down and snuggled into Bear, her big bear who kept getting taller and broader, who was wet from the snow but still lovely and warm.

The breeze on her face, the colours, the cold on her nose, the sun on the snow, the absolute quiet except for the panting of her favourite best friend in the world. Alice cleared her thoughts, let her guard down and enjoyed every second of this moment.

Chapter 42

Alice had gone alone to meet her friends at the train station the following evening, leaving Bear flopping about in the chalet. She didn't know how her mind and body would react when she saw them, but with every passing minute she waited, the more excited she got. All of a sudden it was as if her heart had suddenly realised it was missing them – not as much as it was missing Jill, but enough to notice the gap of where they should be. And now she waiting, on tiptoes to glimpse them as soon as the train rolled in.

They stepped off the train and she ran to them, and all those things she thought would be painful about seeing them – the similarities, the memories, the mirror images they were of Jill, and each other, in so many ways – were not painful at all. They were perfect.

'I've missed you,' she said, holding onto Bahira.

'I've missed *you*. We all have,' Bahira said and pulled back. 'Hi Alice, there you are, we've missed you.'

'You came,' Alice said to Theresa, who was decked out like a snow bunny with pigtails and bobble hat and rosy cheeks.

'Of course we did. Like it or not.' She grinned.

'Thank you,' Alice said, moving to Kemi.

'Anytime.'

'Come on then, before you all freeze.' Alice took a couple of their bags and walked them up the slope while they oohed and ahhed at the chocolate-box chalets and the deep, soft snow.

'This is the prettiest place I've ever been to in my whole entire life.' Theresa was chattering on. 'Ooh, the Eiger Guesthouse looks cosy, can we go in there at some point? I want fondue!'

'I can make you a fondue if you like!' Alice said.

'So you've moved on from junk food?' teased Kemi, gently.

'I have. My friend Marco's mum taught me.'

The three women laughed and Kemi said, 'Whoa, she mentions his name three minutes in – it must be love!'

'What?' said Alice, laughing.

Bahira linked her arm. 'Your mum told us about Marco.'

'Did you kiss him yet?' Theresa asked. 'Because we said we'd report back to your mum.'

'Since when have you three been besties with my mum?'

'Like we said,' said Bahira. 'We missed you.'

Theresa prodded Alice's arm. 'So did you?'

'Well, it *was* New Year.'

Theresa shrieked in excitement.

Alice laughed again. 'Shh,' she said. 'This is us coming up, and he lives just there.'

'We'll meet him, though, right?'

'I don't think I could stop you if I wanted to.'

Alice let them into Vanessa's home, and they filled it up with their presence immediately, gushing over the furnishings, falling over themselves to pet Bear who was in heaven under their gazes as they exclaimed how huge he'd got, their chatter and laughter tinkling through any emptiness.

Maybe she'd been wrong pushing them away. Looking at them now she wondered why she'd convinced herself she'd lost everything when she'd lost Jill. But it was what she'd needed to do at the time. She'd had a tough year, as Lola had pointed out, and she wasn't about to beat herself up for the way she'd coped. She was doing okay.

'Is there anything you guys would like to do for the rest of the evening?' Alice asked, moving to put the kettle on.

'Nothing,' said Bahira, 'But watch the sun go down over this beautiful view and catch up with each other.'

'Agreed,' said Theresa, 'But also fondue.'

'God, this feels like a million miles away from home,' Bahira commented, lying on the sofa facing the huge window, her tea mug on her lap. 'I can see why you like it.'

'I love it,' Alice answered honestly.

'Have you been doing any drawing?' Bahira asked.

'I didn't for a long time, but then I started selling a few pieces in a local café, and I've been making lots of Bear cartoons of him growing up in Switzerland, and then . . .'

The others looked over when she stopped.

'I actually just this last week basically spewed out all my

thoughts and feelings onto the pages of my sketch pads, and it was quite therapeutic.'

Kemi sat up with interest. 'Really? Drawing helps?'

Alice shrugged. 'It helped me. They say writing in journals and things can help with trauma but I isn't good wiv them wordz. So for me it helped to say it out loud but on the page.'

'That's really interesting.' Kemi nodded. 'I've been thinking I need an outlet of some kind that isn't the gym. I've been going at it a bit hard.'

'Because of what happened?' Alice asked with surprise.

'Yep. I've been spending a couple of hours there per day, as if I could, I don't know ... Being strong and fit feels overwhelmingly important right now.'

'I was drinking too much,' Theresa confessed. 'I stopped on the day you left for Switzerland – you inspired me to try and make a change.'

How blind Alice had been, not seeing that her friends were struggling too. 'I should have called you.'

'We were all in our own heads a bit at the time,' said Bahira. She shot a bit of a look at Kemi and Theresa.

'What?' asked Alice, afraid of what they were thinking.

Theresa sat up a little straighter. 'I wish we could have got through this all together, but—'

'Theresa ... ' Bahira interrupted.

'Tell me,' said Alice. 'Let's just be open.'

So Theresa continued. 'It felt like you didn't think we were grieving as much as you. Like you didn't think we understood.'

346

Alice looked at all of their faces. They clearly agreed. 'I think I knew you were grieving, but everything, *everything* I had was focused on Jill. On every detail in life she'd miss out on. On everything she was and would never be again. I simply didn't have anything left to share. Especially once Bear started nudging his way into it.' She paused, collecting up the other thing she wanted to say out loud. 'But I also thought, how could you not be angry at me? I took her from you . . . .'

'When did we ever make you feel like that?' cried Kemi.

'You didn't, but I was . . . under.'

Kemi shook her head. 'Well, please don't think that kind of thing ever again. When it happened I felt so lucky that we didn't lose both of you, but then for a while it felt like we had anyway, and we didn't know how to save you because you kept pushing us away.'

'But we're here now,' said Bahira, practical as ever. 'Because we don't care if you try and push us away. We'll keep pushing back. For you, and for us, and for Jill.'

It was really time human beings stopped giving their insecurities so much credit, Alice thought. When will we realise they're all in our head?

Kemi broke through Alice's thoughts. 'Here's what I think we should do this evening, if you agree, Alice. I say we put on our pyjamas, open all the chocolate in the house and Alice gives us a drawing lesson so we can all let out our feelings. And we can ugly cry, and ugly laugh, and we can talk about how great a person Jill was but also how bloody annoying she always was with being late to everything.'

Alice laughed at that truth. 'I don't know how good a teacher I'll be, but you had me at pyjamas.'

'It doesn't matter what our artwork looks like, it matters that we're having a go together,' Kemi finished. 'What do you think?'

Bear could not have been happier with this arrangement. Within minutes the four women were buckling down for the evening, fresh cups of tea, masses of snacks, PJs on, blankets aplenty, and a big pile of pens, pencils and sketch pads scattered around. And in the centre of everyone's universe, like the glue that held the group together, was the stretched out and sleeping puppy that once belonged to Jill.

Chapter 43

The morning after, Alice took Bear downstairs early, trying to be super quiet and not wake the others. Kemi and Theresa had slept in Vanessa's room (with her permission of course), and Bahira in with Alice.

She saddled Bear up to take him for a morning walk. 'You're eight months old tomorrow, Bear,' she whispered. 'Can you believe it? You must weigh a good forty kilos now, I reckon. You've grown into such a huge, handsome boy, and I'm so proud of you.'

Stepping out into the new day, Alice made next door her first stop.

'Good morning, did I wake you?' she said to a sleepy Marco.

He stood in loose burgundy checked pyjama bottoms, his chest bare and toned, his hair crumpled and his face stubbly. He rubbed his eye with one arm and with the other reached out and scooped her in through the door. 'That's okay, let's go back to bed, come on.'

She laughed at Bear's reaction, who jumped up, his paws flailing against Marco. *What's this? Physical contact? Involve me!*

'This puppy is nearly as tall as me now,' said Marco.

'Sorry to have got you up.' Alice eyeballed Marco's chest. 'Not *that* sorry. What time are you working today?'

'Not until lunchtime. How are your friends?'

'Really good. You want to come over and see for yourself? Come and have brunch with us this morning.'

'Brunch, huh?' He yawned again. 'That sounds great; can I bring anything?'

'Bring the others, unless you want to be cross-examined.' She headed back for the door after a quick kiss. 'See you in a while.'

Brunch was a hit, with the neighbours bringing not only themselves, but juice, bratwurst, eggs and pancakes to add to their already full table of grilled tomatoes, toast, cereals and coffee.

The group intertwined easily, and Alice stepped back at one point, not because she felt overwhelmed, but because she couldn't believe her luck. Bear walked over to her because she was still his favourite person there, and he sat next to her as if he too was surveying the group.

'She does not! Ali, you snowboard now?' Theresa called, after talking with Lola.

'She really does, and she's good at it.'

Alice laughed. 'You sound shocked.'

'Not shocked,' Theresa corrected. 'Impressed. I want to go out on the slopes.'

'I can teach you,' Lola said.

'She's a very good teacher,' said Alice, wandering back over to the table and munching on a leftover half of pancake.

Kemi piped up. 'I want to learn too, but we leave tomorrow.'

'Oh no, I'm all booked today. I could call in a favour at the ski school and see if any of my colleagues could take you?'

'Actually, I had a thought about this afternoon,' Alice piped up. 'Does anyone want to go sledding?'

Alice hadn't been on a sled since she was a little girl, when she and Jill and Jill's toddler brother had been taken by their mums to a nearby stretch of hill in the Surrey countryside after an unusually large winter snowfall. She remembered laughing with Jill all day, going up and down, up and down the hill until Jill had been sick and Alice had fallen off enough times that her mother thought it would be wise to stop.

Theresa had never been on a sled, had never before been on a winter holiday, but was decked out like a pro snow bunny today, snapping selfies in the sun in her pristine matching ski wear, her sled propped up beside her.

Bahira had taken her family on a ski trip a couple of years back and they'd all tried it then ('I remember thinking I didn't have the patience for it on the flat bits,' she commented). And Kemi knew she'd slid down a hill on something that might have been a dustbin lid one drunken evening at university, but couldn't recall if it happened on winter snow or summer mud.

'Are you ready?' Alice asked the three of them. They stood at the bottom of the funicular railway, each clutching a traditional, metre-long wooden sled, ready to head up to the top of the Allmendhubel slope where the bob run began.

'Hell, yes,' answered Theresa, putting her phone away.

They climbed on board the train and oohed and ahhed their way up the mountain, Alice feeling pride for the place she currently called home.

'Can I stay here with you for the next few months?' asked Bahira. 'My family will be fine at home. I want to eat every bit of cheese in all those pretty restaurants I can see below us.'

'Yes of course, stay as long as you want,' Alice said, and although she knew Bahira was joking, she actually meant it. Fancy that.

At the top, they followed the skiers and snowboarders out onto the mountain and Kemi and Theresa's jaws fell into the snow and rolled away.

'Look at this view,' Kemi gasped. 'Jesus Christ!'

'Look at the hot snowboarders,' Theresa added as a sturdy chap in sunglasses and an open ski jacket carved past them and off down the ski slope.

'So according to the map, to make sure we're sticking to the bob run we need to look out for the purple sledding symbols, like that.' Alice pointed at a sign sticking out of the snow next to the entrance to one of the piste basher-cleared runs.

They shuffled their way over there, their boots creaking in the snow and their sleds bashing against their ankles.

'Do we go in a line?' Theresa asked, and they looked at the run before them.

'It doesn't look wide enough for us all to go next to each other,' said Kemi.

'Not with all the cheese I've been eating since I got here.' Alice stepped forward. 'We could probably go two by two, and stop and switch over?'

Kemi put her sled down and it began to slide, so she grabbed the rope handle. 'How do you stop on these?'

'You have to just dig your heels into the snow,' answered Bahira. 'Or plough into the snow bank at the side. Be careful you're not going to career off piste if you take that option.'

Theresa gulped. 'I vote Alice and Bahira go first.' Then she whispered to Kemi, 'Then we can just crash into *them*.'

'Why do I need to go first?' Alice protested. 'I'm just as much as a beginner as you.'

'But your boyfriend is a mountain rescue paramedic,' Theresa shot back.

'Fine,' said Alice. 'Let's go.'

They sat in a two by two formation on their sleds, pausing to make some pictures.

'Hold onto the reins, lean back, keep your legs up but your heels just a little into the snow,' Bahira instructed.

'Let's do this!' Theresa yelled, and Kemi shushed her.

'*Shhh*, you might start an avalanche.'

They sat there, rocking on their sleds, until Theresa asked, 'How do we make it go?'

Bahira, who'd been tucking her hair into her ski jacket, started waddling her feet forwards, pulling the sled with her, like a dog dragging its bottom on the ground. 'Like this. Here we go!'

The four of them swayed from the flat onto the start of the slope.

'Whoooooa!' Alice was the first to fall, the blade of her sled sinking into the softest snow in the centre of the slope and tipping her over. Behind her, Kemi made a leap for freedom so that only the sled bumped into Alice's back. Theresa expertly swerved past them both but then was laughing so much she forget to dig her heels in, and zoomed down a sudden incline and out of sight.

'I'm okay!' She called back from where she was lying in the snow beside Bahira, who had come to a graceful pause.

Panting and chuckling, with snow lodged into their bum cracks, the women attempted round two. The bob run ebbed and flowed from exhilarating inclines to gentle curves to flat plains that they had to waddle themselves along on, causing their hip flexors to ache.

They passed lonely wooden chalets, half buried, and the mountains that encased them became gold-tipped as the afternoon sun began to sink beyond. It was so quiet aside from the slicing of the sled blades through the snow that it almost became relaxing. The four of them were feeling rather smug with themselves for getting the hang of gliding the wide curves, their heels spraying soft dustings of cold snow into the air, which usually landed back on their faces.

It was making Alice's bad leg pang something rotten though, even though on the outside all that remained was her scar. She didn't want to admit it because ... well, for starters she was half way up a mountain and she didn't have much choice other than to keep going. But also she was having fun with her friends, her wonderful, familiar friends who were back in her life. So she ignored for as long as possible the burning ache that was worsened by being pressed up against the wood. Eventually she needed a rest, and ploughed into the snow at the edge, which was much thicker than she anticipated. She disappeared up to her knees.

Bahira was bringing up the lead so came to a stop. 'Everything okay, Ali?'

'Yep, just having a little rest.' Alice twisted around on the sled. 'You're very good at this.'

'Once you've managed to sled down the hill with a child on your lap because they don't want to do it any more, dragging their sled behind you, plus carrying the backpack full of everyone's snacks for the day on your back, this seems a breeze.'

'You can fit two on one sled?'

'Well, you *shouldn't*.'

Alice thought about this for a moment, and then Bahira asked, 'Why? What are you thinking?'

'Nothing.'

'Are you hurt?'

'No, no, absolutely fine.' She extracted herself from the snow but visibly winced when she put weight onto her leg.

Bahira got off her sled and jabbed it into the snow, then walked over to Alice. 'It's your bad leg, isn't it? Does it still hurt you?'

'Not much, it aches a little when I exercise or snowboard.'

'Right then, come on,' Bahira said, and picked up Alice's sled and tied it to the back of her own.

'What are you doing?'

'Taking charge, being the mum, like you've been with Bear over the last few months.' Bahira sat down on her sled, legs akimbo, and patted the small, slatted space in the middle.

Alice laughed. 'I don't think I'll fit in there,' she said. 'You're very kind but I'll be fine on my own sled.'

'Come on, let's give the others a laugh.'

Alice *was* enjoying a laugh these days. 'Bugger it, let's give it a go.'

She climbed on the sled, squidged in between Bahira's thighs and bent her knees so that her feet were up off the snow and on the wood as well. It wasn't much comfier, but it was quite funny. Bahira shunted the two of them forward, and the two of them clung, screeching, to the rope as the two sleds cascaded down the slope like white water rafts. They stayed on, though, almost all the way to the bottom, where they found Theresa and Kemi already clasping three steaming cups of Glühwein, plus a hot apple juice for Theresa.

'That was so much fun,' said Kemi, gulping her drink. 'But surprisingly hard work.'

'Does anyone want to go again?' asked Theresa, and was met with murmurs of 'maybe not's. 'Oh good, I'm shattered!'

Alice said, 'How about we pop back to the chalet? I'll walk Bear, and then we go somewhere to soothe our muscles for an hour or so?'

'That sounds perfect. What did you have in mind?' asked Bahira.

'A simmer in the outdoor hot tub at the Alpine Sports Centre while the sun goes down.'

This revived them, and as they stamped through the snow back to Vanessa's chalet, Theresa said, 'I don't know why you're ever planning to come home, Ali, the "wild" life is really working for you.'

Her friends from home left Mürren late the following morning, happy and exhausted, bruised but so glad they came, and Alice felt exactly the same. They'd all had a great day on the slopes yesterday, followed by a laughter- and memory-filled soak in the hot tub in the evening. And now she waved goodbye to them, under the soft fall of snowflakes, until the train had pulled away and curled around the mountain.

Before she went back to the chalet, where her Marco was waiting with her Bear, Alice took a moment to be by herself. She walked, her hands in her pockets but her heart open, with the slow amble of somebody enjoying nature and not rushing to avoid life. She was proud of herself.

Then she went up the slope, beside the village she'd become so familiar with, and towards the two chalets that permanently had their doors open to each other.

Alice opened the door to her own, and there were her two favourite boys, all hers for the evening.

Chapter 44

From behind her eyelids, Alice was experiencing utter tranquillity. The sun was high in Switzerland's cloudless sky and it was warming her face and seeping into her skin. From her outside table on the patio of the Alpine Sports Centre's Hugs & Cups café, the only sounds that broke the quiet were the muted cheers and the thunking and brushing that floated over from the curling game being played on the ice rink.

Alice breathed in deeply, the sweet vanilla and nutmeg spices from her drink filling her nose. She sipped her *schintiretto*. The hot apple juice swirled with almondy Amaretto was a tonic in the clean, cold air.

It was the day before the four-day Inferno extravaganza hit Mürren, and Alice, Marco and Bear were enjoying the peace and relaxation while they could.

Since her friends had gone home, Alice was feeling more at ease than she had in so long. She looked back at the times over the past six months when she'd doubted she'd ever feel normal again, when she'd had to talk herself out of her own spiralling mindset and remind herself to breathe. And here she was, breathing without even thinking about it most days.

Alice flexed her legs, which were stretched out and resting on Marco's thighs, and he looked up from his book and smiled at her. She took him in, her sun-kissed man with sandy hair and an open smile, and a backdrop of bright blue sky, rugged mountains and snows of pure white and peppermint, depending on where the shadows hit.

'What?' he asked.

From his place lying on the frosty paving slabs Bear looked up and at her too, because of course he was part of the conversation.

She shrugged. 'Just making a picture.'

Marco's smile spread into a grin, which he then contorted into a funny face, making her laugh. She laughed and crossed her eyes and gurned back at him, and Bear sighed and lay back in the sunshine.

Alice took another sip of drink, breathed in and out, and settled back to her place of tranquillity behind the warmth of her eyelids.

Chapter 45

Way, way back when Alice and Bear had arrived in Mürren it was like they'd walked into Narnia. In this quiet, magical world they seemed – almost – to be the only inhabitants. A week later, the best neighbours in the world moved in, and life began popping up like snowdrops. A week after that, it almost seemed busy in this little mountain village.

When the skiers, the spectators, the families and the fans of the Inferno arrived in Mürren, Alice realised just how *un*busy the last three months had felt.

Visitors from all over the world made their pilgrimage up on the cable car or the train in scores. Fresh snow was walked through, restaurant tables were full, skis filled every rack outside the hotels.

Lola had joined Alice on Bear's morning walk, and was talking her through the next few days.

'There's sort of three races overall. Tonight there's a cross-country thing where people do laps of Mürren, then tomorrow's the big slalom. Friday is a chill day where people just rest up or hit the slopes for practice or whatever, but there's the big crazy procession in the evening which I'm going to have to take you to. Then Saturday is the Big Day.'

A group of men in coordinating ski wear came to a stop in front of Bear and after excitedly cooing something in German that Alice assumed was 'can we say hello to your dog', they bent down and took it in turns to ruffle his ears and fawn over him. That was happening a lot on this walk. The more people there were around, the more attention Bear pulled in, and he was loving every second of it.

'So do you think more people will come over the next couple of days, or is this usually it?'

'Oh heck, no, this is nothing. They are going to absolutely flood in during today. I reckon the hotels will be full by tonight. But the day tourists will keep coming in, mainly on Saturday.' Lola glanced at Alice who seemed to be holding Bear's lead very tightly. 'You all right, mate? Are crowds a bit of a thing for you, still?'

Alice loosened her grip so Bear could lollop towards an older couple who had stopped to look at him. 'They're a little bit of a thing, but I'm really doing so much better. And the atmosphere here seems really nice.'

'It is a great feel, anybody local looks forward to this every year. We're a pretty small community, and Inferno weekend is always like having your entire extended family come over for the holidays. In a good way! Lots of familiar faces, everybody is cheering on everybody else. It's pretty great, I hope you like it.'

'I'm sure I will.'

Bear turned and beamed up at Lola, sitting his bum in the snow and being a very good boy, and she stroked his cheek with affection. 'You might want to leave Bear at home for some of it, though. This walk is taking for ever – he's stealing the show.'

The lead-up to the big day was indeed mesmerising, and as Lola had predicted, the village just got busier and busier. The atmosphere was catching, and every establishment leant good cheer to it. The manager of the Eiger Guesthouse had coaxed Alice in for a free beer and some biscuits for Bear, and Lola and Noah had somehow started an impromptu ski disco for complete beginners on the baby slope.

With lovely powdery slopes, endless blue skies and the buzz of two races behind them in the air, come Friday the next day's Inferno was all anybody could talk about. Even Vanessa had called to say she couldn't help herself – she had one day off and was going to travel super early from Zurich on Saturday morning and stay for as much of the race as she could before heading back in the evening.

It was late afternoon and Alice was picking up a few things at the Coop with Marco when David walked through the door, brushing snow out of his hair.

'David, where have you been putting your head?' Marco laughed.

David answered him in Swiss German, and to Alice he seemed a little stressed.

The men spoke for a couple of minutes before David left

with a quick wave to them both. Marco grabbed a bottle of milk and said to her, 'Sorry about that. David says the weather is really turning all of a sudden. It can do that in the mountains. I said I would get the milk he wanted so he can head home.'

'Oh no.' Alice thought of all the people preparing for the parade right now. The plan was to burn a huge effigy of the devil, because apparently that stopped him meddling in the race, and prevented accidents. It wouldn't be easy to torch a soggy Satan.

They stepped outside with their shopping and the sky was thick with dark clouds. It covered the mountain peaks opposite, and the gloom it cast made it feel much later than it was.

The snow was falling thick and fast as Alice and Marco rushed back through Mürren village. Snowdrifts were gathering outside the shops and restaurants, with owners standing by the doors looking at the skies. The high number of visitors were standing, a bit lost, or making their way back to hotels, dragging their skis through the powder.

'People are saying the ski lift is being turned off soon – nobody else can go up but it's bringing people down,' Marco explained, eavesdropping as they passed.

'Wow, so this is quite the sudden snow storm,' Alice said, one hand in his, the other sheltering her eyes from the wet flakes kissing her lashes and cheeks. She peeped up as best she could at the solid grey sky. 'I can't believe we were looking up at blue only twenty minutes ago. Now it's so dark you'd think it was the evening already. It came on so quick.'

'Welcome to the mountains,' said Marco, hurrying them along.

They reached Vanessa's door and when they were under the shelter of the sloped roof Marco turned back to look at the town, his eyes searching, his expression distracted.

'Marco? What's wrong?'

'This is a lot of snow, very quickly,' he answered, vaguely. His face moved to the mountain where he could just make out a few stray skiers and snowboarders taking their time coming down.

'Come on, let's go inside and get dry.'

Alice put her hand on the door knob and had just turned the key when a siren sounded.

Chapter 46

Three low wails pierced the sky and Alice's world tipped. She turned, her eyes searching for Marco, and it was like she was swimming in slow motion, her mind trying to drag her all the way back to August.

Marco's hands grabbed hers and pulled her back from the edge. 'Alice, Alice, are you with me?'

'What's happening?'

Beyond the door Bear started to bark, frantic at the noise and anxious because Alice wasn't coming inside.

'Can you hear me?' Marco insisted, putting his gloved hands on Alice's cheeks and forcing her to look at him. 'Are you with me?'

'Yes,' she blinked. 'Yes, Marco. Come inside.' She tugged at him.

'Alice, I can't, I have to go.'

'Where?'

'On a rescue. That siren means I have to go, okay?'

She clung to him, still trying to shake this fog that was overwhelming her thoughts. 'What's happened?'

He paused, as if not sure whether to tell her.

'*Marco*, tell me.'

'Avalanche, I think.'

'How bad?'

'I don't know yet, the visibility's all gone. I'll be back soon. You go inside, Bear needs you.'

'I can help, let me do something.'

'Listen to me: there's nothing you can do here, and that's okay. You cannot save everyone. Just be there for the one who needs you now, that's all you can do.'

'No,' she cried as he tried to untangle himself. 'Don't go up there, please stay here.'

'I have to go, this is what I do.' He spoke quietly but firmly.

'But ... ' She grabbed for his sleeves, for his coat, the sirens still ringing in her head. 'But I can't do this alone. What if I lose you too?'

He was already pulling away, but he kissed her, his lips warm despite the weather around them, and then backed away from the chalet and held her gaze for just a moment more. 'Of course you can handle this. Don't let the "what ifs" control you.'

Marco turned and jogged back down the hill and Bear's barking turned to a guttural wail, the type of noise Alice hadn't heard since that first night she'd brought him home and tried to leave him to sleep in the spare room.

She scrabbled with the door handle and entered the chalet and had to fumble for the light switch, it was so gloomy inside. But several flicks told her the power was out. Bear was all over her, leaning and licking and catching his breath.

Alice slumped down against the door, holding on to him, running her fingers through his fur. 'It's okay, it's okay, it's okay,' she whispered over and over again, to either the dog or herself.

They sat there for who knows how long, as the sky grew ever darker, the wind howling against the wood of the chalet, the cold air whistling under the door. There were rumbles in the distance and she didn't know if they were thunder or shifting snow on the mountains. Then the chopping sound of a helicopter cut through the falling ice overhead.

Her own demons clawed at the chalet door, reminding her that if anything happened to Bear it would be her fault. She brought him here. She fought back with reasoning – nothing was going to happen to Bear, he was safe inside with her. But the mind has a devilish way of spinning speculation into foregone conclusion.

Bear whined, and Alice talked to him in a sing-song, but wobbly, voice about how she wasn't going anywhere. She told him about how brave Marco was, and how she was working hard to be as brave as him, and as she said it she thought about what he'd said. She couldn't save everyone. And she pushed back harder at her thoughts, breathing in and breathing out, and vowed not to ever again let the 'what ifs' be in charge.

Flashback images of Jill danced in the dark, her face half turned and smiling at her across the sea of people after they'd separated, but Alice pushed it roughly aside and remembered instead a different memory of Jill.

They were at the Women's March back in January. They'd walked and walked and cheered and held their placards high and Alice was so happy because in that moment it felt like history could, finally, start on a new course. Jill had shouted in her ear to be heard over the noise, 'This is so great, but what if nothing changes?'

Alice had laughed her joyful laugh and turned to her, putting her gloved hands on her cheeks and said, 'What if we actually save the world?'

Alice stood up on shaking legs. She was someone who always looked for the bright side, and had always assumed the best, not the worst, was going to happen. Yes it was idealistic, and there would always be plenty of things in the world to try and prove her wrong, but she was damned if she was going to lose that part of herself entirely. It was time to save herself.

This was a storm, she could handle it. Marco was fully trained and would be back soon, and she'd coped with worse than this. She needed to step up now and do the best she could.

Alice moved away from the door and led Bear over to the sofa. She lit the wood burner and the warm glow filled the room. Trauma wasn't going to get the best of her; this other living soul who depended on her was.

'Come on Bear, let's go and sit over here. We're so safe and warm and snuggled in here, aren't we?'

Bear paced, looking back at the door, and whined a little more.

'Come on, puppy,' she coaxed. Eventually he sat half on her, his woolly bum heavy, then he slid down until he lay slumped against her. His ears were still alert, as were hers to be honest, but he seemed to calm. And in turn, so did she.

When the thunder couldn't be heard any more, and the wind had died down, Bear lay his head down on her lap with a sigh. He looked up at her with his big amber eyes, safe in the knowledge that they were both there for each other.

Chapter 47

A short while later Alice heard the faint but unmistakable sound of someone trudging through the snow towards her chalet. There was a rough knock on the door and Lola's voice called out, 'Alice? Bear? You okay in there?'

Bear stirred from where he was dozing on the floor against her thigh but didn't get up, so Alice called back, 'Come in, Lola.'

Lola entered, carrying a torch and bundled up in her snow jacket and salopettes. In her arms were two bulging duffel bags. 'Hey, how are you two?'

'We're okay. I freaked out a bit on Marco, though. Do you know what's going on?'

Lola dumped the bags on the floor and took a seat, rubbing her face. 'Yeah, Noah just came back from the village. The storm caused a power outage on the Schilthorn cable car, and there's like, four hundred people trapped. The conditions mean they don't want to start running it again, and there's a risk of avalanche at the moment but they don't think there's been one so far. Marc will be out with his crew – there are five helicopters airlifting people from cable cars and helping people stranded on the mountain.'

'Jesus ...' Alice sighed. 'Is everyone okay?'

'I don't know. Noah didn't know. It came on so quickly. There's just so many people on the mountain at the moment because of the Inferno that it's not like everyone can go back to hotel rooms, and the cable cars have completely stopped in both directions.'

'So what's happening?'

'The sports hall at the Alpine Centre has been opened up and it's where everyone's being sent to. I'm going to head down there now and see if there's anything I can do to help. I've got some snacks and blankets and stuff. Do you want to come?'

Alice looked at Bear, who was steadfastly snuggled into her.

'The Alpine Sports Centre's open to dogs, you could bring him along. He might be a nice distraction for people. Totally your call of course, I just wondered if ... you know ... misery might want some company.'

The old Alice would have been there in a shot, and she liked the old Alice. If Marco could airlift people from a flippin' cable car, she could absolutely do all she could to help. 'Yes,' she said, standing up. 'You're right. Let's go. What shall I bring?'

'Great. I don't know really. I'm guessing there might be some confused or scared people, including kids. There might be people separated from their friends or family, or even just disappointed people who were looking forward to the procession or worried about whether the race will take place tomorrow. I'm just bringing a few things that might comfort or help them. I have a board game in here and a few old paperbacks.'

Alice pulled on some extra socks and another jumper, then threw in a bag a few items of her own she was happy to part with – thick ski socks, an old hoodie, books, the fleece blanket from her nook. In a flash of inspiration she grabbed her sketch pad and a handful of pens and pencils, and then harnessed up Bear, ready to go.

The walk through the village was eerily quiet and on the ground all the footprints and ski marks from earlier in the day were covered with a thick dump of untouched snow. The snowfall had stopped and the clouds had cleared a little but by this time night was drawing in, and the searchlights from the helicopters were zigzagging over the slopes up to her right.

'They'll need to stop soon, it's too dangerous to fly the helicopters when the light completely goes,' Lola commented, looking up.

'What does that mean for anyone still stuck?'

Lola shrugged. 'I bet they're working really hard to try and make sure that doesn't happen.'

Walking in the door of the sports centre, Alice and Lola saw the size of the operation. There were makeshift signs pointing people to the sports hall, and the lobby area was filled with people, traipsing snow in and out, talking on their mobile phones, queuing up to ask questions from anyone wearing any kind of uniform. The people from the Hugs & Cups café were rushing back and forth bringing free hot drinks to everyone. A paramedic was leaning over a patient lying on the ground and talking to them while they nodded, and for a second Alice thought it might be Marco, but it wasn't him.

A man came out of the ski rental place at the back, carrying a basket of gloves, and spotted Lola.

'Hey, Bron.'

'Hey, Lola,' he replied.

'What can we do to help? We brought some supplies and games and stuff.'

'I think just go into the sports hall. There's a lot of upset people in there so maybe just hang out and chat with them.'

'Do we have any word on the procession or the Inferno that we can tell them?'

'No – we'll hear more once the choppers are done.' He turned to Alice. 'That's a great dog.'

'Thank you,' she said. 'He's pretty comforting. We thought we could loan him out for warm hugs.'

'Good idea.'

They followed Bron into the large sports hall which was filled with people leaning up against the walls, or lying on the ground, and some glued to their phones, hoping for updates. There was an air of glumness, but also one of camaraderie, with packets of biscuits being passed around, and children of different nationalities playing in little groups. One group of nearby kids came running over to Bear when they saw him and took it in turns to hug and stroke him, Bear not minding at all and happily giving out his paws and licks.

'This is Bear, his name is Bear,' Alice explained.

For the next hour or so, Alice walked Bear around the sports hall letting him meet everybody and chatting with people about how old he was, how much he weighed, etc. She could see the worry and disappointment on some people's faces and she hoped that in some small, fleeting way, her big happy dog was providing a little bit of comfort for them, like he did for her, daily, even when she didn't notice.

Alice kept one eye on the door, hoping Marco would walk in at any moment. She just wanted to know he was okay – physically and emotionally. She knew he gave a hundred per cent to his job and did everything possible, but if there were people he couldn't save, or find, it would weigh heavily on him for a while. To distract herself and make time pass, she drew sketches of the kids with Bear and gave them to them, much to their delight.

The rumour started to circulate around the hall that the last of the helicopters had stopped for the evening, so Alice got up from where she was sitting and took Bear back out to the lobby area of the Alpine Sports Centre.

And there he was, her Marco. He stood talking to two men dressed in similar uniforms to his, his brow sweaty and his hair a wonderful, sandy mess. His hands were on his hips and he rolled his shoulders, and she watched him from afar, not wanting to interrupt him if he was still working.

Bear had other ideas though. On seeing Marco he pulled

and stretched and dragged Alice to him, where he mus-
cled right into the middle of the group of men and leapt
his paws up to Marco's shoulders to lick his face. Marco
laughed, and his whole face went from exhausted to happy
on seeing Alice.

'I'm so sorry,' Alice said, apologising for interrupting
them, but also for her breakdown earlier.

'Are you okay?' Marco answered, pulling her towards him
and burying her deep in his arms.

'Are *you* okay?' replied Alice. 'How did it go? Did you get
everybody down?'

Marco and his colleagues nodded at each other. 'We think
so. The cable car is cleared, and we couldn't see anyone
left on the mountain. Nobody has been reported missing
who isn't now back, so we have to have hope that everybody is safe.'

'Let me get you a drink. Let me get all of you a drink.'

'Thank you,' breathed Marco, and she left Bear sitting
on his feet while she grabbed three Styrofoam cups from
the café filled with hot apple juice. The men drank them
quickly and then Marco said: 'Listen, I'm not going to be
finished for a while yet. We have quite a few patients set up
in the *Kinderparadies* children's room and we need to take a
while with them to make sure they're okay and don't need
to go to hospital tonight.'

'All right,' she said, falling in love with him.

'Noah and David are outside, though. They've been helping bring the devil over so it can be burnt.'

'The procession's going ahead?' she asked in surprise.

'No, just the burning. They'll gather everybody outside soon. You should stay and watch.'

'I don't know if people are going to be in the mood for this at the moment, I think they just want to go home.'

He grinned. 'You wait and see. These people know that if the burning doesn't happen the race will surely be cancelled. That bloody devil.'

'So is the race going ahead tomorrow?'

'We will keep the fingers crossed!'

Sure enough, word of the devil effigy burning going ahead had trickled into the sports hall and people were starting to pour out, the chatter volume rising and faces filling with hope. Alice grabbed Marco's hand before he disappeared.

'When you're done, will you come back and sleep at mine?' she asked.

'Are you sure?' He looked down at her and moved an inch closer. 'It might be really late.'

'I'm sure. I'll leave the door unlocked. Come home whenever you can.'

Chapter 48

The dawn was bright – a fresh, clear sky above the mountain peaks of Mürren and the storm a distant memory like a bad dream that had never really existed. Alice awoke, with Marco sleeping beside her, so weary, and Bear a vision of comfort lying on his back in between them.

She breathed them in.

Marco's eyelids opened and he smiled at her. *'Guete Morge.'*

'Good morning. How are you feeling?'

'Achy.' He stretched, then brought his hand up to touch her face. 'How are you feeling? You were pretty scared yesterday, I felt bad leaving you.'

'I'm fine too,' Alice answered. 'But I think I'm going to get some help.'

'Therapy? Oh that's ... hang on a minute, let me tell your dad.' On the other end of the line, Liz leaned away from the phone. 'Ed ...? Ed ...? Alice is going to see a counsellor.'

Alice heard her dad in the background exclaim with happiness, and Liz came back on to say, 'Love, I think that's brilliant. Well done, you.'

Marco had headed home to change and shower, and then they were going to make their way into the village to watch the first of the Inferno racers descend the slopes. The cable car was running, the sky was blue again, the snow was delicate and light, the skiers were back on the slopes and the world kept turning.

'Thanks,' Alice said. 'Everything feels so much better than it did back in August. It's just ... I feel like I broke into loads of bits after it happened, and you guys, my friends at home, my friends out here, Bear, Marco—'

'Marco?' Liz's ears pricked up.

'Yes, Marco. I feel like everyone's helped put me back together and I'm not quite how I was before, but that's okay. But it seems I'm still annoyingly flimsy, and I'm tired of guessing how to fix that on my own.'

'I think you put yourself back together. But anyway, semantics. We're both just so pleased you're going to see someone and get help. Will you need to wait until you get back to the UK?'

'I think I'll try and find someone nearby,' Alice answered. 'Probably not in Mürren because it's tiny, as you'll see for yourself next month, but maybe in a slightly bigger town like Interlaken. I don't want to wait another three and a half months.'

'Ooh yes, our trip,' Liz said. 'We can't wait to see where you've been living, and all your new *friends* ... '

'And that Bear!' shouted Ed.

'But tell us, just how snowy is it? Will your dad need to bring his wellies?'

Alice spent the next fifteen minutes chatting her parents through the simple pleasure of winter holiday packing, snuggled in the comfort of her nook, overlooking her view.

The Inferno atmosphere was on fire. Smiles of happy relief and joyous fun painted everybody's faces, and spectators cheered and rang huge cowbells for everybody who made it to the bottom of the mountain, whether they knew them or not. The skiers themselves flourished to the finish line, spraying glistening powdery snow over the bystanders, much to their delight.

Alice stood with Bear and Marco. Lola was leaning forward waiting for Noah to make it to the bottom. David stood with Vanessa, who had made it, and was cosying up with David like she'd never been away.

'What do you think?' Marco asked Alice.

'I thought I would hate it,' she answered honestly. 'But actually I feel part of the family now.' She grinned up at him. 'I think I'd better enter next year.'

'You do?'

'Yeah. You know, show them how it's done. In fact,' she added, her eyes tracing the outline of the mountain peaks that surrounded her, 'I might have to come back every year.'

Chapter 49

Alice and Lola walked Bear along the Chänelegg Trail as the first signs of spring peeped through the snow. There was no need for snowshoes now, and Bear was enjoying munching on the blades of grass that peeped up through to the sky.

'I just can't believe it's April already and that you go home in a week,' Lola was saying. 'What am I going to do without you?'

'I know, it's going to feel like my right arm is missing, not having you next door any more.' Lola stuck out her bottom lip and Alice slung an arm around her shoulders as they walked. 'Are you looking forward to going back to New Zealand?'

'Ah yeah, for sure. But this winter's been bloody ace.'

'It really has,' Alice agreed.

'You're flying back over in August for Sonja's seventieth, though, right?'

'We wouldn't miss it!' said Alice. 'Imagine if you flew over from the southern hemisphere for a long weekend and we didn't make the effort from just over in England.'

It was so strange to be going home. Alice had long dreaded this time coming around, but actually it wasn't an awful feeling, just a bittersweet one. The fear had melted with the snow, and she was looking forward to seeing her parents, catching up with Bahira, Kemi and Theresa over a bottle of wine, walking beside the Thames, eating 'real' bacon again. She'd be living back at her childhood home for a couple of months, commuting into London two days a week to work from the *Funny Pack* office, which would be a welcome hug. She also planned to visit Jill's mum and dad regularly.

'Did you hear back from any of the publishers yet?' Lola asked.

'Actually, one sounds pretty interested – they think it could make a nice gift book, and they want a meeting when I get back to the UK, so fingers crossed!'

'That's *brilliant*! You'll keep me updated, won't you?'

'Of course! I have been thinking about something else I might do, actually.'

'Go on.'

Alice had read a study once that said humans had a 'hierarchy of needs'. Once you'd filled up on the vitals such as food and shelter, the next thing you needed was security. Then love, belonging and inclusion. Then self-esteem and power. And finally you'd be at self-actualisation and creativity.

Alice formed her words. 'Going to the therapist has got me thinking about choosing happy, which is something I've always tried to choose in life, but as you know I gave up for a

381

while. I want to give other people the ability to choose happy too, so I was thinking of starting some kind of drawing class or workshop, for people who'd suffered some kind of trauma. Not in place of therapy or anything, I am no expert at fixing people, but just to give them somewhere to go, or something to distract them, but maybe then think about training as an art therapist. And I think it's good for me to make connections, in real life. What do you think?'

'I couldn't think of anybody better to do something like that. Those people are going to be so lucky to have you around.'

Alice blushed and gave her friend a bashful nudge. 'Well, it's taken a while to get here, but *I* feel lucky.' She inhaled the fresh air and drank up the view with gratitude.

Goodbyes were so hard, even when they were planned. Bear knew something was up and was sticking to Alice like superglue as she walked through her chalet for the last time, trailing her fingers over her nook, the blankets, looking at the view from the window.

Vanessa caught her in a tight hug. 'Thank you for being here,' she said into her hair.

'Thank *you*. You have no idea how much I needed this.'

'Come back any time, this is your home now too.' Bear nudged his way in between them. 'And yours too, Bear.'

Alice smiled wide, her red lipstick helping to light up her face. 'I can't wait to see you in August.'

Vanessa stepped outside the chalet and took David's hand. They were going for a walk to leave her and Marco alone.

Alice faced him, and the tears came.

'Hey, it's okay,' he soothed, curling her into his arms.

'I'm going to miss . . . everything.'

'Me too. But we won't forget, we made a lot of pictures.'

She laughed. It felt good to let the tears come, drenched with emotions connected to happy times and loving thoughts, because although she was still sad, she wasn't lost any more. Whether she was home, here, or a million miles away, Alice was happy.

Chapter 50

Heathrow Airport. There was something about this place. It was busy and hectic and brimming with hope. As Alice chowed down on a chunk of Toblerone inside the arrivals hall on the warm June day, the man she was waiting for rounded the corner, as handsome as ever.

Although Alice had gone home just with Bear, Marco and she were spending the summer together in Wales, moving into a rented cottage in the countryside, a family of three, where Marco had been awarded a place with a mountain rescue team in the Brecon Beacons. And here he was.

He didn't spot her at first, and paused outside the customs gate to put his passport into his rucksack. She watched him scan the crowd and waited for his eyes to meet hers, giving herself plenty of time to reacquaint herself with his sandy hair, sun-kissed skin, his strong arms as bare in the summer as he left them in winter.

He was here for her. She was here for him. When Marco's gaze found Alice's, and he smiled, it was clear they were both exactly where they belonged. She stretched her arms wide, and ran towards her future.

It was early in August and the hot weather, even here in Wales, was keeping Bear inside in the cool, which suited Alice, who had been using the day to quietly remember the best friend she'd lost a year ago. She had spread her art materials over the kitchen table of the rented cottage she shared with Marco and was putting some finishing touches to the page proofs of her dog cartoon book that was due to be published in time for Christmas.

Marco walked through their door, carrying fish and chips, their new Thursday night tradition, and Alice rose, contentedly, stretching out her back, kissing him, and following him out to their garden where they sat at their patio table and unwrapped their dinner. Bear kept very close, his nose sniff-sniff-sniffing the air.

'I've been thinking,' Alice said, her legs stretched across Marco's. 'I've always been more of a summer girl than a winter girl, but there's something about Switzerland ... I didn't know before that wintertime could be so bright and open and ... warm.'

'Mürren suited you a lot,' Marco agreed, munching on half a chip and feeding the other half to Bear, who loved him more than anything else in the whole world right now.

'I think it did. I felt like I got back to me there, but also transformed into someone who doesn't want to hang around and wait for things to happen or ideas to slowly come to life any more.'

A smile was forming on Marco's mouth, just slightly, in the very corners, like he could guess what was coming but didn't want to assume.

'So I think,' Alice continued, 'that maybe the mountains are calling, and we should answer, as they say. How would you feel about you and me renting a chalet there over this winter?'

It was a 'yes' before it was even a question. She'd known how happy this would make Marco, and there was nothing she loved more than his happy, beaming face. Well, maybe there was one face she loved the same amount, for the same reason.

Last summer, Alice had felt airless, lost in the woods. But in time, with her dog at her side and with a little help, she'd found her way up to the top of the mountain. And while she'd always be a little changed, the version of herself she'd found could see life stretched out before her.

Alice could breathe again.

There's nothing wrong with being afraid.
It's not the absence of fear, it's overcoming it.
And sometimes you've just got to blast through
and have faith.

EMMA WATSON

Acknowledgements

And just like that, readers, here we are together, swooshing to the bottom of the mountain with a happy spray of snow sprinkling the air behind us. I really hope you liked my book, and if you'd like to read any more by me I have a little stack of romcoms published as Lisa Dickenson.

Just a few thank-yous to share now, if I could hold on to your attention for just a few more lines.

Firstly, thank you to wonderful Mürren and the welcoming people who live there. Special mention to Ema and the Eiger Guesthouse team, Constanze and the Café LIV team, Daniela and Nathalie and everyone at Mürren Tourismus, and Karleen and Nick who taught me about snowboarding, and about life in the mountains. This postcard-perfect village snuggled in a duvet of snow halfway up a mountain will always have a place in my heart now.

Thank you Agent Hannah and the Hardman & Swainson team for all your enthusiasm for this story, and for the great *Alice in Wonderland* visual which so perfectly summed it up!

Thank you Viola for all your help in bringing out the best of these characters and giving them life! And a huge thanks to the Lovely Beautiful team at Little, Brown Book Group, and the extended family they work with, in particular Thalia and Charlotte, and Bekki and Robyn. And an essential thank-you to beautiful blogger Simona for helping me with the Swiss-German!

Thank you to Gloria Steinem and to Nick and Jim at Vice for allowing me to use the quote that begins this novel.

I also want to say a warm, hygge-thank you to Meik Wiking for writing *The Little Book of Hygge: The Danish Way to Live Well* (Penguin Life). I read this beautiful little book for research on ways for Alice to find little pockets of happiness, and it actually also ended up helping me through some tough times last year too.

Thank you Phil, the best dog dad, the best travel companion, and the best person ever.

My Paw & Order crew: Belinda, Holly, Bodie and Skipper, who make dog playdates absolute highlights.

Thank you Mum and Dad, and all the Gordons and Dickensons, for being you. And thank you Emma, as always, for testing out my words before I'm ready for others to read them!

To the teams at Jurassic Vets (especially Lovely Vet Peter) and Dogs Trust – thanks for teaching me how to raise a dog, and being very patient when it didn't go to plan. And thanks Hayley and Beverley for introducing our doggo into our lives. You gave me plenty of fodder for this novel!

And finally, the muse for this novel: Kodi-Bear, my very own big, floppy, gigantic Bernese Mountain Dog. I hope you know how much you help life-worries drift away just by plonking a heavy paw on me and smiling. You're more than a dog, you're a heavy lump of happiness. Thanks for inspiring this novel; you can take over my side of the bed any time.

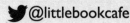